ESSENCE
— OF —
TRUST

Other Five Star Titles
by Melinda Rucker Haynes:

Breach of Trust
The Eternal Trust

ESSENCE
— OF —
TRUST

MELINDA
RUCKER HAYNES

Five Star • Waterville, Maine

Sequel to *Breach of Trust.*

First Edition
First Printing: May 2005

Published in 2005 in conjunction with
Tekno Books and Ed Gorman.

Set in 11 pt. Plantin.

Printed in the United States on permanent paper.

Library of Congress Cataloging-in-Publication Data

Haynes, Melinda Rucker.
Essence of trust / Melinda Rucker Haynes.
p. cm.—1st ed. Published: Waterville, Me. : Five Star, 2005.
ISBN 1-59414-116-9 (hc : alk. paper)
Sequel to: Breach of trust.
1. Time travel—Fiction. 2. Fantasy fiction. 3. Love stories.
I. Title.
PS3608.A96E83 2004

2003065572

[redacted]

For the most "good and pleasant"
Airedale terrier on any world,
Haynes' Glenne Glee, 1988–2003

— PROLOGUE —

Denver, Colorado, Present Day

"You are the best agent in the psychic intelligence business or at least within Datascape Systems International. How can *you* be stymied by this assignment like all the others?" Ian Stoddard asked the uneasy lump of flesh sitting before him. "Perhaps you don't realize how vital the information is?"

Ian glanced up at the light above the conference table. It buzzed like an insect hovering over his head. The long, white fluorescent tubes above cast a bluish pall on the remote viewer's sweat-beaded forehead. The man wisely remained silent.

"If it's a question of proper motivation, be assured that I do know how to motivate employees," Ian said and leaned forward. "Your team's record for accurate hits is unparalleled, until now. What's the problem?"

The remote viewer cleared his throat and started to speak. Ian held up his hand. "Give me no excuses and I'll give you one more opportunity to perform or leave my employ. Your choice."

"No excuses, Dr. Stoddard," the man answered, struggling to hold Ian's gaze. "I can do the job."

"Good. Let's go again, and this time no visuals. I am an auditory exclusive and understand on every level what I hear, as well as what is unsaid. Set your feelings aside and read me the words. I'll hear the hidden meaning. Nuances. Intent. Visual and other input sets up interference patterns that compete with the auditory." Ian sat back, tenting his fingers and smiling benignly.

"That's kind of unusual, isn't it, a remote viewer who gets target info through only hearing, instead of established protocols?" the man ventured as he shuffled his papers and drawings into a loose stack.

"I never said I was a remote viewer." Ian had leaked parts of his story for the psychic intelligence community to put together in a mutating legend that suited his purposes.

"Oh. I guess I thought that since you started Datascape and we're all trained on your method that you were primarily a remote viewer." As the frown cut furrows across his big forehead, he looked like smoke was going to boil out of his ears any second.

Perfect, Ian thought, just where I want you. Composing a reasonable tone, he said, "You might think of me as a super-sensitive, hearing everything across time and space. And yes, it's highly unusual. You can't train anyone to hear or gather information as I do. Most people can be taught to trust their intuition more or to make better-than-average guesses at the outcome of a coin toss. A very few can put themselves in an altered state and become a vessel empty of anything personal, having no wants, desires, or preconceived notions. They can follow a set of rules to allow ideas to form in their empty minds about unknown objects, events, people or locations remote from them. The best of these sensitives, such as yourself, are those I hire."

Ian hardened his voice and continued, "Unfortunately, you, the alleged best, show me a composite of what you all viewed like some viewer trainee. That's when everything goes to hell, because I'm hearing through your personal filters about your viewing experience that you've translated into written symbols. Just report the data. Let me hear it. Don't get into analytical overlay by interpreting for me. Is that clear?"

The man cleared his throat and began, "Okay, I put the team on the Nostradamus quatrain, Century IV-31. *La Lune au plain de nuit sur le haut mont*—"

"Not the French. Give me the English translation of the prophecy," Ian barked.

"I just thought maybe you could hear something in Erika Cheetham's translation that we didn't. In any case, her English version of the quatrain is, 'The moon, in the middle of night over the high mountain, the young wise man alone with his brain has seen it. Invited by his disciples to become immortal, his eyes to the south, his hands on his breast, his body in the fire.' "

Ian held up a finger to stop the viewer and closed his eyes, listening. He heard the woman's thoughts as she struggled to divine meaning in the arcane writings of the cunning old prophet who spun his visions into riddles and anagrams. Letting his mind drift along the mechanical English further into the past of the wet and verdant old French words, Ian heard the sounds change to ripples, as wind across desert sands, dry and brittle, harsh and filled with heat. "Go on."

"We traced the chain of custody of the quatrain to a prophecy that Nostradamus received, which came to him as a papyrus brought back by a French Crusader from the Holy Land. It was titled the *Essence Prophecy of Anubis.* He's the jackal-headed god of ancient Egypt thought to be the guide of the dead through the Underworld."

"Yes, yes," Ian interjected with impatience. "Get to the prophecy. Is it complete?"

"Nearly." The man lowered his eyes from Ian's penetrating stare and pulled a page from the stack.

"Am I to understand that you have nothing more than before?"

"We've got a lot more," the viewer countered. "It's just that there's some sort of interference or block that we keep running up against that we can't get through despite any protocol we use." He glanced up at Ian, his eyes filled with hope that masked the terror Ian heard in his thought. "Maybe you can hear something . . . ?"

"Proceed," Ian said with an abrupt nod.

The man swallowed hard and began to read from the sheet in his shaking hands, "From the Two shall become the One incarnate, an essence of eternal power in complete balance to coalesce at the initiation through a door between worlds, heralding the return of the gods to earth."

Ian heard nothing, save the flat voice of the viewer echoing in his mind. The Two become One with the power. Yes, but how? When? Where? He already knew who. "Continue."

"As you know, that was the content of the papyrus fragment that Nostradamus created his quatrain from. However, his thoughts and beliefs showed us that he somehow understood much more of the Anubis prophecy. Perhaps he used a method similar to ours to get the information." He stopped at Ian's scowl and brusque wave to move on.

"Okay. The following is a compilation of Nostradamus's knowledge or understanding of the prophecy and that of whatever, or whomever, created the so-called *Essence Prophecy of Anubis*." He held up a fan of pencil drawings of straight lines that evolved, sketch by sketch, into swords. "These are apparently the Two mentioned in the text. Two identical samurai swords, oddly enough. They're thought of as the Swords of Balance. What we don't understand is two Japanese-style samurai swords of supposedly vast esoteric power in ancient Egypt, but I guess you do?"

Ian nodded. "Do you have more on the One incarnate?"

"We think it's metaphor—"

Ian slapped the table with his palm and roared, "I don't pay you to think."

The viewer jerked. "As to the One, only the initiated Essence can use the power that's the culmination of some sort of off-planet group's energy. Maybe. They're on earth when he is. I say *he*, because the energy associated with the Essence is primarily masculine. In order for the Essence to coalesce or come to power, all of the group have to give up their own powers to the One, to the Essence, before or at the time of the initiation."

"Then this is the Antichrist," Ian exulted. He jumped up from his chair and began to pace the length of the table.

"No! Dr. Stoddard, not the Antichrist but the great genius; the antidote, if you will, to the Antichrist of the Scriptures and other prophecies. There seems to be a warning about others seeking the Essence's power for themselves or trying to pervert the Essence somehow."

"The great genius or world savior idea is nonsense, and I'll tell you why," Ian began. "These swords that you've mistakenly thought a metaphor or an allegory, they're real. Their power is indeed vast, limitless, in fact. And to hear that this kind of cosmic energy will coalesce in a single being, I know he can be none other than the Antichrist, as Biblical writers have mistakenly misnamed the ancient dark power called Anubis." Ian rubbed his hands together, exhilaration racing through his bloodstream. "His worship is of great antiquity."

The viewer's face became ashen. "Again, Dr. Stoddard, no. You haven't heard the new information. It will prove to you that the Essence isn't intended to be evil. It's the personification of eternal good. There's an additional warning that should the One, who is apparently a child, not complete the initiation before the moment of his twelfth year, then all is eternally out of balance, an opportunity missed to right all wrongs, and the evil will magnify and consume the world."

Ian spun and leveled a glare directly between the man's eyes. "Again you interpret instead of report. Perhaps it's time for retraining. Recycle the lot of you."

"Maybe so," the viewer whispered.

Ian came around the table and put his hand on the man's shoulder. "Don't worry, viewers better than you have failed me and still live, even though they're working directly against me."

The man trembled under Ian's touch. "Are you talking about Integrity Intelligence Services in Seattle that beat us out of the Al-Qaeda contract for the military?"

"Yes, two of my best viewers I let go. They're living proof of the efficacy of my methods and my benevolent tolerance of, let's say, mistakes. They are gifted, as you are not, however. So you'll understand that I will not accept any further misinterpretations of data or errors from the likes of you."

Ian left the conference room, smiling at the fear screaming through the viewer's mind and his futile efforts to block Ian's influence. There were only two that could do that and much more, but now that they were no longer working together, their individualized psychic force was diluted to a minor portion of the eternal power that the One would soon embody.

It was time to take the boy.

— ONE —

Sedona, Arizona
"Return to me."

Rian Farsante stopped dead on the powdery red dirt path lined with stones. She peered into the expanding twilight as a fall-burnished sun dropped behind the brick colored sandstone cliff walls of Encantada Canyon. As the trailside scrub junipers, cedars and sagebrush began to reel in their shadows, the high desert of Sedona hushed to hues of purple and blue.

"Who's there?" Rian asked, turning in a circle. The voice had a familiar quality that she hadn't heard, or felt, in years. Had that someone actually spoken from the canyon's shadows or mentally across time and space?

In answer, the piñon-scented evening breeze brought only the last goodnight squawks of crows and scrub jays and the aroma of cedar smoke. Setting aside her sense of impending recognition and all that it meant, Rian relegated the voice to have come from her imagination or the sweat lodge ahead and quickened her pace up the trail.

The squat, round hut of vertical cedar logs buried a foot or so in the earth supported a conical roof, thatched with scraggly branches. Rian paused before the red and black Indian design blanket hanging over the low doorway and watched a white plume spiral out of the roof's center hole. She released her cares and worries on the rising smoke and ducked into the hogan.

"Welcome, traveler," the shaman invited from the

shadows covering the top half of his body. He waved an eagle feather fan to a seat on the ground opposite the fire pit. "We have waited for you and now begin."

As Rian sank to the woven mat, she closed her eyes and heard the sizzle of water hitting hot stones. Someone began to pound a slow rhythm like a resting heartbeat on a skin-covered drum. Her pulse and breathing matched the resonant pulsations. Sweat sprang from every pore, cleansing her body of toxins.

There were others inside the steaming enclosure, but she sensed their different energies rather than saw their physical forms. They were the usual mix of spa guests: adventurous dilettantes, devoted seekers and the merely curious. And one incredible high frequency she hadn't encountered before—an adept. The shaman, perhaps? Her own curiosity urged her to open her eyes and connect with the master on a visual level. Rian restrained herself. She didn't come to the sweat to interact with anyone; she expected to contact spirit guides that would show her through the higher planes to the Spiritlands.

More wood was added to the blazing fire and water poured upon the superheated stones. Breathing became labored, and Rian's body screamed for escape from the high-temperature torture. Panicked cells and tissues whispered that she might die from heat exhaustion, that her blood would boil in her veins. The accelerating drumbeats wove fire, water, earth and wind into a cacophony that overwhelmed sense and sensibility, urging her spirit out and upward.

A shudder rolled up her spine. Rian gasped as her spirit broke free. Her *ka* soared out-of-body through the crown chakra at the top of her head into the ether, like a streak of pure white light toward the higher realms.

As used to traveling out-of-body as Rian was, the Spiritlands were still foreign to her. They were a different vibration suggested by the drumbeats, unique from the formless ether or wave energy of her accustomed mind travel. She'd worked as a remote viewer, but what she'd done since that initial training and extensive work as a psychic operative to gather intelligence data was far beyond applied technique and protocols.

Once free from the black ops organization that had used and abused her, Rian discovered that her psychic skills were vast and virtually unblockable. She could access thoughts anywhere along the time continuum, undetected, and influence others' behavior, even kill if she had to, by mental means alone. But that kind of power had exacted too high a price. The man she'd been sent to bring back into the fold of psychic spies proved to be her soul mate, her eternal love, and she couldn't hurt him again. She had to save him. Together they discovered that they were more powerful than any other psychic operative in the business and were finally able to escape the man who had trained them. But over the next years of trying to make a life together, they realized they'd never be free of Ian Stoddard. And Spence would never be free of his desire for the esoteric power of the Swords of Balance. As a priest of the cult of Anubis, she'd created the swords for him, then a queen, in a past life in ancient Egypt, and he'd used their esoteric power to defeat enemies of the kingdom. Since that life, the swords had brought untold misery and death to them in subsequent lives, and to the Gabriellis in their different incarnations as well.

The Swords of Balance weren't inherently evil, but when separated and used in the pursuit of personal power, they consumed those who lusted after and wielded them. Spence and Rian had brought the swords together six years ago and lost them in the same moment. But Spence couldn't live without them and had drifted further into the shadowy world of black magic and sexual ritual to try to manifest the swords again and wanted Rian to help him. But she refused and they drew apart. Even the Gabriellis, whom she'd come to love, had abandoned her, so consumed were they with trying to bring him back.

It would be too easy, even now, to follow the ever-present dark inclination and join him. But she would fight it with every breath, every thought, and focus on seeking the light of spiritual inspiration and power and helping others find it, too. Then, perhaps one day when her spirit was traveling the astral plane or the Spiritlands, she would keep on going and never again return to her body in this difficult, lonely life.

She'd never been much for planning the future, preferring to focus on creating in the moment. If she'd been able to live blissfully ignorant of the actual potential being created with every choice, instead of as a remote viewer who could see the results or potentials of a given option, she might have been surprised that things went so wrong, when it seemed they had a chance not to just survive but to put everything right. Ian Stoddard may have released them six years ago at the Great Sphinx of Giza, but they should have known they couldn't escape destiny.

No matter how much of herself Rian had tried to pour into making a life of love with Spence, he demanded more and gave less and less back. Spence couldn't fight the craving for the cosmic personal power the swords offered. Not for Rian. Not for his godson or his best friends. The yang to her yin, her soul mate was losing his way in the dark in equal and opposite proportion as Rian searched for the light.

Away from him for three years now, she still wasn't free, held to earth by even those she'd helped with her healing abilities. They too tried to control her by demanding her constant attention and wanting her to do their mental work for them, just as Spence had. As Rian's reputation as a healer grew, so did the number of those who expected to buy her, at whatever price, as they did all the other upscale services their A-List lives required.

Rian drew further into her inner landscape, searching for the power of her soul, preferring to accelerate her spiritual growth by learning to navigate other dimensions and realms farther from earth's vibration. She could always feel Spence working in the opposite direction, and had learned to protect herself from his mental influence, though it hadn't become any easier over time and space. She loved Spence and that made her vulnerable to him. No matter how much Spence wanted not to, even if he had any self-control or love left for her anymore, he would still use her, hurt her and ultimately kill her again.

"Return to me."

The words decelerated her free flight, the ether wave slowing. Transparent thought forms of totem animals and helper spirits shimmered around her. Rian dared to open her thought. Other forms began to take shape, and she sensed the unique frequency or emotional signature of each.

As had been happening with almost frightening regularity, the higher her spirit soared, the more time spread out in all directions. It was like a holograph, an eternal now of past, present and future, as well as other dimensions and realities. Here, at zero point, she was free and part of the wave, as well as all her aspects and existences. Keeping those distinct was becoming more difficult, and she wondered why she must be separate from all those memories that were pure energy.

The thought or suggestion came to just let go . . . to sever the silver cord connecting her spirit with Rian's body and ascend.

"Return to me," the voice ordered again. His name formed on the sound of his calling to her.

Ian Stoddard.

Fear evolved to revulsion that churned through her stomach. She knew Ian had been psychically and physically monitoring her for years; if not personally, then he'd assigned a team of remote viewers to target her. In fact, he'd never stopped watching her since recruiting her in graduate school and perhaps even before that. She'd been successful at blocking their attempts to read her, but as she'd become more famous and sought after by the public, that opened her to psychic assault from other predators as well as ordinary people who wanted something from her.

Protecting herself mentally became her top priority, so that she could direct her energy to preserving her freedom to use her skills to help people. Ian was never interested in her healing skills. From their first meeting, when she was an undergraduate and he a visiting professor, he'd gained control over her, perverted her talents and convinced her she possessed no other purpose than to serve him and the hideous extension of his corrupt appetites, Datascape Systems International.

Was this audible psychic signal from Ian a notice that he could bring her back in any time and that time was now? He knew that she would never willingly return to him.

"Return, Rian. You were never apart from me, not really," came Ian's reply.

"I've never been with you. *Really*." But she had. Rian tried to redirect her thinking away from him and their past, where she had loved him. Her ascension instantly retarded and she began to spiral toward the darkness.

Fear overwhelmed her, accelerating the descent. She willed her mind blank, for thoughts were immediately actualized here in the astral, unlike those in the dense materiality of the earth plane.

A swirling chaos of color flowed into a red river that pulled her downward. Like funerary masks, the horror-stricken faces of her once-dearest friends, Michael and Dorel Gabrielli, and beloved Spence struggled in the deadly current just ahead of her.

"No! Not them. I won't let you have them!" Rian screamed, plunging faster, following her friends into the dark abyss.

A hand reached for her in the mental freefall. Rian's awareness shifted from the hand that promised safety to her dying friends who needed her. She had to help them!

If they pull you into the darkness with them, all is lost, counseled a disincarnate voice. *Come back now!*

Rian snapped back into her overheated body, every cell convulsing with terror as impotent rage-driven sadness filled her consciousness.

The drumming silenced, but hot blood pounded under her sweaty skin as her lungs floundered. Rian's wide eyes fixed on the center hole in the hogan's roof. She tried to move her limbs and raise herself out of the dirt or close her mouth, which was open in a noiseless scream, but her paralyzed body refused to obey.

"She's not breathing," someone whispered.

"If she's dead," another said in a quivering voice, "cover that face with something. It's like a horrible . . . hell, I've never seen anything like *that.*"

No! I'm alive. Help me, Rian's thought shouted.

"Somebody better do something, or I'm going to freak," a younger female voice squealed.

"Enough!" came a sharp command from somewhere across from Rian. "The woman has been spirit walking. She's very much alive, more than any of you."

A face hovered out-of-focus above hers. "Okay, if you

say so. Should we go for help?"

"No. I will care for her."

Muffled scuffling noises, mixed with lowered voices, as people got to their feet. Rian heard the young woman stage whisper, "You do wack stuff, get all freaked and come back looking worse than dead. What's the point? You can keep the spirit walking. No way."

"Don't you recognize her?" another responded. "She's that famous healer-psychic. The real thing, they say."

"Huh. Well, I'm signed up for her class tomorrow, but I think I'll do the hot stones massage instead." The voices drifted off, leaving Rian aware of lying on the hogan's floor and still not breathing. Yet, she was alive, wasn't she?

A tall, lean man with straight, dark hair hanging around his angular features leaned within three inches of her face, took a drag on a long-stemmed pipe and blew sweet-smelling smoke into Rian's nostrils. "Return now, spirit, to the healer!"

With a resounding thump in her solar plexus chakra, Rian's body sucked in air and her heart echoed a rhythmic thrumming of life. "Wha-what happened?" she asked and attempted to lever herself to her elbows.

He laid a hand on her shoulder. "Stay still a moment and center yourself."

Rian's gaze drifted to the slender fingers. This was a magician's hand of great power, the only one that could have saved her from the abyss. She eased back, closing her eyes, focused on her breathing and waited for answers.

"I am Chevayo," he said, his deep voice conjuring waves of sensation that threatened to inundate her defenses.

Spirit Warrior, his name meant. Then it was he who had saved her in the Spiritlands, if that's where she'd been. Rian licked her dry lips and started to thank him.

He pressed soft, cool fingertips to her mouth. "Wait. To speak now is to put your weakened spirit at risk. Only water should pass your closed lips until sunrise. You can stand now. I will take you back to your casita."

Rian didn't consider arguing with the charismatic man. Her knees wobbled a bit, but he supported her with an arm around her waist until she stood steady. The night air was gloriously cool on her parched skin, but she shivered under Chevayo's watchful support as he walked her in silence back to the resort.

As a visiting VIP lecturer to the resort's world-famous wellness spa, Rian rated a large Santa Fe–style private bungalow on the top tier, with magnificent views of the canyon and its famed energy vortex. Chevayo waited on the porch steps while she unlocked the door. Mouth still closed tightly as ordered, Rian turned back to him and gave a self-conscious shrug.

Chevayo's slow smile lent sensual curves to his face's harsh angles. Rian saw in his brown eyes what he was going to do, but she couldn't move. He stepped close and stared intently, as if to her heart. Rian trembled as his lips caressed her ear, and she closed her eyes as exquisite shivers radiated from the point of contact.

"You cannot hide . . . from your destiny," he whispered, adding a gentle shush as she opened her mouth to defend herself. "Do not defend your fears. Release them. Your friends have their roles to play, that you must not alter. Step into your true power, for you must save the One."

After a few moments of silence, Rian opened her eyes and found herself alone on the porch. However much his seemingly spontaneous disappearance confused her, his succumbing to unnecessary homily when she'd been pretty sure he intended to kiss her was most troubling. How had he been able to get past her defenses to stir up feelings that she hadn't herself allowed in a very long time?

Obviously, she didn't know Chevayo or what he was about, other than his being a shaman with the ability to share a spirit walk. He couldn't know her or her real-life situation well enough to counsel her to turn away from Dorel, Michael and Spence. If the vision could be believed, they were in danger, and no doubt from Ian, just as she was. While Spence could more than defend himself against the paranormal powers that Ian wielded, Dorel and Michael couldn't. That meant their eleven-year-old son Marty was exposed and in danger. She'd always known on some level that Ian's ultimate target was the boy and had tried to convince his parents and Spence to at least consider the possibility. But their best defense, Michael and Dorel believed, lay in attempting to live an ordinary life with an extraordinary son. While Spence hadn't encouraged their view, he hadn't discouraged it either, as Rian had.

Despite what Chevayo advised, Rian had a duty to Dorel and Michael to do everything she possibly could to protect them, whether they wanted her help or not. But first, she must set aside any concern for herself and contact Spence. Only by working together again would they have any hope of defeating Ian for good.

Seattle, Washington

"Tell me you love me," she whispered, resting her forehead on his chest.

I can't. "Trust me. I care," Jonathan Spencer murmured into her hair.

"I can't do this anymore, Spence," she sobbed. "I wanted to believe . . . I thought I'd be able to do it the way you want," she murmured, her breath warm on his bare skin.

He sighed. *You can't do it the way I need it. No one can but her.*

The blonde continued to sob into his chest. "I just can't, you know, do this when you don't care about me like I do you. I deserve better."

He closed his eyes and made soothing sounds as he stroked her smooth, bare back. Jessica was a beautiful, smart woman, and she was right. She deserved much better, someone who would love her. And that would never be him.

His heart and soul would always belong to another.

Spence let his mind drift where it always did. Rian. What they had been able to do together no one would believe. Not even themselves, at first.

Why wouldn't she channel their combined power to create the Swords of Balance? After all, it was the two of them in a different incarnation who'd created the swords long ago. They were his to use as he pleased now, just like when she'd created them for him in ancient Egypt.

The energy bodies of the swords were waiting out in the etheric world to be called into material existence again, but he couldn't do it alone and needed Rian like before. If she could trust that he wouldn't hurt her and only use the swords to defend himself—and her, of course—but she didn't believe him. He knew he could handle the power.

Jessica's crying had stopped, and he kissed the top of her head. "Do you want to stay and just relax, or shall I put you in a cab?"

"I'll go. I've got an early appointment tomorrow."

They dressed in silence, Jessica avoiding eye contact. Spence didn't have to be a remote viewer to know it was over.

Downstairs, he held the umbrella over her and opened the cab's door. She slipped inside and looked up at him through the rain-spattered window. The sadness in her thoughts matched that in her eyes. Spence stepped back under the building's awning and watched the cab pull into traffic.

Rian. Her face flashed into his mind just before his cell phone vibrated in his pocket. He hadn't spoken to her in a couple of years, because she'd stopped taking his calls and blocked his attempts to mentally communicate with her. Now she was allowing—no, initiating—contact. Why?

"Hey, babe, what's up?" he asked, his hand doing a minor tremor on the phone at his ear. He nodded to the doorman opening one of the double doors, and walked inside toward the elevators.

After a moment, she answered. "Spence, have you heard from Dorel and Michael lately?"

Not even, "How are you, Spence?" He made sure the elevator was empty before he got in. "Yeah, sure," he lied. She sounded worried and was allowing him to perceive it. "Hang on. I may lose you inside the elevator."

"Spence, when was the last time you talked to them?"

He thought a moment. "A couple of weeks, I guess. But they're okay, or Marty would have let me know . . . like he does you?" Spence probed.

His godson, Marty Gabrielli, was careful not to take sides, but he did remind Spence, in that odd ascended master way of his, that Spence and Rian were soul mates and their destiny was together. Spence suspected that he kept in close mental contact with Rian, telling her the same thing. The boy had been born special, gifted with unusual knowledge, and as they later learned, possessing memories and skills from all his past lifetimes, many of which Spence and Rian had played a role in, along with the Swords of Balance.

Silence on her end.

"Are you getting something different?" he asked, beginning to feel her concern in his gut. "I didn't think you were working to protect them anymore."

"Despite what you may think and have told them, I care very much about Dorel and Michael. Remember, I believe there is more power in strengthening oneself than in focusing on attack and defense."

"Easy, Rian. I get that you're upset, but let's ratchet down the paranoia, okay? We don't talk about you anymore. What Mike and Dorel think about you, I wouldn't know. I've kept my promise not to view them, and they've agreed not to talk to me about you." He felt her mental hackles rise, and grinned. Even New Age gurus had their hot buttons.

"Paranoia? That's not *my* issue, as you well know." Abrupt silence followed. Spence knew she was clamping pearly whites on her sharp tongue. "Look, can we not do this?"

"Sure, babe. Anything you want," he said, not bothering to dull the sarcastic edge in his voice. He used to regret that getting hurt and losing her turned him into an asshole, but not anymore. The anger worked for him, simmering just under the surface, boiling away qualms of fear as well as any remnants of humanity. Always better to inflict pain than to wallow in it.

"I want—would you just listen, please? I've had a vision that was very troubling."

Then don't chase visions. "Yeah? About what?"

She expelled a breath. "I think it was a prescient warning that Dorel and Mike are in danger. And you were in the vision, too."

A river of red flashed into his mind's eye. He was being dragged along in the turbulence behind Dorel and Mike toward what seemed like a pit of death. Okay, not good as visions went. Now he understood why she'd called him. This wasn't just a random hallucination, it was projected with purpose to Rian.

"Yes, that's what I thought, too," she agreed.

"Who's doing this and why haven't I gotten it?"

"I think it's Ian. I heard him calling to me to return to him. This means he's targeting only me, and I don't know why."

"Maybe he's trying to bring you back in," Spence suggested. "Or could be you've sent some sort of subconscious signal that you want to come back." That was possible. In their worst arguments, he'd accused her of being no better than a Datascape whore who loved her work, because she'd had no problem psychically spying on him and executing whatever degrading assignment Stoddard gave her.

Six years ago, Ian had ordered her to use sex to breach Spence's deprogramming and bring his psychic skills back online for Datascape to use him again. Then she'd claimed she loved him and wanted his love, too. Even though she said their love saved them from the psychic spymaster Ian Stoddard then, Spence never believed he was through with them, especially not with Rian, who'd had a long-term affair with the son of a bitch.

"I see you haven't changed. You're still blaming me for what I did before we were together, though I've more than atoned for what I did to you then. But because you can't change, you won't let me. However, that's only in your own mind, because I have changed, Spence. I don't want to fight your kinds of battles anymore, and I'm not about to be used by anyone, especially not that *son of a bitch.*"

"Ah, I forgot you were listening in to my evil mind." Spence got off the elevator at the penthouse and entered the security code on the keypad beside his apartment's front door.

"Did you?" She wasn't buying that he'd forgotten to shield his angry feelings about her betrayal.

"If you say you don't want to go back, why do you think he's targeting you?" he asked.

"That's just it, I don't know. And the vision really worries me."

She was afraid, and that stirred up the urge to protect her, despite himself. "He's probably just screwing with you. Entertaining himself and letting you know that he's still out there."

"I don't need you to minimize this for me, Spence. I need for you to check on Mike and Dorel," she said stiffly, erecting a shield around her feelings. "I can take care of Ian myself."

Spence didn't believe that. Stoddard's particular twisted malice was imprinted all over this, and he was allowing them to perceive it. That was cause for concern. "Mike and Dorel are fine. Marty would know if they were in trouble, and he'd tell us."

"But it's possible that Ian's able to block Marty, and us."

"Possible. Maybe, if you believe the latest BS from the industry. Datascape has put the word out that they've developed new tech, but exactly what is anyone's guess. They've been mentally projecting suggestions of new, unlimited abilities out to their former clients, most of whom are mine now. I don't think they've actually got the new tech online. They're just implanting a sense of dissatisfaction in my clients, along with anticipation of having some limitless, secret power at their disposal that only Datascape can provide. It's crap."

"Spence, Ian may not have had such personal psychic power or technology when we worked for him, but he could actually have it now. He was able to project audio. It wasn't a suggestion or feeling. I heard him call me. Then, when I was out-of-body in the etheric, I experienced the vision he created. It should only have been my thoughts, not someone else's. Not his."

Spence wasn't convinced. "There are no hard rules for out-of-body travel. It's the ether, the zero-point field of quantum potential and unmanifested energy. Anything can happen in that particle-antiparticle soup. Instead of vision-questing for some elusive spiritual guidance, you should be learning to control the potentials and energy to manifest what we need here. That's the only way we're going to stop Stoddard, you know that. Quit worrying about people who don't want your help. Help me bring back the Swords of Balance and we can kill the son of a bitch."

"I'm not going to get into that once more. You know I don't work that way. I'll never use my gifts against anyone again," she vowed.

"Hell no, why dirty your pure hands when you can leave the filthy business of cleaning up real evil shit to the likes of me," he reacted, grinding his teeth with resentment.

A warm wave of love carried her next words to him. "This is important to me, Spence," she said, her soft, caring voice offering salve to scars he denied. "I would appreciate it if you could at least call the Gabriellis, tell them my concerns and ask if they'll allow our mental protection."

A flare of hope shot through him. "Allow *our* protection, Rian? You and I working together again? Does that mean you're coming . . . home?"

"Oh, Spence," she murmured, "I still love you, but I can't be with you and you know why."

"Yeah," he said and clicked the phone off.

— TWO —

Upper Columbia River Basin, Washington
From the airplane's backseat, Dorel Gabrielli watched between the shoulders of her husband and son. The silver ribbon of the Columbia River wound through the tree-studded green hills a thousand feet below the propeller blur on the deHavilland Beaver's stubby nose.

Of all the aircraft she and her husband owned personally or through their aircraft leasing company, Dorel loved the Beaver best. The fifty-five-year-old, six-passenger, single-engine airplane on floats was not only pure aviation turn-on but a romantic nostalgia piece for an aeronautical engineer like Dorel. The lovely old airplane had carried the three of them safely all over the Pacific Northwest and Canada, and to the getaway cabin hidden deep in the northeastern Washington backcountry, where they were headed now for a few days of much needed R&R. And there was Marty's vision that he wanted to pursue, though she was against it. Michael didn't believe it would hurt for Marty to go on the quest that he'd been dreaming about for the last couple of weeks.

"Okay, M-Man, all set up on final. You've got her," Michael Gabrielli said, releasing the Beaver's controls to his son. Marty took the yoke in both hands and grinned like his dad.

The only differences between her two men were age, size and hair color. Marty was a smaller version of Michael, though if his current growth spurt continued, he'd soon be seeing eye-to-eye with his father, literally though not in attitude. She'd taught him from an early age to enjoy being *special* and wanted him to feel at home in his skin and accept his appearance. He had coppery hair like her own and people weren't always tolerant of differences, if only in hair color. Though she needn't have worried, because Marty had been able to handle whatever and whomever came his way with skill and equanimity since birth.

While he was a normal preteen in appearance, in reality, Marty was anything but.

The Beaver crabbed into a crosswind and the leading edge wing dipped. Marty overcorrected in the opposite direction before bringing the wings back to level.

"Ohhh. I don't know that this is a good idea," Dorel said into her mike from the seat behind him. "Are you sure you want to land in these conditions, baby?"

Her son cringed at the word *baby.* "Mom, I know you think I don't have a feel for airplanes, but remember I used to fly you around in that bull Stearman and did okay, didn't I?"

"Different life, different airplane, Marty. You may have his memories," Dorel reminded, "but remember that Granddaddy learned to fly after the war. Unfortunately, he wasn't that good. There wasn't a plane that he didn't land hard, or ground loop or nearly crash."

Marty laughed, expertly keeping the airplane lined up on approach. "Yeah, but I walked away from them every time."

Michael laughed over the headset. "That's what World War I ace, Billy Bishop, always said." He glanced over his shoulder at her. "Quiet cockpit, remember? Let the kid concentrate, Dorel. Relax, you know how good he is."

Their aged Airedale terrier, lying beside her on the seat, bumped her thigh with his nose, as if in agreement with the men.

"Okay," she said with a sigh and willed her mouth

closed. She tried to ease off on the helicopter-mom thing, reminding herself that nearly-twelve-year-old Marty began learning to fly when he was barely two, sitting in his dad's lap. He was strong and as good a pilot as anyone Dorel had ever flown with, save her husband.

Rather than watch her son fly the airplane down to the river's choppy surface, Dorel let her thoughts soar.

Dearest Michael, by his own account tempered with her good-natured teasing, was the best pilot in the world, who had flown her into and out of terrifying trouble in the past. Though the last five or so years had been mostly clear skies and smooth air. The only turbulence had been their best friends' breakup, and all concerned were apparently getting on with their lives.

They saw less of Spence than they liked, but his business had taken him into very dangerous areas, and she'd rather Marty wasn't exposed to all that. Dorel missed not hearing from Spence's former fiancée, Rian, as Marty did. He kept in touch with her, and Spence, in his own way. Though he made an effort to remain neutral, Michael sided with Spence and, like his best friend, he still didn't trust Rian and hadn't forgiven her for her betrayal of Spence and them when she worked as a psychic spy for Datascape.

When Rian finally gave up on the toxic relationship, she had explained to all of them that she'd done everything she could, short of falling on her sword, to make up for what she'd done years before.

Marty didn't blame Rian, but then he was an advanced soul. Dorel wasn't, and could only relate to her friend from an intuitive and empathetic, female perspective. Spence was generous and kind to his only friends—Michael, Dorel, Marty and even their dog, Katana—but he'd become a strange, haunted man and was getting stranger every day.

Living with him had proved too difficult even for Rian, a psychologist who had thought she could love her former client enough for both of them.

Spence's treacherous work was to blame, Michael believed. Dorel sensed a darkness of soul about her son's godfather that her husband denied and Marty perceived but wouldn't talk about. They both told her to leave it alone. She'd agreed not to interfere, but that didn't keep her from envisioning the couple happy and healthy, even if they weren't together.

Dorel's gaze centered over her son's shoulder when the airplane touched down perfectly on the river. The floats chattered over the choppy surface, checking forward momentum. The Beaver slowed quickly and Dorel relaxed a bit.

"Good job, son. I'll take it now," Michael said, taking the controls to taxi toward the narrow opening of a side channel on the left bank. The semi-hidden entrance was apparent only when directly in front of it. Inside, a finger of water the width of the Beaver's wingspan led to a beach trailhead. They would have to hike from the beach to their cabin deep in the forest.

Dorel glanced at Katana dozing next to her. Like them, the old boy hadn't made the hike since last summer. She hoped he was still up to it. He was in pretty good shape for a thirteen-year-old large terrier, but he was slowing down more every day. Katana was stoic about joint pain or illness, and where Marty went, so did the Airedale, no matter what. The dog would make the moderate five-mile hike even if he had to crawl. Of course, they'd carry the ninety-pound animal before that happened.

"The trees have really grown. The channel looks much narrower," Dorel said. "Hope the branches don't wipe the position lights off the wingtips, or worse."

"You say that every time." Michael laughed, and Marty turned in his seat, grinning with his *Oh Mom* look.

Dorel crossed her eyes at him and made a face. "Well, maybe so . . ." She struggled to control the unspecified worry or sense of impending disaster that she'd been feeling for a couple of weeks. She took a deep breath and rationalized that she was probably just hormonal. Everything had been going so well for them.

"No worries. The beach is just ahead," Michael reassured her. "Marty, get ready to hook us up, if the stake is still there. Yeah, I see it. The lake's really high, though. Not much beach."

Michael chopped power and the airplane coasted, then bumped up onto the strip of sand, the prop clanking to a stop. Marty opened the door and hopped out on the float, tie-down rope in hand.

Katana lumbered to his haunches when Marty opened the door, and climbed over Dorel to get out of the plane. Ever the waterdog, he leapt in and swam in the warm shallows while Marty clipped the rope's shackle-end onto a cleat, then stepped off in the sand and secured the line to the metal stake, taking up the slack.

Warm Douglas fir-scented air and the sounds of jays and water lapping on the floats filled the inside of the gently rocking airplane cabin, as Michael ran the shutdown checklist. Dorel began gathering their gear out of the backseat.

Marty waded to Katana in the water and joined the dog-paddling party around the airplane.

"Marty, though it's too late to make a difference, I feel compelled to do my mom thing and remind you that those wet socks and shoes aren't going to be so great to hike in, you know," Dorel called. She plopped herself in the right seat beside Michael in the pilot's seat. "I wish Spence could have flown us in the chopper. It's very warm and I don't know if Katana will—"

Michael leaned over and silenced her lips with a soft kiss. "Katana will be fine. The weather's perfect and Spence is busy. You always wish we'd flown the chopper directly to the cabin when we first get to the trailhead. But until one of us, namely not me, gets rotor-wing qualified, then we have to depend on Spence to haul our wussy butts to the cabin's front porch. And he's not had the time—"

"Or the inclination," she interrupted, settling back into the seat and crossing her arms.

"He doesn't have *time,*" Michael emphasized, his blue eyes hardening slightly. "You know he wants to, but since he doesn't have anyone but us, his business necessarily comes first. He can't back off now or he'll lose everything."

"I wonder if he hasn't already," Dorel murmured and backed out onto the float, hanging onto the doorframe. "Marty, come get the packs, please."

Marty and she ferried the three large packs to the beach while Michael locked the airplane. The dog followed Michael onto the sand and waited while they all shrugged into their backpacks.

"Better have a last drink, Kat," Dorel said, pointing at the water. "It's a long, hot hobble to the lunch tree."

Katana sniffed and started down the trail ahead of them. They followed the old boy into the breezeless woods, strolling along single file in the dappled sunlight, letting the Airedale set the pace.

"Dad, are we going to Chogan Falls on the way?" Marty asked.

"No, it's off the trail by a good mile and a half," Michael answered. "We should get to the cabin first, make sure everything is all right and get set up. Tomorrow we'll hike in there, if that will work for you?"

"I guess so. But I think I should be there tomorrow for sure. Whatever I'm supposed to do or see won't wait long," Marty said, sounding a little uncertain.

"Don't worry, M-Man, we'll get you there. That's what we came for."

Behind him, Dorel reached up and ruffled his sun-bleached strawberry-blond hair. He was already taller than she and rejoicing in every quarter-inch over her five feet seven inches. With this current growth spurt, her little boy loved to try to look down on her while patting her head, if she made unnecessary mom noises like reminding him to use sunscreen on his fair skin, brush his teeth or get enough sleep.

They'd given up long ago expecting Marty to do anything like a regular kid, and he still didn't sleep much. That worried Dorel but didn't seem to affect Marty adversely. He loved sports and had endless energy and ability, mastering a game, then moving on to another. Currently, Marty was a star multiple-event swimmer on the local team.

When they stopped at their favorite spot, an ancient fir they'd dubbed the lunch tree, a couple of hours later, Katana lay down under the tree and slept while they ate. Marty tried to interest the tired dog in the rest of his veggie sandwich, but the usually omnivorous Katana wasn't interested.

"Smart dog," Michael said, finishing his ham and cheese. "He doesn't like that veg stuff. Katana's sticking with red meat like his pack leader, me."

Dorel snorted. "That dog will eat anything, and has proven that too many times. He's just too tired to eat, but maybe if you offered him a twenty-dollar bill, that might work. Marty, what's the national bank of Katana up to now? About two hundred eighty-six dollars?"

Marty stroked the terrier's brick-like head. "Yeah, about that." The dog loved to eat cash, and Marty's in particular, before he learned to put his allowance safely away. If any money was left where the dog could sniff it out, he'd swallow it. Then Marty would have to follow the dog outside to reclaim the *processed* cash. He truly hated doing it, and they teased him mercilessly about his money-laundering, but Marty wasn't going to let his money go down the tubes and forget about it.

"See if he'll drink some water," Michael suggested, cleaning up the meal debris. Marty poured a cup full from his water bottle and held it to the dog's mouth. Katana pulled himself up and began to drink.

By the time they were ready to go, so was Katana, who sauntered to the lead again. Dorel pulled her cell phone out of the pocket of her cargo shorts. Its screen showed no bars of service, as usual out here, and it was almost two o'clock. She turned it off to save the battery and dropped it into her pack.

At this leisurely rate, they'd reach the remote cabin in three or four hours. Good thing it wasn't dark until about 7:00 p.m. They'd have daylight enough to get the cabin's power plant running and shoo out all the critters that had probably moved in since their previous visit last fall.

"How far to the cabin, Dad?" Marty asked over his shoulder to Michael behind him.

His question struck Dorel as odd, though perhaps he was just making conversation. They'd been hiking in silence, the crunch of pine duff underfoot setting up a slow rhythm as they listened to the birds and wind in the trees.

Michael shrugged. "About two miles, I guess. We should

get there in about three hours. The trail is pretty good. No wash-outs or deadfalls. Is that about what you figure?"

Marty was usually tuned into everything and often shared what he sensed, a game the three of them had played since he was a toddler talking about having been Dorel's grandfather before. Rather than ridicule the child or fear he was possessed by an overactive imagination, they encouraged him to voice what he felt, heard or saw in his mind. The practice had helped him, and them, to trust his intuition.

Yet, they feared for him because of society's inevitable dangerous reaction to their special son, if people were aware of even the most minuscule part of his gifts. Nevertheless, their loving acceptance of his extrasensory perceptual powers had allowed Marty to grow into his extraordinary abilities and still live, for the most part, as a normal child.

"Dunno," Marty answered, who had gotten quieter the farther down the trail they traveled.

Katana dropped into a sit in the middle of the dust trail, licking Marty's hand when he reached the dog. Michael stopped and gave Dorel a look.

"Are you feeling okay? Need something to drink?" Dorel asked Marty, reaching for her water bottle.

"Yeah, water would be good, but I've got mine, Mom. Drink your own. You need it more than I do," he reminded her, pulling his bottle out of the side pocket on his pack. He took a long drink and swiped his red, sweaty face with his arm.

"I asked if you are feeling okay," Dorel pressed, keeping herself from feeling his forehead for a fever. She stroked Katana's wiry-coated head instead. "Got an answer for me?"

"Not the one that you want to hear," her son said, and poured water on his face.

"What's up, M-Man?" Michael asked. Dorel heard that he was trying to keep the concern out of his voice, and Marty did, too.

"Don't worry, guys, I'm okay. It's just . . . different." Marty shrugged. "All I keep seeing in my mind is that big black bird and hearing, 'Chogan Falls,' like in my vision. It's kinda weird."

"Guess whatever it is that's called you wants to be sure you got the message and will get there," Michael said. "Can you tell it, or yourself, that we'll get over there tomorrow? I promise. There's just no way we could make it today."

"It's not driving me crazy or anything. It's just different, like I said. No biggie." Marty tipped up the bottle and took another swallow of water.

"Looks like Katana is ready to roll. Everyone?" Michael asked.

Dorel waited to answer after Marty nodded, and took her place behind Michael on the trail.

For the next three hours they strolled through the warming forest, stopping twice more for Katana to rest and to inquire gently how Marty was doing. Each time he answered no change—just the vision bird and the words *Chogan Falls* going through his mind. He was still okay with his *different* experience. He didn't judge the repeating message that Dorel knew would drive her crazy if it were happening to her.

The sun was settling on the western horizon when they stepped out of the tree line into the grassy meadow. As they crossed to the cabin, she hoped the deer, birds and bears had left some blueberries on the bushes by the stream that wound through the edge of the meadow behind the log cabin, but it was probably too late in the season. She always looked forward to picking fresh blueberries by herself in the crisp dawn and making pancakes for her boys before they awoke.

It was one of their most cherished family traditions. They knew that she always gobbled down more blueberries than ever made it into the pancakes, but Michael and Marty never complained. Instead, they celebrated whatever blue bits they were lucky enough to find in their pancakes as pure serendipity.

Dorel hoped she'd still be greeting the summer sun with blueberry juice-stained hands and mouth out here when she was eighty. And her boys, and maybe a great grandchild, or ten, would be waiting in the cabin for her to make banana pancakes. Because there would never be enough blueberries to feed her berry habit and the big family that Marty, an only child, would certainly have.

"Okay, we're on the arrival checklist. Dorel, you hold Katana. Marty, go to the shed and uncover the collector array, start the batteries charging. I'll issue eviction notices to squatters in the cabin." Michael leaned his pack against a stump and pulled out his .45, just in case the pepper spray that he also pulled out didn't work, like a couple of years ago.

The black bear sow that had moved in during the winter had been most reluctant to leave her cozy den, despite their attempts to lure her out with food. Short of smoking the animal out by setting the cabin on fire, Michael had decided the only way to move the bear was with the bear repellant he'd bought at an outfitter's store. The grumpy bear, who instantly developed a liking for pepper spray, had nearly eaten Michael in a frenzy for more. It was only Marty's timely intervention, by what the then ten-year-old boy described as happy bear talk, that saved his father from being pepper steak. The hungry, but now happy, bear had decamped immediately.

"Be careful," Dorel warned as Marty headed for the shed housing the power plant and Michael stepped up on the front porch. She tightened her hold on Katana's collar as the Airedale began to quiver with excitement.

"Katana may smell something in there," she called to Michael. "Maybe you just better open the door and stand back."

Michael turned and gave her a baleful look. "That dog always smells something. Remember, in his younger days I used to send him in to clear the place out. He's thinking of the good times." He glanced around the porch and at the two front windows covered with metal shutters. "I don't see any large-critter signs. Just those damned mice that have left crap all over the porch and taken over inside."

No doubt. She squatted and rubbed her nose on the dog's head in the softer fur between his ears. "Good and pleasant boy," she crooned, endeavoring to give the canine curmudgeon a better attitude to work toward, "easy now. You're on vacation. Let your dad do battle with the evil mice in your stead. He enjoys it so."

"You bet I do," Michael threw over his shoulder, and unlocked the iron hasp on the thick timber door, pushing it open. He stepped aside, flattening his back against the wall, as the heavy door swung inward. He waited a moment, pepper spray in hand and the .45 tucked in his jeans waistband, and peered sideways into the dark cabin.

Dorel heard a loud click and the slow grinding as the metal shutters began to rise over the windows. Marty had brought the photoelectric cells online just in time. There was usually enough juice left in the bank of batteries to power the shutters at their arrival. The security measures had kept people out well enough, though they hadn't proven entirely bear-proof.

"See anything?" Dorel called.

Katana strained in her grasp, pawing the air with his front feet. Should she let the dog go to help Michael? she wondered and relaxed a little. These weren't the terrifying old days when Katana had actually driven away ninja who'd come in the night to kill them and steal Dorel's sword, a legacy from her grandfather that had brought Michael into her life as well as others who tried to kill them for it.

The loyal dog would still try to protect them, because he was fearless. They knew, even if he didn't, that Katana couldn't hold his own against anything fierce and fast like a bear or mountain lion.

"I don't see anything yet." Michael winked at her and held the pepper spray out like a gun in front of him, "I'm going in, cover me!" He charged inside yelling, *"Aaaahhhh,"* like the Navy SEAL he used to be.

Sometimes he was such a fun goof, but she saw that sexy side of him less and less as they were consumed with parenting and running their business. Life had a way of kicking the romance, and fun, out of it. She supposed that could change if they did as TV counselors suggested and scheduled time to being a couple, focused on each other and their relationship. But planning *we* time felt too contrived and forced to her, like scheduling Saturday as meatloaf night and, oh yes, hot sex night—after the dishes are done, of course.

Dorel still wanted spontaneous, wherever and whenever the spirit moved her, and Michael had always moved her like no other. However, this life together was proving not to be about them, as it had been so many lives through time.

Because they'd discovered that in their past lives together they'd died young and childless, they'd come to believe that this life was to be focused on Marty.

As often happened, she thought of her son and he appeared. Marty barreled around the corner of the cabin. "Is Dad okay?"

"Haven't heard otherwise." Dorel grinned, letting Katana drag her toward Marty at the porch. "Are you barely eaten, Michael?" she called.

"What do you mean, is Dad okay?" Michael asked, appearing in the doorway. "Of course I'm okay, better than, in fact." He leaned over and kissed Dorel on the mouth. "Aren't I?"

"Ew, you guys," Marty complained with an embarrassed smile.

Dorel threw her arms around Michael's neck and kissed him back. Katana strolled into the cabin while Marty continued with kid *yuck* noises. It was that kind of ordinary behavior that made it so hard to believe the boy might be destined to be some sort of avatar, or so said those who claimed to know such things.

While there wasn't exactly a star in the east on that day, Dorel had looked into the newborn baby's blue eyes and seen her beloved grandfather staring back at her. Every day after that had brought similar interesting and sometimes frightening developments into their lives.

But they could always come to the isolated cabin for peace and recharging, to feel like an ordinary family away from the pressures of business, parenting and avatar-growing.

This trip was starting out to be the best yet.

They followed Katana into the one-room cabin that Michael had secured as varmint-free. Dust motes floated in the beams of sunlight cast by the setting sun streaming in the west-facing windows. A cool breeze swirling in from the open door stirred the stale odors of smoke, age-grimed wood and general mustiness. They'd made a lot of improvements over the years: adding a power plant, plumbing and an indoor bathroom and a microwave oven to supplement the wood cook stove.

Michael and Spence had hand-built the log structure as a hunting cabin. Since Dorel had first visited the then-spartan man-cabin over thirteen years ago, the only thing that had been hunted and found there was peace and quiet. Consequently, Spence had come with them less and less, though Rian had often joined them while she'd been with Spence.

They came on this trip because Marty was hunting a vision that had given him, and them, no peace or quiet. He'd started having the lucid dream one month to the day before his twelfth birthday. It claimed more and more of his focus, until Michael agreed that they had to go to Chogan Falls, within a couple of miles of the cabin, as the vision had instructed. Though that had satisfied Marty, who was intrigued and excited about discovering the meaning of his vision, Dorel couldn't help worrying that this action was setting in motion an unstoppable spooling of change that was unpredictable and alarming.

Michael commanded the moving-in process with his usual military precision. Within thirty minutes, Dorel had built a fire in the cook stove and set canned stew to heating in the cast iron skillet, while Marty laid out blue-and-white-speckled enamel dishes on the split log table. Beside the cabin, Michael matched his tuneless woodcutter's whistle to the smack-crack of his axe splitting wood.

"Tell Paul Bunyan dinner's ready," Dorel said to Marty and set a basket of crackers on the table.

They sat at the table and waited. When Michael didn't come in or stop chopping wood, Dorel gave Marty a questioning look. He shrugged and went out to get his dad. The noise stopped, and both returned a few seconds later. Michael washed up in the kitchen sink. Marty sat down, a frown crinkling his forehead.

"Marty Mail not working?" Dorel asked, and ladled steaming vegetables and meat into the boy's plate. He'd communicated telepathically with them since he was a baby. Not doing so was another strange development. She took a deep breath and attempted to relax her stiff shoulders that seemed to have risen around her ears.

Marty wrinkled his nose. "I guess not. Maybe it's because we're having this stuff. The smell knocked my comcenter out."

Michael slid into his chair and reached for a cracker. "I believe it. It's your mother who's in love with canned stew. So we have to partake of the garbage the first night we get here like a sacred rite."

She filled his plate with a superior smile, "It's called a family tradition. We ate this the first time you brought me here, and our eating it each first night in the cabin brings that special feeling back. It's wonderful and I love it."

"Let me remind you that you didn't love it then. You were exhausted and near lame from being on the run from the bad guys. Naturally, when we actually got a chance to eat, you scarfed up every bit of this crap, including mine." Michael lifted a spoonful to his nose and sighed. "Why you ordered enough cases to torture us to perpetuity, beats me. And I thought you loved us."

"Sometimes. Oh, when I went down to the cellar, I noticed that three cases are past their good-by dates. Don't want to waste them, so why don't we haul them into the woods and open the cans? We can feed the critters." Dorel spooned stew into her mouth and closed her eyes while she chewed. "Ummmm."

"Better still, why don't we lay down a stew trail on our way to Chogan Falls tomorrow? Nothing's going to eat that, and we're sure to find our way back." Michael swallowed and held up his hand. "Wait, I'm betting it's great bear repellant. We'll smear you with stew, then you take point. Nothing will come near us."

She stuck her tongue out at him and turned to Marty. "Are we still on for the falls tomorrow, M-Man?"

"Yeah, Chevayo says it's gotta be tomorrow morning," he said, keeping his eyes on his plate.

A shiver went down her spine. "Who's Chevayo?"

"Don't know, but he says I gotta go. It's like life or death or something," Marty said.

— THREE —

In the super-quiet sanctity of his high-tech temple office, Ian Stoddard studied the transcribed *Essence Prophecy of Anubis*. He now knew which voice or vibration to tune his receptive mind to. All that remained was to summon the ancient one by his name that held great magic power and invite the Guide of the Dead to help him prepare for the coming of the One.

Ian had long ago realized that for someone with his skill and innate talent, it was not necessary to speak ancient Egyptian or conduct the complicated rites for summoning spirits. All he needed to do was form an intention, focus on it and match his own vibration to that. He'd engaged, counseled with and fought many disincarnate entities over the years. However, he hadn't summoned one as cunningly dangerous as Anubis before. Extreme care must be exercised in calling upon the dark lord of the Underworld, but only he possessed the power that would bring the One to the earth, the One whom Ian intended to shape and guide, and ultimately rule the world through.

Ian indulged in his own rituals. Such practices helped him consciously change the vibration of his astral body to travel the ether, or spirit world, and contact entities dwelling there and in other nonmaterial realms of existence.

For this summoning, Ian needed specific tools and ritual items that not only summoned the special spirit, but also protected him from possession. He removed an alabaster box from the safe and carried it to the travertine pedestal table in a small alcove shielded by a carved tri-fold screen. Into a turquoise-inlaid gold bowl the size of a woman's cupped hands, Ian sprinkled a sparse pinch of incense from the box. He'd secretly obtained the priceless ceremonial incense, as well as the altar and other required ancient Egyptian funerary artifacts, from a high-level Egyptologist who had the heart of a thief and a distinct lack of moralistic nationalism, in the Egyptian Antiquities Trust.

To the left of the bowl, Ian placed an obsidian figurine of Anubis, the jackal-headed god, that had been found in the hidden room excavated between the paws of the Great Sphinx at Giza. He took a deep breath and brought both palms together in a sweeping arc to his chest. He envisioned his aura or energy field expanding, strengthening to a shimmering, diaphanous, but impervious shield to which no disincarnate being or energy could attach without his awareness or consent.

Ian touched a match to the incense, that combusted with a bang like a firecracker. A puff of yellow smoke swirled the putrid odor of eons around his head, while he focused on the emotional energy wave generated by his intention that would put him in resonance with the spirit entity known as Anubis. Once on corresponding vibration that he felt humming throughout his body and aura, Ian sensed the entity and set the parameters of what he would allow in the contact.

Ian chanted, "I call upon the protection of the great god who rules the Underworld. Guide me, Anubis, that with your help from the Underworld, I may bring about the return of the One to the earth."

"Greetings, priest," Ian heard in his mind. "You remember once again your lord and master. You have done well to call upon me, for those who have held us in abeyance are no more. The way is opened."

Barely controlling his excitement, Ian asked, "You are the god Anubis?"

"Did you not make *paut* to this god?" the entity sneered.

Ian willed his anxious body to continue within the required vibration, for a racing heart fueled by fear would break the connection or give the entity control, if it were stronger than he.

"I made an offering?" Ian asked. If he had unwittingly done so, that would be a grave error, as it could be taken as invitation to the entity to possess and use him. "I only wished to ask for your help. No offering was made."

"Ah, but it was. Did you not send the essence of the gods as breath to the heavens, as when you were my high priest long ago?" the entity asked.

Ian's gaze fell on the altar. Yellow smoke curled from the blackened incense in the bowl. His mind raced his heart to panic. Which was the offering, the bowl or the incense?

The entity laughed in his ears. "Both, and when used in combination, the most powerful offering, as you must now remember. Look closely, high priest of Anubis: this very bowl was created by your command. You prepared the essence of gods' breath within it. These have come to you again by my desire."

"I—I don't remember . . ." Ian mumbled, but memories of Egyptian past lives, as abased slave to exalted high priest, cascaded into his mind, overwhelming him with vivid detail and raw emotion. Before he was lost among the familiar faces of primordial enemies and lovers he began to recognize, Anubis intervened.

"Do not fear, this you have chosen then and now. For what is then? And what is now? The difference of a breath or two. I am the god Anubis and you are my high priest. You have called me to earth by my plan. Let us get on with it," Anubis ordered, his voice taking a stern tone.

Ian inhaled a deep, diaphragmatic breath, rubbed his face and shook out his hands to break his trance state and the connection with the entity. He swept the bowl to the floor with his arm, and the smoldering contents spilled out onto the carpet. He stomped the embers out, picked up the bowl, tossed the Anubis figurine in the alabaster box with the incense and locked the lot into the safe.

"You, priest, are ever the bad-tempered old crocodile. This I forgive you, as you endeavor to serve me," the entity said, sounding as if it were here in the room, right behind him.

Ian spun around. "Go! I banish you beyond the veil between worlds, back to the ether and the spirit world. I do not seek your counsel or aid and will not accept your interference," he stated as his intent. He closed his eyes and focused on his pulse, stepping it up to bring his energy out of resonance with the entity.

Anubis's laughter lashed out like a whip. "Do not try me further, priest, or I shall require your heart for my own. You have called me. I am here. Let us get on with it."

Ian reined in his freewheeling paranoia and made himself calm down and think. "A moment, my lord, I must come to myself," he said to the entity. He was going to have to play along and placate this spirit until he could exorcise it, but now wasn't the time. He couldn't think clearly because of the jumble of Egyptian past lives, the present threatening entity and rapidly-increasing fear tumbling through his mind.

Ian sat at his desk, lacing his fingers on the smooth, polished mahogany top, and began to initiate the mind-chatter quieting and self-control protocols that every remote viewing trainee learned. He'd designed the protocols and hadn't used them in years, but they were the only thing he could think of to use to get command of himself. While he absolutely had experienced spirit communication with entities in his out-of-body astral projections of his own spirit, this obviously powerful entity, claiming to be Anubis, was disturbing in the extreme. It seemed more like a delusion or a psychotic episode than one of trance channeling or communicating with discarnate entities.

"Priest?" Ian heard the entity prompt. "Attend me. I have told you that those who have opposed us are no more and that the way is now open. Are the preparations in place?"

"Who, specifically, are we talking about?" Ian asked the air in front of him.

"The one called Roshi is now with his ancestors and shall trouble us no more."

Ian thought a moment. Roshi? Oh yes, the Buddhist monk friend of Martin Everly, the boy's great-grandfather and previous incarnation. "The old monk was a very skilled meditator and able to mentally project illusions that prevented my team from finding the boy years ago, but that won't happen today."

"Yes, especially now that the Roshi has crossed into the Underworld," Anubis carped.

Ian cringed. "Well, true, but we can find anyone, anytime, anywhere with our present technological augmentation."

"Which the Roshi would also defeat were he in the body." Anubis chuckled. "Do you not remember this one? Was he not the Queen Kalūkuh's magician? It was with his magic, and my swords, of course, that she was able to defeat the invaders of her realm."

Ian scowled, searching memories flashing behind his eyes like a slide show set on fast scan.

"The Roshi is never to be underestimated. He is always the boy's first teacher. In this life, and others past, he was the most powerful of his dark sect of spiritual warlords who did battle with spirits, with those they deem *evil.* It was his magic that sealed the forge of the Swords of Balance and banished me to the spirit world. If Kalūkuh and her lover had taken up the swords and used them in this life, as they were destined, my essence would have coalesced upon the earth then. Now we must prepare the boy."

Ian perked up. "Then I'm right, he is the One."

"His stars show him to be the best vessel for me at this time," Anubis said. "The ancient rites must be completed at the moment before the sun rises on his twelfth year. He will be loath to abandon his body. You, priest, must work your art to enchant his heart to allow my entrance. This is best done bite by bite, old crocodile."

Ian's thoughts churned. Anubis intended to possess Marty Gabrielli and expected Ian to make it happen. If he did that, and Anubis was successful in taking over the boy's body, then that would leave Ian the god's eternal servant. Ian wanted to train and control the boy himself, but Anubis had other plans that Ian was not powerful enough to alter—yet.

Until he could reclaim the skills and knowledge of his priestly past that his consciousness now accepted as true, Ian considered that perhaps it was wiser to serve the devil of the moment until he was able to conquer him without the danger of losing body or soul. He also had to discover the rest of the initiation ritual that would focus the Essence power upon the Gabrielli boy, after he banished Anubis back to the netherlands of the spirit world. In the meantime, he would serve, learn and gather his strength.

"Where would you have me start, my lord?" Ian asked.

"Take the boy from the nest now, as you have planned," Anubis replied and departed.

Ian shuddered in the ensuing silence. How long had the

jackal been stalking his thoughts?

Just after sunrise the next morning and without breakfast, Marty set a fast pace and confidently led the way, as if he'd hiked the rough and often indistinguishable trail to Chogan Falls many times before. This was his and Dorel's first trip to the little-known grotto deep in the eastern Washington forest. Michael hadn't hiked to the falls in many years, and hadn't been that interested in making the trip, but Marty had been insistent.

Last night, when Marty dropped the bomb about someone in his vision insisting that he go to the falls today, they'd tried to pry more information out of him, but he wouldn't talk. Dorel worried all night, her anxiety magnifying with each sound in the darkness outside the cabin. She'd lain awake thinking about how she and Michael had always been so encouraging about Marty's otherworldly excursions and communication. Except for this one that was feeling very wrong. Even the warm sunlight couldn't lift the heavy chill settling around her heart.

If Michael shared her concern, he kept it to himself, but she knew something was up with him, as he'd gotten very talky the farther down the trail they went. He didn't know what they were getting into either. Shouldn't one of the grownups have the courage to tell the boy no? Dorel wondered in frustration. In reality, they couldn't start that kind of parenting now, after giving Marty much of the freedom he'd desired. And he'd always used it well, to his and their benefit.

But this was different, maybe dangerously so, and she had to speak her mind before she took another step. "Stop, guys."

Michael and Marty instantly halted and returned to her. "What's up?" Michael asked, a frown of concern creasing his forehead.

She met Marty's gaze and he gave her a supportive smile. "Mom, it's going to be all right; you've got to trust that. This is the way it has to happen. You'll understand everything soon. We all will."

Dorel put her arms around her son and held him close. "Baby, you've said all the right things but one, that you're going to be all right."

Michael put his hand on her arm. "Let it go, Dorel."

She held on tighter. "I can't until you promise me that what I'm feeling is just low blood sugar or some dumb helicopter-mom thing."

Marty chuckled against her cheek. "Sorry, you couldn't get your blueberry fix this morning, Mom, but we've got to get to the falls by noon. I'm supposed to see something at noon that will be there just for me."

She let him pull away a little. "How do you know this is real and not—"

"Not some evil entity tricking me to suck out my soul?" Marty joked. "It's not, Mom. Roshi told me to expect this."

Michael's jaw dropped. "Before or after he died?"

"I'm not sure, because he doesn't seem dead to me. The communication is the same," Marty said, giving his mother a teasing pat on her head, and moved out of her embrace. "Come on, guys; this is going to be amazing, you'll see."

Michael shrugged and grabbed Dorel's hand. "Let's go. I'm not going to tell him no, like I know you want me to. Besides, I'm curious and want to see what's waiting for us up there. And remember, the Roshi told him to go."

"No, he didn't, Dad," Marty countered. "I said the Roshi told me to expect something."

"That could mean anything," Dorel argued. "You can't tell me that we're out here because a dead Buddhist monk told you to expect something? I thought your vision said for you to be at the falls on this day. And while we're at it, what the hell does Chevayo have to do with all this?"

Without answering, Marty turned and started down the trail.

"Martin Everly Gabrielli, come back here," Dorel demanded, and immediately felt silly because she seldom had to resort to hyper-momism with her son. And it didn't work.

"Follow me, Mom. It'll be all right," Marty called over his shoulder that seemed broader somehow. Could he have grown up without her noticing?

Michael gave her trembling hand a little tug. "Come on, we agreed to this and can't quit now. That wouldn't be the best for Marty."

Dorel reluctantly followed her husband and son as the sun climbed higher in the cloudless sky.

After two hours of tramping through the dense underbrush of the fir and pine forest, they heard the roar of Chogan Falls in the distance. Marty had led them in silence, as if he were being reeled in by something he either couldn't or didn't want to resist. If she weren't so anxious, Dorel would have enjoyed the beautiful, sun-dazzled hike with her boys. But the closer they got to Marty's destination, the more she wanted to turn back for the known safety of the cabin.

In a few minutes, they arrived at the head of the falls that dropped thirty feet to a frothy pool below. They took off their daypacks and sat on the rocks at the stream's edge, waiting for something to happen.

Michael glanced at his watch. "It's not noon yet. We could have lunch. Think we have time, M-Man?"

"Yeah, I'm hungry," Marty answered and opened his pack, pulling out a plastic baggie filled with chips and a ham and cheese sandwich. Dorel and Michael dug out their lunches. As they ate, they chatted casually about everything but what Dorel really wanted to discuss. She held back, waiting for an opening, but Michael smartly deflected her attempts to redirect the conversation.

Marty stopped in mid-chew and stood, roving his sharp gaze from the tumbling water to the opposite bank and behind them in the forest. He tossed the last bite of sandwich into the stream and wiped his hands on his jeans. "It's time." Michael scrambled up and stood next to him.

"How do you know? Do you hear something?" Dorel demanded, getting to her feet.

"Yeah, kinda," was Marty's cryptic answer. "Let's take the packs, because I think we're supposed to go down to the pool." He jerked his head in that direction and grabbed his pack.

"What? Down there?" Dorel stood on a boulder and craned her neck over the edge, her gaze dropping with the curtain of water to the pool below. "Is there a trail down, or do we just find a handy family-size barrel and roll?"

"I think I remember a trail," Michael said, "though I like the barrel-roll idea." He helped her down from the rock and checked over his shoulder, seeing his son wading across in knee-deep water upstream. "Looks like Marty's already got it covered. Let's go."

Dorel pulled him back. "Michael, I've got a really bad feeling about this. Is this smart or even rational, what we're doing?"

"It doesn't matter. We're here because we're supposed to be." He slipped his arm around her and whispered in her ear, "And that's the feeling I've got about this. Now let's go. We don't want to lose him."

Dorel agreed when all she could see of Marty was the top of his red head as he descended between a tumble of boulders on the opposite side of the falls. She followed Michael across the stream and hurried to catch up with her son.

The path was little more than a sort of animal trail through the slippery rocks, and tough going for anything less than mountain goats. At the bottom, they walked through a cloud of cooling spray from the falls-roiled pool. They gathered at the base of a freestanding granite slab that seemed stabbed into the rocky ground like a surfboard in the sand and marking the downstream outflow from the pool.

"I think this is the place," Marty said in a low voice. He slipped his wet pack off, sat down at the base of the slab, his back against it, and closed his eyes.

Dorel started to speak, but Michael shook his head and held a finger to his lips, then eased into a squat not far from Marty. She gritted her teeth and crossed her arms over her chest. No way was she going to sit and wait for whatever.

Marty's eyes popped open and he sat up, pointing. "There," he cried.

Straight across the stream three yards from their position, a huge black bird sat on a tree stump, staring at them.

Michael rose slowly, keeping his eyes on the bird. "Was that there when we got here?"

Marty nodded. "He didn't want us to see him then. Now it's okay." He turned to Dorel. "Do you see the bird, Mom?"

"Of course I see it," she hissed. "Who could miss a four-foot-tall black bird that looks like a Muppet eagle?"

Marty grinned. "Yeah, but I think he's supposed to be a crow or a raven."

Michael nodded but didn't move when Marty began to walk slowly toward the creature.

"Get back here, Marty," Dorel commanded and started

after him. He didn't obey and whispered to her to stay back. She watched helplessly as her only child foolishly approached the stone-still bird that looked like a taxidermist's failed project. Its feathers appeared more hairy than sleek. She couldn't see feet or legs on the black heap with a beak and huge, unblinking black eyes.

When Marty got within five feet of the bird and started to take another step, the animal lifted its great wings, with the span of a hang glider, in warning. He stopped and raised both hands, palms open, and dipped his chin in greeting. The bird blinked and folded its wings.

"He's going to let me talk to him," Marty called back to his parents behind him. "Please stay there. I'm perfectly safe, and this is what I'm here for. Don't come near or try to talk to him or me, okay?"

Not waiting for his parents' agreement, Marty asked, "Are you Chevayo?" The bird's energy felt the same as the one that had identified himself as Chevayo in his waking dream yesterday as they hiked to the cabin.

"It is I," he heard the voice from yesterday speak in his mind.

"Are you really a bird?" Marty asked, and sensed laughter in response.

"Do I not appear as a raven?"

"Not a very good one," Marty returned. "More like someone in a bird suit, though the wings are massively cool. Would they work?"

"If I wished them to, yes. But, as you know, there are other ways to break the bonds of earth. I appear to you in the form of the raven as a beginning of the transformational work of soul alchemy that you, Initiate, will undertake. I, Chevayo, am honored to be your spirit guide. These are the primary stages, as symbolized by this black bird form that I take, of your journey from the consciousness of the physical senses that tie you to the body into the dark, inner world of the soul."

"That sounds kind of hard. Do I have to do it?" Marty asked, wrinkling his nose. This wasn't feeling very fun anymore.

"It is what you and your group have chosen." The bird perched on the log like a stuffed animal, unmoving and silent to physical ears.

"And you're my guide. Does that mean I'm going to need help to do this thing?" Marty persisted. He knew something big was coming, but this sounded almost impossible. Almost like he'd have to leave his family and go off with this fake raven.

"Yes, if the mission is to be fulfilled."

"What if I don't want to do soul alchemy?" He thought he would go ahead and ask, but knew it was a done deal. Childish tempers were not tolerated in soul matters.

The sense of laughter radiated from the raven. "Okay."

"Okay, that's it? All I have to say is I don't want to, and I don't?" There might be hope yet to be an ordinary teenager.

"Of course not, but I wanted you to have a sense of choice. This course was chosen by your group long before your present incarnation."

"How long? Like when I was Dorel's grandfather?" He remembered scores of his past lives, and always wanted more information about any others, like Rian had helped him remember.

"The culminating soul cycle began in ancient Egypt."

"Can I ask you some questions?" As long as he had an actual spirit guide here, he might as well take advantage of it.

"Ask, and I will choose which are best to answer for your present growth."

Marty laughed. "Great. I guess asking you for the lottery numbers is out, huh? Anyway, I can do certain things like remember my past lives and the skills I had from them. I can communicate telepathically with people and animals. Oh yeah, and I can see or sense people's energy, but I think I could help them, too. Like heal them, because I can tell what's wrong with their health on an energy level that eventually shows up in the body, but I don't know how to change that. Can you teach me?"

"You already have such skill, which will be found and developed on your soul journey within. There you will learn to trust yourself to help whomever you choose and to accomplish, with pure, selfless intention, your heart's desire. But be warned, heart's desire is never a material thing."

"I knew there was a catch." Marty grinned. "I come here, talk to a huge black bird that tells me I'm going to be able to do and get anything I want—just not here on earth, right?"

"A humorous attitude will be of great solace to you in the days to come." The bird shifted on the log and closed one eye like an owl.

Marty squinted at him. "That doesn't sound so great."

"I do not wish you to fall into fear. Do not allow it, but know that fearful-appearing events and people are entering your experience within a day. You must prepare yourself for battle and loss. Remember that the body dies but the soul is eternal. Just as you communicate with those in other realms now, so you may continue as you expand your consciousness. Control your emotions or they will step down your vibration and you will become deaf and blind to those who would help you.

"Do not be deceived by appearances. Listen, sense the intention of each that you encounter. It will reside in their energy field: either a dark blotch or a spark of light. Control your thoughts, for he will seek to do so by every means available to him. And he has help from the dark realms—"

"He who?" Marty interrupted. He rubbed his arms as a shiver of recognition dashed down them.

Ignoring his question, the bird continued. "Know that all events are unfolding by sacred design for your growth and that of your group. You are beloved and protected. I, Chevayo, am never farther away from you than a thought of peace."

"You say something bad is going to happen and you won't stop it?" Marty raged, taking a big step toward the bird. It instantly ruffled its wings and squawked. He stopped, hearing his parents running toward him, and spun around. "Stay there, Mom, Dad. I'm okay. Just a couple more minutes."

When he was sure they'd stay put, he turned back to face the black bird. "Sorry, I didn't mean to lose my temper. It's just that I don't want anything to happen to my parents."

"You must guard your emotions. Do not be deceived by appearances. See such things as the illusions that they are, as designed to manipulate you. Control your thoughts, or someone else will."

"I don't know if I can do this," Marty whispered, his voice quivering.

"Such is always the first step of the journey within," Chevayo answered. "Now go, with great love for all things in your heart. I will come to you again at your summons."

Marty closed his stinging eyes and rubbed them. When he opened them, he saw through the blur of his tears that the bird had disappeared.

— FOUR —

The lead remote viewer burst into Ian's office unannounced. "Dr. Stoddard, we've got it! The rest of the prophecy. And there's new information that changes everything."

Ian laid his pendulum on the worldwide grid map in front of him and looked over the top of his readers, pinning the excited man with a baleful stare. "Have you now?" He gestured to the armless, straight-backed chair in front of his desk, designed to render an occupant a couple of inches lower than Ian's eye level.

The viewer, aware of Ian's intent to put subordinates entering the sanctum of his office in a state of unease that enabled obedience, eagerly took his place and began. "We've found a different origin than the one we first understood. It was hidden in the translations. The original author is not of the Anubis sect at all. It's far older than that. We were able to get through an interference pattern that proved to be energetically encoded in the translation when the prophecy was usurped by the Egyptian priests."

Ian tented his fingers and smiled, exhilaration tingling across his shoulders. "Clever, very clever."

The viewer beamed. "Yes, sir. Researchers have found that Egyptian names had magical power, numbers were symbols possessing active force and their properties sacred attributes. That in mind, we pursued the line of inquiry, as some research suggests, that the ancient Egyptian magicians or adepts were able to manipulate energy and sound waves to virtually move mountains. As the team worked with the prophecy, a verbal pattern or auditory wave began to emerge, the scheme of which we overlaid to the text of the papyrus. We were able to get on that energy wave and trace it back to the priests in a preparation chamber beneath the Sphinx, where they created their version of the prophecy."

As the viewer explained the process, Ian heard the ancient priests, led by himself, chanting and embedding the magical words and symbols in the papyrus, so that those who would translate it would be mesmerized, subject to the arcane intention of the cult of Anubis to bring the god to earth.

"Obviously, Dr. Stoddard, when the papyrus came into Nostradamus's possession, instead of intuiting the real prophecy, the seer actually channeled the entity known as Anubis. And that is what has happened each time someone has tried to translate the papyrus, until the original prophecy was completely bastardized and misunderstood to be the coming of the Antichrist. We realized then that we had to protect ourselves from the entity's influence. With that realization, we were aided by one of the highest—most divine, if you will—energy wave forms we've ever encountered. In fact, we agree that the energy can only be described as hyper-dimensional love."

Ian smirked. "Are you saying you've found God?"

The viewer blushed and looked down at his hands. "I don't know, sir. But it's an energy being that, just by approaching its frequency with our very limited perceptual skills, we felt moved or transformed . . . by the completely nonjudgmental love we experienced from it. It was like—"

"Kissing the hem of Christ's robe, perhaps?" Ian jibed and stood.

The man raised his eyes, looking past Ian, his expression bright with faith. "Yes!"

Ian turned his back on the viewer and gazed out at the

downtown Denver skyline, considering the next step. The remote viewing team had some sort of religious or conversion experience. They were of no use to him now, for they would suddenly be filled with conscience and clear-cut ideals of right and wrong. This would produce nothing but a moralizing analytic overlay of each target they were assigned in the future.

Ah well, team housecleaning was long overdue, anyway. So be it. He rolled his tight shoulders and smoothed his tie, and turned back to the viewer with a benign smile.

"You say you have the real meaning of the prophecy?" he asked and settled into his leather executive chair again, relaxing into its cushiony support.

The viewer blinked and cleared his throat. "Well, yes. I thought I'd told you—"

"What you said was that you think you found the origin of the piece, but you said nothing of its meaning," Ian prompted, honing a chiding edge on his tone.

"Oh, right. I guess I was so excited that I forgot." His grin trembled at the corners and he bit his lip. "As we discovered, the prophecy is about the coming of the One called the Essence to earth. Now, it's the actual ritual that we've finally discovered that allows this to happen. The Anubis cult intended to use it for their own purposes and changed it to suit. In their understanding and application of what we know as quantum physics, astrology, astronomy and lost arcane wisdom, they believed that the opening between dimensions will occur at a given time. If a magical ritual is conducted by a priest of Anubis at the correct alignment of the stars, which they believed to be energy bodies that exert a force of influence on all beings, that will allow for a soul exchange at a given location or energy vortex. Anubis will come to earth again."

"And this was the intention embedded within the

prophecy?" Ian asked, stroking his chin with his little finger. If Anubis could be believed, then as the god's high priest, Ian had prepared the papyrus for his future incarnation. Fine, he believed that now, but what was the exact ritual and how could he keep from being enslaved by his old master?

"The Anubis cult's intention, but not that of the Essence, which is the information the incredibly high vibration *being* that we encountered helped us to decipher." The viewer leaned forward and spoke in earnest. "We have the entire ritual and it's to be used for the good of mankind, to bring this great genius to earth. We were instructed to give this information to no one but you."

Breath hung in Ian's lungs. His mouth moved but no sound came. Finally, he struggled to his feet and the viewer stood, too, an expression of concern on his face as he reached a hand toward Ian.

"I—I'm fine. Sit. Tell. More," Ian managed, gripping the edge of the desk to steady himself.

The man remained on his feet, poised as if he might have to catch his fainting boss. "First, let me tell you that the being warned me to destroy the team's viewing notes. I have told none of them what I compiled from the individual viewing sessions. The target, by your order, was blind to everyone but me. Each only knows what he viewed, but he does not know what it means, only that he had an inspiring experience with an unusual entity. The being actually seemed to counsel me as I compiled the data that the information was for you only. I'm to tell you, and then I'm going to forget everything."

You certainly will. Permanently. Ian eased into his chair. "Very good, continue."

"Let's take it line-by-line, beginning with, 'The moon, in the middle of the night over a high mountain.' As he was under the influence of the hidden Anubis spell on the papyrus, Nostradamus left out something very important, the time and place for the initiation ceremony."

"Which are?" Ian's pulse pounded in his temples. He knew the time was near, but not exactly where.

"I'm pretty sure it's two weeks from today at the full moon before midnight—"

"Pretty sure?" Ian hissed in irritation.

"Well, that's what every viewer reported, and the entity seemed to confirm it to me. I don't know any other way to verify it, so I can't say with absolutely certainty," the viewer defended, his eyes widening.

Ian waved away his excuses. "All right, where?" He glanced at the grid map of worldwide lay lines on his desk that he'd been working with before the viewer came in. His pendulum had been circling on the American Southwest . . .

"Sedona, Arizona." The man held up his hands, shaking his head. "I know, it sounds crazy that something this momentous would take place in the *woo-woo* capital of the United States. Again, we all got the same location in our viewing sessions—the energy vortex in Sedona at Encantada Canyon."

He should have known. Rian was there and he'd been working to influence her, draw her back to him. All the pieces of his life—his actions, feelings, compulsions, intuitions and years of constant monitoring, then working with and against the Gabriellis, Spence and Rian, were all for a purpose, the scope of which he hadn't comprehended until this moment. He alone would command the powers of a god upon the earth.

When Ian didn't respond, the man continued, "Let's move on to the 'wise young man.' This is a boy of eleven years and eleven months of age." The viewer looked away. "A boy of your acquaintance. You've had a team on him and his parents . . ." his voice dwindled at Ian's sharp intake of breath.

"Yes, move on."

"The boy's astrology charts perfectly match those that Nostradamus drew for the great genius, though we don't know how he knew to do so." The viewer waited for Ian to comment.

"What about 'his disciples' mentioned in the prophecy?" Ian asked, holding his pendulum over the grid map. It began a narrowing circle of Sedona, Arizona. *So, now you agree to show me what I ask for,* he mentally derided the pendulum. It began to swing vertically, its signal for yes. Ian dropped it in disgust and focused on the viewer's thoughts, roiling with excitement, awe and a good bit of fear.

"The disciples are his supporters, which we understand as his parents, the godfather Jonathan Spencer and his former girlfriend, Rian Farsante. They must also be present at the initiation, where they invite him to become immortal, and we believe that they must willingly give themselves up for him in some way, perhaps through oath and ritual. Though the Anubis cult requires that the disciples give of their own blood, sacrificing themselves. One can't imagine that a great genius would require a blood sacrifice in his return to earth," the frowning viewer said with scorn.

Shows the limits of your stunted imagination and lack of intellect, Ian thought. "And the ritual? Do you have the exact words and procedures?"

"Remember the two samurai swords? They must be used together in the ceremony, but as to the rest of it and the wording, well, no." The viewer arose, clasping his hands behind his back as if they were being bound. "Dr. Stoddard, the distillation of this target viewing is this: The boy, Martin Gabrielli, is destined to be the greatest living being on earth since the Christ or Buddha. From epochs ago, that enlightened, ascended being was destined to incarnate now. Those who are to help him do that are assembling and, at the time, will know exactly what to do to make that happen. I think you are one of them and that when the time comes, you will have your part to play." The man extended his hand. "May I shake your hand, sir, and wish you Godspeed."

Such a gesture caught Ian totally off-guard. He stared at the man's trembling hand a moment, then arose and shook it with a sincere though humble smile. "Thank you, son, your good wishes mean a great deal to me."

Ian allowed a small sigh as the viewer left, fairly aglow from virtually consorting with gods. After those fond good wishes, it was going to make him a bit glum killing the fellow.

He reached for the phone and enabled *scramble* before inputting a number that he hadn't called in nearly fourteen years. Two short rings preceded the tentative, "Hello?"

"Inada, Ian Stoddard here. It's been a long time."

"*Hai,* Ian-*san,* many years. You honor me with your call. How may I serve you?" the smooth, almost-accentless voice intoned.

Ian envisioned the Japanese business magnate older now, though his ego and fortune securing his ageless passage through an international jet set life of wealth and privilege. Ian heard in the man's thoughts that he was still consumed by the one thing he couldn't buy or steal—the Defender Sword.

"My friend, the sword has returned. Your enemies have hidden it from you. But now you will find it again, that is, if you are still interested," Ian said.

Inada breathed into the phone. "*Hai*—yes."

"I will call you back with the exact location within an hour." Ian hung up and prepared to initiate the targeting protocol to locate the Gabriellis.

He leaned back and closed his eyes, allowing thoughts to flow through his mind without resistance.

Years ago, Inada had hired Datascape Systems to find the priceless samurai katana known as the Defender Sword. Ian's teams had traced it to Dorel Everly, who was then on the run and being helped by Michael Gabrielli, a former Datascape viewer. Inada had tried to steal the sword from her and her defender, Gabrielli, and nearly been killed himself. After that, Inada had retreated, but hadn't given up hope of obtaining the sword. Ian had promised him that somehow he would secure the ancient weapon for him. Good thing Inada was a patient and trusting man, because Ian had no intention of ever giving up the powerful Defender or the Guardian Sword, when and if they materialized again. They truly were the weapons of the gods.

Of course, the Gabriellis didn't have the swords, but Inada didn't know that and would take care of the Gabriellis, allowing Ian to get what he wanted, the boy.

The next morning Rian didn't see the shaman as she entered the Wellness Kiva at 7:30 a.m. She was disappointed, though accepting. Perhaps he had other bad-tripping spirit walkers to attend to. Though even a shaman had to eat, so she might see him at breakfast.

She made her way across the broad expanse of polished slate floor to the reception desk and spoke to the turquoise-smocked concierge. "Good morning, can you tell me if the shaman Chevayo is staying at the Kiva or at the resort?"

The concierge consulted a computer screen tucked beneath the edge of the chest-high counter. A shimmering waterfall trickled down the flagstone wall behind her. "No one by that name here at the Kiva. Let me check the resort . . .

sorry, no listing." She smiled up at Rian. "Does he go by another name?"

Rian shrugged. "I don't know. He was the shaman leading the sweat last night, so I thought he was staying here. Maybe he's an employee?"

The young woman shook her head. "Not of the Kiva, anyway. He could be a guest speaker, like yourself, but local and commutes each day from town. Shall I check with the seminars' registrar?"

"No, that's all right. No doubt I'll see him around, if that's the case," Rian said. "Which way to breakfast?"

The concierge pointed to one of the broad, flagstone passageways that was a spoke of the circular, domed Gathering Place. "Just down there past the Aqua Place. You'll see the Eating Place, a big round bar with the chef and kitchen in the middle. There will be a name tag for you at your stool. Have a lovely Wellness Kiva day, Dr. Farsante."

Rian thanked her and enjoyed her short walk through the Kiva's serene beauty, drawn by the delicious aromas and happy-sounding voices. Before she entered the Eating Place, Rian took a deep breath and compacted her aura safely around her, shielding herself from negative influence or attack. There were many kinds of people at these events, most honest seekers and good souls, and there were those who were anything but. Best to be aware and protected, which is what she taught her students, too.

Rian guessed there were over thirty people seated at the circular bar when she entered. An empty tall, upholstered stool sat directly opposite the chef's station. The place of honor, if there was one in a round table? That had always been a point of interest for her, energy-wise, though King Arthur and the knights worked that out, apparently. She smiled and nodded to those turning to look at her and checked the beige tag tied with raffia to the stool's back. Dr. Rian.

"That's me," she said with a self-effacing shrug and hoisted herself onto the cushioned seat. Rian put the turquoise linen napkin across her lap and smiled at the chef. The room had gone quiet and everyone stared at her. She wasn't sure what to do next, so she stuck her hand out to the chef and said, "Good morning, I'm Rian. What's for breakfast?"

The short middle-aged man in a tall, white chef hat that, with his attitude, made him seem six feet tall, shook her hand, barely, and pointed to the hand-printed menu sitting in the peach-colored stoneware plate before her. "As you see. What may I prepare for you?"

Rian winked at the guest next to her. "What's everyone else having?"

Most of the diverse group laughed and resumed their conversations. The chef and his staff began to prepare stone-ground maize and quinoa griddle cakes with prickly pear syrup and other exotic, supposedly healthy foods. When she asked for eggs over easy and sausage with hashed browns, a cheer went up.

The chef served up his answer cold and without meeting her gaze, while he chopped pine nuts into tinier bits. "That is not on our wellness menu. However, we endeavor to serve our guests. In that regard, I shall send one of my staff up to the resort's main kitchen or to McDonald's, whichever is your preference."

The older woman in an earth-toned yoga garb next to her elbowed her ribs and whispered, "At these prices, make it from the resort. It would come to fifty bucks with tip, and maybe mileage, for a sausage biscuit, and that doesn't seem right to me. While you're at it, get an order for me, would ya?"

Several other less devoted adherents also chimed in. A very miffed chef directed one of his minions to phone in the order to the resort's main kitchen, then completely ignored the heretics. He devoted himself to lauding praise and fresh lentil meal scones drizzled with guava and lime reduction upon the believers. Despite the chef's open disgust and others' thinly-veiled envy, Rian and her confederates enjoyed their artery-clogging breakfast with gusto.

She finished her breakfast and left the table before the others to prepare for her morning session. The assigned seminar room was bright and airy, opening onto a shady patio with a center fountain and edged with green shrubbery, trees and a variety of flowering plants. An overhead wood-bladed fan hanging from the center of the tent of rough-hewn timbers swirled the scent of mint, rosemary and other herbs through the patio and into the whitewashed meeting room.

Rian set up her laptop, synchronized her presentation to the digital projector and checked sound levels on the audio system. As she set out stacks of handouts, meditation CDs and her books for sale, people began to drift into the room and select their seats at the long tables covered with turquoise cloths.

Several times throughout the day, Rian noticed a large black raven land on the patio's block wall and walk around to the willow tree in the corner by the French doors. He hopped onto a low branch and cocked his head, as if trying to see into the meeting room. She was completely intrigued by the bird's odd behavior and finally mentioned it to the class after the afternoon break.

Yes, they'd noticed the raven. There were lots of them

around the resort. Nothing unusual in that. But Rian couldn't help wondering if it were trying to communicate with . . . someone.

No one asked her about her experience the previous night, even though she thought she recognized one or two from the sweat lodge. And since they didn't bring it up, she didn't either, though she wanted to ask if they'd seen the shaman today. But as open and receptive to her process of Light Seeking to connect with their higher selves as this group was, they were in resort mode—massages, herbal wraps and with a dose of discovering past lives as hopefully famous, rich people.

As she sent the last student on her way and organized her materials for the class the next day, she saw the raven hop off of the branch and stroll through the open French door. Rian stood very still, barely breathing. The raven fluttered his wings and squawked as he looked at her.

Suddenly she was overcome with the need to talk to Spence, to see if he'd gotten a hold of Mike and Dorel as she'd asked him to last night. "You wouldn't be telling me to do that, would you?" she asked the raven. It flew out the window and over the patio wall.

After a long, tedious dinner with the conference organizers and VIPs, Rian walked up the concrete path to her casita. Someone in dark clothing waited on the porch, sitting on the low wall, his face shadowed from the pale-yellow porch light.

"Hello?" Rian called and stopped. She reached out with her psychic sense to perceive the intention of the man who waited for her.

He unfolded from his seat and stood, the sharp angles of his face and shining black hair bathed in light. "It's me, Chevayo. Just making sure you're okay. It's late and dark out to be strolling around alone."

"I can take care of myself," she said and joined him on the porch. He stepped back while she unlocked the door, this time not taking her eyes off him, so he wouldn't disappear like he did last night. She pushed it open and turned on the foyer light. "Want to come in?"

He shook his head, retreating into the shadows, and sat on the wall again. "I like it better out here, where it's cool and I can smell the trees. It's almost piñon time."

She left her laptop and bag on a chair inside and leaned against the doorjamb. "What's piñon time?"

"When the pine nuts are ripe. I used to gather the cones with my mother and brothers and sisters when I was small. Even the grandmothers helped. It was work and we'd get sticky with pitch, but it smelled so good and the nuts tasted . . . like heaven," he said, a wistful tone riding his words.

She couldn't see his eyes, but sensed a sadness or longing in him. "Where did you do this pine nut gathering?"

He shook his head. "Where? Oh, at home. Four Corners area."

"Are you a Res kid?" She moved toward him slowly, feeling an odd kinship with him.

"No, I never lived on the reservation, but know many who have."

"Are you Native American?" Rian asked, now within an arm's length of him, and felt the warmth radiating from his body. He smelled like sunshine, pine trees and sacred cedar smoke. Still, she couldn't see his features clearly.

"I am Chevayo," he said, cocking his head to look at her.

"Ah. That's a great name. Means spirit warrior, doesn't it?" She wanted to reach out, touch him, stroke his gleaming raven hair, anything to connect with him and his incredibly vibrant, multihued aura that glowed around him like the aurora borealis.

"Yes." With that, he stood and faced her, the outside light illuminating only his piercing black eyes looking into her soul. "Last night I warned you to keep your silence and release your fears. Neither of which you did. This has put you and your friends at greater risk. You would have been best served to meditate and gather your strength, and must do so still. However, now that you have communicated with him, you have brought him into play before his time. This alters the course and must be dealt with."

Rian's hand hung in midair. Icy dread rose in her throat. "What are you talking about?" she choked out.

"I speak of your lover in this life and others, your soul mate in a cycle of eternity."

She couldn't take her eyes off his, though they burned as if blasted by a hot desert wind. "Spence?" she whispered.

Chevayo nodded. "You have again endangered him, and all, by your willfulness."

As if he'd slapped her with a two-by-four, she retaliated with instant gut-harbored fury that rattled up her throat and vomited from her mouth. "To hell with you. I'm not to blame for all the evil in the world, especially not that particular evil. What Spencer or anyone else does or doesn't do isn't my fault, not my responsibility, and I don't give a good goddamn. Now get the hell off my porch and leave me alone."

The unblinking black eyes stared at her. The rest of him wasn't moving either.

As quick as her anger had flashed, it receded, leaving behind a sludge of remorse. Never one to trade in *I wish I hadn'ts,* this painful moment she really wished she hadn't lost it. Her own aura was so screwed up after her ugly outburst that she couldn't sense anything but her own noxious radiation.

What if he told anyone that Dr. Ascended Sweetness and Light Seeker was a total fraud who couldn't take criticism and had cursed him with the mouth of a Tarantino film star?

"I do not deal in such things," Chevayo said in a holier-than-thou tone, as if answering her fearful thoughts.

"How nice for you. Now, look, I apologize for verbally scourging you. Let's just say goodnight and not presume upon each other again, shall we? Bye bye now." Her anger may have detonated, but if this guy said one more word, a secondary explosion was imminent and she didn't want to do a damn thing to stop it.

Chevayo stood, still holding his gaze on her. "You are angry because you embrace your shortcomings, your failures, as if they are a sentence, a punishment meted out by someone else besides yourself. They are not. You do not believe this, however, and that is why you suffer alone. You chose to share this life with him again, so that you could fulfill your soul's desire and that of your group. You are dangerously close to failing in both. This you also know."

He raised his hand and touched his forefinger to her forehead between her eyebrows, at the third eye. Her eyelids fluttered closed as if he commanded them. Chevayo said, "Open now to your path, your destiny. With your inner eyes you see all things, all times. You listen for guidance and, so enlightened, do as you are led. I, Chevayo, am your spirit guide. Listen and act in body and spirit."

"What am I to do now?" Rian heard herself murmur.

"Gather your strength. Protect yourself with the pure white light of Spirit; then, and only then, shall you open a door to your soul mate. Rest now. I shall come to you again soon."

Rian opened her eyes and Chevayo was gone.

— FIVE —

The early October day dawned unusually clear and warm for a Seattle autumn. The late-morning sun streamed through the east window of Jonathan Spencer's bedroom, waking him from a sleep of the dead. He staggered out of bed and closed the drapes, shutting out the headache-producing light. The room returned to darkness and Spence to his bed, though not to sleep. Like nearly every night, he didn't fall into deep REM sleep until just before dawn, only to get up and start his long day on two or three hours' rest. Today, he'd apparently overslept and didn't feel the better for it.

He couldn't pinpoint exactly when the dreams started, after not having them for years, but if he had to guess, it would have been about the time Rian bailed on him. She was the one who had been responsible for his nightmares in the first place, and the one who took them away. Could be she was up to her old game. The rational part of him that still loved her questioned that conjecture. Why would she do that? What would she have to gain?

Maybe she was working for Ian again?

Spence gritted his teeth, rubbed his irritated eyes with the heels of his hands and stared up at the ceiling, seeing nothing except the troubling images from the dream that he'd just had. Maybe he wasn't really awake? He got up and opened the drapes again. Still bright sunshine pouring over the downtown cityscape and sparkling off Elliot Bay in the distance.

His vision suddenly went black and he grabbed the windowsill to keep from falling. Maintaining equilibrium was forgotten as the scenes overlaid each other in a sickening collage behind his blind eyes. Spence's knees buckled and he sat down hard on the carpet, helpless to stop the horror show of his mind.

A huge black bird hovered above a forest in the starless night and landed in a clearing, spilling giant, evil robots, like a Japanese cartoon, onto the ground. They marched relentlessly and circled a log house with a tiny candle in the window. The biggest robot crashed down the front door and rolled inside, crushing the occupants, a man and a woman. From under the ground, an indestructible, colossal monster arose and consumed the robot in fire, swallowing the candle in the window. The monster took wing and flew south, calling, "Return to me. Return to me."

Spence cried out and rolled to his side, vomiting bile. The images burned into his visual cortex, making him fear that he would continue to see them superimposed upon his real life at every turn. Unable to use his strangely paralyzed legs, he dragged himself with his arms to the bathroom and into the shower. He lay on the cold tile shower floor and reached his fingertips to the cold knob. A thousand needles of freezing water sprayed down on him and he turned his burning face up to the deluge.

The cleansing water washed away the negative images clinging to his energy field. The terrifying visions abruptly ceased, leaving a contaminated wasteland in their place instead of his usually sharp, perceptive mind. Already, he couldn't remember the vivid detail of the waking nightmare, and he wouldn't have cared, except what he could still remember seemed to beg him to try to make sense of all of it.

Spence turned off the water and found himself able to

stand. He dried himself off and opened the shower door, planting his feet solidly on the dry tile, grounding himself with each breath. When he felt steady, he walked slowly to the bedroom and dressed, considering what to do next.

He'd have to remote view this vision to discover where it came from, because it sure wasn't his own creation. Someone was projecting it to him. Perhaps the same someone who Rian said was calling to her to return to him? Or Rian herself? As he shaved around his goatee, he realized there was more gray among the brown whiskers: premature, of course, and a product of his damn hard life. Or so Rian had teased when he'd found the first one.

He set the electric razor down and peered into the mirror at a haggard face that he hardly recognized. His eyes were bloodshot and shifty. Shit, there's the face of a haunted man, he thought, and grabbed a bottle of prescription eye drops, tipping it over each eye in turn. At least he could mask that problem with good drugs, which he hadn't been able to do with any other part of his life, and it wasn't for lack of trying.

If Rian knew the shit he'd been up to. He stopped himself. Of course, she knew, because she'd been spying on him. That's why she'd called, trying to get him involved with the part of his old life that she approved of and control him from afar without having to actually commit to being with him. He snorted. Telling him to call Mike and check on him. That would piss Mike off, because he was a big boy and he sure as hell didn't need anyone checking on him.

Rian was just trying to screw with them all again. Marty would disagree . . . Spence stared at his reflection as he recognized that he hadn't heard from Marty like usual. How long had it been? A couple of hours, or was it days? And Rian hadn't heard from him either. She was worried about that, not about screwing him literally, as he'd hoped, or even figuratively. Spence's gut twisted and he raked his bottom lip with his teeth.

Spence walked to the bed and sat, closing his eyes. He gathered his energy and expanded his aura thirty miles south to the Gabrielli acreage in rural King County. He sent the vibration of intent to contact his godson and waited. Like a no-contact sonar echo return, nothing came back except his own signal. Marty wasn't receiving. That had never happened before.

He expanded his aura farther and reached out with his energy body again, targeting Marty wherever on earth he might be in this timeline.

Spence's spirit dropped in on a scene that sent chills of horror through him. It nearly broke his state and popped him out of the remote viewing trance. He viewed the Gabriellis' Airedale, Katana, roar in pain, pulling his black-swathed attacker to the ground as he collapsed, his teeth still embedded in the man's leg as the dog died. Spence willed himself to detach and slammed back into his body.

"That can't be," he declared aloud, as if words of doubt would vanquish what he'd just witnessed. Had he viewed a future event or was it happening now, if at all? If he couldn't contact Marty, and that was cause for real concern, maybe he could locate Mike or Dorel because they rarely let the boy out of their sight. Where they were, he would be. And Katana, too, he reminded himself, and felt a rush of anxiety that would be difficult to detach enough from to silence his mind chatter in order to remote view.

The moment he stopped trying and relaxed into his neutral intent, he felt his aura expand and his spirit fly free from his crown chakra. Flying low over treetops along a broad reach of fresh water he recognized as the Columbia

River, he turned and followed a narrow inlet to float above a Beaver beached in the sand at the edge of the woods.

The Gabriellis had gone to the cabin!

Spence thought the destination, but instantly popped back into his body as if he were slammed by some kind of force field. Someone had created a thought form of energy to block psychic intrusion or spying. They'd probably set the Katana death thought form as an emotional deterrent to disrupt a viewer's vibration at the perimeter. For those who got by that, then they brought out the big illusion the likes of which Spence hadn't experienced before except in his, and Rian's, own mental warfare of thought forms and remote influencing.

He stretched and took several deep, calming breaths. Now that he knew what was stopping him, he could breach it and discover why. And who. But it happened again, exactly as before, and Spence blasted back into his body without a glimpse or other sensation that would give him information about the Gabriellis.

Apprehension jangled in his chest as he hit speed dial and called Mike's cell phone. When that rolled to voicemail, he tried every other number he had for his friends. They were completely incommunicado. And they wanted to be, logic suggested, but his gut told him their trip might have started out that way, but not now. They were in trouble.

Spence dialed the FBO at Boeing Field and told the fuel desk attendant to get his chopper ready. He started coffee brewing, went online on the terminal in the refrigerator door and filed a flight plan to Kettle Falls, Washington. With a little luck, he'd be landing at the cabin in time for a late dinner, which he hoped wouldn't be Dorel's favorite of canned stew leftovers. His friends and Marty would be glad to see him. They'd take the old dog for a short hobble, and he and Marty would sack out under the stars, telling each other ghost stories of past lives they remembered. And all this shit he'd just been through would have been just another bad dream. Though from all indications, for that ideal past scenario to be present reality, they'd all need a lot more than luck.

Despite his complaints that it was too early, Dorel tucked Marty into his sleeping bag on the camp cot under the window, where he could watch the stars, and kissed him goodnight. She patted Katana's head and stroked his soft ears, making cooy-lovey noises, as Marty called the affectionate sounds that she heaped with abandon upon furry-and-otherwise family members.

They'd had a very long, eventful day and even though it was barely nine o'clock, the adults were tired, and Marty wasn't. Michael already snored from the double bed. He'd thrown off the zipped-together sleeping bags and uncovered his broad chest and shoulders. Dorel gazed at her strong, still-handsome husband, feeling happy and safe, and very much in love with him. More every day.

She pulled the screen across the dying fire rather than add more wood. It was warm in the cabin, though the temperature had fallen rapidly since sundown. There would probably be frost on the meadow grass at dawn. Crawling in beside Michael, she pecked a kiss on his cheek, which made him smile, and lay down, pulling up the slick nylon covering.

"Nite, Mom, I love you," Marty whispered. "Tell Dad I love him, okay?"

"You told him already; besides, he's asleep," she reminded him and turned on her side, her back to her husband.

"Yeah, but I want you to tell him that he's very strong,

no matter what, and whisper that in his ear with the cooey-lovey, okay? He needs to hear that."

It might have been an unusual request, but she didn't question it. Marty was always tuned in to them, knew how they were feeling and what they needed emotionally from each other. When they were frustrated or angry or even afraid, he knew and always said the right thing to them that helped them. Dorel turned back over to Michael and raised up on her elbow, putting her lips next to his left ear. "Darling Mikey, my dearest sweetie, your wonderful son loves you and wants you to know that."

"Wants you to *remember* that," Marty corrected.

"Wants you to remember that he loves you and that you're very strong, no matter what," she said, and finished with a tender kiss on his temple.

"Love you too, M-Man," Michael murmured.

"I heard, Mom. Thanks. You're strong, too," Marty said. "Nite."

Dorel said goodnight again and tried to relax, but her mind wouldn't make the right connection with body. It wanted to worry about what Marty's words might really have meant. Soon Marty's little sleep sounds joined the snoring chorus of Michael and Katana. Ordinarily, Dorel would have drifted off and probably joined them, as her boys swore she did, but not tonight. She waited awhile, then carefully got up without disturbing Michael and wrapped a blanket around her shoulders over the sweatshirt top, sliding into her flip-flops. The door swung open silently and she stepped out onto the porch, closing it to just a crack.

Marty wasn't the only one who loved stargazing. She'd taught him, or maybe it was he who'd taught her, because her grandfather had given her a telescope for her eighth birthday and a large star chart for her bedroom wall. She'd wanted a chemistry set, but soon found that her grandfather had made the right choice.

A bright shooting star streaked across the sky from the west. Dorel leaned out so she could see past the porch's covering roof. Incredibly, the star got brighter rather than burning out . . . and it had changed direction. It was coming toward the cabin. The muted whop-whop of an incoming helicopter reached her ears and she listened harder. Sounded like a Huey. Spence!

She stayed put as the chopper hovered a hundred feet off the ground about twenty yards from the porch, its spotlight searching a bright path to the cabin below. Out of instinct, Dorel ducked back in under the porch, her engineer's trained ear telling her that chopper was indeed a Huey, but a twin turbine-engine K model. Oh, my God, it was landing!

Dorel whirled and charged into the cabin, slamming and bolting the door behind her. Katana met her, barking wildly, spurting around her to get at the door. Michael was already on his feet, pulling on his hiking boots and Marty sat up in bed, peering out the window into the bright light.

"What the living hell is that?" Michael yelled over the roar of the landing helicopter. "That can't be Spence."

"Get your gun, Michael. I think we've got trouble," Dorel said and threw off her blanket. "Marty, get your shoes on and get away from that window."

"There's a whole bunch of men . . . Dad, they're ninja!" Marty cried, his nose pressed to the glass.

Dorel and Michael locked gazes for a moment. "It can't be, Michael. Not again. Please, God, not again."

Michael grabbed Marty off the cot. "Get your shoes on and grab your pack. We're going out the tunnel in two minutes!"

The three scrambled to ready themselves to escape while Katana barked himself hoarse and clawed deep furrows in the door. Dorel pulled the dog away and they assembled in front of the tall cabinet, where Michael would release a hidden mechanism that lowered the cabinet's false floor like a dumbwaiter. From the secret cellar below, they'd be able to crawl through a long tunnel to the tree line and escape.

It had worked before, but not this time.

The cabin door blew inward off its hinges and six black figures stormed in, backlighted by the helicopter's spotlight shining on the cabin.

Michael and Dorel roughly shoved Marty behind them into the cabinet, and turned to face their attackers. Katana wrenched free of Dorel's grasp and charged, hitting the lead ninja full in the chest. The man fell with Katana on his chest, ripping at his throat. Another struck at the dog with a samurai sword, and knocked him off as the fallen man rolled to his feet. Though bleeding badly from the long gash down his back, Katana spun and grabbed the ninja's leg, sinking his teeth to the bone. The man screamed and dealt a death blow to Katana's neck with his own sword.

"No!" Marty screamed, broke through his parents' shield and ran to his dying dog on the blood-slicked floor. Dorel dashed to grab him back, but two of the men, covered in black with only their eyes showing, jumped between her and Marty; the other four, swords held in front of them at the ready, advanced on Michael.

Michael pulled his .45 out of his sweatpants waistband, easing the hammer back, cocking the gun and pointing it at the ninja menacing Dorel. "Stop or you're dead."

The bastard that killed his dog lunged for Marty, but Michael shot him between the eyes. He dropped in a dead heap beside Katana's body that Marty had thrown himself on, wailing uncontrollably. The remaining five froze.

"Dorel, get Marty," he ordered, keeping his eyes on the ninja beginning to thaw and creep into some kind of new attack position. Michael jammed his free hand at them, waggling his finger. "Uh-uh. Want to join your dog-murdering pal there, assholes? Make a move. I'm gonna love killing every goddamn one of you."

"You should already have done so, Gabrielli-*san.*"

Dorel heard the voice from long ago and shuddered with the unwisely postponed apprehension that there was no escape from the past, or destiny. Her heart breaking, she stroked her son's tear-damp cheek and spoke softly, hoping he would hear over his crying, "Marty, you must use whatever power you have to save yourself." She forced herself to leave her grief-stricken son and go to Michael's side to face their old enemy together.

The middle aged Japanese man, previously meeting them in battle dressed in full shogun regalia, now wore a custom-made business suit. He stepped inside, found the switch and turned on the overhead light and pushed between his men, who parted and took up flanking positions behind him. Hiroshi Inada, sophisticated and elegant, surveyed his disheveled captives with a contemptuous smirk.

"What the hell do you want, Inada?" Michael demanded, turning his .45 on the man whose expression of disdain mutated to open hatred. Dorel gripped Michael's arm, warning him to watch his mouth. Inada was insane, but she'd driven him away once with the right words. Perhaps she could again.

"I want what is mine. Let us dispense with arguing. Give me the Tsuji sword now or I kill your son." He shrugged and swept his hand out in a conciliatory gesture. "No bartering or trickery. Easy. Your son's life for the sword."

Terror roared in Dorel's ears. "No! We don't have them."

"Them, Everly? I do not understand. I speak only of the sword left to you by your grandfather, the Defender Sword. Is there another?" Inada asked, his unlined face showing a slight scowl.

"There isn't another, and the Tsuji sword doesn't exist anymore," Michael declared bitterly. "We cut it up and that pissed you off, remember, asshole?"

Inada shook his head. "Yes, unfortunate and wasteful. But I understand that was a decoy, a fake. You have hidden the real sword from me. And now I shall have it or," he said, pulling a sleek, chromed .22 Ruger from inside his jacket and pointing it at Marty, "I start with your son, and if that does not persuade you to give me the sword, then I have to kill your wife."

Dorel took a tentative step toward Inada. "Please, you are a reasonable man, Inada-*san,* but you've been misled again. The sword disappeared when Michael returned from the dead. You know that it is true, because you killed him and yet here he is. He died that night. But after you left the house in peace and all things were forgiven, he returned. Alive. He came back to me alive, Inada-*san*. Then somehow the sword reassembled itself and disappeared in a flash of light. I know it all sounds fantastic, but it's true. You know it is. We don't have the sword anymore. No one on earth does," she said with conviction that she prayed would sway him. All the while she spoke, she'd inched toward her son, weeping over his beloved dog, putting herself between Inada and Marty.

In a fluid motion, Inada turned and fired. The gun popped and Dorel flinched, looking down at the dot of red on her chest. She looked from her aghast husband to Marty, jerking to stand and reaching out for her, as her vision went black and her knees buckled. Dorel fell at the feet of her son.

"Nooooo!" Michael cried and dove to catch Dorel, the .45 forgotten as it dropped to the floor.

His father grabbed up his mother's lifeless body and began rocking her against him. Marty went cold, tears drying in the drought of feeling brought on by excessive trauma. He turned grimly to the murdering Jap, his former incarnation as a World War II military intelligence officer who'd witnessed the atrocities of the Imperial Army taking command of his eleven-year-old body. "You have died more than once pursuing this forbidden venture. The sword is not for you."

Inada's eyes narrowed as he gauged the boy speaking like a man. He crooked his finger, beckoning him forward. "Who are you?"

Marty stepped around Katana's body, brushing past his father. "I am he who received the sword briefly held by your bloodline, but it is not for you," he growled.

Michael came to himself enough to realize that Inada was drawing down on his son. He eased Dorel's body to the floor and made ready to throw himself at Inada.

"Ah, I see, you are the bearer. Give me the sword now," Inada commanded, pointing the gun at Marty's forehead.

"It is not for you," he repeated, holding himself tall and straight.

Inada cocked the .22 with his thumb. "You will give it to me, or," he turned the pistol on Michael, "I will send him to join your mother in hell."

When Inada's gaze snapped back to Marty, Michael leaped. He heard the report, felt the sharp blow between his ribs and staggered, falling short of his target. Marty gasped and ran to him, crying, "Dad! No, no, not my dad." His boyish arms weren't strong enough to support his dad's heavy frame. Michael felt himself slipping away, and dragged the boy down, too. His breath was fire in his chest and warm blood trickled down his stomach.

Marty's tear-streaked, red face hovered above his. His mouth moved but Michael heard nothing but the roar of a jet engine in his ears. His last breath flowing out of him, Michael murmured, "Wait for me . . ."

Marty struggled out from under his father's body and fought to his feet. He charged Inada, head down and fists swinging. The men peeled him off Inada and threw him to the floor, holding him down by his thrashing arms and legs. Impotent rage boiled through him, igniting a frenzy of cursing. He spat every deadly oath at them that he'd ever heard in any life. He wanted them all dead and he would make it happen, even if he had to kill them from the grave.

Inada leaned over him sprawled on the floor, poking his nose with the gun barrel. "You *gaijin* dishonor yourselves even in death. How poorly you die."

Marty bucked and growled, staring daggers of hatred into the man's eyes. Inada drew back, his eyes betraying a trace of alarm. "You are not to be reasoned with, I see. Sword-bearer or not, you will give me the sword now and I will kill you quickly. If not, we can persuade you very painfully and slowly. I think a small one such as you will not suffer well, and I promise to keep you alive for as long as it takes to get what I desire."

A burst of gunfire erupted with flashes from the doorway. The lights went out and the ninja holding Marty down fell like dominos, one sprawling across him, pinning him to the floor. Inada shrunk back, firing at the men pouring through the door. He dropped his gun, grabbed his stomach and cried out when he was hit, crashing into the table.

Marty could see nothing in black moving and hoped they were all dead. He watched as a leader dressed in fatigues stepped over the bodies and stopped in front of Inada sitting on the floor. He shined a bright flashlight into Inada's blinking eyes and grunted. The man raised his other hand, holding a gun like Marty's dad's .45, and delivered a single, loud shot to the man's head. Inada slumped sideways, his unseeing eyes wide with terror.

"Let's get this cleaned up," the executioner ordered and turned, shining his light down on Marty. "Are you alive, son?"

"I think so," Marty said in a weak voice, vaguely wondering if he was about to wind up like Inada, and he didn't care.

"Let's make sure you stay that way. Give me a hand over here," he called to his men flashing their lights around the dark cabin. Two of them hauled the dead ninja off Marty and the leader gave him a hand, pulling him into a sitting position. "Are you hurt?"

Marty shook his head. "But my mom and dad are. Can you help them?" If he pretended they were just hurt, maybe they wouldn't be dead.

"Medic, check those two. See what you can do," the man said, indicating the dark lumps on the floor with a sweep of his flashlight.

In just a couple of seconds, the medic called back, "Sorry, sir, there's nothing I can do. There's a dead dog over here. Do we bag it, too?"

"Yeah, take him. Son, do you want to take anything with you from here? Truthfully, there's not much left."

Hearing that he was now completely alone was too much to bear. Marty shook, with the anguished sobs overwhelming his mind and body. Darkness invaded his heart, eclipsing the light of his soul. He felt like he was drowning, and no one in this world or the next could save him.

"Hang on, son." The man put a hand on his shoulder. "It's hard, but you'll be all right in time. Now, come with me. I'll protect you. There are more of these guys on the way."

Marty went silent as shock insulated him from the excruciating pain of loss. When they tried to move him out of the cabin away from his family, he balked. The leader waved them off and told Marty he could wait and go to the helicopter with his parents. He handed Marty a bottle of water and told him to drink it.

Marty complied, sipping the water mindlessly as he dully watched the men quickly zip his mom and dad and Katana into black bags like they had the other dead people. The row of body bags extended from the back wall to the door, ten in all. He began to worry because he wouldn't be able to tell his family from their killers when they were moved outside.

He stood next to the last three bags, guarding them, and followed when they were carried out to the waiting helicopter.

The leader helped Marty inside and buckled him into his seat despite his protests to watch the bags get loaded, and sat beside him.

"They're onboard, son. The first to go out the door," he said. His voice and manner were kind, inviting trust.

"No. They were the last three bags," Marty argued, confusion clenching his stomach as his ears began to ring.

The man smiled sadly and shook his head. "It was very busy in there. Theirs were the first, I promise. Those last bags weren't anything you'd want. The man who killed your parents was in one of them. I'd like to kick it out the door into the river after we're airborne."

Tiredness crept up on Marty and he tried to pay attention while the man was talking, but it was hard. "What?" he asked, his heavy eyelids fluttering.

The man smiled. "Here, lean on me, you're exhausted."

Marty let his head rest lightly on the man's shoulder. "What's your name?" he mumbled, unable to fight the heavy drowsiness overtaking him.

"Ian, and I'm going to take good care of you from now on."

— SIX —

"Rian, wake up. Something terrible has happened and I need you. Call me."

Rian jerked awake and sat up, agitated and a little afraid. She was used to controlling her dreams during sleep, the same as she did in her awake lucid dreaming, but when a spectral Spence loomed up unbidden in her path as she dream-flew over the Spiritlands and shouted at her, it was very disturbing. And wrong for him to intrude upon her that way, which he'd promised not to do anymore.

Weary, she glanced at the clock's glowing yellow numbers on the bedside table. Oh, God, only two in the morning. She rubbed her eyes, listening to crickets chirp to each other in the dark outside her bedroom. She got up to close the terrace door on the racket. Bugs of any kind were disgusting and she didn't think their noises were at all charming. As she slid the door closed, she noticed a raven perched on the wood railing of the deck. It cocked its black head at her as if to question what she was doing.

"What are *you* doing out in the middle of the night? Aren't you supposed to be tucked up in a tree somewhere waiting for the sun, so you can dump on people and raid trashcans?" she grumped, shutting the door and locking it.

The raven ruffled its feathers, cawed and took off, leaving Rian with the distinct impression that she was supposed to do something important besides verbally abuse the fauna.

Call me! Spence's voice boomed in her mind.

Why the hell don't you call me? she mentally shot back at him and climbed into bed. She lay in the rumpled sheets, feeling each wrinkle and bunchy crease. Unable to find a comfortable spot as she flopped and turned, she engaged in deep breathing to initiate her self-hypnosis process, and tried imagining herself in her sacred safe place. Nothing worked to put her back to sleep.

He's screwing with you and has an interference wave pattern homed on you, accused the part of herself that really hated Spence. Tired and cranky, Rian didn't argue and sat up, turning on the lamp. What the hell. He deserved a wakeup call. She reached for her cell phone and punched in his number.

It rang several times, and she was about to hang up when Spence answered on a very poor connection. "Spence? Are you there?" she asked, straining to hear and pressing the phone to her ear. He was probably partying in some noisy after-hours club on the seamier side of life somewhere.

"Rian. Bad happened. Cabin is shot . . . dead . . . Marty . . ." was all she heard of his answer, but enough to jolt alarm through her.

"Spence, can you move so I can hear you better?"

"Unblock your number and I'll call . . ." The connection dropped and Rian looked at the phone's screen. She'd forgotten that she'd blocked his calls and reset the phone to receive, because he sounded serious, and the intuitive tingling at the base of her skull confirmed it. More importantly, Spence's fear was real. No wonder he had to use the mutually prohibited means to contact her.

She waited several tension-building minutes and almost hit recall to phone him again, but the phone chimed in her hand. It was he. "What took so long?" she exclaimed, trying to lighten her hold on the phone that she gripped so hard her hand began to ache.

"I'm in the chopper, orbiting the cabin. It's the only place I can get a good signal," he explained, his voice competing with engine and wind noise.

"I didn't get anything you said except something about Marty. What's happened?" she asked, trying to control her increasing anxiety. She didn't want to spontaneously leap out-of-body, propelled by fear to the ether, where she would be of no help to anyone as a victim of her own dreadful illusions. Spirit travelers manifested what they thought in the out-of-body realms much faster than in materiality.

"Have to give you the short form. There was one hell of a battle at the cabin. Mike and Dorel are probably dead and Marty taken—"

"No!" she cried, nearly squeezing the phone in half. "I don't feel this. I don't see it. It's not true. I'd know if something happened to them, Spence. I'd know."

"Take it easy, Rian. It's not your fault," he said, his voice heavy with frustration. "Something's going on here that we can't . . . I don't know, maybe Datascape really does have the tech they say."

"What's that got to do with this? You can't be thinking that Ian's done this."

"Hell no, he'd send someone like you and me," Spence barked.

She flinched at the truth of that. Though she'd been Ian's best viewer and trained as a psychic assassin like Spence had been, she'd never been ordered to use that particular skill. Spence had.

"I'm telling you that this has Datascape spec-ops smeared all over it. A fast strike team hit the cabin, I'm guessing about two hours before I got here. Big firefight, and Mike probably took several of them with him. Lots of blood and the place totally screwed up; no bodies, though. But they did leave a couple of empty shell casings behind—special sniper load, hollow points. A Datascape hit squad signature, if there ever was one. Looks like Ian wants us to know who did it."

"Oh, Spence, Ian's an amoral son of a bitch, but he wouldn't do what you're suggesting." She couldn't let herself believe the man she'd once idolized and loved was capable of such evil.

"Believe what you want. It doesn't matter. I didn't call to get up in your Ian-screwing business. Just thought you'd want to know about Marty. Guess I was wrong," he jabbed in an ugly tone that hit her like a punch in the face, a hurtful *déjà vu* that she knew was his intention. He'd never had to get hands-on physical with her, when he was so adept at psychic and emotional abuse. She wasn't going to allow him to start again.

"If you want to continue to talk to me, you will take that intention to injure me out of your thought, your mouth and your field. Do it now or I hang up, Spence, and will not communicate with you again," she warned, her thumb poised over the button.

He didn't speak for a moment, then she felt the air between them clear. Rian sensed the dark patch in her own aura that he'd created with his angry intention quickly disappear when he severed his energy connection that fed it. "I'm sorry, Rian. I love you. I don't mean to hurt you."

She heard the honest remorse, but she didn't drop her guard. Trust and verify, that was her motto when dealing with Spence. His cripplingly traumatic childhood and Byzantine adult experiences resulted in a distorted view of the world that left him too wounded and too angry for her to trust him with her life or her love ever again.

"Thank you for doing that. Now, let me ask you, why did you go to the cabin?" she asked.

As he told her about a weird dream that he thought was projected by Ian, she saw in her mind's eye what he'd gone through. "I remembered I hadn't been in contact with Marty, and that was strange. So, I viewed their place outside of Auburn and they weren't there. Then I dropped into this bad scene with their dog being killed. That could have been real-time or a view of the future, I don't know, because I also viewed the Beaver beached at the trailhead. When I tried to call them, there was no answer. They were at the cabin, Rian. Their stuff is still there, even Katana's food dish. Shit!"

"What's wrong?" she asked, hearing an alarm horn.

"Got an engine oil overheat warning. Gotta land this pig and let her cool down. I'll do some more checking and give you a call back." He paused and she knew what was coming. "Why don't you come on back now? We've got real trouble and we'll handle it best together."

"I'd better stay here until we have a better idea of what's really going on. I'll Light Seek when we hang up. You call me back in, say, an hour and a half, and we'll compare. Then we'll go from there, all right?"

"Forget the spiritual seeking-the-Light crap and use remote viewing protocols on this one. It's going to be bad and you need to be objective. That isn't going to happen with that viewing Light stuff you do." The call dropped and Rian turned her phone off, trying to calm herself. He was wrong. She could get the information her way, without having to squirm around in the twisted minds and nervous systems of those who did this. She and Spence had gone far beyond the protocols of technical remote viewing long ago, and to opposite ends of the psychic exploration spectrum. She wasn't about to invite the hellish darkness into her life that he delved into.

But he was right about one thing; she would need complete, detached objectivity to distant view the Gabriellis' location, activities and emotional states for the last twenty-four hours. She'd have to protect herself with the Light. Or if she found them and didn't control her emotional reactions and analytical mind, she'd misinterpret what she viewed by overlaying it with assessment falsified by her strong feelings. She'd be severely traumatized, and possibly incapacitated. And that would help no one.

Most trainees and even experienced viewers found unprejudiced remote viewing was difficult to achieve under ideal conditions. Rian had overcome the inclination to project meaning upon sensory input, on what viewers called nonlocal data. However, at this untimely moment, she found herself already very afraid of what she would see.

Spence brought the B-Model Huey helicopter down a few yards nearer the cabin than he'd landed when he'd first arrived. He ran the shutdown checklist and turned off the landing lights.

Tomblike quiet shrouded the area and he had to force himself to climb out of the pilot's seat. Once outside, he reached back in under the backseat and pulled out his Uzi, checked the full magazine and grabbed a long-barreled, heavy flashlight that he could also use as a club if he had to. He slung the submachine gun onto his right shoulder, wrapping his arm through the sling, and closed his fingers around the grip.

He didn't turn on the flashlight until he eased inside the cabin. The odors of blood and gunpowder, combined with wood smoke and shit, hit his nose. He fought the urge to gag as he played the circle of light over the ravaged room, revealing broken furniture, shattered glass and log walls pockmarked with bullet holes. The floor was sticky with drying blood and other evacuated body fluids. He recognized Mike and Dorel's ransacked backpacks, their contents spilled across the blood-spattered sleeping bag on their bed, further evidence that they'd been here when the attack came.

There was nothing of Marty's to be found in the cabin and only one place left to check. The cellar. He prayed that he'd find the three of them hiding safely below or the tunnel's entrance open, an indicator that they'd escaped.

Spence stepped carefully around the smears and puddles to the cabinet and nudged the unlatched double doors with his flashlight. They swung wide and two tall, black bags fell forward, nearly knocking him down, but he leapt back.

Jesus, body bags. Ian had left him goddamn body bags.

He held his breath and listened. Nothing, inside or out, that he could hear. And that wasn't good. Spence leaned over and held the light on the black heavy-mil plastic bags that had fallen across each other. He knew he had to unzip them, make sure. Letting the gun hang from its sling strap, he dug the zipper tag out of the top of the track and pulled it down a couple of inches.

A thick strand of Dorel's coppery red hair spilled out.

Spence gasped a horrified sob, clapped his hand over his mouth and fell down on his ass beside the bags as anguished fury wracked him. Just as quick, like throwing a switch, the grief and tears turned off, replaced with icy detachment. He wiped his face on his sleeve and stood, letting the Uzi slide off his shoulder, and laid it on the floor with a flashlight that he positioned to shine on the bags. He pulled Dorel off the other that he knew held Mike, straightening both side by side.

Something ancient crept over him, instilling a duty to his friends to remove them from those pathetic death sacks and clean them up. They would not want to enter the afterlife, leaving behind bodies broken and ultimately defeated by their enemy, who lived to scorn them. He'd douse their funeral pyre and torch it, a fitting send-off for gallant warriors.

And then he would find Ian and kill him.

Spence glanced at the cabinet against the wall, and decided he had to go below to the cellar. Marty might be down there, though he didn't sense the boy's energy.

He picked up the flashlight and got inside the cabinet, twisting the clothes-hanging rod a half-turn in its brackets. The floor lowered smoothly to the cellar. He stayed on the dumbwaiter and roved the light over the walls lined with metal shelves stacked high with boxes of canned goods and other foodstuffs, supplies and bottled water. The escape tunnel's opening was still covered by the upright tool chest. No one had moved it or gotten in or out that way.

Returning above, Spence prepared to pull the bags off Dorel's and Mike's bodies. He knelt and completely unzipped hers first, then started on the other, drawing down the chest. Two hands jammed out and grabbed his neck, squeezing off his air. His gaze trailed down the long arms to meet a wide-eyed gaze.

"Mike, it's me, Spence," he choked out, clawing at the steel fingers trying to break his windpipe.

The frantic wildness of Mike's eyes subsided in a flicker of recognition, but his hands didn't yield.

Am I going to have to kill him to keep him from killing me? Spence thought, and clasped his hands in a fist, slamming them upward sharply inside Mike's stiff arms, and broke the chokehold. He staggered to his feet and backed off as Mike clutched at his legs. "It's me, goddamn it. Stop."

Mike raised up on his elbow, holding his bloodied side with one hand. “Spence? Thank God! Where did you come from?” His gaze slid to Dorel beside him on the floor. “Oh God, it really happened.” Either from shock or pain, his friend began to weep, his shoulders rounding small and shaking.

Spence crouched and put his arm around his friend. “What happened, Mike? Who did this to you?”

Mike got control of himself and began to tell his story. Every time he mentioned Dorel, he looked at his wife’s body and broke down again. “Inada shot her first, then me, when I tried to save Marty.” He tried to get up, but Spence restrained him. “Did they get Marty? Is he here?”

Spence shook his head. “No. I think they took him, but it wasn’t Inada. Ian’s team took them out, I’m pretty sure, and I think he kidnapped Marty. I don’t know why, but we have to remember that he tried once before and has hovered in the background, waiting. My guess is he’s counting on working a trade—we bring back the swords and Marty comes home.”

“Home? Marty’s not coming home. They think they’ve killed us both. They don’t plan to let him go. That’s not the plan, Spence. Think about it,” he said vehemently and grimaced, leaning into his wound.

“Better let me take a look,” Spence said. Michael raised his sweatshirt and Spence peered at the tiny wound in the center of a bruise the size of a fist. “Really small. Some kind of special round.” He moved around behind Mike and raised the shirt, shining the light on his back. “No exit. Probably still in there. That’s not good.”

He rubbed his beard, thinking, and squatted beside Mike again. “But if that’s all the blood you lost and still passed out, that’s weird. Maybe you weren’t shot with a regular round, but with a wax bullet that held a knockout dart. It'd hurt like hell, make you think you were dying, then the drug kicks in and for all intents and short-term purposes, you're dead."

They looked at Dorel at the same time. Mike reached for her, but Spence said, "I'll do it," and swiveled to face her. He touched two fingers to the pulse point on her neck and willed a beat of life from her. He shook his head and put his forefinger under her nose. After a moment, he allowed himself to believe that he'd felt something and nodded at Mike. "Maybe."

He looked down at the small bloodstain in the center of Dorel's chest and gently lifted the sweatshirt's bottom. The bruising around the tiny hole between her bare breasts was larger than Mike's. He could see that the bullet hadn't gone all the way in, stopped by her breastbone. And it was still oozing droplets of blood. Dead people didn't bleed.

Spence used his fingers to pinch the object from her skin and held it under his flashlight. He rolled it between his fingers. "Yeah, some kind of wax."

He leaned back over Dorel and yelled in her face, "Wake up! You're okay. Wake up!"

A sharp intake of breath was followed by a moan. Her pale eyelids quivered but they didn't open. She was still heavily drugged and barely breathing.

"We've got to get her to a hospital," Mike said and tried to get up, but fell back.

"Take it easy. Too much of that crap is still in your system. Must be some kind of muscle relaxant. Keep talking to her. I'll get the oxygen from the kit." Spence dashed out to the chopper and pulled out the first aid kit.

When he returned, Mike cradled a limp Dorel in his arms, rocking her. "Wake up, baby. Come on, we've got to go get Marty."

 [redacted]

"Don't know that I'd tell her that right now," Spence advised. He laid the clear plastic mask over her nose and mouth and turned the valve on the oxygen bottle.

Mike shuddered as he peered around the cabin. "It's so dark in here, I feel like I'm still dead. There's some bulbs under the sink. Let's get some light on."

Spence got up. "You're not going to feel any better when you can see it, let me warn you," he said, groping inside the cabinet. After he pulled out a two-pack, he found the lamp on the floor, replaced the broken bulb and was instantly sorry.

The cabin looked like ground zero.

"Turn it off," Mike roared, then lowered his voice. "I don't want her to see it like this."

"I think we ought to get the hell out of here," Spence returned, switching off the light. "I'd kill you myself, if you let me wake up to this."

"Maybe you're right," Mike said in the dark. "I think I can stand now. And she's breathing, coming around. Help me carry her out to the chopper."

It was a struggle to keep his patience and mouth shut as he watched his former fellow SEAL officer repeatedly stumble and nearly fall, trying to carry his wife to safety. It would have been better if Mike had just let Spence carry her by himself, but he was too proud, and determined to have it his way. And Spence let him be.

Dorel roused a little more as they strapped her into the backseat. Michael sat beside her, supporting her limp body against his. Spence made one last sweep through the destroyed cabin, looking for Mike's wallet, but came up empty and grabbed a dishpan on his way out. He returned to the chopper, bled off a gallon of turbine fuel from the tank sump into the plastic dishpan and carried it back inside and splashed it around.

"What are you doing?" Mike demanded when Spence removed the flare gun from its holder.

"Gonna have a Viking funeral," Spence said, and started to walk back toward the dark log house.

"Wait, you can't burn down my goddamn house," Mike yelled.

"My house, too," Spence reminded him over his shoulder. "We're never coming back to this place again, and I'm going to make sure," he said under the fierce desire to raze the past and reinvent now from the ashes.

"You'll burn down the whole goddamn forest!" Michael objected, his voice strident with condemnation.

"Yeah," Spence said and pointed the flare gun toward the open door and fired. A white streak shot into the cabin and exploded the fuel into an inferno that lighted the whole meadow.

Spence calmly replaced the flare gun in its holder and stood at the open crew door, watching the fire punch through the roof and blow out the windows.

"You're one crazy, stupid son of a bitch, you know that?" Michael ranted and continued to swear. He threatened to kick Spence's ass, but began to cool down as the mesmerizing flames consumed their cabin.

The fire contained itself to the building and didn't spread to the shed or tree line. When they'd sited the cabin years ago, this broad clearing was specifically chosen for its natural firebreak feature. Within ten minutes, the old log structure's roof trusses burned to a black skeleton and crashed down, knocking the smoldering remnants of the porch flat. In thirty minutes, only one or two small flare-ups remained within the four smoking, chinked log walls. They would smolder for days until the fall rain wetted them through; then they'd cool and begin to rot in the winter snow.

"You owe me a cabin," Michael snarled. "Now let's get the hell out of here and find my son."

The vintage Huey dusted off, providing them a higher view of the ruin below, but they couldn't see much in the darkness. The sun would come up in four hours, and if there was still smoke in the area, or the glow of the flames was seen by some insomniac bow hunter or backpacker, the Forest Service would send out a spotter plane to check it out. Spence's shoulders tightened at the thought of government pukes, or anyone, poking around in his business.

Self-recrimination chewed at him, claiming he'd brought it on himself by burning the contaminated cabin, a futile gesture. But it felt so damn good.

It accomplished nothing, his conscience challenged. Spence knew he shouldn't have given in to the dark urges, the destructive inclination eating more of his soul. . . . But you don't want to, the violence within taunted, and Spence let it go, vectoring the Huey on a westerly course back to Seattle, while Dorel slept in Michael's arms.

After landing at Boeing Field well before sunup, Spence insisted that Mike and Dorel come home with him instead of back to their place, where Ian might be waiting. Dorel didn't say much, still too groggy to argue. Mike, however, had other plans.

"I'm worried about her. We better take her to the emergency room," Mike said as they held Dorel between them and drag-walked her across the tarmac toward the parking lot. Her lolling head and rubbery knees made for slow-going and Spence worried that they were drawing attention, and possible interference, to themselves.

"She's okay. Let me carry her. It'll be faster," Spence said, glancing around. The airport was quiet and deserted, except for two package freighters parked on the apron at the brightly-lit hangar. The men swarming around the airplanes loading cargo containers wouldn't be able to see across the runway, so no worries there. But you could never tell who might be watching from the control tower or from one of the parked airplanes or hangars.

"No, I can carry my own wife," Mike growled and slid his free arm under her legs, jerking her up. She smiled and snuggled her head under his chin. Despite probably feeling as terrible as he looked, his friend wobbled determinedly toward Spence's black Escalade, sitting in a dark corner far from the brilliant lot lights.

They argued all the way to Spence's penthouse, but he refused to take Dorel to the hospital. "Be reasonable, Mike," he said, pulling into the gated underground garage. "We smell like smoke. You two look like victims of a hostage rescue gone bad. We go to Harbor View and the cops come. One, and probably both of us, get arrested, best case, on simple wife abuse. Worse, they're going to get a little upset that your son is nowhere to be found." He glanced in the rearview mirror at Mike's grim face. "Are you getting the picture, here? The bad old days are back with a vengeance."

"They were never gone," Mike mumbled and looked out the window.

Staging a convincing show of three drunks enjoying a movable party for the omniscient surveillance cameras, they finally arrived at Spence's front door. Once inside, Mike guided a semi-waking and nauseous Dorel to the bathroom to clean up.

Spence poured a neat single-malt scotch into a venti-sized Starbucks travel mug and sagged into his black leather recliner that was a castoff from Rian's old office. He keyed the remote control, and the blackout drapes skimmed open on the view of Elliot Bay surrounded with twinkling lights.

He stretched his aching neck and shoulders, hoping to delay the headache that was building from the stiffening muscles, and sipped the smoky-flavored drink.

Mike wandered into the living room, clasping a towel around his waist, revealing the impressive bruising on his side. He followed Spence's gaze. "Yeah, it hurts worse than it looks," he said with a lopsided grin and gestured to the towel. "I need some clothes."

Spence didn't get up. "Get what you need in my closet."

A few minutes later Mike returned, wearing a pair of faded jeans that exposed his white skin a couple of inches above his ankles. "I put her to bed in the guestroom. You're right. She's going to be okay," he said and strolled to the sliding glass door to the terrace.

Spence saluted him with his empty cup. "I'll drink to that." He got up. "Want one?"

Mike shook his head. "Better not. Don't want to mix alcohol and whatever that crap was they shot me with."

Spence refilled his glass and returned to his chair. "Yeah, I get that." He took a drink and set the cup on the chair's arm. "Better tell me what happened."

Mike sighed and nodded. He took a seat on the white sofa and began to tell his horror story with an emotionless voice, while he looked down at his hands wrestling each other for a white-knuckled hold.

Spence listened quietly, making mental notes. When Mike finished, he waited a moment, then told his friend how it really was. "It wasn't just Inada's deal. Ian sent him. I don't know why he's gone to all this trouble, when he could have just offed you guys and taken Marty with no trouble."

"No, he couldn't," Mike countered. "Marty would have known and stopped him."

Spence looked at him. "Mike, did Marty know or stop him, or Inada, for that fact, this time?"

Mike frowned and shook his head. "No."

"There you go. And here's why. Neither Rian nor I had heard from Marty in a couple of days. We couldn't view him either. That can only mean that Ian's got psychictech that's blocking us all. I think he's putting us through this shit because he wants to force us to bring back the swords; then he'll work a swap—Marty for the swords."

The color drained out of Mike's gaunt face. "What the hell do we do now?"

Spence reached for his phone. "We bring Rian home."

— SEVEN —

Ian had stared for hours at the closed-circuit TV monitor's screen, watching a live feed of the boy sleeping. He seemed a pale and delicate wax figure lying on a hospital bed in the stark safe-room.

Marty Gabrielli hadn't twitched even a finger since they'd brought his unconscious body to Datascape's high-security complex. Perhaps the dosage that had been calculated on his parents' averaged body weights had been a little heavy for his size, but he'd survived it. That was the important thing, for it could have so easily gone the other way if Ian hadn't personally anticipated and arranged for every possible contingency, including Inada's wanting to use his ninja and personally slice up the Gabrielli clan like lunchmeat with his own samurai sword.

Instead, Inada had been truly honored when Ian presented him with the loaded specially-made chromed pistol, along with his personal well-wishes to recover his sword.

The operation had gone perfectly according to his plan—

"*My* plan, old crocodile," the entity imposed on Ian's thought. "But I shall forgive the slight this once."

Ian's hands gripped the chair's hard metal arms as his gaze darted around the empty control room. Mocking laughter rang in his ears.

"Yes, it is I, your master Anubis, come to praise his high priest."

Ian slammed the door on his private thoughts that he'd unwisely left unshielded and opened a guarded communication with the entity. "Thank you, master."

"Your first bite has won a small prize, priest. He is undersized, this one, only a boy," Anubis said, as if he were gazing out of Ian's eyes.

"A very powerful boy who will grow tall and strong," Ian reminded him.

"When will you begin to prepare him?"

"Already, master. Subliminal suggestions are being implanted in his brain as he sleeps, and the drug we'll continue to feed him will make him receptive to my—our—wishes." Ian felt the entity's restless impatience as uneasiness in his own body. If he weren't very careful, Anubis would soon demand total power over him. "I must continue with preparations so that all will be as it should by the full moon."

"You have my leave to do so, old crocodile. Your god knows how your plotting and planning consumes you. But believe this, priest, you do what you do for me. No one else," the entity warned and swept out of Ian's consciousness with a haughty flourish.

Ian reached into his pocket and pressed the on switch activating his two-inch-square titanium-cased field transducer that amplified his personal frequency to the highest cycle possible and formed a protective shield around his aura. His was a miniature of Datascape's new psitech frequency generator that they'd beamed at the boy for the last four days. The machine was programmed to detect and disrupt, with a lower dissonant wave, a single target's personal frequency. They'd directed it at Marty, knocking any extrasensory powers out of phase and therefore out of the so-called divine range, so the boy was psychically blind. So far the psychic technology had performed to the drawings and specifications of the Tesla technology from which it was derived.

Ian wasn't absolutely certain his own transducer would block a discarnate entity, but he'd keep it on just in case, and would soon find out if it worked when Anubis decided to drop in on him again. The one drawback was that he couldn't extend his energy to remote see or influence while his transducer was operating. With that thought, he turned it off again.

Datascape R&D continued to promise that he would soon have an improved multi-phase model, allowing him to send and receive while in shield mode. He needed the new psitech now that this operation was rolling. He'd soon have to combat Spence and Rian, and if they actually worked together again, they would be problematical to defeat. At the same time he had to train the boy and hold Anubis at bay. Very, very difficult, but exhilarating and certainly worth betting his fortune and his life on.

He glanced at the time displayed in a small box at the bottom right of the monitor's screen: 8:00 a.m. Denver time. Spencer would have found the surprises that Ian left for him at the cabin and gotten a hold of Rian by now, begging her to come back to help them find the boy. She wouldn't go. Rian would be returning only to Ian, or not at all.

Ian allowed a chuckle of satisfaction. His former employees, Rian, Spencer and Gabrielli, were all so predictable and therefore completely manageable because all, including Gabrielli's wife, deluded themselves. The four hid the obvious from themselves: that they weren't ever free, and they weren't ever ordinary folk living a life the American way. They were, and always would be, his personal creations to play with as he pleased.

The boy began to roll his red-crowned head and move his limbs. His eyes were still closed, but the cardio and

EEG leads hooked up to him showed that he was awake.

Time to make a new friend out of a potentially undefeatable enemy. Ian walked out of the control room and down the hall toward the detention area where Marty Gabrielli was waking up and would be looking for a shoulder to cry on or someone to blame and kill.

Ian intended to be the shoulder, fatherly and comforting.

Rian's Light Seeking mutated into the worst remote viewing session she'd ever had. The horrendous scene at the cabin so disturbed her that she couldn't stay locked on target and repeatedly popped out of trance in defense of her own emotional stability.

Soaking wet with sweat, she finally gave up and stumbled to the bathroom to vomit repeatedly and then crawled into the shower, sitting on the tile floor, unable to stand. Still the visions wouldn't stop. She continued to spiritually writhe in Michael's and Dorel's fear and anguish as they died over and over on the screen of her mind. No amount of water or soap could wash away the imprint of horrendous sensations on her psyche. She didn't know how much time had passed until she climbed out of the shower and looked at the clock on the counter.

She'd lost four hours!

Why hadn't Spence called?

Rian made her way back to bed, wet and exhausted, and tried to dial Spence but couldn't get service on her cell phone. She reached for the room's phone on the bedside table and dialed Spence's home number, hoping it hadn't changed since she'd last called.

A recorded voice mail greeting advised her to leave a message or call back later. Just as she was about to hang up in frustration, Spence picked up.

"Spence! Why didn't you call?" she exclaimed, massaging her forehead with her fingertips. The pain refused to be rubbed away.

"Couldn't," he answered and started to explain what had gone on at the cabin.

She stopped him. "I know, I know. I can't tell you how sorry I am. I'm sick about Mike and Dorel, Spence. Really sick."

"Rian, they're okay. Mike's right here and Dorel's in the guestroom. Didn't you get that in your viewing?" he asked.

Rian shivered and she ran her fingers through her wet hair. "No. No, I didn't. I got in a loop of the Japanese maniac killing Dorel and Mike . . . but he didn't, right? What did I see then?"

"Oh, he shot them, all right, Mike says, but used some kind of special bullet with a knockout dart load. He doesn't know what happened to Marty, but from what I turned up at the cabin, I'm telling you that Ian set this all up. He's taken Marty and I think he's using him as bait," Spence said, his voice tight and cold.

"Bait for what?" she asked, drawing a blank.

"You don't know? How could you have missed this? What the hell were you viewing, Rian, your ass? Or weren't you even trying?" he spat in her ear.

Rather than enable him to further abuse her by arguing, she redirected the conversation. "Let me talk to Dorel."

"She's asleep."

"Mike, then. Put him on the phone," she demanded, aggravation burning in her stomach. Spence hadn't changed, he'd only gotten worse.

When she heard Mike's voice, welling tears spilled down her cheeks. "Oh, Mike, what can I say? I'm so sorry. What can I do to help bring Marty home?"

"I honestly don't know, Rian," he said, his usually strong voice soft and filled with sorrow.

She wiped her cheek with the back of her hand and sniffed. "Is Dorel all right? What I viewed was so horrible that to find out that you're okay is . . ." she choked back a sob, ". . . overwhelming but so great." Her voice broke and she let the tears flow.

"Shhhh, easy, Rian. It's okay. Thanks for caring so much. I'll let Dorel know you called."

"Wait, Mike," she choked out. "I want to get Marty back, I do, but I can't come there like Spence wants. It wouldn't do any good. If Ian really has Marty, he'd take him to Denver, not Seattle, though I'll say that I can't see him there or anywhere. It's like he's dropped into a black hole. There's one good thing, though. If he were . . . dead, then I'd be able to perceive him, you know? I'd get him crossing over, and after."

"Yeah," Mike agreed. "That's what Spence says, too. You're probably right about him being in Denver. None of us are thinking straight right now. We need time to regroup and think this thing through, but I don't know that we've got it. What I do know is that my boy is out there somewhere and—"

She heard Spence snatch the phone back. "Rian, it's simple. Ian wants the swords. That's never changed. Remember he said he'd wait until the swords came back to us, like they always do, then he'd take them? I figure he got tired of waiting and decided to make things happen on Ian time."

"How can you be sure he has Marty?" she reasoned with him. "Could it be possible that Marty ran away from the cabin after he thought his parents were killed? Or Inada could have taken him. I didn't get anything that happened after Mike and Dorel were shot, did you?"

Spence huffed into the phone. "No, but if you'd been there afterwards, you'd understand what I'm talking about. This whole operation has been executed for maximum emotional impact on all of us, probably Marty, too. Ian wants us worked up and not thinking, just fearing and reacting; then we get *handled.* At least, that's the way I'd run it, and he's the one that taught me. And you."

Spence always had to remind her of her despised, foul past with Ian that he wouldn't allow her to forget because he couldn't.

"And you think he's doing all this so we'll bring back the swords?" Rian asked. "Think, Spence, that doesn't make sense, because there's no evidence that he'll be able to use them, even if he has them. We created them for ourselves, no one else."

"And Mike, don't forget. He's used the Defender Sword through that cycle of lifetimes he and Dorel were locked into. The only way we'd find out for sure if Ian can use the swords now is to view and trace the entire chain of custody of the swords from their creation to now. We don't have time for that."

Spence could be right on both issues, especially the crucial time factor. Why had Ian chosen this time to do this, if he had? She couldn't accept Spence's warped perception of the situation, and must verify it herself.

Obviously reading her thoughts, he carped, "We don't have the time for you to dick around in the fallacious ozone until you see the freaking light." She started to shield herself, but he bellowed, "No, Rian, don't block me! We've got to work this together. I'm smart enough to know that Marty needs you probably more than he does me. We need you to come home. We're all depending on you."

Spence was spreading it on with a trowel. Bastard. She swallowed back the lump of building resentment and tried to redirect what had degenerated into a quarrel back to a reasonable conversation. "And Marty, Dorel and Mike have my commitment to help them in any positive way I can. No one wants to hang onto past mistakes or bickering. Everyone desires to work together, in their own way and best methods, using their strengths. And I promise to do that."

He snorted with disgust. "Are you running for goddamn office? What a shitload of platitudes. Only you would attempt to reframe a life-threatening situation that required your commitment with doubletalk so that you commit to zip. Thanks for nothing, Rian."

He didn't hang up. She heard him breathing heavily, waiting for her to engage; then he'd get his hook-up—she'd be angry and he'd get off on it. Rian waited a few seconds, clearing her intention to retaliate, and beamed back a high wave of peace so strongly focused, like a laser, that it should have him hearing harps and seeing white bunnies hopping through a sun-splashed field of daisies.

Spence's breathing in her ear calmed. "Yeah, okay, I get that." He chortled. "Jesus, Rian, celestial music?"

"Uh-huh, just for you," she answered, putting a grin in her voice. "Now, again, I'm not saying that Ian isn't at the bottom of this or that everything isn't as you've said, but consider a moment. If he's truly done these things, there has to be a bigger, grander reason . . ." She had no idea what that might be, but something at the edge of her consciousness hinted that answer was out there in the ether, if she had the courage to search for it.

"Okay, so you said. What do you suggest, then? Not bring back the swords? That's your idea, then the only thing left to us is to target Ian and try to remote influence him into releasing Marty. Or I can kill him. That would get us the same result and I'd enjoy it a hell of a lot more," Spence said.

"Let's keep our heads and do some obvious practical things at this point. Have you tried to connect with Marty?"

"Yeah. Nothing still. Could be he's being bumped offline and kept blind. Drugs or tech, maybe both," Spence posited.

Rian shivered. "Spence, can Mike hear you?"

"Yeah," he said, his voice tight.

"Then don't say anything more about what you fear may be going on, okay? Mike has to calm down. We all do, or none of us will be able to perform. Like you, I believe that we'll all need to be at our best, and you've got to help bring Mike back online. His remote viewing skills . . . well, I just don't feel them, do you?"

After a moment he lowered his voice. "No, not much, but you know as well as I do that he hasn't lost them. You can't lose this shit once you start, but you can ignore it, push it way down and kid yourself that if you act and live like everyone else, you are. That's where he is now. But I'm aware that he's groping around, wondering if he can get the skills back in time."

She agreed. "Like us, he hoped he'd never have to use them again and that it was over."

"You mean like you believed. I didn't. Ian told us that day at the Sphinx, when he didn't kill us outright but let us go, that it wasn't over. If you've really believed otherwise, you guys have kidded yourselves like the rest of the sheep-people out there. Believing what you're told, buying into the illusions that powerbrokers like Stoddard want you to have, so they can control every thought you have. They keep you pacified with slaving in the corporate fields to pay for shit you don't need, so they can live like kings by the sweat of your brow," Spence preached, warming to his usual conspiracy rhetoric.

She sighed. They'd been over it a million times. Just because she chose to use her psychic gifts differently and, to her mind, more positively than he, in pursuit of spiritual awareness and freedom, didn't mean she was a sleepwalking member of the entranced masses.

"Okay, Spence," she said quietly. "When you can tell me that three of you, together, have formed a viable, workable plan to find Marty and bring him home, I'll come."

A sharp rap sounded on the casita's front door. "Hang on," she said, grabbing her robe. "There's someone at the door. I'll be right back." Not waiting for Spence's answer, she tossed the phone on the bed and shrugged into the silk wrap. On her way through the living room, she heard the birds begin to stir in the early dawn and a raven's raspy caw. A single knock cracked on the door again. Could be the early-morning delivery of the newspaper and fresh orange juice. But they hadn't knocked the other mornings.

She peered through the view hole at the indistinguishable form blending into the tall bushes beside the walkway across from her porch. "Who's there?" she called.

"Chevayo," came a voice soft as a gentle breath across her ear.

The space between her brows began to itch. She fingered it lightly. He'd touched her there last night, hadn't he? And said something about gathering strength before dealing with Spence . . . just what she hadn't done. And the mysterious shaman was again at her door.

Rian cracked the door and stuck her head out. "Morning. You're out early."

Chevayo moved out of the shadows onto the sidewalk.

He was dressed in black jeans and a white cotton long-sleeved shirt buttoned at the throat and the cuffs. His dark, straight hair was slicked back off a high forehead that accentuated his hawk-like nose, and tied at the neck with a leather band. Out-of-the-box new western boots crunched beige pea gravel as he stepped off the sidewalk onto the short path to her porch. A black- and white-beaded medicine bag ensconced between two large turquoise nuggets was suspended on a rawhide thong from his neck. He extended a newspaper and willow basket holding two bottles of orange juice to her.

"I bring news," the austerely handsome man said, a dry smile hinting at the corners of his mouth.

"Ah, and you deliver, too," she said, letting the door swing wider. Rian took the paper and basket and backed inside, holding his gaze. "If you'll excuse me, I'm actually on the phone."

"You must invite me inside," he said sternly and raised a slim hand, the motion stopping her from closing the door.

It was entirely alien—his words, the odd inflection heavy with intention that she felt in her third eye rather than solar plexus, the sudden shift in his demeanor. In the sacred space between breaths, she thought to rebuff him. Even there his determination found her. He would not be rebuffed.

Rian lowered her startled gaze and stepped aside. Chevayo crossed in front of her and stood in the middle of the foyer while she bumped the door closed.

"Do not agree to return. You are not ready," he counseled and fixed his umber gaze on her forehead.

She felt his gaze burning into her third eye and, summoning her force of will, tried to turn her face away.

His eyes glittered and he lifted his arrow-straight finger

to her face, bringing it to within an inch of her forehead. "Will you see what will happen, if you go to him now? How you will fail, because you refuse to follow the soul path?"

"Please, he's waiting for me on the phone. I—I have to talk to him," the plea rolled easily off her tongue and she knew it was Spence who'd projected it to her. Two powerful men were obviously battling for her mind, to influence her for their own purposes. That infuriated her. They didn't care, and maybe even relished, that she was virtually helpless to refuse them.

"Tell him you are not ready," Chevayo said.

"I can't move. Let me, and I'll tell him," she promised, willing herself to break his hold on her.

"By your intention, your will manifests." Chevayo's finger made an electric, activating connection with the skin covering her third eye. She stumbled back as if pushed, her head clearing as a purifying sensation blasted through her body.

In a crystalline moment of truth, Rian went to the bedroom, took up her phone and informed Spence, "I cannot help bring Marty back at this time. I cannot be with you now. I will contact you when I am ready on both counts."

The call dropped without her pushing the off button, and Spence's encroaching connection to her aura broke off abruptly. Rian walked back into the living room where Chevayo waited for her. "Now, you tell me why you are doing what you're doing and why I should let you continue."

He gestured to the wrought iron glass-topped table and chairs on the terrace. "The sun will rise in minutes over the mesa. Let us greet father sun together in the harmony of trust."

She smiled. "Only if coffee is part of the hello, my

friend. Go ahead and start whatever it is you do. I'll be there directly."

He gave a single nod and slid the glass door open, stepping out to the flagstone terrace facing the red-and-tan-sandstone eastern wall of Encantada Canyon. Rian set the coffeemaker up and returned to the bedroom, dressing quickly in rust-colored silk pants, black sandals and a sleeveless mock-turtleneck black top. She draped a length of antique Japanese hand-embroidered silk in jade and rust tones over her shoulders. She didn't bother to use the straightening iron on her long, black hair, twisting it into a chignon and holding the sleek bun in place with a large, ivory dragon comb.

She placed the coffee pot, orange juice and two cups with cream and sugar on a tray and carried it to the terrace. Chevayo stood at the railing, looking down into the broad ravine that separated the top tier of casitas from the rows below. He turned when she approached the closed screen and slid it open for her. She set the tray on the table and began to serve the coffee as he returned to face the yellow-red glow of the sun peeking into the canyon below.

Rian didn't ask how he took his coffee, because when she'd opened her mouth, he'd opened his, beginning with a low, resonant humming. As she stirred cream into the steaming black brew, his voice rose in pitch and cadence. He lifted his long arms in a reverent open-palmed salute and began to float a beautiful chant on a melody of the spheres.

A musician herself, she took great pleasure in Chevayo's inspiring, masterful song of praise and wished she'd pulled her Andean flute out of its case in the closet. She still could but didn't want to miss one exquisite moment with him. She closed her eyes in the rising sun's golden light, imagining the beloved instrument as her lips, her tongue, and let her heart sing.

Spirit sounds flowed down from the higher dominions through the tops of their heads, amplified in their hearts, flooded their bodies with intense high wave energy and poured from their mouths as inspired creation.

By the time their chorus trailed off on the breeze and she opened her eyes to see him lower his arms, his face aglow like an angel's, Rian sensed that the entire canyon quivered with blessing. This exalted state was what she wanted to achieve, how she wanted to feel forever, having never approached such ecstasy in this life and any others she'd recalled.

Now, here with Chevayo, she'd flown to heaven effortlessly on the music of her heart. He'd been her wings, lifting her, fortifying her spirit to reach into the divine.

And she wanted more.

"There is no wanting," he answered her unspoken desire. "There is no more, for it empties itself endlessly upon you."

She lowered her abashed gaze and picked up a coffee cup. "I haven't felt like that, ever. Thank you."

"Do not thank me. It was your creation and I thank you." He continued to survey the canyon, tilting his head at the different morning sounds.

"That's very kind, but I know what you did. Just like the other night at the sweat, you helped me. This morning your song boosted me up on that wave and I rode it to the Spiritlands," she said, and took a sip of tepid coffee.

"Not the Spiritlands, Rian. It is the majesty of your own soul that you have experienced," Chevayo said. "It is now that you remember and must be ready."

Rian braced herself, her fingers tightening on the delicate cup trembling in her hand. "Ready for what, Chevayo?"

"You must stop the god's return to earth."

The cup dropped and shattered on the flagstone floor.

"You must manifest the Swords of Balance, forestall those who would take the power for themselves, yet with their help defeat the god and his high priest so that the Essence becomes the Initiate."

She felt his curious stare on her and tried to control her reaction. "Oh, of course. Is that all?" she tried joking. "Just one little thing, how am I supposed to do that?"

"You must use the skills that you have learned from all your experiences. The moon will rise full in a few days. The Initiate will be ready, but if you are not, all will fail. Take responsibility for who you are and what you have chosen," he said. "And we shall begin now."

— EIGHT —

The gorgeous symphony streamed into Marty's consciousness like warm sunlight, cleansing and nurturing his energy field, elevating his emotionally shocked and depressed vibration. The heavenly music permeated every cell and membrane of his body and he began to awaken from his long, dark sleep.

As the revitalizing sounds faded, before opening his eyes, he became aware that he was not in his own bed, at home or at the cabin. His head was fuzzy, as if wrapped in cotton, and his senses lethargic. A ringing, like hundreds of tiny bells in his ears, distracted his self-analysis, along with a headache that got all his attention. He slitted his eyes and the bright overhead light amped up the pain in his head.

"Good morning, son," a friendly voice greeted him.

Marty squinted at the tall man smiling beside his bed. He focused as best he could and the man's blurry features sharpened. The one who'd helped him last night . . . "Oh!" he wailed, covering his tearing eyes with his hands.

A gentle hand rested on his shoulder. "Easy, son. I know it's hard . . . to let it go . . . and don't remember that they're dead . . . you aren't alone."

Trying with all the strength he could muster, Marty couldn't remember more than flashes of horrible images that the man's words seemed to provoke. His mom and dad were dead. And Katana! The more Marty wept, the colder his heart became, the pain of loss receding to a dark void, frozen of feeling.

"Feel better now," the man said. "Go ahead and sit up. I bet you're hungry and thirsty."

Marty pulled himself up and wiped his face dry on the hospital gown's sleeve. He grimaced with the movement.

"What are you feeling?" the man asked with a concerned frown.

"Mr.?" Marty began, rubbing his aching forehead between his eyes and spiking upward.

"Call me Ian. Are you in pain?"

"Yes, sir. My head kind of hurts."

Ian picked up a tiny white paper cup and poured water from an iced jug into a plastic glass. "Here, this will help."

Marty frowned at the white tablet in the cup. "What is it?"

"Perfectly harmless and good for you. Trust me, you'll feel better in an instant. You've been through a lot that most men couldn't stand. You deserve to be happy again . . . and you will." He rattled the pill in the cup, his brown eyes shining with compassion as he handed it to Marty.

Marty took it from the man called Ian, feeling a sense of trust and connection with him, then tipped the pill into his mouth, followed with a gulp of water. Strangely, the headache magically improved. He quirked a smile at Ian. "Wow."

Ian laughed, the sound making Marty feel even better. "Wow, indeed. See, just as I promised. Shall we have breakfast? How about pancakes?" He swept back the sheet, motioning for Marty to get up.

"Is it okay? I can get out of bed?" Marty asked, a little unsure, glancing around the hospital room, then back at Ian.

"Of course. Because I say so. You can do anything you want."

Marty grinned and swung his feet down, hopping onto the cold tile floor, a breeze flapping his gown. "Uh, I need my clothes." He grabbed the back of the gown together over his naked bottom.

Ian opened the white metal bedside table and pointed. "Right in there. If they don't fit, not to worry. We'll find something else."

Marty quickly dressed in the white boxers that were a size too large and a black cotton jumpsuit that zipped up the front with long legs he had to roll up. He slid into the huge rubber flip-flops that were like skis on his feet. "Okay, but I look like an inmate from the county jail. These don't fit very good. Where'd this stuff come from?"

Ian turned around and tried not to laugh, his hand covering his mouth. For some reason he was reminded of Spence. Marty frowned, trying to remember where Spence was. "Ian, I need to call my uncle to come and get me."

"Right after breakfast, Marty, we'll get started," Ian said, placing a hand on his back and guiding him to the door.

The blueberry pancakes made Marty cry, maybe because they weren't that good, not like Mom's. There was no one else in the dining room at the other white-covered tables. Just Ian sitting across from Marty, urging him to eat while drinking green tea, because it was better for you, he said. Ian talked about a bunch of stuff. It was kind of interesting, but Marty was distracted, like there was something he should be doing or had forgotten. Something . . . or someone calling to him.

"Beware the dog," popped into his head. Marty dropped his fork, glancing around the room for the source of the voice.

"What is it?" Ian asked with a troubled look.

Marty shrugged and picked up his fork, dragging lines in the puddle of brown syrup on his plate. "Nothing."

"Oh. You looked like you had a thought or wanted to say something?" Ian said, then went on about being on the Olympic swim team and taking the gold in the 200-meter breaststroke, back in the old days.

Marty dully wondered when that was. Ian didn't look real old, but definitely older than Dad. Tears sprang into his eyes and he whisked them away when Ian wasn't looking. A sick, hollow feeling opened in his stomach. He couldn't remember why he was here eating blueberry pancakes without . . . them.

After breakfast, they walked down the hall together, Marty shuffling along in his flapping clown shoes and half-listening to Ian chatting about a bunch of different adult stuff.

"Here we are," Ian said, stopping in front of a door with a security keypad beside it. A red and white sign said *Restricted Area, No Admittance.* He took a card out of the breast pocket of his leather jacket and slid it into the pad, still talking. The door unlatched and Ian pulled it open, motioning him through.

He stepped inside a short passageway that led to a central command station where two people with headsets watched several computer monitors. Ian didn't say anything to them as he ushered Marty past them into a room opposite the station and closed the door behind him.

"Take a seat at the table, Marty," Ian said and pulled out a chair across from him. The stark white room was cold and bleak, with only a gray metal table and two gray chairs.

Marty sat on the hard chair and met Ian's bland gaze. "What's this place, some kind of interrogation room?" he joked.

"Good, I thought you were asleep again. Yes, it's a debriefing room." Ian swept his hand around. "Nothing to distract you. No noise. No color. Just you and me. And the truth."

Marty shivered. Ian was going to say it. Say his parents were dead and he couldn't let him do that. "Do you work here at the hospital—if it is a hospital. Is it?"

Ian's solemn expression didn't change and he didn't answer the question. "You know, Marty, we have to talk about it. You owe them that much. They'd want you to tell me all you can and let me help you." He touched Marty's shoulder. "You want that, don't you," Ian said, nodding.

Marty dropped his eyes to his hands in his lap and nodded.

"Good. Let me tell you first that I blame myself for their deaths—"

"No!" Marty interrupted, jerking his head up. "It's not your fault. It's mine. I made them go to the cabin. If I hadn't done that, we'd be home instead of me here and they'd be . . ."

"Why did you insist on going to the cabin?" Ian asked.

"Because, well, I just wanted to," Marty evaded, wondering if he jumped up and ran to the door if it would open or be locked.

"Didn't they want to go?" Ian persisted.

Marty gave a quick shrug. "Not so much. They're busy and I've got school . . ."

"Yet, you wanted to go to the cabin anyway, and they agreed? Why?"

"I couldn't sleep, okay?" Marty yelled. "They thought if they took me there and I saw it, I'd be able to sleep."

"Saw what?"

"The thing. From my dream," Marty mumbled, wishing

he'd never had those stupid dreams.

"Ahh, yes. I understand. Your parents were very supportive of your special skills, weren't they?" Ian said, nodding slowly, his lips pursed as if he were studying Marty and liked what he saw.

Marty nodded, too. "Yeah, but it got them killed, didn't it? What good is being able to remember that you were some old warrior or pilot or a grandfather and not be able to keep your parents from dying, or making it happen because you wanted to find out some dumb secret?"

"And did you find the secret?"

He jumped up, knocking the chair over. "Shut up! I don't want to answer questions and I don't want to talk about this anymore. I want to go home." His heart banged in his chest, making his head throb as he glared at Ian, looking so distant and cool.

"To an empty house? The authorities wouldn't allow you to live there on your own. They'd put you in juvenile detention until they decided what to do with you, while they sold your parents' home and possessions. Not much to go back to, I'd say."

Marty reached the door and turned the knob. Locked. He leaned his burning forehead against the cold metal. "No. My uncle Spence will take me to his house. My—Rian will come . . ." his voice drifted off and he began to wonder why he hadn't heard from Spence. It wasn't unusual to go for a couple of days without his responding to Marty's mental messages, but he realized he hadn't communicated in days. Or Rian either.

"I need to call my uncle," he said, but had the sick feeling that he wouldn't be allowed to and didn't know why.

"We've been trying to contact Jonathan Spencer since we learned about the attack on your cabin. He's nowhere to be found. I'm sorry, Marty. I've been doing everything I can to help you, and I'll continue to do the right things for you," Ian said behind him.

Could something have happened to Spence, too? Marty wondered and locked his knees to keep from falling. "I—I have an aunt," Marty said, turning around stiffly, "Well, not really an aunt; she's a good family friend, like my godmother."

"Yes, I've been calling her as well, son. She hasn't responded." Ian waved him back to the table. "Come, sit. You look like you're about to fall down and we don't want you to hurt yourself further, do we?"

Marty shook his head and returned to the chair, since he wasn't getting out of here, but he would, just as soon as he could find Spence or Rian. "You think something's happened to Spence and Rian, too, don't you?"

"Truth?" Ian asked.

Marty said yes, not so sure he wanted to hear it.

"Yes, it's possible. That man who killed your parents wanted something—"

"The sword," Marty spat. "He killed them for a sword that doesn't exist. I heard my mom try to tell him that, Dad too, but he wouldn't listen and . . ." The awful picture of his parents' murder blasted into his mind like an Omnimax show with surround sound. "He shot them."

"Yes, he did, but your parents taught you that people don't really die. Not the spirit anyway." Ian gave a soft chuckle. "Of course they did, and why am I telling you, since you remember many of your past lives. You do, don't you?"

Marty squinted at the bright light hurting his eyes. "I guess, but not so much lately."

"Oh? Why is that?" Ian asked, leaning forward.

"I used to, but I haven't thought about anything in days. You know, couldn't hear anything." He shook his head, feeling foolish for sharing the family secret. "No big deal."

"Oh, but it is. It's huge, as they say. You're a very gifted young man and I want to help you, because I helped your father, trained him. I owe it to him to take care of his son," Ian said, looking like he might cry too.

"You knew my dad?" Marty asked, his stomach unclenching a little. "Did you teach him in the Navy?"

Ian nodded. "Yes, I did."

"Were you an instructor pilot or did you teach at the Academy?" His dad hadn't talked much about his Navy days, other than how much he'd enjoyed flying.

"It was during his special ops duty that we first met," Ian said, and glanced at his watch. "Are you thirsty? Don't want you to get dehydrated. Maybe you're hungry. You didn't eat much of your breakfast."

Marty said no and impatiently pushed for more information. "Did you know him when he was in the SEAL teams?"

"It was after he was transferred out to a special intel unit to develop his mind or intuitive sense to see and gather information at a distance. It was called remote viewing. I was his trainer and targeting officer."

Marty rocked back. "You—you're Ian Stoddard!" he sputtered in horror.

Ian held his hands up and smiled. "Yes, I am. Very good." He reached across the table and grabbed Marty's arm, holding him in the chair. "Get control of yourself. There are things I must tell you, and you must be calm to understand." His hand tightened on Marty's arm. "Are you mature enough to accept that you may not have all the facts, or all the truth about me and a great many other things?"

Marty tried to jerk his arm away. "My dad doesn't lie. You do!"

Ian released him and sat back, crossing his arms. "All right then, let's take stock, shall we? What exactly have I lied to you about? I've rescued you, killed the man who murdered your parents and tried to kill you and I brought you to safety." He rolled his shoulders and sighed, his index finger pointing at himself. "Where's the truth?"

It made no sense. He heard the words, saw Ian say them, but he didn't understand the way they went together or the jumbled feeling the sounds left in him. Marty rubbed his smarting eyes with the heels of his hands. Thinking was getting too hard and it hurt, too. He shook his head. "I don't know."

"That's right," Ian said like Marty had given a correct answer. "You don't know Ian Stoddard and your father didn't either, or he'd have listened to me when I warned him about the three of you being in danger."

Marty frowned. "In danger from what?"

Ian stood and smiled down at him. "Old friend, you and I have had many lives, many adventures together in the past. You've helped me. I've helped you. Over and over. Now you need me again. Remember, and let me help you as I always have." He beckoned to Marty. "Don't think that because your enemy is dead, there aren't others waiting for and working against you. There are many, I'm afraid, but I will not let them get to you without a fight. Just like always. Trust me. I'll help you get your old skills back and we'll face them together."

Marty got up and followed Ian to the door, where he stopped and put an arm around Marty's shoulders. "You're not yourself. Not to worry. It's been very hard for you this time. But that old, bad life is gone. Use this terrible tragedy as steel in your hand and cut away the chains of the past that imprison you. You will become all that your father knew you would be, and more. Trust me. I will do all I can to father the best in you, Marty."

Confusion bounced back and forth in Marty's head like a ping-pong ball. He let Ian take his hand like a little kid and walk him back to his room. Marty said nothing as Ian handed him another pill that he swallowed, and got in bed as ordered.

"Sleep well, son."

Just before lethargy pulled him down into silence, he heard a whispered, "Beware the dog."

Rian's spirit settled gently back into her body. She sensed that Chevayo still stood beside her and considered how well he and she matched each other. Of course, the shaman had great psychic skills, but it was more than that. They actually communicated on every level, after she accepted that his appearing here and now to teach her was not coincidence but fate, or at least something wonderful unfolding in the plan for this life.

They made beautiful music together that stirred profound longing in her. She didn't want to leave Chevayo's side. Just being with him this last hour on her terrace was like meditating at the feet of an ascended master at a sacred site, like the Great Pyramids at Giza or a mountaintop monastery in Nepal. She was filled with incredible energy, better than any sex she'd ever had. She began to wonder what making love would be like with a spiritual adept. Tantric? Transformational? She'd never experienced tantric sex but had understood that it could lead one to bliss and the higher states of consciousness. Perhaps he was the one who could take her there.

Suddenly the thought entered that it was time to go or she would be late to teach her Light Seeking class at the Wellness Kiva. Rian took a deep, centering breath and opened her eyes, glancing at Chevayo's strong profile. He was still flying out there. She didn't want to disturb him and moved quietly toward the terrace door to go inside and collect her things.

"Go," he said behind her. "I will await you here."

That probably wasn't the best idea, given the sizzling thoughts she was having about him, and meditating further with Chevayo wasn't one of them.

"You could come to the Wellness Kiva with me. We break for lunch at eleven-thirty, if you didn't want to sit in. Or I could meet you somewhere else?" Some place public and safe—for both of them, because she was quite certain he was thinking about her in the same way. One usually didn't generate such thoughts by themselves, but by picking up on an intention or availability projected by someone else.

The shaman turned to her and they locked gazes. Of course, he'd read her intention. Was she sending signals she wasn't aware of? Apparently so. She squelched the rising embarrassment and smiled. Hell with it. It is what it is.

Chevayo also smiled. "There will be no danger in my waiting for you here. But if you are worried, perhaps it is best that you don't go to your class. Stay here and continue to meditate and gain strength."

"No, that's okay. I feel great. Teaching always strengthens me, the shared energy. While it's nowhere near the charge of meditating with you, and not much could be," she said with a self-conscious grin, "it's the best I can do right now, I believe. And I have to fulfill my obligations."

"You are obligated to help your group. These that you

try to *teach,*" he said with a sneer, "attach to your aura with their problems and false expectations that they want you to fix, instead of taking responsibility for their own lives and what they have drawn into them."

She opened her briefcase on the coffee table and began to stuff papers into it. "Yes, there are those who do that, but if I can inspire one or two to seek the Light, then my being there is worth it, don't you think?" She zipped the bag and shouldered it. "As much as I'd like to sit on that mountaintop with you, I can't live a cloistered life, no matter how much I want to. I believe that I came here to help people."

Chevayo stood in front of her. "Are you sure that's why you're here, living this life—to entertain weekend seekers who will have an ecstatic moment, then return to their automated lives of tranced-out consuming?"

His words burned into her heart. She'd had the same hopeless, desperate doubts about the effectiveness of her work, but what else was she to do? Quit hoping to make a difference? Become like Spence and chase money and power? She wouldn't do either, and she couldn't do other than what she managed to do right now.

Chevayo wrapped his arms around her shoulders and held her close. "You are here to bring the Essence to the earth. That is why you must be strong and not distracted by your past, or even your present. You felt the music, the highest frequency of eternal Love. That is where you have to operate from, to prevail over those who battle you for the power of the Swords of Balance."

Rian sighed and raised her head from his sheltering chest, looking into his fathomless charcoal eyes. "Enough cryptic shamanizing, okay? You know what's happened to Marty, don't you?"

He dropped his arms and stepped back. "I know the One, the Essence, yes."

"Good for you. Unless you mean that Marty is the One that you're referring to, that wasn't all that helpful and certainly didn't answer my question," she complained in frustration.

"He shall be initiated as the Essence, yes."

"Is he okay?" she asked, hope rising for the first time since Spence's frantic call. Spence! Oh lord, she had to go home and help him.

"No! They must come here," Chevayo countered. "By then you will be ready."

"Then you do know where Marty is," she accused him and grabbed up her phone to call Spence with the news. "Tell me."

"I know, yes, but if you interfere at this point, he will be lost. Events must be allowed to progress, do you understand?" He put his cool hand over hers clutching the phone. "Trust me. To do so is to trust yourself."

She wanted to, but better to trust the man she still loved to help Marty rather than the one who had failed him, herself. "I can't." Rian pulled her hand away, grabbed her bag, dialing Spence as she left the casita.

"Hello, Rian," the smooth voice said into her ear and she stumbled, grabbing the porch's railing for support.

"Ian! How did I get you?" she demanded, her voice and body trembling.

His laugh was soft and dangerous. "Like always, because you wanted to."

"Like hell. I'm hanging up," she said, her finger on the button.

"No! Not if you want to find a certain boy wonder," he barked, stopping her.

"Spence was right. You did take him, didn't you? For God's sake, why, Ian? He knows nothing," she said, trying to keep the pleading out of her voice. He despised that sort of show of emotion and would use it against her.

"Rian darling, you do want to know where Marty is, don't you? Isn't that why you called me instead of Spencer? He isn't any use to you. Never was. I, however, am, because actually Marty and I are becoming very good friends. He's going to help me, you see, where you and Spencer would not, and of course Gabrielli wouldn't, listening to that obtuse wife of his. I'm tired of waiting, Rian. I'll have the swords now, if you please."

"You know damn well that I don't have them," she protested, her mind in turmoil.

"Of course, but you can bring them back, manifest them, can't you? That's all I want, just the two swords, unless of course you want to return to me as well. Then we'd be one happy, little family, wouldn't we?" Ian's intention oozed into her ear.

"Family?"

"Yes, my darling, you, me and dear Marty. Quite the picture, isn't it? The most powerful psychics in this world wielding the Swords of Balance. Imagine, there's nothing we couldn't have. Nothing we couldn't do. The world would be ours, and then out into the ether and other realms. Return to me, Rian; bring me the swords and help me train this boy."

"Never!" she shrieked. "I'll find him and kill you, you megalomaniacal son of a bitch."

He laughed at her again. "Have it your way. But I had to offer to take you back, didn't I? That's only fair, given that we meant so much to each other once. However, now that's out of the way, I can proceed. Bring me the swords and I won't kill the boy. You won't find him, so don't even think about trying. You should have realized that by now anyway."

"We will find him, Ian. Your ridiculous covert suggestions not to try are wasted on me. I'm the master, remember? I can find you anyplace, anytime—"

He interrupted her, "That would have been true, my darling, say, last week? But be honest, haven't you been a bit preoccupied with your Spiritlands travels or oddly incommunicado with Marty, even? That's because I've got it, Rian, the psitech online. I don't need remote assassin scum like you and Spencer anymore. With my own skills amplified, and shielded with the tech, why, the world is my oyster, my domain, mine for the taking and I'm taking it now!"

My God, Spence was right again, she conceded, barely able to stay on her feet, she was so distraught. "If that's so, why do you need the swords?" she taunted him, in vain no doubt, but she had to have time to think.

"Why? Because I want them. I want to find out for myself if they bestow the potential to command the universe like the legend says. And they must, because Spencer, and you and Gabrielli, have killed scores of people to possess them, proving that legend. And who would know better than the swords' creator, eh, Rian?"

"I don't believe that the swords give anyone power or anything else. Power comes from within, from one's connection with Spirit," she said, but knowing she lied and Ian would know it, too.

"Yes, that's right, oh great, though counterfeit, guru. Spread the balm of sacred bullshit liberally upon the poor, unenlightened masses; then perhaps you will actually come to believe it one day. But don't waste your breath or overrated talents on me. It angers me and you don't want to deal with an angry Ian, now do you?" Ian threatened, and the line went silent.

"Wait! Ian, don't hang up," she yelled into the dead phone.

Chevayo appeared beside her, putting a steadying hand under her elbow. "He will call again. But you must not agree to give him the swords. Yet."

— NINE —

For a scheduled transport, the G-Train ran more on time than most, due to its restricted access to only those holding Top Secret Violet. No Ultra or Q clearances could even access the G-Train's schedule, let alone book passage. The four-passenger car mag-lev train's manifest had been full for this trip, but Ian bumped an Air Force four-star general and his adjutant by simply flashing his Datascape photo I.D. with the tiny violet triangle in the upper right-hand corner.

The general's security badge had the requisite violet triangle in the bottom left corner that ordinarily would have given him priority over nearly everyone, but not over Ian. Datascape had been a primary contractor on the construction of the tunnel system. His team of remote viewers sighted the best routes for the laser tunneling machines that turned rock walls into glass. They'd shielded the operation from the public and everyone else with no need to know with thought forms, projected subliminal suggestions, planted news stories and movies with so ridiculous a premise and full of violence that the public succumbed to the embedded intention of mindlessness every time.

Ian acknowledged the general with an apologetic nod and ushered Marty to the platform, where they were the last to board.

He motioned Marty to take the window seat, though there would be nothing to see but himself reflected in the window on the downhill run from Denver to the secret underground base a mile beneath the surface of Encantada Canyon in Sedona, Arizona.

"Are we really going all the way underground?" Marty asked, his heavy-eyed expression showing a faint flicker of interest. He blinked at the lights of the station fading behind them. "Is this like a bullet train or something?"

Ian smiled. "Yes to both questions. We'll be there in less than two hours."

Marty roved his glassy gaze to the passengers, mostly men, in a variety of uniform types, and business and casual dress. "Are they going to the same place we are?"

"Some, yes, others at different installations or stops along the way," Ian answered, keeping his voice low. They'd already drawn attention, for there were seldom children on these trains.

"To do what?" Marty asked with a hooded look.

"Secrets, Marty, secrets. You don't want to ask and certainly don't want to know. It would be very dangerous for both of us. You never know whose interest you're going to draw. There are those who obviously want to kill you, and we don't know who may be helping them. Inada was one of many whom your father crossed swords with in the past. I'm doing everything I can to keep you safe, and you want to help me do that," Ian said. "Why don't you settle back and get some rest?"

Marty did as he was told and Ian began to relax. They would be secure within the Sedona base that was technologically shielded from every sort of surveillance, though not from remote viewers who knew where to target. Even then, official debunkers had trained the media and the public that the existence of a vast, nationwide transportation tunnel system and hidden bases were the stuff of mad conspiracy theorists and UFO nuts.

Within the vortex canyon, he could begin Marty's training as they began stepping up the frequency, bombarding the boy in preparation for the full moon's initiation. That, coupled with the whirlpool of the canyon's high level energy, could bring his skills back online before the full moon. It was a delicate balance of physical and behavioral management. If Marty's personal energy was suppressed by the drug and he was too drowsy, the energy transfer would mismatch and give Anubis control instead of Ian.

". . . ware the dog," Marty mumbled in his fitful sleep.

Ian jammed his hand in his jacket pocket and checked his personal field transducer—still on. He hadn't sensed Anubis, but perhaps the entity was in direct communication with the boy? That would not be good, not good at all.

Spence finally argued an exhausted Mike into agreeing with him, but talking sense to Dorel was impossible. No matter what he or Mike said, she had a fearful reason why they couldn't do it.

"We fly to Sedona, pick up Rian and come back tonight," Spence repeated and rubbed the back of his tight neck. Jesus, she was stubborn.

"And why come back at all? Marty's not here," Dorel declared, pacing the living room, her reddened fingers wringing the tied belt of Spence's blue terrycloth robe that he'd let her borrow while Mike washed their clothes. She'd already tromped down the nap on the area rug in her endless circling.

"I don't know that," Spence interjected, calling to Mike in the utility room. "Do you know that, Mike?"

"What?" came his response, muffled by the sounds of the dryer running.

"Never mind," Dorel yelled and flopped down on the

sofa. She rocked herself, head in her hands, and moaned, "Why, why, why is this happening?"

Spence sat beside her and slipped his arm around her slim shoulders. "I don't know, honey, but it's going to be all right. We'll get Rian and then it will all come together."

Dorel looked disbelief at him. "Like the last time? I'd rather hang than go through that again."

"You may just get to do that if she doesn't help us, and if Ian doesn't beat you to it," Spence jibed. "Come on, Dorel, this is the only way. I really feel that Marty wants us to do this." He didn't feel shit from Marty, but her thinking he did would move her, because she wasn't feeling anything from her son either.

"If Spence is getting something from Marty on this, we better go with it. I'm just glad that since he's hearing from him that means he's still alive and okay," Mike said, carrying a short stack of clean, folded clothes.

"Wait, Mike, I didn't say that," Spence said, dropping his arm off Dorel, guilt for lying to his friends chewing at him.

"The bloodstains aren't coming out of your stuff or mine either. We better get some clothes, but I don't think we ought to chance going to the house," Mike said and glanced at Spence. "We taking the BBJ?"

Spence shook his head. "Nope, the seven thirty-seven is too heavy for the runway in Sedona. We've got to get your Beaver back."

Mike slapped his forehead. "I forgot about that. I'll send a couple of delivery pilots, Bob and Greg, up to get it in your Huey, if that's okay with you? Though I have to say that I really question your devotion to those Vietnam-era choppers. Bob's I can understand, he flew one of them in Nam, but you? Beats me. In any case, he'll love the ride and

Greg will bring my plane home if it's flyable. Then we can fuel it on a short turn."

Spence agreed, still feeling like a rotten son of a bitch. These people, his only real friends, trusted him with their lives and their son's. Nothing he could take back now, it was a done deal. He'd have to make sure that all worked out like he promised, starting with bringing Rian home, one way or the other.

"There's the King Air two hundred that just came off of lease," Dorel suggested. "We need faster than the Beaver, and the King Air is the only plane we've got in local inventory that will have no problem getting in and out of that airport. Unless you want to charter?"

Spence and Mike shook their heads. "Mike, while you get a hold of Bob, I'll call and have the King Air fueled and file a flight plan. We ought to be able to depart in about ninety minutes, wouldn't you think?" she said, taking charge.

They left her alone to do what she did best, organizing everything and everyone within a fifty-mile radius. Mike headed out to buy Dorel some clothes and other personal things, leaving Spence to try to stay out of Dorel's way.

True to her estimation, they went wheels-up in the twin-engine turboprop ninety minutes later out of Boeing Field and turned south, climbing to cruise at 25,000 feet. Their estimated flying time was approximately four and half hours to watch the landscape slide by and make small talk about everything but exactly how they hoped to find Marty.

Dorel and Mike assumed Spence had a plan, and he had no choice but to let them think he did. He wasn't about to tell them that his best idea so far was to get Rian to help him bring back the swords. Then they'd have some real power and could take Ian out. If Dorel knew what he intended to do, she'd work directly against him with anger and fear that she couldn't control. That wouldn't do anyone any good, except Ian. He could count on Mike to be one merciless operator when sufficiently motivated, and out of Dorel's influence.

"I've never been to Sedona," Dorel said over the intercom and looking out the right side window. "I hear strange things happen there in those energy vortexes."

Mike, in the left seat, reached over and patted her knee showing beneath the short denim skirt riding way up her thigh. Spence thought Mike had done pretty well picking the outfit. Dorel hadn't said much and kept pulling at the bottom of the skirt. The pink sweater top didn't seem to be the best color with her red hair, but she always looked good. Though Spence couldn't remember ever having seen her wear clothes like this. He grinned, knowing that Mike was going to pay when she got him alone for dressing her in his high school chickie fantasy outfit.

It got too quiet in the cockpit again as Spence sensed Mike and Dorel reliving their terrifying ordeal at the cabin. He had to keep his psyche shielded against being swept into their stultifying fear. The worst to bear was their broken-hearted dread that their son was dead. Though Spence didn't believe Marty was, at least not yet, he worried what would happen to himself if that happened. Would he completely lose the last shred of humanity left in him? He'd be a lost soul, for sure, and no one would give a good goddamn. Especially not him.

"Where is Rian staying?" Dorel asked, not soon enough to keep him from spiraling into the pit.

"Huh? Oh, at some exclusive spa, Encantada Canyon Resort, I think it's called," Spence said, and stretched his tense body as best he could in the small passenger seat.

"She knows we're coming?" Mike asked.

Mike knew damn well she didn't, officially, though she'd gotten Spence's intention the moment they climbed in the airplane. "Yeah," Spence said, wanting to plant his foot in the back of Mike's seat.

"Spence, I love you, you know that, but I think you're kidding yourself. Rian told you she wouldn't come home. What are you going to do, kidnap her?" Dorel asked, without turning to look at him.

"Of course not. I hoped to charm her into the airplane with my winning smile and pure sex appeal," Spence said lamely. "Seriously, I don't have a freaking clue what she's going to do when she sees me."

Mike and Dorel exchanged looks. "Don't worry, bud, we'll protect you from the evil ex-almost-Mrs. Spencer. Or Dorel will, because Rian won't screw with her because she's Marty's mom and therefore holy. You and I, however, are screwed," Mike said.

They all laughed, but Spence knew what Mike said was true—Rian hated his guts, and he'd given her all the reason in the world.

Once they'd reached altitude, the weather was clear and smooth all the way from Seattle. The King Air touched down at 6:00 p.m. sharp and they'd parked in transit, rented a car and were on their way in the rose-tinted dusk thirty minutes later. Spence tucked the low-end plastic sedan into the line of crawling traffic on the main drag through the endless strip mall on both sides of the road. Tourists wandered from shop to café to bar to art gallery to psychic reader, and ducked in and out between the slow-moving cars to reach the same stores on the other side of the highway.

"Jesus, what a zoo," Spence grumped, drumming his fingers on the steering wheel.

"What's the street we're looking for?" Mike asked Dorel in the back seat.

Spence glanced into the rearview mirror at her tracing the streets on a map in her lap. "Sandstone Drive, then Encantada Canyon Way," she said. "The turn is about three miles ahead. And Spence, the man at the rental counter said we wouldn't get past the gate if we weren't guests or didn't have a reservation. I should call the resort, don't you think?"

"Yeah, go ahead if you want, though I can send them a let-those-fine-folks-in suggestion," he said, screeching to a rocking stop at a light and throwing them forward against their chest restraint belts.

"No, you just focus on driving," she harped.

"I can do both; tell her, Mike," Spence said and split his attention toward the resort. A picture of an adobe and tile-roofed gatehouse appeared in his mind. He projected his energy and the gate opened wide. "Okay, done. No need to call," he said and lifted his hands off the wheel. "And look, Mom, no hands!"

"Jerk," Dorel said. "Your turn's coming up on the right."

He pointed the car down a two-lane blacktopped road that ran through low hills dotted with grayish-green, short, sparse trees and scrub bushes. The road was virtually deserted until it dipped down, crossed a wide sand wash and continued up the rise. Spence slammed on the brakes to keep from rear-ending a stopped, topless, pink Hummer with *Magical Mystery Vortex Tours* painted on the side and filled with sunburned people. The driver, in a stained yellow duster and crumpled dirty hat like a trail-hardened cowboy, gave Spence a leisurely wave to pass as he continued to point ahead at a U of red sandstone cliffs in the hazy distance.

"Oh my," Dorel said, as Spence gunned by. "Vortex tours? You think they're going where we are?"

Mike said he didn't know and Spence didn't care. He just wanted to get there, worrying about what would happen when he did. Would Rian and he start throwing verbal and literal lightning bolts at each other straight up or wait a civil ten seconds or so?

No official road signs advised them that they were on the right road; only a series of small turquoise-colored wood arrows pointed the way until they topped a rise. The road snaked down into the red and tan cliffs through the canyon's mouth, blocked with a six-foot-high wall broken by a small adobe guard hut in the middle of the gated driveway. A minimalist sign on the guard hut announced: *Welcome to the Encantada Canyon Resort* in tasteful gold script on a turquoise background.

When Spence approached the hut, the cross-bars were down on both sides and an SUV sat on the in-drive, its driver talking to a guard uniformed in desert khaki. He stepped inside the hut, came back with a clipboard that he checked, then raised the gate and waved the SUV through. The bar came down again as Spence moved forward.

"He isn't going to let us in," Dorel warned. "I'll tell him I lost the reservation or something."

"Wait," Mike shushed.

Spence looked straight ahead and kept rolling. The guard smiled and waved them through as the gate went up.

Doral blew out a breath. "Every time you and Rian do something like that, I can't believe it's going to work."

"That's why you can't do it," Spence said, and glanced at Mike. "You've got to get your skills back online real quick."

Mike sighed. "I know."

The road narrowed as it wound through the extensive resort complex. No direction signs, other than the turquoise arrows with room numbers on them, appeared on the smaller paved tracks branching off the main road. Spence slowed and ducked his head to see out the passenger window at an austere, blocky building like a dusty rose-tinted cliff dwelling on the right, with a *Wellness Kiva* arrow pointing into the driveway.

"Think that's where she'll be?" Mike asked, jerking his head toward the building.

Spence shook his head. "I don't feel her. She's been there, but not now." He looked up at the tiers of individual Santa Fe–style buildings rising from the west cliff's feet. "She's up there," he said and turned into the next track.

A turquoise and white surrey-topped golf cart careened down the paved pathway and squealed to a stop in the powdery dirt beside the car, sending up a puff of reddish dust. "Sir, you can't drive from this point. It's closed to private vehicles. Can I show you to the parking lot and give you a lift back to your casita?" the young driver, dressed in the same khaki uniform as the gate guard, asked with a friendly smile and practiced deference.

"Sure, thanks," Mike said, leaning across Spence.

"Just back up to the main road and follow me, please," the driver said, and waited for Spence to back out.

Spence put the car in reverse. "What did you do that for? I had it handled," he griped at Mike and began to back the sedan.

"I didn't want you to zap him or something. He looks like a nice enough kid, just doing his job," Mike said, winking at Dorel.

Spence followed the golf cart up a steep incline to the resort's main multilevel complex, surrounded with tennis courts and pools, and drove into the one open space in the terraced parking lot at the driver's direction. Spence opened his door. "From now on, let me handle this. Do not speak or think," he said pointedly to Dorel.

They climbed in the golf cart, Spence up front with the driver and Dorel and Mike in the back seat.

"Are you just checking in?" the driver asked, pulling out and stopping at the lot's entrance.

Spence said, "No," and stared at the space between the kid's cow eyes. Focusing his intention like a laser, Spence projected into the kid's open and somewhat chaotic energy field, *Take me to Rian Farsante's room.* The driver blinked and pulled a two-way radio out of the holder on his belt.

"Jason, what's Dr. Farsante's casita number?"

"Piñon Pine 281," crackled back in answer.

He said thanks and took off, pedal to the metal, up the path, climbing through rows of casitas and chatting with his passengers like an old friend. The cart whizzed around a corner, throwing them against each other and grabbing for something to hang onto, and up a concrete sidewalk exactly the width of the vehicle.

Spence caught glimpses between the individual pueblo-like cabins of this topmost row of the resort spreading below. Dorel and Mike kept quiet, as he'd ordered them to, but he felt their dreamy reaction to the beautiful and unique setting. Before they approached 281, the last casita, he told the driver that they'd walk from here. They got out and waited until the driver backed down the sidewalk and disappeared.

Dorel rubbed her arms, shivering. "I know it's crazy, but I almost think I can feel Marty here." She glanced at the casita. "Like Marty's going to open the door and—" her voice broke and Mike pulled her into his arms.

"Shhhh, it's okay. Go ahead and feel that way. It's better for us, isn't that right, Spence?"

Spence nodded, feeling the same way as Dorel. Marty's essence was as close as he'd ever perceived it. For a crazy second he wondered if Rian were hiding Marty with her, because her energy was mixed into what he perceived. And another ultrahigh frequency that he hadn't encountered before was with her. His gut tightened and hands fisted as the urge raged over him to kick the goddamn door in.

The overhead yellow light snapped on at the same time as the landscape lighting that was tucked into shrubs, shining up into trees and illuminating the sidewalk and the three of them. They automatically moved into the shadows, keeping casita 281's closed door in sight.

"Nice place," Mike murmured as he surveyed the area, Dorel clinging to his arm. "Quiet. No one coming. You got anyone watching us?"

Spence said no, but that ultrahigh wave had already reached beyond the casita and contacted them. Strange thing was, it wasn't threatening but neutral and assessing, almost inviting, but that could be an illusion, a trick to pacify the unwary.

Spence rolled his shoulders and stuck out his chin. Well, hell then, let's get to it, he thought, and nodded at Mike. They crossed to the porch together, with Dorel bringing up the rear, and stopped. Spence eyed the overhead light and it winked out, dropping darkness on them. Focusing his power, he raised his hands, prepared to defend against or attack whatever awaited him on the other side.

The door swung inward, revealing a tall, spectral figure blocking the entrance. Ultrahigh frequency energy radiated from it like a supercharged halo or pulse weapon. Spence squinted and put up his hand to shield his eyes, until he realized a nanosecond later that he wasn't seeing with his physical eyes. The energetic mega force had shut down his rational left brain processes that locked him into earth's space-time and connected directly to the ancient brain's amygdala in the anterior extremity of the temporal lobe, the seat of intuition and the paraphysical senses.

A completely irrational notion that he beheld the face of God exploded in his solar plexus. Defenseless, Spence reeled back and fell into Mike and Dorel.

"Spence, what's wrong?" he heard Dorel cry as she grabbed for him.

Mike held him up with his hands under his armpits, hissing in his ear, "Get a grip!"

With an intake of breath, his spirit and body integrated with a snap at the crown of his head, sparking down his spine like electrical current. Spence struggled to find his feet, pushing off Mike, and opened his eyes.

"Spence?" Rian asked, materializing in the doorway and reaching for him.

He couldn't speak, only gawk at her. Always exotically beautiful, with her slightly olive-toned skin, athletic figure, shining dark hair and luminous blue eyes, Rian was still sexy as hell, but now exuded an angelic or spiritual quality that was to his mind and taste a forbidden and irresistible combination.

"Is he okay?" He watched Rian's full lips move as her seductive half-lidded eyes turned away from him to Mike and Dorel, then glided to him. She wrapped him in a sweet embrace so full of love that he almost wept.

Too fast, he heard Mike clear his throat, preparing to rob him of this precious and rare moment of absolute happiness.

"Gotta say, Rian, I don't think this was the reception

Spence was expecting," Mike said with a chuckle and pecked a kiss on her cheek.

Rian returned Mike's kiss. Her arms dropped off Spence as she turned to hug Dorel. A creeping possessiveness begrudged the old friends their greeting, making Spence struggle to stave off the jealous urge to drag Rian back into his arms where she belonged.

She told them she was glad to see them and invited them inside. Dorel and Mike went on through into the living room while Spence waited for her to lock the door. Rian turned around and took his hand between hers.

"What just happened out there?" she asked, concern hovering behind the welcome in her eyes.

Spence's defenses slammed down like an iron gate over his vulnerable heart. "Where's your friend?" he asked, cutting his eyes toward the living room.

Rian frowned as if she didn't understand English. "What?"

"You know, the guy with big skills that sent me a pretty damn compelling message, or maybe you've learned some new tricks, huh?" He couldn't look at her or he'd buy into that disarming innocence she wore like a chaste, white wedding gown. Spence sidled to the archway to the living room and stuck his head in, seeing only Mike and Dorel across the room at a sliding glass door to a dark terrace. No one else. Unless he was in the bedroom?

Rian gave an exasperated huff. "As usual, there's no one, Spence. Go check for yourself," she said and swept by him. "Can I get you something to drink?" he heard her ask his friends.

He would not show weakness and remembered that he didn't care if she had the entire male staff hiding under the bed. While Rian told Mike and Dorel how sorry she was about Marty, Spence leaned against the wall, casually sliding his gaze to the built-in wet bar where Rian began to mix drinks, the Southwestern-inspired furniture, the Mexican *horno*-type fireplace with gas logs burning cheerily and around to a short hall that had to led to the bedroom.

Rian caught him. "Go ahead, see for yourself, so you can stop generating that nasty sludge. Do you want a scotch?"

He nodded and made himself move to the fireplace and sit on the wide, plastered hearth seat. The minimal warmth from the flames barely counteracted the chill settling over his shoulders despite his leather flying jacket. Spence took the scotch that Rian handed him with a curt thanks and listened in silence as she let Mike and Dorel endlessly retell their tale of horror. Spence ground his teeth to keep from hurling his empty glass into the fireplace with a shout of: "Get over it and let's do what we came for!" He stood and asked where the bathroom was. Rian pointed to the hall with that smartass knowing look he hated.

Waiting until he was out of her sight and he'd entered the hall, as if Rian wouldn't sense his probing, Spence extended his aura into the bedroom—an empty king-size bed, chair, desk, dresser, closet with clothes and another bathroom, but no man. No trace of the ultrahigh that had confronted him on the porch. When he returned to the living room, the three had moved out to the terrace and were engaged in a heads-together hushed conversation. How freaking cozy. Rian was working on them, no doubt about it.

Spence leaned against the doorjamb and crossed his arms. "Ready to go, guys?" They jerked their heads in his direction and broke out of their huddle.

"Rian thinks Marty's here, too, Spence," Dorel proclaimed in excitement. Her expression of hope was hard to take, because she was opening herself to more hurt when it became evident that Marty wasn't here and that they'd wasted valuable time, all due to Rian's betraying them again.

"She didn't say that, exactly," Mike said, and gave Rian a look.

"What I said was that I felt him more now than I have in days. But I don't know if he's here; it's as if he's broadcasting from . . . underwater, or something," Rian said, rubbing her bare arms against the crisp air.

"Well, I don't get that at all. Maybe it's a hormonal thing special to you ladies in the estrogen sisterhood?" Spence said with a grin he meant to be teasing, though he was an asshole and there wasn't enough charming intention in the world to change that.

They all scowled at him, but he persevered. "I think we're getting a little distracted here. Don't get me wrong, I'm glad you can feel better about Marty, but remember why we came," he directed to Dorel and Mike.

"*You* came here," Rian emphasized in a solemn tone, "because this is where we're all supposed to be at this time. Marty will come to us. And so will Ian."

— TEN —

Spence shot his anger like a prickly barb at her. "You don't know that Marty and Ian are coming here!"

Rian raised her hand in a subconscious defensive reaction and turned her right side to his attack. She wasn't about to let his resentment attach to her.

"In fact," he continued, "if you want to get real, then I'm telling you I know the exact opposite. Ian's running from us, not to us."

"I think Rian's right," Dorel said softly. "I know I can feel my son, and I believe he's trying to communicate with me. It's very faint, but I'm getting it."

Rian saw Mike's stricken expression and realized he, like Spence, wasn't receiving Marty. Perhaps they weren't listening for him, because they were so adamant in their belief that they had to do something active or physical and strategic. They wanted to exact retribution, to draw blood, make Ian pay for what he'd done to them. As long as they gave in to the lower emotions of hate and revenge, they would only draw that to them.

"Mike, I feel it getting stronger every moment. Marty is here in Sedona. Somewhere, I promise," Rian said, ignoring Spence, and swept her hand to include Dorel. "Perhaps Dorel and I are able to sense this because . . . well, it may be an emotional or sensitive female thing. You know intuition is opened via the higher sentiments of love, compassion and empathy. In any case, that's what you once taught Dorel, right?" she said with an encouraging grin.

Mike threw his hands up and plopped down on the sofa. "I don't know what to think. I've seen my old enemy kill my wife and shoot me. We get magically resurrected by my best friend and then the son of a bitch burns down my cabin, telling me that another and, if you will, more deadly enemy has kidnapped my son. And in order to find my son, we're supposed to come here so the two of you can either kill each other or kiss and make up, which doesn't look all that promising at the moment. Now my wife, back from the dead, has got skills, baby. She can *feel* my boy here in the land of crystals, psychic channelers and vortex tours."

He rubbed his face with his hands and sighed, leaning his head back on the cushion. "Thing is, guys, what troubles me is despite what everyone but me is apparently feeling, we haven't heard anything from Ian. No demands. Nothing." Mike threw a pointed look at Spence. "No real evidence that it was Ian who even took Marty, but everyone's got feelings, lots and lots of feelings, as the song goes. I always hated that damned song."

Rian took a deep breath. "What I haven't said is that I'm getting flash impressions of Ian's signature, along with Marty's. He's ready for the next step, and we must be very careful."

Mike frowned at Dorel. "You, too?"

Dorel shook her head. "No, just Marty, and actually it's more than a feeling, it's a picture. Remember his Junior Bear that he loved so much when he was five? He left it behind when the Roshi took him to the Sangha, because Ian could trace him through his attachment to the stuffed animal? That's what came into my mind when we got to the resort. Like we could trace him, too, with that bear . . ."

"I'm sorry, Dorel honey, but that sounds like wishful thinking to me." Spence jerked his thumb toward the terrace outside. "You're right in the middle of one of the most powerful energy vortexes on the planet. The earth's electromagnetic and other dimensions' subtle energies intersect here with people's own fields and magnify their emotions and issues. It all makes for a volatile combination that manifests in all kinds of weird reactive behavior to feelings," he said, nodding at Mike, "many of which are misunderstood projections of people's own illusions."

"That may be true for some, Spence, but this wasn't an illusion. Marty wanted me, us, to know that he's near and under similar conditions to the last time Ian came after us." Dorel turned to Rian with a pleading look. "Don't you think?"

Rian nodded. "Yes, I do, but I don't believe we're going to be able to prove our *feelings* to them. They'll have to experience Marty here themselves. That can only happen when you let go of your own mistaken projections about what is happening and why," she directed to Spence and Mike.

"Oh right, I'm self-deluded. The ole vortex is screwing me into the ground like all the other wannabe psychic trippers, huh?" Spence snorted. "Problem with that little theory of yours is that I'm not affected; I get this place—the energies, the lay lines, vortex dimensional doorways—"

"What do you mean, dimensional doorways?" Mike growled.

Spence's eyes went wide. He wiped his hand over his moustache and down his goatee, holding his throat. "That must be it! That freaky son of a bitch is working something through the Encantada vortex's doorway . . . but why . . . and what's Marty got to do with it?"

"It's about the swords, isn't it?" Dorel asked.

Rian saw fear in her friend's eyes, its cold hand threatening to reach out and claw at her. Why hadn't Chevayo mentioned this when he was counseling with her earlier? He'd said her friends were coming and that they were all being drawn to this place at this time for a high soul purpose. He said nothing about the Swords of Balance, only that they must be united and of one mind to achieve their calling for this life. The implication was that even Ian, and Inada, were all part of the plan.

"Hell, yes, it's about the swords. Always has been," Spence barked and sent a mean squint Rian's way. "He's maneuvered us here because he wants the swords. Does he think he can make us manifest them out of the ether here at the vortex, or what? I don't get it, but you must. You know him better than we do, and you did say we're all here because we're supposed to be," he dumped on her again.

"Yes, that's how I understand it, but not the specific intention of Ian in regards to the swords or how. Just that we're called together here for something very important and that means all of us: Marty, Ian, you, me, Dorel and Mike. It's an ending and a beginning." Rian rubbed the frown lines on her forehead with her fingertips. "I don't know that it's really about dragging something down to the earth or manifesting the swords at all. More like an ascension . . ."

"There she goes again, folks, floating off into the ozone just when you really need her," Spence grumbled, shaking his head and sweeping his almost collar-length hair behind his ears. Rian noticed his hair was sable brown, almost black, like the tint on his fingernails. Her breath caught. What dark influence was Spence under that was pulling him deeper into the sinister side of the occult?

Mike got to his feet. "Do you think you two could give us a break from your personal axe grinding for awhile?" He gauged Spence, then Rian. "Here's how it's going down for me. You two are the biggest problem we all have. Now, if Dorel thinks Marty is here or at the South Pole, we're going to go with that until she or I think something different. I don't care what you or Rian think. Dorel and I are staying put until we figure out a better plan. You two can go fight this out in heaven or hell or wherever, but don't bother us until you've got a constructive plan. In the meantime, we're going to go get a room here. Come on," he said to Dorel.

"No, wait, Mike," Rian said.

"Sorry, Rian, I'm hungry and really tired, of you guys in particular," Mike said, taking Dorel's hand and leading her out of the living room.

Rian caught up with them in the foyer. "You can't get a room here at the resort, Mike; they're full up."

"Then we'll go back to town," he said.

She smiled. "No need. I told them today that I was expecting guests. They've made the adjoining bedroom available. Come see. It's very nice and there's a private terrace and entrance. You won't even have to see me," she said, and motioned to them to follow her.

She opened the door in an alcove beyond the wet bar and on the opposite side of the living room from her own bedroom.

Mike and Dorel stepped inside the large room. "Oh, it's really nice. Thanks, Rian," Dorel said, giving her a hug.

Mike nodded and said thanks, too. "I'm going to get a shower and then I think we need to eat. *I* then can think about this a little more sensibly."

As he headed for the bathroom, Dorel glanced behind Rian at Spence lurking in the living room. "Can we get a rollaway for Spence? He can sleep in here with us—if he wants to."

"There's a Murphy bed behind those doors by the bar. He can sleep there."

"Are you sure that's a good idea?" Dorel asked, keeping her voice low. "He's changed a lot, Rian. You see how he looks and how angry he is. We've seen less of him these last few months and I have to tell you, I'm happier that way. Mike's busy and he doesn't think much about it. He's an accepting kind of guy and figures Spence is a big boy and can take care of his own business. I know we haven't helped you with him as much as we could have, but I don't know what we'd have done or even can do now. He may be dangerous. At least his behavior is erratic, as you've seen. Actually, I've worried he's doing drugs, but Marty and Mike don't think so. They think he's dealing with personal demons and that he'll work it out, though I'm not as optimistic. I hate to put you on the spot like this, but what do you think?"

Was this the time to tell her about Chevayo and what he revealed to her today? Rian felt a resistance in her solar plexus. "I'm not sure right now, Dorel. I need to observe him, to think objectively about it, but that's so difficult because I have to be open to him and all his stuff while shielding myself, you know? At the very least, it's complicated and could be a complete disaster, given how far he's moved to the dark side."

Dorel's fair complexion paled. "You can't think he's consorting with evil or satanic stuff, do you?"

Rian expanded her aura to shield both of them and glanced over her shoulder, not seeing Spence, and whispered, "When did he start dyeing his hair?"

"What's that got to do with anything?" Dorel hissed back, her frown growing.

"It's just that he's really got a Prince of Darkness thing going on with the dark hair, and it looks like he's dyed his mustache and goatee, too. And the black fingernails? Dorel, those are all indicative of—"

"Of what?" Spence's oily voice asked. Rian startled, cutting a sideways glance, and there he stood not four feet from them. How had he managed to sneak up on them?

"Spence, do you want us to get you a rollaway?" Dorel quickly asked. "There's lots of space for you in our room."

"Is there now?" He sauntered past them and squinted into the invitingly restful bedroom. "Not for me," he said with a baleful smirk. "I'm more comfortable with something, oh, I don't know, darker?" He walked to Rian and stopped in front of her, so close she felt his warm breath on her lips. "Isn't that right, babe?"

Rian's pulse hammered. Her breathing shortened to minute gasps. She barely held on as the huge surge of Spence's intense sexual force steamrolled over her.

"Aw, Jesus," she heard Mike exclaim from the bedroom. "Are you two still at it? Dorel, come in and close the door. Let them work it out one way or another."

She wanted to scream at Dorel to stay with her, but her mouth wouldn't move. Dorel ducked her chin and scurried into the bedroom, closing the door behind her. Even in the shadowy hall, Rian clearly saw Spence's ruthless expression and his hazel eyes heavy-lidded with lust, his intention plain. He wanted her right now, right here, and was going to have her.

Rian could stop him if she wanted to, but she couldn't summon the resolve. A dim realization arose that she was succumbing to the long-repressed sordid need as raw, unrestrained sexual want undulated up from the base chakra between her legs.

"That's what I thought." Spence gave her a smoky grin and jerked her roughly to him. "You want it as much as I do and more, don't you, babe?" he whispered huskily against her hair and slid his hands down her back, cupping her butt, hauling her against his hard crotch. He slammed his mouth on hers and stabbed his tongue between her opening lips.

A muted moan escaped her and she ground against him, twisting her hands into his hair. He yanked her off her feet. She squeezed her legs around his waist and, with his mouth still smashing hers, he stumbled toward her bedroom, kicking the door open. Once inside, she reached over his shoulder and punched the door closed before he threw her down on the bed. He straddled her on his knees, unzipped his fly and pulled out his erection, jamming it in her face. "This is what you want, isn't it? But I want something from you first."

Breathing heavily, Spence gritted his teeth and tore at her silk pants with one hand as the other ripped her top upwards. It caught on her chin. "Take it off," he growled and dragged the pants down her thighs, followed by her black bikini panties.

She felt the panties rip away as she clawed off her top and reached to unhook her bra. His hand flashed out and ripped that off, too. She fell back naked under him still kneeling over her, his hard erection bobbing above her face. Before she could take it, he climbed off and stood at the end of the bed.

Panting, he pulled off his lizard cowboy boots and skinned out of his tight jeans and low-cut black silk shorts. He pulled the black V-neck cashmere sweater over his head, baring his hard-muscled, lean body glistening with sweat. His skin was smooth, hairless, including his crotch. He followed her stunned gaze and looked down at himself. "Now, let's talk about what I want from you."

Rian bit her lip and clutched her fingers into the bedspread. Whatever he wanted . . . she knew that she wasn't only going to do it, she'd want to.

He grabbed her wrists, pulled her to her feet, holding her hands to her sides, hovering his wet lips over hers. "I want you to use me, abuse me. Like the first time. That's how I want it from you," he murmured against her mouth, hungry for him. "That's how you always want it, isn't it? You screw me and I take it."

Rian nodded, breathless, her whole body alive and aching against him. She couldn't think. Only feel. Sensation sprang from his touch, igniting desire that oozed from deep inside her and crawled over her skin.

"Say it!" he ordered, his dark gaze glittering as he dug his fingers into her skin.

She wrenched her hands from his hold and laid her palms on his chest. "Shut up and take it," she growled and shoved hard.

Spence lurched backward onto the carpet. She fell on him, pushing him flat, and pinioned his hands beside his head. She pushed herself down on his erection, keeping her upper body out of reach above him, not allowing his touch. Pent-up ferocity roared through her tension-filled body and she pumped up and down on him, her hair tumbling out of its twist and sweeping his chest.

Not a word was spoken, nor any hint of loving tenderness expressed one for the other.

He noiselessly writhed and bucked under her, eyes wide and locked on hers, each reflecting the taut craving of the other. She pressed her teeth into her bottom lip, working hard to pleasure herself on him. He watched her rapidly peaking to climax before him and stopped mid-thrust, trying to steal it from her, but she threw herself prone upon him and hung on at his waist, rocking her hips in short, tight thrusts that he couldn't escape.

"Damn you," Spence swore when her pulsing climax overtook him, and he grabbed her hips, lifting her off as he rolled to his knees and forced her on hands and knees, slamming into her from behind so hard she clamped her mouth closed to keep from crying out and giving him the pleasure of her pain. He bent over her, squeezing her breasts mercilessly and biting her shoulders and neck. He swore abject filth into her ear as he climaxed in shuddering spasms. And Rian came again.

Spence pulled her back into his lap and wrapped his arms around her, nestling his face in her hair as the last tremors of sensation rolled through her. Her breathing slowing and taut muscles beginning to lose tension, she leaned back against his chest. He was still hard inside her and traced her nipples with the tip of a black fingernail, then trailed it down her stomach into her sex, massaging in gentle circles of arousal, and whispered, "It's been a long time, but you can do better than that, can't you, babe?"

She started to question what he meant, but he put a hand over her mouth as his other deftly fingered her to wracking climax so fast that she cried out, stiffening against him.

"Yeah, that's how it is with you and me," he murmured in her ear and traced his tongue around the inside. "I touch you and you come. I think about you and you come." He turned her around to face him and guided her legs around his waist: his voice, his smell, his touch mesmerizing her. Drunk with sensation, her head lolled and eyelids fluttered as she began to move up and down on him.

"Are you ready to give me what I want?"

Rian answered with a breathy, "Yes," unable to deny him anything as he tongued her skin and stroked his hands over every inch of her, bringing her to climax again and again. Completely spent, she collapsed off him onto the carpet and rolled on her side, breathing raggedly and slick with sweat.

He moved in and spooned her back, skin to skin from neck to calf, his rock-hard erection pressing against her buttocks. "Are you ready now to give me what I want?" he breathed against the back of her neck.

"Do-don't. I—I can't again," she said weakly but couldn't make herself move away from him.

"Yes, you can," he said, draping his hand across her arm and cupping her breast. His touch, words and hot body pressing against her back rekindled fire in her root chakra, making her body want him again, but her mind reeled in confusion.

"Please . . ." she protested as he pulled her flat on her back and mounted her.

"Give me what I want," he said, holding himself on his hands above her.

"I have," she cried and rolled her head back and forth, tears squeezing between her eyelids and running down her cheeks as he heartlessly screwed her.

He shook his head, quickening his stroke. "Not yet."

Her body obeyed him and she rushed toward climax, straining against his crotch. He stopped abruptly and she teetered on the brink. "Don't . . . stop," she breathed, clutching his firm butt.

"Focus," he coaxed above her. "Focus on giving me what I want and I'll give you," he gave a short teasing thrust, "what you want."

"What do you want?" she groaned, still moving against him, but he lowered himself flat on her, his weight holding her still.

"Form your intention, see the swords, call them to you. Our intention will come into alignment and, combined with the energy we release in climax, the swords will manifest," he said, nose to nose with her.

A light knock sounded on the bedroom door. "Rian? Is Spence in there with you?" Mike asked.

"Don't answer him," Spence whispered against her mouth.

She jerked her head to the side. "He'll come in, if I don't," she hissed, pushing at him.

"Uh yeah, Mike, can you give us about thirty minutes?" Spence called, his voice wink-wink suggestive.

"Oh. Sure. Didn't mean to bother you. Just wanted to tell you that Dorel and I are going to get something to eat," Mike said. They heard him walk away and the casita's front door close a few seconds later.

As if walking out of a dark theater into the light of day, Rian reassessed the man invading her body. She went stone cold from the inside out, summoning force of will, and shoved him off of her. She scrambled to her feet, taking a stance to defend herself against attack.

Spence sat up. "What the hell's the matter with you?"

"Approach me again with this black arts sexual stuff and I'll put an end to your *practice* with a dull knife. Now get out of my room," she seethed, holding her position as he got up and gathered his clothes.

He went to the door and opened it, turning to look at her. "I need the swords, Rian. That's the only way to bring them back. You know that. And if you were honest with yourself for once, you'd realize that you aren't the celibate spiritual leader type at all. You like to screw, and me in particular, because I take you where you're afraid to go. Thing to remember is," he said, leering at her, "you taught me."

When he closed the door, her knees gave way and she slipped to the floor, sobbing into her shaking hands. After a few moments, she pulled herself up and took herself to the shower. She turned the water on as hot as she could stand and scrubbed her body red from head to toe with a scratchy loofa that she repeatedly saturated with a bottle of bath gel.

Rian soothed lotion over her tender, sore body, expecting that bruises would appear by morning. She dried her hair to hang straight, parted in the middle, and pulled on a warm cream-colored turtleneck sweater, matching pants and ankle-length boots with three-inch heels. Wrapping a brown cashmere shawl around her shoulders, she tossed her hair back off her face, compacted her aura around her physical body and opened the door.

Spence sat in the dark corner of the living room, staring into the fireplace. She made herself walk to him. His eyes were closed, making his face look a little less haggard. Perhaps he was sleeping, and she decided to let him be. She started to walk away and he stirred.

"Ready to go eat?" he asked, rubbing his eyes, as if he were waiting for a date.

"Yes." She wanted not to look at him or even be near him. It made her feel too vulnerable and embarrassed.

They left the casita and walked along the lighted path toward the main lodge. Spence swaggered along, hands in his leather jacket pockets and head up, alert and interested. She was self-conscious with him now. Each gesture, fleeting expression, fluid movement, even his smell, freshened the memory of his hands and mouth all over her body. She hastened her step to put some physical distance between them, but he paced her.

They didn't speak during the ten-minute walk, which was as uncomfortable as it was desired.

He held the massive stained glass door to the reception lobby open for her and she entered, walking quickly across the slate floor to the Terrace Place restaurant. She saw Mike and Dorel outside on the terrace at a round wrought-iron and glass-top table set for four. Rian slid the heavy glass door open and stepped out into the chilly air, waving at the Gabriellis.

"Spence! Glad you're here," Mike said, getting up. "Help me move another one of those heaters over here." He pointed to a tall, stainless steel propane heater with a broad top like a coolie hat.

"Why aren't you sitting inside where it's warm?" Spence asked and helped him wrestle the lighted heater to their table.

"No room, but it's great out here. Just look at the stars. Don't see those much this time of year in Seattle," Mike said.

"So, you and Spence get everything settled?" Dorel asked with an impish grin as Rian sat down across from her.

Rian shook her head. "Have you ordered?"

Dorel sat back with a quizzical frown. "No, we were waiting for you. We've had some nice drinks though. Have you tried the prickly pear margarita?"

"I don't drink much anymore," Rian said, shifting in her chair away from Spence as he sat down next to her, and saw Dorel and Mike exchange a look.

They ordered dinner and made small talk like the rest of the vacationers dining on the terrace beneath the waxing moon. Rian remained reserved and quiet, letting Spence entertain his friends with *remember when* stories that didn't involve her.

"Hey, there's a wizard," Dorel said, leaning to see past Rian into the lodge.

Rian didn't turn, but smiled at her tipsy friend and continued to stir her black bean soup. Mike uh-huhed his wife and took issue with some part of Spence's recollection of a particular Navy mission.

"Really. Look, he's wearing a wizard coat," Dorel urged, pointing.

Rian turned to look. A tall man wearing an ankle-length multicolored patchwork coat stood inside with his back to the terrace, hands clasped behind his back. He turned and gazed directly at her. "Ian!" she cried and leapt up. Her heavy chair clattered over backward onto the flagstone floor.

"Ian?" Mike and Spence demanded in unison, then saw him, too, and bolted to their feet.

"Oh my God, it's Marty," Dorel exclaimed.

— ELEVEN —

Spence reached the sliding glass door first, colliding with a knot of elderly women struggling with it. Mike pulled it open for them, waving them through. Spence pushed through the unhappy ladies, keeping his eyes on the wizard coat weaving through the Sun City refugees clogging the reception area.

By the time Mike and Rian caught up with him, Ian had disappeared as if he'd never been there.

"We can catch him. Don't let them take Marty again," Dorel shrieked as she ran by them and ducked between seniors coming inside. Mike hustled after her, followed by Spence and Rian.

Outside, Dorel ran a few steps in every possible direction, calling for Marty. Spence told Mike to stay with her and motioned to Rian to check the parking tiers. She charged off and he went in the opposite direction, down the broad stairs to the pools on the lower level and on to the tennis courts, and came up empty. He jogged along the sidewalk past the dark putting green where people gathered around a big barrel telescope. Spence slowed and eased into the fringe of the group but didn't see the wizard coat. Or Marty. Just a bunch of star-struck tourists wrapped in resort blankets and raving about the rings of Saturn.

Spence hurried back to the top and met Rian coming out of the parking lots. "Did you see Marty?" he asked as they trotted back to the lodge.

"No. Just Ian, and now I'm not even sure about that," she said.

"Yeah," Spence agreed, replaying the whole scene in his mind.

Dorel saw them coming and broke away from Mike. "He can't have just disappeared. You have to find him. They must have taken him to a room or car," she said, frantic. "I'm going to call security."

Spence grabbed Dorel's shoulders, restraining her. "You can't do that, honey. We don't want them in on this."

She fought to pull away. "They'll understand and help me get Marty back," Dorel cried, looking to Mike for support.

"No, they won't," Mike said with frustrated finality and took her out of Spence's hands. "That's never worked for us before, and will only make things worse for all of us. We can't find him if we're in jail," he said, lowering his voice as a well-dressed couple strolled by, looking the four of them over warily.

"We better go back to the casita," Rian said, tucking a strand of shimmering hair behind her ear, and put her hand on Dorel's arm. "We'll be safe and out of sight there."

Despite Dorel's irrational pleading with them to continue searching for Marty, whom no one but she had seen, they were able to get her back to Rian's casita without drawing too much attention. Spence sensed that they were being observed and kept checking behind them and into every dark corner along the way.

Once safely inside the casita, Dorel broke down. Spence stayed clear of Rian's and Mike's efforts to comfort her and gritted his teeth at her wailing. Was he the only one who trusted that Marty could take care of himself as he had done so many times before? They were wasting too much energy that needed to be directed to targeting Ian, his plan, and to manifesting the swords.

He watched Rian bending over Dorel, stroking her hair and making cooing noises. If they only knew Rian like he did. Knew what she really was and what she was capable of, it would scare them to death. It scared Rian plenty, and it should. Though why she continued to fight her natural propensities, pretending they didn't run her life from deep in the murky domain of her subconscious, he couldn't understand. She needed to better allocate that energy she wasted maintaining her secrets, but if she did that, an uninhibited Rian would be unstoppable. She had more natural talent and psychic ability than anyone he'd ever met, and he meant to use it.

"Dorel, I didn't see Marty, I told you," Rian said. "When I finally looked at who you were talking about, it was Ian I saw in the coat. How about you, Spence?"

He thought a moment. "Rian screamed, 'Ian,' knocked her chair over and I caught a glimpse of someone that I took for Ian. Mike?"

Mike nodded. "Pretty much the same." He picked up Dorel's white hand and kissed it. "Tell me again what made you think you saw Marty?"

Dorel jerked her hand out of his. "Not *think* I saw, I *did* see him. The crowd sort of parted and he stood there looking at me." She sniffed and wiped her eyes with a tissue. "He was so pale and looked tired."

"As if he were sleeping?" Rian asked, squatting beside Dorel's chair.

"Yes, possibly," Dorel said with a shrug.

Rian stood up, deep in thought. "He could have been astral projecting himself to us—well, to you," she said to Dorel. "But why would the three of us see Ian instead?"

"Because he wanted us to," Spence reasoned. "He's playing a game with us, projecting what we want most to see. Showing us that he's in control. And this verifies that he does have Marty. Dorel, you may be right. They could be here in Sedona. Although, thought knows no material bounds, so Ian could have broadcast his thought forms from anywhere."

"No, Ian's here," Rian countered. She rubbed her arms and shivered. "Though that wasn't he that I saw in the lodge, but a projection, as Spence said."

"If that's so, why did I see my son and you three saw his abductor? It doesn't make any sense," Dorel complained.

Spence smoothed his hand over his moustache, down his goatee and neck. A foggy impression in the back of his mind was coming clear. "Rian, are you still sensing Marty's energy, as you said earlier?"

She blushed and shook her head, avoiding his gaze. "Not since . . . earlier."

"Dorel?" he asked, monitoring Rian's discomfort out of the corner of his eye.

"Yes! More than ever," Dorel proclaimed. "I didn't realize it until you asked. I suppose that's why I know he was in the lodge."

"Well, I'm still not getting him," Mike said. "I think Rian has it right. Marty was asleep and astral traveling, sending his essence out to his mom." A vein stood out on his tense forehead and he rubbed the back of his neck. "Wish I'd seen him instead of that bastard Ian."

"We didn't see Marty, because we can't," Rian said from the terrace door, her back to them as she faced the night outside. "Like minds. We receive or perceive what we send out." She turned around, crossing her arms. "The three of us are operating at a stepped-down or low frequency. The fear, hate, anger and other negative emotions that we're hanging onto are generating that wave and making us vulnerable to similar waves from others. That's why we saw Ian, while Dorel saw Marty."

Rian gave Spence a sharp look and continued, "When we give in to our darker inclinations, we open ourselves to commune with all manner of evil."

Her words stabbed at him, punishing him, so she could retreat to her cloister for eternal penance for sinking low enough to love him. "What if that's simply our nature?" he lobbed back.

"We aren't evil. Each of us is a divine part of the holographic universe," she argued.

"Even Ian?" he persisted in yanking her chain.

She nodded and pontificated, "Unfortunately he's chosen an evil path, but he isn't inherently evil or even the embodiment of it."

"Unlike dirty ole evil Spence, right, your holiness?" Spence quirked a sarcastic grin and raked his gaze down her shapely body that he'd completely possessed less than two hours ago. That infuriated her and he reveled in her out-of-control emotions crashing over him like a tsunami.

Dorel cut off Rian's sputtered comeback. "Pleeeeeze shut up, both of you, or you can go straight to hell with your fighting and makeup sex crap. Because while you're screwing around, my son may be about to die."

She was right. He'd lost sight of the reason he was here, to find Marty. Properly chastised, Spence apologized to Dorel, including an oblique apology to Rian. Mike shrugged it off, his features slack with exhaustion.

"We all need some private meditation time, in our own way, of course," Rian said, opening louvered double doors and pulling down a queen-size Murphy bed. "Spence, you can sleep here. I'm turning in; goodnight all." She went to her bedroom door and turned. "Dorel, are you still doing yoga? I greet the sun at about seven, if you'd like to join me."

"Sure, I'd like that. 'Nite, Spence," Dorel said and trooped after Mike to their room, leaving Spence alone with an empty bed in an empty living room. Not the evening he'd planned, but at least she slept only a few steps away from him instead of a thousand miles. She'd be back in his bed for good and the swords would be his again. And that plan was coming together perfectly.

"Priest, attend me," Anubis's voice ordered and Ian awoke with a start. "You have hidden yourself from me."

Ian gathered his wits and rubbed the sleep from his tired eyes. "I'm here." His personal field generator's LED glowed red on the bedside table. So, the entity could not only breach it, he was aware of Ian's intention in its use.

"Khensu, the moon god, sails to fullness soon. Is the boy prepared?"

"Working on that," Ian mentally answered with a yawn.

"It is time for another bite, old crocodile. Take the mother into your safekeeping, but do not let her near the whelp," Anubis commanded.

"As you wish. There is another matter, master. This body does not remember the ritual for transformation and asks your aid so that I may prepare properly," Ian inveigled with proper subservience.

Anubis's laugh was a low growl. "You need only know that all must be assembled and giving of their own free will their blood to the vessel. The Swords of Balance that resided for millennia within my temple shall be embodied as I assume the vessel. You shall free his spirit, but he must want to go and invite me in."

"The ritual words or special artifacts?"

"Think not of these, for the time, the place, the sacrifices and the vessel are your only concerns," Anubis said imperiously.

"And the Swords of Balance? Are they to come to earth?"

Mocking laughter filled Ian's head. "That which has been called the Defender Sword appears as I do, priest. You best remember something of your service to me, or I shall have little use for you," Anubis snarled.

"Understood, master," Ian answered, keeping his thoughts neutral.

After a few moments, the entity moved out of his consciousness. Ian got out of bed and pulled a cotton robe on over his pajamas, moving to the adjoining bedroom where Marty lay sleeping in a single bed. He stared at him for a few moments, probing the boy's brain activity. Marty was about to drop into another active REM cycle of sleep, which was probably when he would attempt to breach the drugs and psitechnology to contact his mother again. He hadn't expected that from him, a stupid underestimation.

Ian had targeted the four and projected his thought form to them above him at the resort, incentive for them to stay put and expend their energy trying to find him. And doing so, they would unconsciously lower their defenses, even a fraction, but enough to allow Ian access. In his out-of-body viewing of their reaction to his appearance, Ian found it odd that the boy's mother had seen her son instead. Until he realized he'd perceived Marty's astral body, too.

These events revealed two dangerous flaws in his plan. The entity could overcome Ian's personal psitech defense structure, and the boy's spirit was able to bypass his drugged and electronically-shielded body to astrally travel. Any time now, Marty would naturally learn to lucidly direct his ethereal body within the sleep state. Ian couldn't allow him to realize that tremendous power on his own. Marty must think it a gift, a bestowal that only Ian could grant through his beneficent guidance of the young avatar in the making.

Covered with sweat, Spence threw off the sheet and pulled on his shorts and jeans. He padded across the cool slate floor to the terrace door and slipped outside. The pine-scented air chilled his skin and cleared his head. He leaned on his hands on the wood railing and stared up at the canyon walls. The almost full moon skimmed the topmost mesa and rose into the midnight sky dusted with stars.

Crickets and other night sounds abruptly ceased. Spence caught a movement out of the corner of his eye in the scrub below the terrace. A lean coyote slunk out from a cluster of manzanita and oak bushes, head down and hunting.

"Stop," Spence thought at the animal.

The coyote froze, front paw lifted, raised its nose, scenting the breeze, and turned its head in Spence's direction. The animal promptly sat on his haunches five feet from the terrace in the pine duff and dead leaves as if he had a reserved seat and looked up. Spence's eyes locked on the hunter's. An energetic link like a pencil-thin red line shimmered between them.

"Hello," Spence whispered, excited at this unusual opportunity presenting itself to him.

The coyote's head dipped once in greeting.

"How's the hunting?" Spence asked with a delighted grin.

"It proves fruitful," darted into Spence's mind and nearly bowled him over.

The creature answered him! He'd never used his remote

viewing abilities to communicate with animals, though he knew that others did, or so they thought. He'd assumed they'd channeled their own imaginations or other trickery-inclined entities that liked to play jokes, appearing to the gullible as real fairies, gnomes and other lawn art nonsense.

He ventured another question at the animal that the rational part of his mind yammered wasn't real either. "What are you hunting?"

"You," came the answer.

Spence staggered back to the table behind him, groping for a chair. Steadying himself, he wondered what the hell he was doing out here in the dark and cold interacting with whatever psychosis this represented.

The coyote's haughty, superior attitude flashed out with impatience. "You I have found. Do not cause me to regret it."

Now that was familiar, Spence thought. Who, and when, had he encountered this particular vibration before? He eased to the railing and looked down at the coyote, still there as if waiting for him.

"Why are you looking for me?" Spence asked, half playing along with his delusion and wondering at the answer.

"Khensu readies himself." The coyote's head turned to the moon and gave a sharp yip that startled Spence, raising goose bumps on his arms. "The queen is called to serve her god. Once again, the swords shall be hers to vanquish her many enemies. The time draws near."

"What queen?" Spence asked. He was almost certain now that he was channeling his memories. But why? Was he consumed with wanting the swords so much that he created talking coyotes to tell him to remember a past life where he possessed them?

"Queen Kalūkuh, as you well know. I warn you, do not trifle with the god who guides men safely through the Underworld, or not . . ." the coyote answered testily.

Maybe his subconscious was trying to tell him something that he'd forgotten or repressed. That's what Rian would counsel, as well as to go with it. "What do you want?"

"That which you do," was the cryptic reply that came into Spence's mind.

"So, both of us are wanting the swords?" Spence tested the voice in his head, his gaze fastened on the motionless coyote below.

"Your servant created them for you, usurping my powers on earth. These I wish again. You must command your servant to bring them to you, as before."

No mistake about that. "My servant, as you call her, has a mind of her own and nothing about her is about helping me out, I can tell you," Spence griped, shaking his head in disgust.

"Command her!" roared inside Spence's ears. "Are you not her ruler?"

"Not anymore," he admitted.

The coyote got up and shook itself. "Your high priest seeks to deceive us once again. He will have the swords for himself. If you cannot command your servant, he will possess them *and* your lover." The animal took a couple of steps toward the terrace and stopped, looking up at Spence.

"What are you?" Spence called down.

"Your god, Anubis. Ally yourself with me and make ready to command great power once again." The coyote turned and disappeared into the brush.

I'll be damned. Spence clamped his hand over his cold lips, closed over chattering teeth. He shivered and retreated indoors to consider what had just happened.

"This is a new low, even for you," Rian said from the hallway and snapped on a lamp by the sofa.

Spence grinned at her and started for the kitchen. He needed a drink. "Got any good booze, or even any bad?"

She strode to the wet bar, her sheer baby blue nightgown swirling around her ankles and hair flowing over her bare shoulders like a dark stream, leaving the scent of jasmine in her wake. Rian pulled out a full bottle of scotch and poured it into a cup from the coffee service tray until it overflowed. She handed the mess to him instead of tossing it in his face like he knew she wanted to.

He transferred the cup to a dry hand and licked his fingers one by one. "Mmmm, my cup runneth over with damned good scotch, I'd say. Thanks."

She crossed her arms under her breasts, the sheer fabric stretched to almost see-through over taut nipples, and glared at him. "So, you've conjured Anubis, have you? I'll go ahead and ask why, just to hear you verbally confirm that you are officially in league with the devil, as they say."

"Signed in blood and sold my soul," he joked and swallowed a fiery gulp. She didn't respond, but her expression went tight and grim. "You're not seriously thinking that was an actual entity?" he scoffed for effect.

"Yes, I am." She gauged him with narrowing eyes. "You're not sure what that was, are you?"

He shrugged. "A projection of my subconscious desires or demons, wouldn't my favorite shrink say?" He wouldn't have to tell her what he believed or even think about it. She was getting it real enough already and would tell him.

Rian paled and put a trembling hand to her lips. "Oh, God."

"That's what *it* said it was, you might recall. Just after the old dog told me to command my servant, and I take that to be you, to bring back the swords or my former high priest would have them and you." Spence tossed back another big swallow, gritting his teeth against the burn down his throat. "Now what would you say that was out there in the dark, howling at the moon? You got that part, didn't you?"

She shook her head. "No, but the noise woke me and I saw, and heard, you and it talking."

Spence cocked his head. "You heard both of us?"

"Yes, distinctly, and the misshapen auras around you contained the same dark blotches and joined with that red ribbon," she said and sat down on the edge of his bed.

He eased down beside her, careful not to touch her. "I thought the whole scene was all mental, telepathic."

"It could have been, but I definitely heard both of you as if you were speaking out loud," she said, holding her hands, prayer-like to her lips. They sat in silence for a few moments; then she slapped her hands on her thighs and rose with determination. "Yes, it was Anubis, can we agree on that?"

Spence said okay and waited for her next reasoned pronouncement. She always problem-solved this way—orderly, factoring in all the human personality BS, driving toward consensus and finally arriving at a conclusion or course of action. Good thing her complex process happened in nanoseconds, or he'd have killed her the first time she made him go shoe shopping with her way back when they still could live together.

Standing in front of him with the light shining like an X-ray machine through her thin gown, revealing her nude body underneath, she distracted him so much he wasn't listening. And he knew she'd said something else.

"That's just my point," she huffed. "You don't listen to me."

"Sorry. Why don't you go put on a robe or something?" he suggested. "Then I'll pay attention."

She tried to maintain her scowl, but a smile crept from the corners of her mouth. "I guess you meant that to be flattering?"

"Did it work?" He finished his drink and stood.

"Uh-huh. I'll be right back," she said and dashed into the bedroom, returning in a couple of seconds shrugging into a long, white terrycloth bathrobe, with the resort's turquoise medicine wheel logo on the breast pocket. She tied the belt tightly around her small waist. "I bet you can hear better already, right?"

"Unfortunately, yes," he poured another drink. "Want one?"

Rian shook her head and settled on the sofa, waiting for him. He wasn't sure where she'd be comfortable with him sitting and decided to go for distant cool. He leaned his butt on the bar, crossed one bare foot over the other and sipped scotch.

"You were saying?" he said, squinting at her, the light hurting his eyes.

"We're drawing these negative entities to us, can you agree with that?" she asked, leaning forward.

Where was she headed with this? "Go on," he said.

"As I said before, we're operating on a lower vibration than we should, at least I am. My aura feels like I'm wrapped in heavy goo, weighing me down so that I'm on the same level or correspondent vibe with noxious energies like Ian and negative entities like Anubis," she explained, obviously meaning he was, too.

He clicked his tongue against his teeth and nodded. Now he got it. "You're saying that I've pulled you down here in the shit with me."

"I'm saying that our earlier sexual encounter or energy exchange, if you will, disempowered me because I allowed down-and-dirty lust to knock me off my spiritual path," she said, her eyes not quite pleading for his understanding.

"Yeah. Making love with me is like screwing the devil, right?" he ground out.

"What we did to each other in there," she jerked her head toward the bedroom, "had nothing to do with love. It was about control over someone else, like any other form of abuse." Rian came to him, her eyes glistening with tears and took his cold hand between her warm ones, clasping it to her breast. "Spence, my darling, what we make is war on each other, not love. If we can't foster respect and the purest intention for each other's happiness and well-being, then we must let each other go."

He looked deep into her sad eyes. "I can't . . . let you go."

"And I can't let you destroy me, along with yourself," she said and wrapped her arms around him, burying her face in his neck.

In the grip of his physical need, he didn't dare touch her, using all his resolve to keep from sweeping her into his arms and onto the bed. He wanted to be able to caress her gently, murmur words of sweetness and caring, but couldn't summon them from the void within. He was too far gone, lost. And no amount of incorruptible, sacred love could redeem him.

"That's not true," she spoke softly against his throat. "I know you love me and that love will redeem you, if you choose to allow it."

Spence put her away from him with a harsh laugh. "Yeah, if I choose. That's the rub, isn't it, in the whole *love will save you* thing. I'm supposed to have a choice. You want to know something that I haven't admitted even to myself until right now? I don't, Rian. I can't afford that kind of weakness. Like you, I've been a humbled saint and an exalted sinner though many, many lives. And powerful sinner is the appropriate choice for this life. And it's mine."

Rian hugged herself and backed away from him. "Then let me go."

He shook his head slowly. "Sorry, we need you. You've got to give me the swords or Ian gets them. And you."

Rian jerked her chin up. "I won't permit that."

"No choice. It's a done deal according to the coyote. You've seen what Ian can do now." He'd felt the entity's power and, while he believed that what it said about Ian was true, there was still something, some other agenda Anubis wasn't sharing. "Come tomorrow, it's game on. You've got to help me or do nothing, which will help Ian. It's your choice."

"I feel like we're tied to the wheel of karma, ratcheting around to some point where we'll all have to play or pay. I don't understand," she said, shaking her head wearily. "I just don't understand."

"Who does?" Spence gruffed and climbed in the Murphy bed. "Turn off the light on your way out. I've got to get some sleep," he said and turned onto his side away from her.

"Goodnight, Spence," she said, her voice soft and sorrowful. The light snapped off and her door closed, leaving him alone in the darkness.

— TWELVE —

The next morning Rian woke before sunrise. She dressed in gray knit yoga pants, a long sleeved top and soft leather low-cut yoga shoes and wondered if she ought to wake Dorel. When she was ready and her friend hadn't appeared, Rian greeted the sun alone on her terrace.

As the sun rose over the mesa, her spirit soared heavenward on her song, as Chevayo had taught her, and amplified in the ether's highest realms, returning to her.

"You've shaken off the shackles that held you down yesterday," Chevayo said.

She opened her eyes to find him beside her, dressed in the same clothes as yesterday, arms raised and face peacefully radiant. He somehow knew what she'd done last night. She wanted to hide. "I'm . . . well, I don't know what to say," she said, ashamed.

"I do not judge you, or him. Each judges themselves alone, that is the way. To judge another is to feel the sting of guilt. Let it go, for it never was," he said with a kind smile.

"Thank you," she said, grateful for the acceptance she felt from him, despite her self-consciousness.

"The trickster paid you a visit last night, I see." He leaned against the railing and looked down at the scrub jay pecking around the scraggly rabbit bushes below.

"Oh, yes, the coyote," she acknowledged. The shaman seemed to know all. "You have taught me many things and seem to know much more—everything, as a matter of fact.

You aren't a simple shaman, are you?"

He turned his gaze on her. She closed her eyes and basked in his attention as beautiful images and sweet sensations flooded into her mind. "Ohhhhhhh," she breathed in ecstasy until the visions gently faded.

Rian opened her eyes. "Oh yes, more than a simple shaman, I'd say."

Chevayo motioned her to stand beside him in the corner. "He looks for you, but I must have a few words first."

"Spence?" She leaned to see around the barrier on the opposite side, between her terrace and the living room's. Chevayo put a hand on her arm in warning and she pulled back. "Oh, okay."

"You will not see the coyote again, but he will try to come to your soul mate," he said. "You must not let the coyote have him. You must fight for him, bring him into the light with love."

Her heart sank. "Fight for him? With an evil entity? Spence is so far gone, he'd let Anubis have me if it meant he could possess the swords again."

Chevayo gave her a stern look. "You will not sacrifice yourself as before, when you were servant lover to a queen. You must teach him the transformational love you have learned throughout your lives. While your soul learning has ascended up the energy centers to the spiritual crown chakra, he is caught in the root chakra of sexuality, pain, pleasure and survival. From this unenlightened basis, he endeavors to use the sexual power rising from there to create the swords, but he needs your present body's female, creative Kundalini energy to merge with his to do so. This you refuse him, and rightly so, because his intention is impure."

"Can he make me do it like he tried last night?" Spence had overcome her sensibilities and reserved self-preservation easily enough last night and encouraged her body to betray her spiritual path.

"You are asking if you are strong enough to withstand his seductions without falling into the abyss with him," Chevayo said and opened his hand. Five brown shelled piñon nuts sat in his palm. "I have brought these for you."

"Breakfast?" she teased, taking one and rolling it between her thumb and forefinger. She pressed her fingers together, but the shell was too hard. Holding it between her teeth, she bit down, feeling the shell crack. She pulled the creamy white nut out and popped it in her mouth. It tasted a bit like turpentine and disappeared in a chew or two. Seemed like a lot of work for such small, though essentially tasty, reward. "Nice, thank you," she said.

"Yes, it is much work, but worth the effort, for one learns many things from the task. And that is the true reward of any endeavor. Your soul mate is worth your effort."

Old wounds sent a panicked message to her heart and it stepped up its beat. "You don't know what he's done to me and others. I can't enable him or allow him to do that to me again."

"I do not ask you to accept his abuse, his fear that always seeks an outlet and a like vibration. I ask you to use the eternal power available to you to remind him of his connection to the spiritual dimension. He is too much in the body, and this is his downfall. He must remember that to receive and utilize the vast creative power of love. He must commit to live a more conscious life, as you have. Loving is not simply sexual mechanics but the merging, the perfect balancing of the cosmic male and female principles. In doing this, harmony and equilibrium are created. Loving thus becomes a sacred act of transformation."

"You're talking about tantra," she exclaimed. She'd

been studying the principles of sacred sex as a pathway to the higher spiritual realms for a couple of years now, though she hadn't practiced it as she'd chosen to live celibate.

Chevayo nodded. "Tantric loving focuses not only on the body, but the mind and spirit, in order to increase joy and closeness. Your soul mate has forgotten that a loving relationship should be filled with delight and bliss. You and he will never manifest your highest desires if your loving is not balanced and enlightened."

She could never approach Spence with this. He wouldn't listen. Instead, he'd blast her with his potent sexual energy that his proclivities had perverted and that he justified as uncontrollable desire for her.

"It will not be easy, but I shall help you. So will the events that are unfolding even now. They will motivate him to open to you, for there will be only pain left that he may turn to. He will discover that to pursue the dark path does not bring freedom and power, but enslaves one. The coyote reminds him of this, though he still believes that he can control the dark powers that he conjures," Chevayo said, his voice matching the grave expression on his angular face.

It suddenly occurred to her to ask him about Marty. "You already know what I'm thinking, I believe, and you probably even put it in my mind. But do you know anything about Marty? I haven't been able to contact him, though I did perceive his presence . . . for a short time," she said, avoiding his gaze.

"Yes. The One is preparing." Chevayo stood and gave a prayerful hands salute to the risen sun and bowed to her. "They are at your door. Go now."

Rian dashed into the bedroom and heard the banging on her locked door. She fumbled with the bolt, casting a glance at the terrace where she'd left Chevayo. He was gone.

"Rian, are you in there?" Spence's voice boomed over the pounding.

"Yes, yes, hang on a minute," she answered. The lock unfastened and she turned the knob. The door shot open, spilling Spence, and Mike behind him, inside, nearly knocking her down.

"Is Dorel with you?" Mike asked, his frantic gaze roving her bedroom.

Rian said no and stepped aside, allowing the men full access to the room. "What's wrong?"

Mike, dressed only in jeans like Spence was, came back in from the terrace. "Where else could she be?" he threw at Spence, looking long-night rough and worried.

"I've checked everywhere. Maybe we should search the grounds," Spence said.

"What is going *on?*" Rian demanded, steeling herself against the next horror that Chevayo said was on its way.

Spence stopped dead and glanced toward the terrace. "That guy was here again, wasn't he?" he accused and turned his mean gaze on her.

Spence could perceive Chevayo? That would mean that Chevayo allowed it. Perhaps that was the help the shaman promised, opening Spence to the higher energies? "Maybe she went for a walk?" Rian suggested, hopeful that was the case.

"No, she said that she was coming here to do yoga with you after she got the juice and paper off the porch for me," Mike said. "I must have drifted off and, when she didn't come back with them, I went to the kitchen. She wasn't there and the juice basket was still on the porch. I asked Spence if he'd seen her."

"I didn't, not while I was in bed anyway. She could have come through to the kitchen when I was in the shower,"

Spence said with a pensive rub on his moustache.

"We better look for her," Rian said. She opened the dresser and pulled out a zip-up hoodie that matched her yoga set.

Mike agreed and hurried away to dress. Spence stopped in the doorway. "You didn't answer me. He was here, wasn't he?"

"You're the psychic spy," she snapped. "You tell me." She grabbed her keys and phone, glancing at the clock as he stormed out. They had an hour to look for Dorel, before her class started at nine. If she searched with Mike and Spence, she wouldn't have time to meditate to Light Seek and use her spiritually enlightened remote viewing process to locate Dorel, which was exactly what they all needed to do rather than physically hunt for her. Though for Mike, she'd go through the motions, while using the movement and united focus on Dorel as a walking meditation to raise her own vibration and project that beneficial, supportive energy to him and Spence.

"Your mother cries for you. Go to her, calm her with soothing words that all is happening as it should. Like you, she is where she must be for now. All will be well," the huge black bird said. He opened and closed his eagle-like beak, making clicking noises, and shifted from one taloned foot to the other.

Marty's astral body circled a few feet above the bird perched on a sandstone boulder the size of a small car near a circle outlined in the chalky dirt with red rocks.

"I can't find her," Marty said to the bird. "I don't know where I am . . . or how."

"You are at the medicine wheel, the door between worlds. Your body lives far beneath the surface here, waiting for the initiation while you prepare yourself. Remember and you will find yourself," Chevayo's thought winged into his mind.

He immediately found himself hovering on the ceiling in the corner of a sparsely furnished room. A tall, slim boy with red hair lay sleeping in a single bed below. "That's me!"

"That is your physical form, yes," the bird said. "It is not truly you."

"There's something the matter with me," Marty worried. "What is it?" At the moment he thought the words, he zoomed inside his body, where his organs' own vibrations were discolored and slow. A silvery haze surrounded his brain like an opaque helmet and he wondered why. The answer appeared instantly in pictures of Ian giving him drugged food and water and using some sort of machine that hurt his head.

"As you see, you think, *where am I,* and find your true self and your vessel for this journey. Their methods cannot affect your true spirit body, which is your soul, and will have no effect on your physical body when you believe in your own power and don't believe what they tell you. Remember the wound or illness appears as a different-colored spot on the energy body first, then materializes on the physical body's equivalent. Change the vibration to remove the affliction from the energy body, and it disappears from the physical."

Marty wondered if he wanted to change his hair color, could he just think it and he'd have cool, dark hair like his dad. He felt Chevayo's amusement as a tickle of lighter energy.

"You selected your vessel's physical attributes before you appeared in this life for very good reasons."

"So that means I can't change anything I don't like, once I get here?" Marty thought with disappointment.

"It means that you are the creator of your earth experience. Each thought you have creates, a good bit slower on the earth plane than in the spiritual, which is due to earth's dense vibration. But no matter, if purple hair is your desire, you can manifest that like any other thing or condition you choose."

Marty looked down at his sleeping body and imagined a silver can labeled *black paint* pouring on his red hair. A can popped into the air a foot above the bed and tipped, but nothing came out. The lid was on tight. He tried over and over to make the lid open. Finally the paint can disappeared in a flash, leaving him frustrated and losing altitude as his spirit self was drawn back to the prone body in the bed.

"Help," he cried to the black bird fading from his mind.

"Great help is gathered for you. Call upon it. Think and create." The hushed words, as if spoken into a pillow, followed him down.

Marty jerked awake, face buried in his pillow and gasping for breath. He flopped over on his back, his dream still fresh in his mind, and started reviewing it until he sensed that he was being observed. Should he let them know he sensed them? No, better not.

He scooted to the side of the bed and hung his feet over, kicking them in a disjointed rhythm, and began to hum tunelessly, instinctively setting up a distraction wave with his own bioelectric energy. He even threw in the thought of a couple of dancing bears just for fun and waited to see what would happen next.

"Good morning, Marty," Ian said, opening the door. He still wore the cool leather flying jacket and tan Dockers like Dad liked to wear and carried a tray with some covered dishes and a tall glass of OJ.

"Where's the bathroom?" Marty asked, eyeing the tray. He was hungry, but something about the food . . .

"Just outside. We're sharing with the other rooms on this floor, I'm afraid," Ian said with an apologetic smile and set the tray on the end of the bed. "To the left, two doors down."

He walked out into the wide corridor barefoot and in pajamas. None of the busy adults hurrying by even noticed. Marty finished quickly and thought about exploring on his own to see how far and where he could get, but got the urge to go straight back to the room instead.

Ian was sitting on a plastic chair at the desk when Marty entered. He nodded and pointed to the tray. "Looks pretty good. I know I enjoyed mine, though I don't think you're the eater that I am. But I'm sure there's something there to your liking."

Marty sat cross-legged on the bed and picked up his spoon. The sugar-coated crunchy cereal was his favorite and the waffle with whipped cream and strawberries made his mouth water. But he wasn't going to eat any of it. Not even the juice; that was probably drugged, too, he decided, suddenly remembering his whole dream.

"What's wrong?" Ian asked. "Can't face the food yet? Have a little orange juice. It'll raise your blood sugar and make you feel much better," he said, sounding like some kind of doctor.

Marty shook his head with a frown, rubbing his belly. "My stomach hurts. I'd like a drink of water."

"Sure," Ian said, gesturing to two bottles of water on the nightstand.

Marty took one and twisted the plastic top. Someone already had opened it. He put the bottle to his lips and pretended to drink, careful to think about how good the water tasted.

Ian smiled and settled back in his chair. "There are a few things I'd like to get straight between us, so you won't misuse your time and mine. First, because of your devastating ordeal, I needed you to rest and build your strength, so the food was drugged, but not anymore, nor is the water. Yes, the bottles have been opened, but that was just a little test for you to keep you interested in the game."

Marty narrowed his eyes. "What game?"

"The power and glory game. I'm responsible for you now and want to engage your mind, bring out your talents, give you new skills and a better sense of how and when to use your own gifts. And why do I want to risk my life, my career, everything I hold dear, to do this for an orphaned boy, you might ask?" Ian asked.

The word *orphan* knifed at Marty's heart. He couldn't talk for the sobs gathering in his throat and shrugged, keeping his eyes on his hands so Ian wouldn't see his tears.

"Because you're destined to be the greatest leader that this world has ever seen, and I have pledged to your parents to help you become that," Ian said.

Marty jerked his head up. "When did you tell them that? Last thing I heard my dad say about you sure wasn't anything about you being my guardian or anything. He doesn't—didn't trust you."

"True, and for good reason. I treated him, and your uncle Spence, and Rian, too, very badly. But what they didn't know, and I was forbidden to tell them, was there are certain powerful rogue elements within world governments and business that wanted, and still want, all of you dead. They knew, from experience I must say, what your father, Spencer and Rian were capable of—"

"You said *were!* Does that mean Spence and Rian are dead, too?" Marty cried.

Ian pressed his lips together and looked sad. "I can't honestly say, Marty."

"Then they could be alive and trying to find me, I know it," he said, hope pushing away the tears.

"Yes, they could. And if they are, I'll welcome them here with us. Then we can all safely work together against those who killed your parents and want our deaths," Ian said with conviction.

"But why here? What about those people outside? Who are they?" Marty asked.

"They're friends, fighting against tyranny and world domination by forces of evil that are very real. There are hundreds of us like minds in this complex and at others around the world." Ian leaned his elbows on his knees and looked intently at him. "Do you understand how important it is for you to stay safe and work to improve your skills?"

"Why do you think I'm supposed to be some kind of world leader? I'm just a kid who has weird dreams and knows what people are thinking sometimes," Marty objected. He had to make Ian understand. "Lots of people can do that."

"No, they can't. How many people do you know, with the exception of your father, Spencer and Rian, and me, that can move things with their minds, or create suggestions of things that aren't real but people believe are? How many can travel outside their bodies at will? Or remember their past lives and use the skills they learned then? Not many, Marty, not many at all."

"Well, maybe not, but how can being able to do that stuff save the world like you're talking about?" Ian was crazy if he thought some mind tricks could stop armies or people with lots of money. Inada had sent many assassins to kill his mom and dad before he was born, then killed them himself a few days ago. And his dad used to be able to do the kind of stuff Spence and Rian could. What good did that do him? He died anyway.

"Your father chose not to use his gifts," Ian answered his thoughts. "Your mother asked him not to because she feared that it would lead him to the dark side, and he respected her wishes. I promise you that with training you will be able to use those powers, and more, to save other kids so they won't lose their parents like you have. Your father and mother wanted you to achieve your potential. Isn't that why they raised you as they did? They knew you were special and destined for greatness. And that is why they asked me to safeguard you if anything happened to them."

Confusion settled over Marty like a fog. "But . . . I don't know . . ."

"That's okay," Ian said and stood. "Go ahead and eat your breakfast, or not. Or you can go down to the cafeteria where you can be sure to get something drug-free on your own, though I'm sure all the adults that you'll see eating there will probably seem like drugged-up zombies to a bright kid like you anyway. I won't even go with you. Just point you in the direction." Ian bounced his eyebrows and grinned.

"That's okay, you can come," Marty said. "But I've got to get some clothes on."

"In the dresser there," Ian said. "I'll wait for you outside."

Marty dressed quickly in new blue jeans, a brown and puke yellow tie-dye T-shirt that made him seasick and some Nikes that actually fit. He smooshed his freaky hair down with some bottled water and left the room. Ian was talking with another man about his same age out in the corridor until Marty walked up and he excused himself.

Ian led him through several turns to several different corridors, chatting all the way. Just as Marty wondered if they'd taken a wrong turn, a short A-frame signboard sitting in the middle of the corridor had a red arrow under the word *Cafeteria* pointing to open double doors. The smell of bacon wafted out and made Marty's stomach growl.

"I'll get some coffee and take that table over there," Ian said, nodding toward a round table set for two by the big window framing a view of a windswept lake and mountains. Ian followed his gaze and laughed. "Oh, don't worry about that. It's a photo designed to help you forget that you're nearly a mile underground, which is an idea that is troubling to many people. But not to you, of course."

Marty told him that he didn't have a problem with it and joined the short line for omelets to order. After he loaded up on bacon, sausage and a Spanish omelet with double cheese, Marty carried his heavy tray to Ian's table.

He'd gobbled down half the food when Ian started to talk in a conversational tone that was easy to listen to. "If you don't mind, while you're eating, I thought it would be good to talk a little about auras or energy fields. Of course you know a great deal about that subject, but it might be good for me to perhaps fill in some blank spots about the subject that your parents may not have covered."

Marty swallowed a glob of hot sauce-spiked egg. "We didn't talk about it much," he said.

"Rian? Spence? Did they discuss this with you?" Ian asked, his expression bland, but Marty sensed he was very interested in what he did or didn't know.

Marty shook his head. "Not so much." He stuffed the last of the bacon in his mouth and chewed, chasing it with a long drink of apple juice.

"Ah, all right then. I'll just start in and you wave me on if you've heard it before or get bored," Ian offered, and set his half-full cup on the tabletop in front of him and began telling him that the human aura was a three-dimensional energy field and that all things had an energy field.

"Yeah, I can usually see them," Marty said.

"Good!" Ian glanced around the cafeteria. "See that fellow over there in the blue jogging suit? Can you tell me the shape of his aura?"

Marty bit the corner of a piece of toast and defocused his eyes at the youngish man's back a few tables away from them. "Um, like an egg or oval?"

"Yes, and how far does it extend from his body?"

Marty frowned. "Maybe about five feet, but it's not very strong or bright around his back. Kind of weak." Before he could stop himself, his energy popped inside the man and he saw grayish lungs. It made him want to puke. He shook his head and stuck his tongue out. "Ugh, he's a smoker. It doesn't look good in there."

The jogger got up and carried his tray to the trashcan, an unlit cigar between his teeth. Marty met Ian's delighted gaze and they shook their heads, chuckling.

"Excellent," Ian exclaimed. "Do you mean that you actually can view inside the physical body without following RV protocols or going into trance?"

"Guess so," Marty said, pushing away his plate, his stomach still queasy from his inside tour of jogger man. "But I haven't always been able to do it. It's kind of a recent development."

"Yes," Ian said, gauging him. "Well, let me go on and we'll see what else develops. Did you know that ancient masters could extend their auras out from their bodies for miles, and their ritual practices were designed to keep their auras strong, healthy and vibrant?"

Marty said no. Ian suggested that one day soon they would begin to systematically explore his past lives to catalog skills developed back then and available for Marty to use now. "I fully expect that we will find that you are one of the so-called ancient masters," Ian said.

"Can you see my aura?" Marty asked.

"See? No." Ian sat forward, his elbows on the table, and tented his fingers. "My gifts are different, nothing like yours, but still rather unique and valuable. We're all wired a little differently by our DNA. You *see,* is that right?"

When Marty nodded, Ian continued, "You see energy, getting a visual impression. I hear it. If I wish, I can tune into anyone in this room; or if I have a picture or name, some identifier like that, I can target anyone anywhere in the world, and off-planet, too," he added with a sly smile. "I guess you could say I'm a mega-clairaudient." He leaned closer. "But you can do that, too, can't you, son?"

He wasn't sure and had to think about it for a moment. "Well, maybe. I hear stuff, too, but . . ."

"No worries," Ian said and bumped his fist lightly on Marty's shoulder. "I'll help you. We'll start with the basic remote viewing training, just as a refresher and a diagnostic procedure so that we know what we've got to work on, then we'll progress naturally into the advanced skills that are going to knock your socks off."

Ian's enthusiasm was contagious and Marty began to get excited, too.

"Great! Come on then, let's get going," Ian said, pushed to his feet and took Marty's tray.

Marty followed him across the cafeteria and waited in the entrance while Ian dumped his tray at the trash, idly watching passersby. Ten feet away, a big, black short-haired dog with pointed ears like a Doberman trotted into view, stopped mid-corridor and looked at Marty.

"Hey! A dog. How cool," he said to Ian and started out to pet it.

Ian stopped him with a hand on his arm, his expression hard. "There's no dog. Look again."

Marty did, but the dog was gone.

— THIRTEEN —

They searched the entire resort grounds and up into the trail along the foot of the eastern mesa, but could not find Dorel. Spence couldn't believe it when Rian announced she had to go teach her wanna-be guru class. Mike was pissed, too, but he was more diplomatic, telling her to go on and they'd handle it.

Rian danced off to class and Spence ground his teeth to dust keeping his mouth shut. There was nothing else to do but return to the casita and figure something out. He intended to target Dorel and, maybe with Mike remote viewing at the same time, they'd be able to get a lock and breach the psychic technology that he was sure Ian was using. Or maybe the best tactic was to target the psitech itself, trace the chain of custody to the brain that created it.

Housekeeping was still working on the casita when they arrived, and Spence suggested they go wait at the top-tier casitas' private pool just beyond a chest-high hedge at the end of the walkway that he'd seen during the search. The west third of the pool's broad deck bordered a tall rock wall and the rest of it opened to the valley below as if hanging in space. No one was around when they entered. Spence turned the *Closed for Cleaning* sign face-out. He walked around to Mike, who'd collapsed in a chair with his head in his hands and his shoulders shaking, and sat down on the end of a padded chaise lounge a couple of paces away from him. He didn't want to intrude on his friend's grief. The guy had earned every right to cry as much as he wanted.

But it wouldn't change anything.

His wife and kid would still be gone and he'd be weaker for having indulged himself, instead of focusing the emotion at his enemies and destroying them.

Spence waited as long as he could, and was saved having to say anything stupid to Mike when he saw the housekeeping cart leave the casita. Mike was still at it, but Spence wasn't going to leave him here by himself. That could be dangerous. Given all the emotions he'd been generating, anyone could get a lock on him. He walked over to his friend and cleared his throat. "The room's ready. I'm going to go get a cup of coffee. Come on, you need one, too."

Mike wiped his face and stood. He averted his red-rimmed eyes and nodded. Spence motioned for him to go first and followed him back to the casita. Entering warily, they split up and checked each room. Spence made coffee while Mike went to his room and came back with a pad of paper and a pen and sat down at the kitchen table.

After Spence poured the strong coffee and set the cups on the table, he sat down across from Mike. "Okay, what do you want to do now?"

"We view them and go get them," Mike ground out.

"We can target them and find them, but go get them? With what? All you've got is that antique .45. That and my Uzi can take care of quite a few and I can prep them with psychic warfare, but we've got some heavy technology operating here. He's targeting us with that, I'm pretty sure. For all I know, Dorel could be right here and we can't see her because we're being technologically presented with an illusion that our brains are believing instead." Spence got up and brought a bottle of Jack Daniels back from the bar and topped up his cup. He started to pour into Mike's, but he shook his head.

"Think you ought to be drinking when we're going to view?" Mike chided. "Booze and drugs lower your vibration, slow things way down."

Spence grinned and took a big gulp. The hot coffee burned the shit out of his mouth, but he didn't flinch. "I do this for a living, you know."

"You mean drink?" Mike snorted.

"No, asshole, psychic intelligence gathering. I'm a first-class operator, drunk or sober. Makes no diff out in the ether where the big boys play, but you wouldn't know that," Spence boasted good-naturedly.

The smile slid off Mike's face and he shook his head. Spence punched his shoulder. "Hey, I was just kidding. You were a hell of a viewer back in your day, best on the team. Nobody had anything on you."

Mike's eyes glittered. "You did."

This again. Spence set down his cup and took a deep breath that he hoped would extinguish the flash of temper building in his gut. "Yeah, well, we all make choices. It wasn't forced on me, or you. It was offered. I said yes and you said no. End of story."

"It wasn't just a choice, I couldn't do it. You could and did," Mike said flatly. "And over the years I've wondered if that choice you said you made back then hasn't made our lives what they are today."

Spence pushed back from the table, hands gripping his knees. "I am not responsible for Inada coming to kill you or Ian taking your son."

Mike held up his hand. "But you are responsible for the reason they've done what they've done. You created the sword—make that *swords*."

Spence's mouth fell open in amazement. "Jesus, you're holding a life of mine thousands of years ago against me now? Hell yes, actually Rian created them and I used them. So have you. You and Dorel hooked yourselves up for a shit-load of lives in that so-called eternal trust of using and losing the Defender Sword, my friend. But you probably blame me for that, too."

Mike began to grin. "It might be a little harsh to hold someone's past life against them, especially one that long ago."

Spence relaxed his fisted hands. "So you don't blame me for the eternal trust thing you and Dorel had going?"

"My frustration is that we don't seem to get away from the problems the swords cause. Just when we figure it's over, something new and terrible goes down. The cycle goes on and on," Mike said, and abruptly pushed the coffee away from him. "From one life to the next, apparently. God, when will it stop? If I thought this was really eternal or endless, I don't know that I could go on, you know. What would be the point of trying to live a decent life, raise kids, never cheat on your wife and pay your bills? Why not just screw it and live—"

"Like I do?" Spence said with a wink and saluted him with the bottle. He took a swig and held it out to Mike.

Mike shook his head. "Pass. I can barely think now, I'm so screwed up. I've got to get my wife and kid back; then maybe we'll just disappear."

"Join some secret, remote viewer protection relocation program?" Spence joked and took another hit on the bottle. "Problem with that is it ain't secret from the psychic spies targeting you."

Mike snorted, nodding. "Yeah." He sat up and dragged the paper and pen over. "Let's get at this."

For the next two and a half hours, Spence worked Mike through a series of protocols and exercises that would help to bring his rusty skills back online.

"Let's take a break," Mike said, rubbing his eyes with the heels of his hands. "I've got to get something to eat." He glanced at the bourbon bottle that Spence noticed was significantly less full than when he'd sat down earlier. "And so should you."

Spence agreed and ordered two Southwestern burgers from room service. The food arrived at the same time Rian walked in, looking beautiful and vibrant, far above the fray of the material world of lost wives and sons.

"It was the last class, so only a half-day," she explained when he questioned her unexpected appearance. "Teaching always fills me with energy."

"You want to share?" Spence offered, ready to cut his burger in half.

"No thanks." She put her arm around Mike's shoulders and asked how he was doing.

"Spence has been prepping me for a session after lunch. We're going to target Dorel and Marty, maybe the psitech, I don't know. Got any ideas?"

Rian started to pull out a chair and sit. "Let me think about it while you finish." She took her tote bag and briefcase into her bedroom and closed the door.

Spence didn't know what she had to think about. It was pretty clear-cut, unless she was going to want them to try some of her Light Seeking methods, which couldn't be that much different than what he did.

As if she knew they'd finished, Rian opened her door and came to the table when Spence set the room service tray outside on the front porch. He sat down and the three of them looked at each other.

"So?" Spence prompted. "Any revelations?"

Rian's smile was indulgent. "A couple of impressions, yes."

She turned to Mike. "Is Marty having a birthday soon?"

Mike slapped his forehead. "His twelfth is the day after tomorrow."

She asked Spence when the full moon was. "Isn't it full now?" he said.

"It looks almost full, but I mean officially," she said.

Spence shrugged. "Would that be in the paper somewhere, maybe the weather page?"

Mike was already on his feet and heading for the living room. He came right back, the folded-out paper between his hands. "Tomorrow night at eleven fifty-six the moon goes full, here in Sedona anyway," he said, putting the paper under her nose. "Why?"

"I intended to find where Dorel and Marty would be twenty-four hours from now, rather than their present location, which might be shielded somehow. I suppose I was hoping that whatever technology or process that was making me believe that I couldn't see them would have to be focused within tight parameters of a given *now*," she said to Mike.

"And wouldn't be able to multitask to another location or time," Spence finished for her, and Rian nodded.

"When I dropped into my meditative state and flashed out-of-body on my intention, I got a strange series of images or impressions. A full moon. Party balloons, which actually could have been the full moon and vice versa, so I don't want to overlay the data. I'm just reporting."

"Did you sketch out what you saw?" Mike asked.

"No, I don't use that process anymore. Mine is less structured, more free-form impressionistic, but I rarely get into analytic overlay of the data. I don't try to project meaning on what I experience. I let the data speak for itself," Rian said.

"Okay, so what's this data saying, the moon and the balloons?" Spence asked, trying to conceal his impatience.

"I can only say what it means to me. Dorel and Marty are outside at the full moon, and it's some sort of celebration." She looked from Spence to Mike's frowning face and blushed. "I said it's my impression and I didn't have very much time."

Spence put his hand on hers. "It's okay. To a by-the-numbers remote viewer like Mike, your process and data are flaky psychic-hotline remote viewing. But there's something I'd like to get clear on. Remember the coyote? He said something about the full moon, too. You wouldn't be getting a loop of amassed data, would you?"

She pulled her hand out. "Yes, I remember the mention, and no, I'm not mixing or overlaying data."

"Now, take it easy. I'm just asking, like any good targeting officer," Spence said, giving her what he hoped was a winning smile.

"There's more," Rian said. "Do you want to hear it?"

"Of course," Mike jumped in. "And Spence does, too."

"Gathered in a circle with the moon and balloons, I saw a raven and an Anubis figure," she explained to Mike.

"What do you think that means?" Mike asked in more careful words than Spence would have, which was why she was ignoring him and talking to Mike.

"The Anubis figure is self-explanatory. That entity has already appeared to Spence and ordered him to produce the swords. I think that means Ian, Dorel, Marty and Spence and I will be in the same place at the full moon."

"Why you and me? How do you get that?" Spence asked.

"We represent the swords or they, us."

"You're talking about interpreting dream symbols. That's dicey, Rian, and not exactly objective," Mike argued. "Besides, what about me? Where am I supposed to be while you all gather at the full moon? Or didn't you get balloons, a bird or airplane for me?"

Rian leaned over and hugged him. "Oh, Mike, I'm sorry. I was being very insensitive. Of course, it's all symbols out there, out-of-body in the Spiritlands. I just didn't have enough time for more."

"What about the raven, what's that mean, you think?" Spence asked.

She pulled herself up and looked him straight in the eye. "The raven is my spirit guide, Chevayo."

"So that's what you're calling him," Spence groused. He was right with his first assessment; there had been a guy sniffing around her. And no ordinary one, at that; he remembered the high form wave that met him when they'd first arrived at the casita. Who the hell was this guy?

"Actually, I don't call him by name, though I perceive him as a native shaman. He told me that his name was Chevayo, which means spirit warrior," she said, refusing to hit his bait.

"What's the raven? Why do you associate that with this shaman?" Mike asked what Spence wasn't about to.

"I didn't put it together until this meditation that I just did," she said, speaking directly to Mike. "Since I'd gotten here to the resort, I'd been seeing the raven, and then the shaman seemed to show up just after that and counsel with me, and disappear."

Spence couldn't keep quiet. "You think your shaman or raven is going to fly in for the festivities at the full moon?"

Rian gave him a sugary smile, but her eyes were stone cold. "Yes. You bring your dog and I'll bring my raven. And a good time will be had by all."

"Nice, smartass. I'm just trying to get some information

here," Spence said in a lame attempt to cover his jealous poke at her.

"Fine. Allow me to enlighten you about totemic animals or signs—the dog, or coyote, and the raven that we've been shown—or do you know all about that?" she asked deadpan.

"I don't," Mike interjected. "If it's got something to do with getting my wife and son back, I want to know everything."

"I can't guarantee an actual causative relationship of these signs to the return of Dorel and Marty," Rian said cautiously. "But like any other sign or metaphor, there's a meaning or a lesson to be derived from its appearance in one's life. Perhaps because of the spiritual path I'm on, I received the raven as a sign for the presence of my guide, who knew that I would relate to that symbol's meaning, and opening me to his help."

"I get that, but what does a raven or coyote mean?" Mike persisted and flattened his palms on the table.

"In many cultures and traditions, the raven is a powerful sign, with the ability to shift into other domains of awareness, out of time and space. The raven has mystical powers and is thought to be the maker of the material world, or so some Native Americans have believed. Its appearance to someone is considered an omen of change coming into their life," Rian said, a peaceful beauty smoothing her features as she spoke.

They sat quietly for a few moments, Spence the first to break the spell her words had woven among them. "I think we all know we're in the middle of big changes, and we don't need a shaman bird or a coyote to tell us that when the obvious bad, nasty signs are all around us, you know?"

"Jesus, Spence, will you shut up?" Mike barked. "Stop

speaking for *all of us*. Pry open that steel trap mind of yours and give her a chance. At least she's trying to help."

Spence held up his hands in surrender. "Shutting up, sir!" he barked back and threw Mike a stiff salute. He wasn't going to say another goddamn word. Let them chase down their *let's talk about feelings* blind alley and waste their time. It was nothing to him. But when it came to getting the job done, they'd both be right back begging him to save their asses.

"You've got a spirit guide and . . ." Mike prompted her.

"I think if the three of us were to specifically target these signs or data that I received in relation to Dorel's and Marty's location at the full moon, we'd get something useful," Rian said, and gave Spence an inclusive glance.

"You two can go ahead, but I'm going to set up a psychic parameter that will stop them, or at least slow them down, while you guys view," Spence offered, despite his irritation and promise to himself not to get involved in their ridiculous touchy-feely stuff. But someone had to protect them if they wouldn't protect themselves, because he felt they were being targeted right now. In fact, Ian's psychic eavesdropping on them had never stopped.

Rian lifted a dark brow and pursed her lips. With a nod of approval, she said, "Good thinking, Spence. I've been lax about that lately. Too much going on and I'm distracted."

"That's his plan," Spence said and got up. "I'll go do my thing out on the terrace, so you guys can split up in here. Mike, we're not going to do a blind targeting this time. The intention is to locate Dorel and Marty, and you can start with that." He looked at Rian. "It's best for you to rework your own data, don't you think, and let him view on his own and see what he gets?"

"I suppose you're right," she said. "Mike, you can stay

here at the table and I'll go to my room, or the other way round, if you like."

"I go to your room?" Mike asked with a wry smile. "No, I'll stay here. Our bedroom . . . it'd interfere, I couldn't focus."

Rian stood and gave him a hug. "I understand." She checked her watch. "Let's limit this first-go to sixty minutes?"

They agreed and Spence took himself out to the terrace, closing the slider behind him. He sat at the table, but it didn't feel right. Better to do this on his feet, he determined, and walked to the railing to survey the landscape. There was no coyote waiting to talk to him when he looked down to the slope below. A red-tailed hawk circled high overhead and scrub jays squawked from pine tree to bushes to rooftop. Rian would probably say that the jays weren't blue birds of happiness but signs that they were going to get their asses kicked by a band of camp robbers.

Spence shook his head and chuckled, then rolled his shoulders, took some breaths. He shaped his intention and created a thought form of an impenetrable bubble of harmonic frequency. He designed the bubble to disrupt any intruding personal energy field with a destroying dissonance wavelength. The thought form ballooned out and started to expand across the valley. That would potentially protect and kill a lot of people, if he let it. Spence deflated the bubble, reducing the energy shield to a tight coating over the casita, and continued to focus energy into it while his friends worked inside.

"I have a surprise for you," Ian told Marty after they'd finished a round of racquetball and headed to the locker room. The boy had displayed incredible athletic ability and won easily, though he said he'd never played before. There was probably nothing on this earth that he couldn't do or learn. The eternal power of the universe seemed to animate him. Ian couldn't imagine what the boy would be, or how he might handle him, after the initiation.

Marty wiped his sweaty forehead on his terrycloth wristband, twirling the racket in his other hand. "What initiation?"

The boy had read his unguarded thought. "It's your twelfth birthday soon, isn't it?" Ian said, filling his thoughts with balloons, gifts and other celebratory regalia.

Marty smiled. "Yeah, tomorrow or the next day. I've kinda lost track of the days down here."

They entered the locker room and went to their lockers. Ian turned his back, giving Marty privacy while he undressed, chatting about the game until the pair in the next bank of lockers left. Ian wrapped a towel around his waist and proceeded to the showers. After a few moments, Marty slipped in and took the farthest stall away from him. The boy was extraordinarily modest, but perhaps most were at his age. Ian didn't remember caring one way or the other when he was twelve, but then again he didn't remember being twelve, either. He finished quickly and was dressed by the time Marty returned to his locker, scrubbed and redder than usual.

"I'll meet you back at the cafeteria," Ian told him. "I can use a pick-me-up after you ran me around so badly."

Marty blushed and grinned. "You'll get better. Practice helps a lot."

"Thanks, but I've been playing every day for the last ten years and that *was* my better," Ian said with a friendly wink and left him to get dressed.

In less than ten minutes, Marty wandered into the cafeteria, saw Ian and came straight to the table. He got up and asked what Marty wanted.

"I think it's pretty cool that all this stuff is free and that I can have anything I want," Marty said. Ian agreed and walked away to the counter to get Marty's food.

They were going to have to begin implementing basic nutritional rules designed to augment the boy's intuitive platform after the initiation. Until then, he could have whatever artery-clogging concoction he wanted, including the hot fudge and pineapple sundae with gummy worms that Ian ordered for him.

Marty hunched over the heap of ice cream and inhaled it, as Ian averted his gaze to focus elsewhere. Surely, he was raised with some manners? Ian let mentally slip.

Marty snapped his mouth shut, sat up and said, "Sorry."

"That's all right," Ian demurred. "Didn't mean to be critical. I'm just not used to being around kids—I mean, young adults."

Marty glanced around at the other diners. "Yeah, I can see that." He began to eat again, a little more slowly this time.

"Now, let's talk about your birthday. Did you know that in some ancient and aboriginal cultures, some of which you might even remember, a boy's twelfth birthday was considered very special, a rite of passage into manhood?"

"Like when they leave him out in the jungle or forest and he has to live on his own for a couple of weeks?" Marty asked, scraping his spoon around the empty parfait glass.

"Yes, some did that. Others used circumcision or body piercing, scarification or tattooing, combined with very solemn ritual and rites of initiation, to induct the boy into the cult of men. It was a sacred duty and privilege for all concerned and looked forward to by the boy and his tribe."

Marty stopped rattling his spoon, his eyes narrowing as he pinned them on Ian. "Okay, but I'm not in a tribe . . ."

Ian laughed. "No, of course you aren't. What I'm talking about is making your birthday special and thought it might be fun for you to celebrate in a very unique way you're really going to like."

"Not if it has anything to do with knives or other sharp stuff and me," Marty said, a wary glint in his eyes.

"I won't lie to you. There are some sharp things, as you say: fire, full moon, people dancing around with swords. Everyone having a great time." Ian leaned forward, dropping his voice. "But it's all pretend! Like an interactive computer game."

Marty began to smile. "Yeah? You're giving me a game machine? That is so cool. I really miss playing."

Ian shook his head and put his finger to his lips. "Shhh, not so loud. We don't want anyone to hear." He cast his gaze around the few people left in the cafeteria. "A computer, and something else, a full-size virtual reality interactive pod. You've heard of the TV show 'Star Trek.' Remember the holodeck? The crew went there for a full sensory experience of any situation, culture or time created by a computer? Did you ever wish the holodeck was real and that you could use it?"

Marty nodded slowly, his mouth slackening and eyes taking on a trance-like cast. Ian leaned closer, his voice steady and rhythmic, and looked deeply into Marty's eyes. "It *is* real."

"No way," Marty's lips mouthed.

"Yes. It is absolutely real. You know that many science fiction marvels on TV or in the movies are based on actual secret technology that the government is hiding from the public. The holodeck is one of them. And we have it, a couple of levels up from us right here," Ian said, jabbing his finger at the tabletop between them.

"Can we go there now?" Marty asked, clearly believing everything Ian said.

"Not at this moment, no." Ian moved back a little. "The holodeck—we call it our RTVRPod—I know, yet another meaningless acronym."

"No, it's cool. Real-Time Virtual Reality Pod. Says it all," Marty enthused, moving closer as Ian played him.

"I suppose so, but what I was saying is that the RTVRPod is a busy place, as you can imagine, and you must reserve time in it days ahead. But as luck would have it, one of my employees has been sent on a special assignment and his reservation opened up. He wanted you to have it for your birthday. How about that!" Ian beamed at Marty, who nodded, exactly pacing his own reinforcing nod.

"How come he did that for me?" the boy asked in wonder.

"Marty, everyone knows what happened to your parents and we're not going to let that stand. I can promise you that. Now, I want to ask your permission before I program your session. I thought, since this is a very special occasion for you, and after all that's been stolen from you, that you might enjoy a birthday party where your parents and Spencer and Rian are all present. We could all celebrate together like we know they'd want, and pretend, if only for a little while, that things were like they used to be. Would that be all right with you, if I set that up for you?"

Tears streamed down Marty's face. He pressed his trembling lips together and nodded.

Ian patted his shoulder. "Thank you for allowing me to do this for you. We'll have a grand celebration tomorrow night."

— FOURTEEN —

"Rian! Open up. Mike's gone," yelled Spence, pounding on her door.

Rian shot back into her body and rolled off the bed so quickly that her spirit didn't have time to assimilate completely. She staggered, disoriented, to the bedroom door that shouldn't have been locked.

"What the hell did you lock it for?" Spence raged in her face when she managed to get it open.

"I—I didn't," she mumbled, trying to will her shallow breathing into full, deep breaths that would empower her body.

He finally looked at her and grabbed her shoulders, pressing down with his palms. "Breathe and center!"

At her sharp intake of air, her spirit fully integrated with an almost audible *pop*. "Thanks."

Spence held onto her, his tired face deeply lined with desperation. "I've looked everywhere. He's disappeared just like Dorel. Like he was dematerialized out of here. How can that be? I set up my shield thought form and fortified it nonstop the whole hour to protect you guys, like I said. I did everything right, but it was wrong. Always wrong," he said, hanging his head.

She'd never seen him so shaken or hopeless and put her curled finger under his chin and gently raised his head. Holding his distraught gaze, she assured him, "It's okay."

He scowled at her like she was crazy and dropped his hands off her shoulders. "Okay? I screwed up. They're gone. How is that okay?"

"I could defend my *faux pas* by saying I'm not going to agree with your erroneous self-blame. While that's true, I didn't know what else to say to you. It was stupid, but sometimes I do stupid things, okay?" Rian sighed and rubbed her forehead, where a low-grade headache throbbed between her eyes. Tension. *Surprise, surprise, look how you're reacting to all this,* she berated herself. "What do you want to do now? We could look for him."

He stared her down. "Are you getting him at all?"

She extended her consciousness over the resort and beyond. "No, not close anyway."

"Me either," Spence said. "So physically looking for him around here would have the same results as our search for Dorel."

Rian agreed and asked again what he wanted to do. His misshapen, splotchy aura showed that Spence was in spiritual crisis and soon would be in physical pain. It was difficult for her to withhold the loving comfort he so badly needed. But he would misconstrue her caring touch and empathetic words as a readiness to bring back the swords.

"I'm fresh out of ideas. Except for one . . ." He ran his hand through his hair and avoided the compassionate gaze that she beamed on him with tender affection.

"Bring back the swords, right?" she said, and his hopelessness morphed to done-deal anticipation in an instant.

"The swords' combined power will give us the ability to breach any technology and whatever else Ian or anyone can throw at us," he said, his demeanor carefully eager.

"How can you be certain of that?" she asked, shaking her head at his wishful thinking, and walked to the living room to put some space between them, but he followed.

"I'm not sure of anything, but I'm willing to give this a calculated try. You've got to consider that why else would

Ian and a negative entity both want the swords? Because they know the swords have massive arcane power, the extent of which we can only guess, and attempt to rediscover," he said behind her, his passion probing for an unguarded opening in her aura to penetrate and attach.

Rian moved her body away from him, trying to order her mind to do the same. He came up behind her and brushed her hair back, skimming his lips over the sensitive skin of her neck. "Let me in, Rian," he murmured. "I need you so much."

Loving becomes a sacred act of transformation. Chevayo's voice floated through her mind like a feather on a delicate breeze. Apparently now was the time and perhaps the only chance she'd get to help Spence manifest his desire in a way that would actually empower both of them and transform him. And if the swords should materialize, it would be *meant* to be. She turned around and put her palms on Spence's chest, exerting a light pressure to hold him in place.

"You need me to bring the swords back. The truth, say it," she said, looking up at him as he wrestled with the idea.

"That isn't the only reason. I love you," he began.

Rian laid her fingertips on his lips. "Truth. Say it."

He blew out an exasperated breath. "Yeah, okay. I need you to help me materialize the swords, but I do love you and need you, too," he added, as if he'd just remembered that a woman liked to hear that sort of thing before the condom got unwrapped.

"And we materialize the swords how?" She dropped her hand back to his chest. His heart beat beneath her palms, and she was nearly overcome with the loving connection established from that point and going straight to her own heart.

He watched her, obviously feeling what she did. A gorgeous smile spread over his mouth and lit his hazel eyes with gold. "We make the best love this world has ever seen. From the incredible high level energy we generate, our intention zooms out to the ether to resonate with the essence of the swords, and draws them to us on the corresponding wave. They manifest according to our thoughts right here on the material plane. Just like the first time we did it. Creating the swords, I mean," he said, eyes twinkling with excitement.

Rian grinned. "Sounds simple enough." She raised her face to be kissed, half-closing her eyes.

Spence bent his head and crushed her mouth, sticking his tongue down her throat, and grabbed her breasts. Rian gagged and shoved him back, swiping at her bruised mouth with the back of her hand.

"That's your idea of beautiful love?" she huffed; then, seeing his anxious, guilt-ridden expression, made herself calm down. She remembered that Chevayo said teaching Spence the necessary transformational love would be a lot of work, but supposedly worth the effort.

"I just got carried away," he said with a repentant cringe. "I'm sorry."

She took his hands in hers. "Spence, you tried it that way with me before. And what you wanted to happen didn't. It's going to take more than down-and-dirty sex to get what you want. There's a spiritual aspect to real lovemaking. Think a moment about the swords. They're called the Swords of Balance. To me that means they represent the yin and yang. Light and dark. Male and female energies. Together. In balance. To hope to materialize them through lust alone, well, I don't know if that can happen—at least not for you and me, anyway."

"It did the first time," he countered and gave her hands

a light squeeze. "Yeah, there was love between us, as I remember, in that life and in the creation of the swords in particular, but there was a hell of a lot of ritual Egyptian magic, too. It's all about generating the correct energy, the right vibration, and ritual, chants, specific words and movements that are designed to do that. Ritualistic sex is the most powerful energy generator and has been used for millennia in the dark arts to conjure and control."

She gave him a disgusted look and dropped his hands. "So?" Why had she listened to a shaman who talked about tantric sex in the first place? Spence had probably projected the experience just to get her in the mood.

"I did not," he answered her thought that she'd foolishly left open and unprotected. "Though if the raven said you should have sex with me, we better get to it, don't you think?" He shined a naughty smile on her. "I think I like your talking raven more than my coyote—better options package and people skills."

Rian laughed. "You are such an incredible jerk. Very clever, but a jerk." And a very cute, loveable one that she adored when he was happy and gentle. But that was almost too long ago to remember.

He slipped his arms around her and pulled her gently to him. "Yeah, I'm a jerk, though I'd have used a stronger anatomical term if I were you describing me. Despite the crap I've put you through and the way I've treated you, I am the jerk who loves you."

Rian embraced him, stood on tiptoes and touched her lips to his. He kissed her back as sweetly. She put her head on his shoulder and they stood quietly holding each other for several precious minutes.

"All right," she said against his neck. "I want to make love with you. My way." She held herself away a little and looked into his eyes. "Allow me to love you without objective or motive, the only intention to give you pleasure and share bliss."

His eyes widened. "I know I should say something profound, but the blood just left my head and all I can think of is yes."

"Why don't you take a shower while I make some preparations?" she suggested with a smile, feathering her fingertips down his bare arms as she moved out of his hug. He backed away, pulling his sweater over his head, and charged into the bathroom. "Don't come until I call you," she said.

"Right," he said and shut the door.

In her own bathroom, Rian relaxed into a rose-scented warm bath and allowed her consciousness to drift to seek the past, as she'd learned to do when she was a psychologist practicing past life therapy. She soon found herself within the naked body of Seta, high priest and sword-maker to Queen Kalūkuh of Egypt. He was preparing himself to take part in ritual lovemaking with his queen that would eventually lead to their manifesting the Swords of Balance.

Within the palace temple of Anubis that was also his residence, Seta knelt on the smooth marble floor before a large stone basin decorated with magical symbols and filled with cool, jasmine-scented water. Seta dipped his middle fingers in blessed oil of sandalwood and, starting at the top of his shaved head, traced protective symbols on his skin, redipping his fingers in the oil together and returning them to his body in precise parity. When each sacred point was anointed, Seta brought his hands to the crown of his head and chanted powerful words of protection and to heighten his receptivity to the gods and his queen.

He placed the tips of the fingers of his two hands exactly sideways, middle fingers touching, over his mouth that murmured the spell of speaking only truth and providing pleasure. At his heart, he laid his crossed hands and invoked love only for his queen.

His two forefingers delved into his navel as he blessed mother Isis who made his seed strong. Both hands wrapped around his rigid manhood, Seta called upon Osiris to keep him hard and sturdy as a tree. He repeated the pattern of touching each part nine times, chanting specific sounds to heighten his spirit's and body's responses to his queen.

Rian came back into her body fully aroused and ready to make magical, transcendent love with her man. She rubbed jasmine lotion over her damp skin and slipped on a lacy white mini-negligee. Gathering candles, incense, essential oils and a bowl of warm water, she arranged them on a tray and set it on the floor. She pulled the duvet off the bed to the floor next to the tray and covered it with clean, fluffy towels, placing a folded blanket nearby. Rian drew the heavy drapes over the terrace door, darkening the room, and inserted a CD of her own ancient Egyptian mystical flute music into the player. She adjusted the volume and took an appraising look at her temple of seduction. The candles needed to be lighted now, she decided, and did so.

Rian took a deep breath and opened the door. Spence stood just outside, handsome and smelling designer fragrance masculine. He held two glasses and an open wine bottle in one hand and his other clutching the ends of a small green striped kitchen towel together around his waist. "I didn't know what the dress code was, so I decided on the towel, which will be handy for serving the wine, as you see." With a wicked grin, he jerked the towel off with a flourish and draped it over his arm. "What do you think? Does it work?"

"Uh-huh, and you could hang it there, too," Rian said,

dropping her gaze to his crotch. She stepped aside, sweeping her arm to invite him in.

Spence let out a long, low whistle. "This is great." He edged around the duvet and looked at her. "Where do you want me?"

"Let me take these and you can get comfortable there on the duvet." She took the glasses and wine, leaving him the kitchen towel, and knelt on the duvet next to the tray and set them on the floor. Spence hopped in the middle of the towels and sat down cross-legged, dropping the towel into his lap, where it became an instant tent.

Rian stayed on her knees, Geisha style, almost touching his knees, and twisted the cap off a small, brown bottle of essential oil. "This is one of your favorite scents," she said, passing it under his nose.

Spence inhaled, holding her gaze. "Mmmm, jasmine. Smells delicious, like you." He caught her hand, kissing the inside of her wrist. She slowly pulled her hand out of his and tipped several drops of oil into the bowl of warm water and stirred it with her finger. She lifted her slick finger to his chest and drew a smooth line down his belly and stopped at the top of the covering and looked up at him with a slight grin, removing her hand.

Rian sat in a lotus position facing Spence. "Our love-making will achieve incredible ecstasy if we take the time to awaken our energy."

"Mine's awake," Spence said, giving her a sizzling look.

"I can see that, but just wait. You're going to love what we do together," she said and held her hands out, palms up. "Let's start by connecting energetically. Put your left palm under my right and your right over my left." When disappointment dashed through his gaze, she added, "You're going to experience the most incredible sex, unlike anything or anyone you've ever had, I promise you."

"Can't argue with that," Spence said and slapped his palms upon hers.

"Let's allow our eyes to close and focus on creating a circuit of energy between us," Rian said and closed her eyes, taking deep, even breaths. She imagined a silver cord of energy extending from her heart chakra to Spence's heart. Within a few breaths, she felt his acceptance and the connection completed and begin to grow. An electrical current pulsated between them.

After a few minutes, she opened her eyes and told him to open his. Spence's body, his face were illuminated with tranquility and love for her. Her heart and body urged her to make love with him now, but she couldn't. He wasn't ready.

"Now that our energy is connected, let's energize each chakra in a body-to-body meditation." Rian grasped his hands and pulled herself to sit in his lap, wrapping her arms and legs around him. "Put your arms around me. That's right. Starting at the base chakra, let's focus our breath and intention on each energy center, up to the crown chakra, opening like a lotus flower."

"If this is going to take very long, I need to move my foot. I'm sitting on it," Spence said and shifted around a bit under her. "There, that's better."

She smiled at him and kissed the end of his nose. "Didn't the connecting energy feel great? And you didn't even realize that it took fifteen minutes, did you?"

He shook his head. "No, it felt great. Still does."

"Excellent. Let's begin." She hugged him gently, her open hands on his smooth back, and put her cheek against his. She felt him breathing deeply and matched his inhale and exhale, lengthening the space between and visualizing the energy of breath flowing into her base chakra between her legs. The energy center slowly opened and begin to spin faster; then she moved her awareness to the next, just below the navel, and on up the next four centers to the crown chakra. An explosion of wave form energy in the violet range rippled through her body and aura, joining the rainbow of vibrations emitted from all the opened chakras.

Her cleansed and magnified energy merged with his in an extravagant amalgamation, and they became aware of each other at the same time. Rian slitted her eyes to behold the rainbow-hued glow around their bodies as Spence opened his.

"We're ready to progress to the next level," she murmured and told him to lie down on his stomach while she moved off of him to the tray. She poured massage oil into her hand, warming it a moment between her two hands, and began to massage the tight muscles of his shoulders and back, letting the soft, sensual music orchestrate her movements.

"Touch is an intense, personal means of communication," she said in a low, melodic voice. "Hands of love touching, caressing the body express a deepness of feeling more profound than mere words. Respectful, tender touching can strengthen intimacy, both physical and emotional, relaxing the body, erasing tension and bestowing cerebral tranquility. Loving touch invigorates the body and arouses sensuality and stimulates the skin to its full capacity of sensation."

Rian kissed him between his shoulder blades as she massaged her hands over the small of his back and onto his firm buttocks. "As you can feel, massage with a loving touch is a perfect gift that a lover can bestow upon a partner."

She opened her negligee and lay down on him, undulating her body to massage his.

"Mmmmm," Spence groaned in obvious enjoyment, his hand groping to touch her. She sat astride his buttocks and opened her legs wider. He skimmed his fingers inside her thigh, mainlining sensation straight to her root chakra and she almost climaxed. Focusing her attention back on him, she eased off of his back onto her knees and asked him to roll over.

Rian leaned over him and began to nuzzle and lick his flat belly, teasing kisses down almost to the base of his erection. His hands reached for her and she put them gently at his sides.

"Let me touch you," he whispered, his empty hands clutching at the towels beneath him.

She began to massage his legs, starting at the insides of his thighs, covering every inch of skin down to his toes and back up, speaking words of seduction as she went. "Not many men have been allowed to enjoy the whole body sensuality that women do, and so they become detached, centered on the genital area, ignoring the whole body that is an erogenous zone to be explored, stimulated and enjoyed."

Rian let her negligee fall off her shoulders and reached her hands to Spence. He grabbed them and pulled himself to a sitting position and her astride his lap. He lifted his hips to penetrate her, but she moved off him, shaking her head.

"Not yet," she whispered. "Every part of the body is sensitive and worthy of arousal—starting with the fingertips." She took his fingers one by one into her mouth on the pad of her tongue and sucked each gently.

She guided his awakened hands to hold her in a gentle embrace and cupped his face in her hands, her gaze on his mouth. "The mouth, the lips and the tongue are so erotically sensitive that a kiss becomes ecstasy, like the act of making love. Close your eyes and feel."

After a second of hesitation, Spence's smoky eyes closed and she tenderly brushed her lips on his forehead, lightly kissed each eye and down his nose. Rian let her eyes close and focused on the sensations of her tongue tracing his soft bottom lip, the tickle of his moustache on her top lip as she delved into his mouth, savoring each pleasure as he deepened their kiss. They fell into synch, their hearts opening to each other and energy fields intertwining.

Spence lay back and she followed upon him. His erection slid into her easily and he laid his hands on her bottom as she snuggled against him. They lay quietly together in deep unity, Rian gently rocking her pelvis against him to keep him hard without over-stimulating him, so that he stayed focused on their communion. In the following moments of stillness, they gazed lovingly into each other's eyes, their breath rising and falling in perfect synchronization, uniting them on an energetic level.

Spontaneously, without thought or effort, they moved together as if dancing on the wind, the sense of merging hearts and minds lifting them higher and higher. Individual sexual energies dissolved into a single harmonious wave of ecstasy that carried them as one into an eruption of sensation that expanded and forever altered their coupled consciousness. They let go together into the pulsations of blissful release, surrendering themselves to each other, becoming one in body, soul and joy.

Rian lay peacefully in Spence's loving arms as they returned slowly to themselves, still intimately connected with breath and body.

"I love you," he murmured against her temple.

"I love you, too," Rian answered. She tilted her chin up

and looked at his face, shining with inner tranquility. His whole demeanor appeared changed: lighter, balanced, whole. Rian knew she too was changed inside-out from their tantric experience of sacred loving and that she glowed with soul *chi* as he did.

Spence looked at her with adoring eyes. "I've never felt . . . like this. I hope, well, whatever this is that I feel, I hope it lasts . . ."

Little by little as they lay in each other's arms, thoughts of the past and the future nibbled at their bliss. It was time to deal with now. Rian caressed Spence's stubbled cheek and kissed him longingly. He tightened his embrace and kissed her with the same intensity, as if he too feared they'd never be together again.

Rian reluctantly eased out of his arms and went to the bathroom. She took a quick shower, put on the terrycloth robe and combed out her hair. When she came back into the bedroom, the candles were snuffed and the duvet, that had been the altar of their reuniting passion, empty. Spence was gone.

Fearing that they'd taken him, too, she ran past the empty hall bath and into the living room. The lamps were on, showing that his sweater and leather jacket lay together on a chair and his boots were on the floor, as if he'd just kicked them off there. But Spence wasn't there. Her hands went to her mouth against the scream climbing her throat. An intermittent noise like low voices reached her ears and she looked toward the terrace. One drape was drawn back and the sliding glass door was open about six inches. Dusk had settled shadows on the terrace, but she was certain someone was out there, the energy was so strong, and familiar. And becoming aware of her!

Rian pulled her aura in tight around her body and

stepped to the slider, pushing it open, peering out. Spence, wearing only jeans, and Chevayo stood face-to-face on the terrace and turned to smile at her, as if they expected her. And of course they did.

Relief soothed her alarm-tightened muscles, allowing her to take a deep calming breath and she stepped outside. "Spence, you scared me to death," she directed at him.

Spence jerked his thumb toward Chevayo, whose grin was less idiotic than his. "Sorry, but we've got company."

"Yes, I see." She nodded to the shaman and raised her eyebrow at her darling Spence. "How'd this happen?"

"Well, in case you were wondering, though I'm not saying that it was my first thought after—you know, but we didn't get the swords," he said, his forehead creasing with a tiny frown over his twinkling eyes. "Looks like we got him."

She chuckled and kissed his cheek. "Do you know who *him* is?"

"Yup." Spence winked at her. "It's the shaman raven, which is no doubt your preference as opposed to what I was trying for—at first, or thought I was," his voice trailed off. He blushed and rubbed his moustache and goatee self-consciously.

She put her arm around Spence's bare waist and looked questioningly at the shaman, who continued to beam happiness at both of them with his warm and friendly dark eyes.

"Spence sees me now because his consciousness is altered, elevated to a balanced and resonant high-level vibration. The negative entity calling itself Anubis cannot attach to or influence him, or you, as you remain within this frequency band. Entertaining or allowing thoughts and actions of lower vibrations will resonate with like and draw them to you."

"What about the Swords of Balance? We aren't able to

materialize them since I've *changed,* as you say, can we?" Spence said, disappointment or worry in his tone.

The shaman spread his arms and for a moment Rian thought she saw great black wings, and glanced at Spence. He saw, too.

"The wave form energy that you call the Swords of Balance have materialized once," Chevayo looked pointedly at them. "*In you.* You must maintain your now-balanced and conjoined auras with the highest quality thoughts, words and actions of love, and in doing so, you are the embodiment of the power of the Swords of Balance that you sought."

Spence and Rian cleaved to each other to keep from staggering under that pronouncement.

When she could speak, Rian asked, "What are we supposed to do with this power?" Spence, still slack-jawed with shock, said nothing.

"You must keep your soul pact to unite your consciousnesses at the specified time with the others of your soul group and fulfill your individual soul missions as well as your soul group's mission, that culminates tomorrow night after eons of preparatory lives," Chevayo said gravely and pointed at the dark shape of the eastern mesa across the valley. "At the full moon tomorrow night, the door between worlds will open at the Encantada Vortex medicine wheel for a brief moment. The wisdom of the ages will pour through and combine with your soul group's energy to transform a boy at the moment of his twelfth birthday to the Essence, the One of prophecy who will save this world."

— FIFTEEN —

Spence's serene composure began to slough like a reptile shedding skin as the shaman spoke. He looked at Rian listening with a rapt expression and seeming to hang on every word the man said.

"Marty is the boy you mean, isn't he?" Rian said to Chevayo and squeezed Spence's hand, her excited touch instantly bringing him back to high awareness and oneness with her.

"Yes, and you know this because you have opened to your soul group memories," the shaman said, then swung his dark gaze to Spence. "You must hang onto your illumination, for it comes under attack even now. The jackal awaits and tries to contact you again. This is why you feel a lowering of your vibration that threatens to drop you into turmoil again."

Spence's higher consciousness immediately validated Chevayo's warning, sensing that a lower energy hovered near, just out of phase, probing for a link-up to his field. "Yeah, that feels like him," he said and strengthened his connection with Rian, returning her loving touch with a gentle pressure on her soft hand in his. But he worried if they'd be able to keep their elevated connection going.

Rays of gold flared in Chevayo's aura. "Life in the earth school is like a river, constantly flowing and changing. Each moment offers choices—to struggle against the current to the past which is gone or try to swim faster than the river into a future not yet arrived. Or one may choose to float along, trusting that the river will take you where you need to go and that all experiences along the course are exactly what your soul has chosen. You must trust your soul, Spence, to know your worth."

The shaman got to the heart of the matter, Spence admitted. Of course, he didn't trust himself. After what he'd done and what had been done to him during this rotten life, trusting himself to do something, anything, right wasn't possible. But the way he was feeling now after the shift in his consciousness, doing the right thing seemed possible.

"It is more than possible, my friend," Chevayo said with solemnity. "You are at the crystalline moment of your destiny, your reason for living this life. See that you perform well, for your soul group depends upon you."

Ordinarily such a "don't screw up" admonition would have fired his defensive anger that he'd then use to forge courage and determination to get the job done. But the anger didn't come. Maybe because he didn't know what he was in for, and he asked, "You talk about my soul group and I'm guessing that Rian," Spence glanced at her, "and I are in this group with Marty and maybe Dorel and Mike?"

Rian stared at the shaman as if she were viewing the face of God. "And you."

Chevayo shook his head with a small grin. "Only in an advisory role." He nodded at Spence. "Yes, the One and those who agreed to be his parents in this life. And there are others playing different roles as well."

Rian put her hand to her mouth and gasped. "Not Ian!"

Chevayo told her yes. "And the one called Roshi, who has returned to the group and offers his help from out-of-body. Even though one chooses to incarnate on the earth or other worlds, their oversoul or higher consciousness remains in the primary grouping of like vibration that you will understand as a soul group. That is a very limited, material way of explaining the exalted spiritual realms known as heaven, paradise, transcendence, Nirvana, Valhalla or the Spiritlands."

A vision arose in Spence's awareness of a group of energetic forms in correspondence grouped in a circle with their backs to him. As he focused on one, the individual turned and Marty's oversoul energy smiled at him. One by one they all turned and greeted him, including his own oversoul. Spence was stunned by his pure spirit that emanated absolute, unconditional love. His body couldn't handle that level of feelings and he began to weep as the last light being turned to greet him. "Oh my God, it's Inada," he gasped.

Spence jolted back into alertness in Rian's comforting embrace. "Shhhh, it's okay," she crooned and stroked his cheek.

"Remember that every soul makes agreements with other souls prior to incarnating to teach and learn. They all play roles for each other for this purpose. And when they return to their soul groups after leaving the body, they are often surprised to find their worst enemy or dearest lover happily greeting them," Chevayo said. "Before I became what you might understand as a guide or a teacher, I experienced a tragic, to me anyway, death as a young warrior," he said with a wry smile. "Mind you, when one is fresh from an earth experience, one is disoriented because you are still vibrating at the lower rate. This passes quickly as one again realizes parity with the higher frequency. In any case, my spirit rose into the Light and I soon found myself surrounded by my soul group. And who should be the first to greet me with loving laughter but my enemy who had ordered my murder." The shaman shrugged and laughed merrily.

Rian grimaced. "I think you took the whole thing rather

well. Don't know that I could have been so accepting of a revelation like that."

"You have had such experiences yourself that you'll recall, if you wish to explore beyond your past lives to your subsequent returns to your soul group. For myself, let me say that when planning for the learning opportunities in that life as a warrior, I chose to learn certain lessons that had to do with sacrifice of self for a greater good. I persuaded my soul group friend to teach me that lesson. Besides, I'd taken a similar role for him, and I say 'him' because his energy signature, in material terms, is primarily masculine, in another of our mutual incarnations. But one forgets these reasons and goals when again born to the earth and the human struggle."

"Rian has told me these kinds of things when working with me on our mutual past lives, but I can't help thinking, as Jonathan Spencer, that if I ain't getting out of here alive, and if life, if you'll pardon the expression, is so great on the other side, why would I choose to come back here?" Spence asked. A shiver dashed over his skin as the freshening evening breeze swirled dust and a couple of dried leaves into the terrace's corners. "Let's go in."

When Chevayo said he preferred to stay outside, Rian said she was okay with it, too. Spence asked if she'd like a jacket and she shook her head. That meant he'd have to tough it out.

"You can light the fireplace," Rian said, pointing to a smaller version of the living room's whitewashed stucco *horno* in the corner. Spence went inside, pulled on his sweater, and grabbed a tiny box of resort stick matches. After he lit the gas log, he turned around, hands behind his back to catch the warmth, and tuned in to what Chevayo was saying to Rian.

"On a material level, few have such an understanding. However, as you know, in the spiritual realms there is no body to feed, clothe or satisfy and no reason to strive against other souls. All have their own lessons to learn and that is what is important," Chevayo said, and threw Spence a compassionate look. "Yours is a soul that always chooses the hard road, filled with strife and sacrifice, because that is the best learning."

Spence sighed. "Man, I'm so tired of that. I must be a masochistic fool to keep doing it the hard way. So I have to ask, when do I smarten up and get to have a kicked-back life?"

"Complete this one well, and there will be no need for you to return," Chevayo said, but Spence thought the shaman didn't look like he thought that was going to happen.

"Chevayo, did Ian abduct Dorel and Mike and can you tell us where they are?" Rian asked. Spence felt like a selfish jerk, thinking of himself when he should have been concerned about his friends.

"They are held unharmed until the initiation tomorrow and will appear at the medicine wheel, as will the One."

"I think what Rian is trying to say is can we rescue them, and Marty, because he's probably being held at the same place, right?" Spence pushed for information that this shaman, or guide, or whatever he was, should know. "We must do something."

"All you can do now is to direct your best efforts to meditation. Observe the silence between breaths. Cherish each blank moment of the practice, for something sacred is about to be brought forth. And you are the key to its birthing," the man advised like a maharishi lecturing a boisterous pupil.

Spence suppressed the tiny wiggle of irritation, thinking that yesterday he'd have demanded a more concrete plan that involved guns and a whole lot of psychic ass-kicking.

Chevayo and Rian laughed, apparently mentally eavesdropping on his self-assessment. She walked to Spence at the fireplace and pecked a kiss on his lips. "Your mind is a thing of wonder, my darling."

"Thanks," he said, "I think." He kissed her back before she moved away to stand by Chevayo.

"You're sure everyone will be there tomorrow night?" she asked, and the shaman nodded, telling her that things were unfolding as they should. Rian wondered aloud what time they should go to the vortex and if they should scout it ahead of time.

"There is no need. I will guide you there at the appointed time," Chevayo answered and glanced up out into the dark, looking like he was getting ready to go. "Beware the dog. He will try to tempt you again. Do not allow him entrance," he said to Spence. To Rian he added, "Let go. Trust that all is as it should be."

Spence half-expected the shaman to spread his arms and launch himself into the darkness like a spirit raven, but Chevayo bid them each goodnight and left by the front door.

Chevayo's departure wasn't the awe-inspiring reassurance that they might have wanted, but it was what it was, Spence concluded, and shut the door.

Marty was playing a game at the new computer when Ian poked his head in the boy's room.

"How's it going with the *Prince of Time* game?" Ian asked. "Is it good? Probably too easy for you, I'll bet."

"No! It's cool. Really hard," Marty exclaimed with his

eyes riveted on the twenty-five-inch flat-panel display less than an arm's length away from his nose. He bobbed and squirmed, punching keys and twisting the joy stick as megawatt speakers on the desk boomed with a bizarre cacophony of computer-generated noises.

"Great, have fun. Just wanted to say goodnight," Ian yelled over the din. "See you tomorrow."

Marty didn't answer and Ian closed the door with a self-satisfied smirk. The game was working perfectly, beyond their expectations, the readouts showed from the sensors on the joystick's grip and various keys. The tiny camera in the monitor recorded the boy's facial expressions and pupil dilation rate while another transmitter beamed a subliminal frequency designed to create new neural pathways in the brain that would change his behavior and responses to certain stimuli. The more Marty played the game, the more control Ian gained over him. Marty would play all night, and Ian would let him, because the programming machine entrained that desire in him and reinforced the behavior with vivid sensory input.

Ian went to the lab to watch Marty on the closed-circuit video feed. He relieved the observer and sat down at the control panel and rubbed his tired eyes, thinking about how he was going to pull his intricate plan together. He only had actual hands-on control of three of the players. Spencer and Rian could prove problematic if they worked together, as unlikely as that was, but he still had to consider that possibility. Tomorrow night just before it was time to go to the medicine wheel, Ian would have Marty semi-anesthetized for transport, along with his parents, until the time for their appearance. Then he'd awaken Marty, telling him that they were in the holodeck, and let it all play out from there.

Ian scowled and pushed back from the panel. He was not

one to leave anything to *play out*.

Anubis had told him not to concern himself with the ritual. And when Rian and Spencer arrived? Or what if they were waiting in ambush for him?

These kinds of variables made Ian nervous. Of course he could retarget the field generator they used on Marty to shield the medicine wheel and block any psychic attempts to stop him, but there were no guarantees it would work against formidable mind mechanics like Spencer and Rian together. Gabrielli might be able to overcome his present drugged state to join his rusty powers with theirs.

Marty would be open and receptive, which he had to be to receive the vast energy aligning to enter him. He could turn his powers against Ian, too.

And what if he couldn't convince the four of them to give up their energy, which no doubt meant their lives, willingly to the boy? Would he have to shoot one of them as an inducement? It wouldn't matter; they'd try to save Marty to the last one standing and try to kill Ian, too, despite the firepower his team trained on them. So, the four die and Marty lives. Then what? Does he receive the cosmic power, wholly, partially? At all?

Too many unknowns and what-ifs. And he still hadn't decided how to deal with Anubis, especially since the entity had proved he could overcome Ian's personal shield.

"Yes, that is true, old crocodile. I go wherever I please and no incarnate former high priest shall stop me," Ian heard Anubis growl as if the entity were materializing in the control room.

Ian sat up and cast his gaze around. An irregular wisp of diaphanous haze floated at shoulder-level five feet from him. He bolted to his feet and backed around the chair, putting it in between him and the materializing entity as he mumbled every chant of protection and warding he could summon.

"Yes, fear. That is the invitation I seek," Anubis said, the haze coming nearer.

"Stop, dark spirit. I cloak myself in light impenetrable," Ian wheezed, all but crossing his forefingers over each other at the entity's advance. His long-harbored doubts and qualms secreted within his body and mind gathered into a long, low undulation and snaked out to the reciprocating force.

Anubis sucked up the terror between them so quickly that Ian felt the invading entity as his own constricted next breath and choked out, "No-o-o."

"I told you not to concern yourself with these particulars. These are not the affairs of priests but of gods. You think to deceive and use a god? That is not possible, for it is I who will use you," Anubis said, hovering within inches of Ian's heart chakra.

"But you need the boy's body and me to help you possess it," Ian argued, desperation shivering in his voice.

"I shall accomplish that as your teeth, old crocodile. As such, I need not concern myself with your artful dance of deception, where you would have the boy's power for your own." Anubis laughed; the sound like knives stabbed at Ian. "And what would you do when the door between worlds opens? Stare in amazement and beg them to sacrifice themselves freely to the One?"

"What about the Swords of Balance? You said they were you, that you have their power. Does that mean you're going to manifest as them or simply be the power that can force them to complete the ritual?" Ian tried to clear the fear from his mind and think quickly. "Then you need me to help you wield them."

"In a different way, yes, since the unexpected has occurred. He who was queen and she the priest sword-maker have reconciled, joined their forces again. Now the breached force of the swords has combined in perfect balance of eternal power. From the Underworld, I commanded the male or dark energies of the Defender Sword of legend, while light or the female force known as the Guardian Sword lay idle. Through time and use, the Defender strength grew until the makers came together again in that life and banished both to the higher realms. Now they have reunited, embodied in the makers, and shall remain theirs as long as they are true to their covenant of balance."

Then Spencer and Rian possessed the vast power swords that he coveted. Ian seethed, gritting his teeth.

"Yes, old crocodile, your teeth are weakened, though not for long, as you will soon see. You must force discord between these two, separate and so weaken their power," Anubis said.

"If they have the power of the swords, technology or direct mental influence or interference can't stop them," Ian cried in despair.

"Perhaps. If the mother or the father were made to anoint the One with their own life force, the two would struggle against each other for retribution—one wishing to exercise the aggressive Defender power that always seeks outlet, while the other presses for peace. So divided, they shall be overcome and their power taken."

"A blood sacrifice?" Ian cried. "You want to kill the parents in front of the boy? How is that going to make the others *willingly* give their energy to him? If you kill any of them when they are in fear, their essence may be captured and infused in the One but will taint or lower his vibration."

"Yes, to that of my realm," Anubis said. "A god must

have a sacrifice, priest, as you well know. And yours shall be the first."

With his next unguarded gasp, Ian sucked the entity into his mouth. His eyes bulged. Lungs stopped and vision twinkled black as his heart paused, squeezing pain into Ian's chest and down his left arm. On the brink of death, his heart pulsed once, then began a slow, arrhythmic beat that spread the ancient dark force of Anubis throughout his body and brain.

Ian became aware of a spreading evil that had consumed his right side and now slowly moved into the left side of his body. He realized he wasn't dispossessed of his body yet, and that some of his soul force still remained.

"Of course, old crocodile," Ian heard inside himself as his own voice. "You are needed to operate this body as well as perform other duties as your god requires."

"But why do this?" Ian cried. "Your power is in the infinite Underworld—"

"My power is drawn from belief, and there are few worshipers in that darkness of late. I want more power, priest. Even you can understand that."

"The moon's coming up," Spence called from the terrace the next night. Though he and Rian had spent the better part of the last twenty hours making love and in meditation together, strengthening themselves, seeing the lemony full moon rise gave him a twinge of edginess. The feeling was probably just excitement or readiness, because he was filled with a true sense of stability and confidence for the first time in his life. Now that he and Rian were together again, nothing could tear them apart; he was certain, because he would die before he'd let that happen.

Rian was more the other half of himself and he her other

half. They were one. Whatever she wanted him to do or be was what he wanted. Their minds were in accord on all things. He had never experienced such harmony and peace in any life, because from the life in which they'd used their love to create the two swords until now, he and Rian had never come to love each other unconditionally. Now that they'd claimed the love of all their past lives, they could focus on building a life together in this one and begin to heal the old soul wounds. It would be as if the Spence and Rian of just two days ago never existed. As if they could change the past as well as their future. And maybe they could.

"I want that, too," Rian said, appearing beside him, and stared at the huge moon. She was dressed in a white turtleneck sweater over black jeans and white tennis shoes. "Though I wonder how our lives will change after tonight." She turned and pulled him around to face her, embracing him with her head on his chest. He stroked her hair down her back and kissed the top of her head.

"Yeah, me too, though I'm getting pretty focused on now, and a couple of hours from now, too. How about you? Okay?"

"Uh-huh, just trying to hold on to my vibe and stay grounded. But I'm so incredibly open that my awareness is expanding almost exponentially, as yours must be too. I feel like I'm going to float off and disappear like Marquez's character in *A Hundred Years of Solitude*, who ascends to heaven while hanging laundry," she said.

"Wow, I'm impressed. You must have been a lit major. I, however, was a simple systems engineer and we don't do books. So I don't know about your obscure literary reference, though taking off to heaven sounds better than doing wash any time," he joked.

She leaned back and gave him a lifted-eyebrow look. "It wasn't a way to get out of doing the laundry. She became so spiritually transformed that she floated away, and people saw her go. So hang onto me, okay?" she said and smacked a kiss on his mouth.

"Gotcha." Spence hugged her tightly. "If you go, I go."

"It is time," Chevayo's voice came to them from below the terrace. They looked over the railing to where he stood, and Rian said they'd be right down. Spence put on his leather jacket while she grabbed a white knitted poncho, pulling it on over her head.

"We're going to have to talk about all this black. Is it time to lighten up a little and lose some hair, too?" she said with a grin and stroked his goatee, then flipped her fingers through his hair on his collar.

"Maybe. Let's just get through this first, then we can talk about makeovers and a key to the condo, okay?" he said, and opened the door. Chevayo surprised them waiting on the pathway.

They descended through the tiers of casitas to the main lodge and by the tennis courts in silence. Once out on the road, they kept to the side and crossed the parking lot adjacent to the Wellness Kiva to a locked gate in a fence that marked the edge of the property. Rian stuck her room keycard in the lockbox, the latch clicked and she pushed it open, Chevayo and Spence following her through to the wood trailhead marker. The bright moon cast a silver sheen over the trail and surrounding brush, washing out the desert tans, reds and green with hues of gray. The dark brown-appearing red rock mesa loomed a hundred yards away and Chevayo started up the trail. After a few minutes of easy walking, they reached the foothills and turned south toward the open end of Encantada Canyon.

Several times Chevayo halted, peered into the darkness and listened carefully, then motioned for them to follow. When he stopped again a few minutes later, he whispered that they'd be going off-trail and free-climbing from here.

"It will not be difficult, but will take longer than the direct trail to the medicine wheel. We want to approach unseen and before the others," he said.

"Won't Ian be able to target us coming in?" Spence asked, staring up at the crotch between two sandstone pillars about a hundred feet above them and a quarter of a mile away.

Chevayo shook his head. "The vortex is chaotic tonight with the incoming unstable shift, and that causes interference for him, and us," he admitted. When Spence started to protest, he added, "We are more or less on equal footing—"

"Yeah, we're blind," Spence hissed.

"And deaf. Remember that Ian is clairaudient," Rian whispered.

Chevayo stepped off the trail over a short clump of sagebrush and began to climb through the huge slabs of rock and boulders on a diagonal that took them around to the back of the mesa. When they'd almost reached the top, Chevayo crouched between boulders and waited for them. Spence gave Rian a hand up and they squatted next to him.

"The first ones are arriving. You will see your friends are among them," Chevayo said, pulling his head back down. Spence inched upwards to put his line of sight just at the edge of the shielding boulder.

A Datascape rapid strike team of five men in desert camouflage eased onto the fifty-foot-wide clearing in a chevron formation, sweeping the area with lights mounted atop automatic weapons, toward the circle of rocks in the middle. Dorel and Mike, hands behind their backs, were prodded along in the middle of the formation by a sixth. Spence had to help Mike and Dorel now.

Chevayo pulled Spence back down. "Control your thoughts. If I can perceive your turmoil, someone else might be able to as well."

"I thought you said there'd be interference and we couldn't get a read on each other," Rian whispered as she crouched by Chevayo.

"There is, but you must remember that you now embody great unified power. To think it is to have it, but within the present conditions it is uncertain what you might create. At the very least, you'll broadcast a wave that may appear as a flaming arrow to our position," Chevayo warned. "You must both control your thoughts."

The shaman crept back up to observe. In a couple of minutes, he sank down and advised them that Dorel and Mike were sitting inside the medicine circle and seemed to be all right. The armed men had taken up positions outside.

"I wonder why Ian and Marty aren't there," Rian said and moved to look over the boulder. "Here they come. Oh! There are two more men walking Marty between them. There's Ian. How strange . . . his aura—"

Chevayo and Spence pulled her back down together. The moonlight may have washed out her complexion but her beautiful face glowed with wonder as she put her fingertips to her mouth.

"What did you see?" Spence whispered and grabbed her trembling hand.

"She has seen the jackal," Chevayo said with a cryptic smile.

— SIXTEEN —

"What does that mean, she's seen the jackal?" Spence said.

Rian saw that he was beginning to be concerned and drew his hand to her lips for a quick kiss of the fingertips. "It's Ian's form or body, but he's barely there. It seems Chevayo is right. The negative energy that appeared to you has possessed Ian." Spence's brow creased with a frown. "I'm not afraid. Just amazed at what I can see and still feel so centered and above it all."

"I don't know that's going to help them much, or that we want to detach from this and do nothing," Spence said.

"It is not inaction that she speaks of, but from a lofty perspective of power, where the emotions and intentions are viewed as different vibrations that may be re-modulated as needed. Trust your skills," Chevayo said, and stood up in plain view of those below.

"There! In the rocks. Come down with your hands up." Rian heard the cry from below and tightened her fingers on Spence's hand.

"Approach this with joy for the One and the earth," Chevayo said to them. Rian and Spence stood up together and followed him down the slope. The lights spotlighting on them as they made their descent made it difficult to see where to put a foot or hand. Chevayo didn't lose his footing, but Spence had to belay Rian's stumbling more than once to keep her from slipping.

When they reached the foot of the slope, five men rushed forward and surrounded them, aiming their weapons at their hearts. Still Rian didn't feel fear, and she sent an encouraging smile to an angry Mike and Dorel, who were clearly terrified for their son, now standing beside Ian in the center of the medicine wheel's concentric rings, outlined with rocks the size of a man's fist.

Her attention focused tighter on Marty. The bright moonlight showed that he wobbled as if he were drunk or drugged, which he must be, because he smiled idiotically from his bound parents to Spence and her. How else would Ian be able to handle Marty except with drugging him? Rian projected a lucid, centered beam of energy to Marty. His dazed expression slid off his face with the stupid smile, as he shook his head and pulled himself up to stand tall and square.

"Marty!" Dorel cried out.

The guard on her jabbed his rifle in her back and barked, "Shut up."

"Ian? What's going on here?" Marty asked with a frown, and started to take a step out of the inner circle of the spoked wheel toward his mother.

Ian's hand whipped out, grabbed his arm and jerked him back. "It's the holodeck, Marty. Relax and let the program run. It's great, you'll see."

Marty shook his head again and rubbed his face, casting a suspicious gaze furtively around them, as Ian announced that he'd created a holodeck program for him after a *Prince of Time* game. Rian flicked a glance at Spence, and he gave an almost imperceptible shake of his head. Chevayo stood in front of her and Spence, as if to shield them. She couldn't see his face, but sensed, as a tiny plume in his aura, a mild interest in the scene unfolding before them.

"The moon comes full, Anubis," Chevayo interrupted and stepped forth, sweeping aside the rifle shoved at him.

"The time is at hand. Move out of the initiate's circle."

Ian swung his head toward him, still holding onto Marty's arm. "Who the hell are you to tell me what to do?" he growled.

Marty looked at Ian in horror, seeming to realize that it was not Ian who spoke.

Chevayo chortled. "Yes, beware the dog, and now you see him for the trickster that he is."

Ian wrenched Marty's arm behind his back and he cried out in pain. Rian cringed at Dorel's scream as she strained against her tied hands. Spence and Mike lunged forward at the same time, blocked by the armed guards, who slammed them backwards. Mike fell into the dirt and Spence against Chevayo, who caught him.

"Do not be deceived by this illusion," Rian heard Chevayo hiss at Spence as he scrambled upright.

"Marty, the trickster has no more power than you give him," Chevayo said, and moved forward again, stepping into the outermost circle. Rian cast a glance at Spence, now held back by his arms. He jerked his head at her. She followed Chevayo and no one stopped her.

"Who are you?" Ian demanded, still holding Marty.

Rian stepped in front of Chevayo. "Let him go, Ian, and move out of the way," she said, the hairs on her arms tingling as if lightning was in the air.

Ian cocked his head at her and struggled to speak. "Don't—go nearer. Kill you," he ground out, shaking his head.

She placed her foot in the next circle, only six feet away from them. Marty twisted his arm out of Ian's grasp and tried to shove him aside, but Ian grabbed his hair, jerking his head back, and put the short barrel of a .38 revolver to his temple. "I'll kill him right here if there's one more move or word out of any of you," he growled, his surly gaze locked on Rian's. Marty tried to break free, but Ian cocked the .38, pressing it harder into his flesh, and told him not to move.

"Put them all right here on their knees," Ian ordered his men and nodded to the edge of the circle where he and Marty stood. The men menaced them with their assault rifles, herding them into a semicircle, and forced them to their knees in the red dirt. Rian saw out of the corner of her eye that the team backed off and took positions outside the medicine wheel, their guns trained on the five of them kneeling at Ian's feet.

They'd shoved Rian down between Mike and Dorel, with Chevayo on one end and Spence on the opposite end, next to Mike. The Gabriellis' terror was palpable as they stared fearfully at their son. Rian's calm detachment perceived everyone's negatively-charged emotions spiking out in every direction, any sense of individual energy signatures unidentifiable, the air was so permeated with noxious thoughts.

Ian smiled up at the full moon that cast a deathly pallor over his wolfish features and swept his evil gaze around the semicircle. "All right then, who wants to be the first to sacrifice themselves to the One?"

"No!" Marty cried, his eyes wide with horror. Ian twisted his handful of red hair until Marty shut his mouth and stood still.

"Those assembled have already agreed to link their energy bodies to his when the door between worlds opens. It is done as a group," Chevayo said quietly from the end of the line. Mike and Dorel looked aghast at the shaman.

"It's all right. Control your thoughts," Rian whispered to them. Mike and Dorel swung their incredulous gazes to her, their minds asking what could they have possibly experienced in the last few days or here tonight that in any way indicated that it would be all right, much less they'd be able to control their fear?

Ian crawled his gaze over them and stopped on Rian. "He asks that I give you a final opportunity to return to him, or me, as it were. Seems the old crocodile wishes his lover and protégé to return and help raise the boy," he said with a nasty laugh and dipped his chin to her. "Well?"

"The One has nothing further of value to learn from you. You have taught him with this experience, as was your agreement," Chevayo said in an even tone.

"What's going on here, Spence? Rian?" Mike interrupted, throwing her and Spence a desperate look.

"Shut up! Or you're first," Ian roared at Mike, then glowered at Rian. "I hear doubt in your thought. He doesn't wish me to say more, but I feel our need for you . . . to help train the boy. And the natural place for one such as you is with your own kind."

"We drive the demon out together," Rian heard Chevayo say in her mind, and realized that Spence heard it, too. "Now."

The three stood as one. The gun blazed. Abruptly, Rian felt the bullet penetrate the chest and her centered wholeness split off. But she realized that it was not she who was shot, when Spence fell face-first into the dirt. Rian's guttural cry went up with Dorel's scream, and she threw herself at Spence, rolling him over. A dark, glistening splotch in the middle of his sweater grew as his eyelids fluttered. She grabbed him out of the dirt, holding him close, willing her own life into him.

"Spence, Spence, please don't leave me," she cried softly into his ear, and drew back to look at him, wiping the blood from the corner of his mouth.

A divine smile illuminated his face as he opened his eyes and drank her in. “Shhhh, it’s okay, Rian. He owed me the favor. Let me go . . . I love you,” he said in a long sigh that trailed off, and he was still.

“Noooo!” Rian keened, rocking his body against hers. She perceived his sparkling spiritual essence rise out of the top of his head, hover lovingly around her like a final embrace, then rise heavenward. And with him went her heart.

A dead coldness rippled over Rian, freezing all emotion to an icy mass that manifested in hard steel against her back. She closed Spence’s sightless eyes with her fingertips, laid him down reverently and straightened his clothes, zipping the jacket over the bloody stain. Rian smoothed her hand over Spence’s hair, brushing it off his now-peaceful face. She leaned over and placed a last, gentle kiss on his cold lips, then got to her feet.

Rian locked her gaze on Ian and reached her right hand over her head into the back of her poncho’s neck. She wrapped her fingers around the handle and pulled out the naked samurai sword. Ian’s expression sharpened, and a collective gasp filled the medicine wheel.

“No, Rian, don’t,” Chevayo yelled, holding out his hand. The men closed in, and Chevayo whirled to the Datascape strike team. He swept his arm at them with the sharp command: “Stop!” A pulsation of plasma separated from Chevayo’s huge aura and enveloped them like a shockwave. The men lowered their weapons and stood as if they were petrified wood figures. Mike and Dorel scrambled to their feet, but Chevayo stopped them.

Rian grabbed the sword’s cord-covered handle with both hands, holding it effortlessly in front of her, the moonlight glinting off the blade. “Let him go,” she said to Ian. “This is between you and me.”

Ian shook his head, pressing the pistol barrel harder into Marty's temple. "Bring me the sword."

She shook her head slowly. "It's mine and I'm going to kill you with it."

"Rian, whatever you might achieve with the sword will only turn to dust in your hands," Chevayo said beside her. She took a step that put him behind her.

"Rian, you can't save Marty with the sword," Dorel called out to her.

"She's right, Rian. Give me the sword. I know how to use the sword, remember? Like I did with all the others he sent after me. He was smart enough not to come after me himself," Mike said behind her.

"No, Michael. You swore not to use the sword ever again," Dorel cried.

"He's got our son, Dorel. Am I just supposed to let him kill my son?" Mike answered, his voice full of anguished rage.

"Listen to them, Rian," Ian said with a reptilian smirk. "You can't hope to actually strike me with that before I put a bullet into his brain, do you?"

Chevayo stepped between her and Ian, his back to her. "This is an ancient feud that will not be settled here. The time for the initiation is at hand. You can feel the vortex changing spin to align with the other dimensions. We must all gather round the boy and open to the incoming energy."

Ian's eyes shifted to Dorel and Mike clamoring at Chevayo. Rian leapt around the shaman and swept the sword in a streak of silver, cleaving Ian's gun hand off at the wrist. The gun discharged in a contraction of the finger on the trigger. Rian sliced the sword upwards as Ian released Marty and grabbed his wrist, screaming. The blow sliced deeply into his side. Marty staggered forward to his parents and Rian stood over the crouching Ian, raising her weapon to take his head.

"No!" Chevayo cried and put a hand on her upraised arm. "That is enough. Anubis deserts the body even now."

Rian watched with disinterest as the aura around Ian contracted to his form like a bodysuit, only to expel a dark jagged smudge out of the top of his head that dissipated in the moonlight.

Ian raised his pain-filled gaze to her. "It wasn't me. I wouldn't have hurt the boy, or you. You must believe that."

She just wanted him dead. "You brought the gun to the party and you killed Spence. End of story."

"We must gather in the center circle," Chevayo said to Marty and his parents, who protested that they didn't understand and should be allowed to run with their son. But the shaman wouldn't allow them to delay, and Marty seemed to understand that he needed to stay, even though he didn't say anything. He simply broke their hold and their bonds. Marty moved to the center of the circle next to Ian, crumpled in the dirt. Chevayo motioned Dorel and Mike to stand on either side and face Marty. He put a hand on Rian's, grasping the sword, and pulled her arms down. She dropped the sword to her right side and let him bring her inside the circle with them. He helped Ian to stand with his arm around him, and they faced Marty, too. Rian locked her eyes on Ian's glassy gaze.

She heard his labored breathing and felt the energy force draining out of him. He was dying. Slowly and in a lot of pain. And face-to-face with the one who killed him. Better yet. His fear fed her and, as if the sword itself wanted to taste him again, she felt it grow warm in her hand.

Chevayo turned his eyes on her. "You will only murder yourself," he warned, and her hand went cold again.

To the others he said, "You all remember your soul agreement this day to commit your spiritual force to bring the One to earth. You wonder at this now, but in moments the door between worlds will open. Complete illumination will descend and the One is initiated with the wisdom of the ages that will come upon all."

"Everyone but Spence," Rian growled, her gaze slipping to the dark form on the ground behind Ian. Her heart broke in a rush of sorrow and loss that nearly knocked her to her knees.

"He was the first, as was his desire, to complete his mission and help you all," Chevayo said with great compassion.

A tearful Marty held out his hand to Rian. Crying softly, Dorel lovingly took her hand, and Mike, tears streaming down his face, slipped his arm around Dorel's shoulder and nodded to Rian. Their outpouring of love washed over her. She gave in to the sorrow wounding her soul and let the tears flow. The sword dropped from her hand, clattering against the ring of stones at her feet, and she reached for Marty's offered hand.

Chevayo shifted his gaze heavenward and began to chant an atonal combination of sound. Their joined auras expanded in a flash of brilliance that lit the area. A pillar of dazzling plasma shot down through their arcing corona and straight into Marty. He was drawn up, lifted off his feet, arms outstretched, into the radiant stream.

Blinded by the light, Rian lowered her eyes to the others gathered around her. Everyone, including Ian, all gazed wide-eyed with rapture at Marty hovering in the emanation above them. Yet their gaze seemed soft-focused, filled with visions of their own, and their faces shone with exaltation. Rian turned her face away at the dreadful realization settling over her like a heavy cloak. She wasn't to share their illumination. Clamping her eyes closed, Rian gritted her teeth against the anguished cry arising from her soul and fisted her hands at her sides, holding her breath.

"Return, spirit, to the healer," Chevayo said, and Rian startled. Only darkness greeted her when she opened her eyes, but she felt his breath on her face.

"I—I can't see you," she said, reaching out a hand. She realized that she was no longer standing, but lying on the ground.

"Soon you will see," he said, and lifted her into a sitting position.

She clutched at his arm, straining to make something out of the blackness in front of her. "I didn't see it. I didn't get the illumination," she sobbed.

"Your vital essence, your soul, felt lost when your soul mate's essence left this plane, so you would not see, because you believe you have lost your equilibrium, your balance. Your whole soul shall be retrieved, and you will see the way again and prepare it for the One," Chevayo told her, but it didn't give her any peace.

"Where am I?" she asked, turning her head as if she might see. She cocked her head and heard shuffled feet and whispering.

"At the medicine wheel still. The team is taking Ian with them. He must protect the One with certain arrangements before he joins your soul mate."

Rian gasped and struggled to stand. "Where's Spence? What about Spence?"

Chevayo helped her get up, but held onto her hand. "They have taken him, too. Ian wished it, to care for his friend's earthly remains."

"No! Ian is our enemy. Why did you let him take Spence from me?" she screamed, but he put a hand over her mouth.

"Shhh, we cannot be discovered here. The initiation has already drawn unwanted attention. We must go." She felt him turn, and he called Mike to help him with her, as if she were some heavy baggage.

"Rian, it's me," Mike said next to her. "I'm going to put my hand under your arm, and we're going to walk you out of here, okay?"

"Mike! Please don't let them take Spence. Please, he's mine. You don't understand; you can't take him away from me again," she begged to the air, as the two held her between them.

Suddenly a hand touched her high on her chest at the base of her throat, filling her with extraordinary warmth and serene well-being. "Spence never left you," Marty's sweet voice said. "His love is right here with every beat of your heart."

Rian gasped a sob and sagged between them, her tears flowing freely and cleansing all the pain and damage from her soul and body. She lifted her face and felt the full moon's glorious rays seep between her eyelids and bring the light of true illumination, a brief glimpse of eternity. And she understood. Rian opened her eyes and saw Marty's glorious face before her, radiant with love and benevolence.

"I can see!" she exclaimed, and tugged her arms free and threw them around Marty. "Thank you, thank you."

"We have to go, Rian," Mike said, putting a hand on her back; and she released Marty, wiping her eyes.

Chevayo and Marty started down the trail with Mike, and Dorel grabbed her hand. "Come on, my friend. Chevayo says he has a lot to tell us."

The trail was so easy it was as if they flew over it. They made it back to the resort in much less time than it took to sneak to the medicine wheel. The pathways were deserted and no guests were about, as they stepped up on the porch and Rian opened the door. Chevayo ushered them into the living room, motioning Mike and Dorel to the sofa with Rian. Marty stood next to him.

"You have each received according to your needs. You now know why you chose this lifetime, to bring the One to the earth," Chevayo began. "Though your soul group mission is achieved, your individual missions to learn and teach are not." He smiled wryly. "Or you would not find yourselves in the body still."

Questions tumbled into Rian's mind, and she glanced at Dorel and Mike. Same there.

Marty walked to his parents and squatted down at their knees. Rian's breath caught with excitement. Something huge was about to happen.

"Mom, Dad, I've got to go with Chevayo," Marty said. Dorel gasped and grabbed his hand, as if to keep him with her. Mike shook his head, throwing a disbelieving glance at the shaman.

"Marty must now learn to become the man who will lead the world into peace," Chevayo said.

"We can teach him," Dorel said, including Rian in her sweeping gaze that went to Chevayo. "At home, where it's safe. You can come to our house, live with us." Marty stood up, kissed his mother and moved back to stand with Chevayo.

"It won't ever be safe for him, will it?" Mike murmured, clenching his hands on his knees.

Chevayo shook his head. "There are those, much more powerful than Ian ever hoped to be, who now know that the One is initiated. They will search the earth for him."

"Won't that mean that they'll still be looking for Dorel and Mike, too?" Rian asked, frowning, then remembered the sword. "Did someone pick it up? My sword? I can protect them with it."

"Disappeared," Mike said with disgust. "That was the first thing I thought of, when you collapsed and Chevayo told Ian to leave. I searched, but it wasn't there."

"Someone must have taken it," Rian exclaimed.

"The sword materialized on Rian's hatred and sorrow. When she let that go, the sword went as well," Chevayo said. "So, to answer your offer of protecting them, yes, you must, but with your skills of healing and mental projection. The three of you must stay together and prepare the way for the One. He is no longer your only son," Chevayo said pointedly to Dorel and Mike. "He is the redeemer the world has been waiting for. You may regret this choice that you made so long ago, but simply remember that you wanted to do this great thing, to take part in this wondrous world transformation. That was the soul view of which you had a glimpse just an hour ago. Think upon it, recall it often. It will grow and continue to encourage you.

"The three of you shall live together, travel the world spreading the news, preparing the minds and hearts of men to receive the One. And, at the ordained time, you will join him," Chevayo said with a delighted smile.

In stunned silence, they stared at Chevayo and Marty for a few moments. Rian took a deep breath, sending the thought of self-sacrifice and acceptance of their shared destiny, that bound them together in an eternal soul trust, to Mike and Dorel. The three of them arose together and embraced Marty.

"Do you feel okay? I don't know if I can let you go," Dorel said, clinging to him.

"I feel fine, Mom," Marty said, kissing her cheek. "Not like I used to, but more alive somehow. Full of energy, I guess." He laughed. "That was quite a download I got. I'm excited, too, but it'll be hard to be away from you and Dad. Rian, too. I'll keep in touch, though." He glanced at Chevayo. "I'll be able to talk to them with my thoughts, won't I?"

Chevayo nodded. "Rian will help them learn to safely communicate with you, too."

"I'll miss you, M-Man. I understand what you've signed on to do, but . . . it's difficult to think of my son going through all that." Mike grimaced and shook his head.

"I know, Dad," Marty said, giving him a hug. "It's just hard right now to understand it all, but you'll remember more and more. I've got to learn and do a lot of stuff, and I guess Chevayo is the only one to teach me. Right now. If I stay with you, then we'll all be in danger and I won't be able to do what I'm supposed to. We'll all be together again . . . soon."

"How soon?" Dorel asked, as Marty stepped out of their embrace. She reached for him, and he held her hand while he kissed Rian on the cheek.

He turned to Chevayo and asked, "Can I come home for the holidays?"

"Not this year, Marty. I want all of you to know that you aren't without help or protection. If at any time you are in need, please, simply bring my name or Marty's to your mind, and we will answer." Chevayo smiled at Rian. "Your balance has returned, and you are not alone. Remember that you and your soul mate are one still."

Marty gave them each a last kiss and personal farewell, then joined Chevayo outside the casita. The three of them watched the shaman and the Essence-in-the-making disappear down the path. Rian perceived her friends' desire to not be left behind. They wanted to run after their son.

Rian felt the same, and more. She'd love to run after her old life, chase it down and fill it with love that she'd been too foolish or selfish to accept or express. Rian Farsante's life had ended tonight at the medicine wheel, and she hadn't realized it until now.

The next morning, as the King Air took off into the rising sun, Rian sat back and watched the desert below disappear beneath the airplane's wings. In the pilot's seat, Mike reached over and took Dorel's hand, guiding it to his lips, and she smiled with love at him.

Rian looked at the empty seat beside her. From the infinite expanse of paradise, Spence's gentle smile shined into her heart and she knew that her soul mate would always be with her. From this moment forward, she would be the reborn Rian Spencer, the perfect balance of an earthly amalgamation of two souls, and dedicate her new life to lovingly preparing the world for the Essence of Trust.

— EPILOGUE —

Hilltop, Blue Water Canyon, Arizona

The grizzled Indian dressed like a cowboy stopped the old jeep at the end of the rutted dirt road. Marty glanced around at the high desert terrain. They were out in the middle of nowhere flats dotted with short, fat evergreens that Chevayo called junipers.

Chevayo shook the man's hand and climbed out of the open four-by-four, motioning to Marty, who jumped out of the back into the chalky dirt. He reached in among the discarded pop cans and other junk and pulled out the big blue-nylon, frameless backpack that Chevayo had given him this morning when they'd left Sedona. He'd stuck his hand in a bush and, like magic, had pulled out the fully-loaded pack. That was the first of many weird events, like the Indian just happening by as they'd reached the top of the northern end of Encantada Canyon.

They watched the jeep disappear back down the empty road. Chevayo told him to shoulder his pack. "The trailhead is over there," he said, jerking his thumb at a clump of skinny bushes and junipers. Marty followed him through the brush and would have fallen, if Chevayo hadn't pulled him back from the edge of a deep canyon that yawned some hundreds of feet below his toes.

"We're going down there?" Marty asked, glancing over the brink and adjusting the straps on his heavy pack.

"Yes, the trail is steep and not used very much, but there are handholds along the way. Just be mindful of each step, where you put your foot, and it will be fine," Chevayo said, and stepped off onto a narrow track that didn't look anything like a trail.

Marty eased himself down to the trail and put his weight on his lead foot. It slipped in the gravel and he got dumped on his butt, sliding along for a couple of feet until he grabbed at a rock sticking out of the sheer wall on one side of the trail.

Chevayo didn't stop and disappeared around the bend. Marty tugged himself to his feet, made sure they were planted before he took a step. No slip. He hurried to catch up with his guide.

After a few minutes, he began to get the rhythm that the trail required and settled into it. The canyon below the switchback trail seemed to stretch for miles, and he wondered if anyone was down there somewhere. He could see some green bunches and thought there might be water, too, the canyon was so deep.

"Yes, there's water, and a falls too, but we're going way beyond that," Chevayo said over his shoulder.

"How far?" Marty asked, feeling thirsty.

"Very," was Chevayo's cryptic reply.

"You haven't told me why we're coming here," Marty said and reached for his water bottle. "Do you want a drink?" The shaman wasn't even wearing a canteen, much less a heavy pack like Marty, who figured he was probably carrying Chevayo's stuff, too. The thought made him kind of smile, and he took a swallow.

"No, thank you. You drink enough, though."

Marty capped the bottle and put it back in the top of the pack. "So, why are we taking this big hike?"

Chevayo stopped and waited. When Marty reached him, he slipped his fingers under the backpack's front straps and lifted. The load temporarily lightened; Marty straightened, looking up at the shaman.

"At the bottom of this canyon there is a sanctuary, a hidden place known to a chosen few. There you will live and learn, until it is time to move along to the next place," Chevayo said.

"Will you stay there, too?" Marty asked, hopeful.

Chevayo nodded. He pulled his fingers from the straps, and the heavy pack ground down on Marty's shoulders. The shaman patted the pack and gave him a wry smile, then turned back onto the trail, striding out.

Jamming his thumbs under the straps and pulling up, Marty shifted the load higher and resumed his trudge down the trail, his knees cushioning each jarring step. Instead of asking the shaman to slow up, he called out, "What's the name of the place we're going?"

"The Secret School," floated back to Marty on the warm desert wind, and he quickened his pace on the difficult path to catch up with his guide.

— ABOUT THE AUTHOR —

MELINDA RUCKER HAYNES likes to pretend that she learned to write fiction as an education research project grant writer, though she assures readers that academia was not where she discovered how to spin tales of eternal love. Her previous writing work has included published education research, technical, informational and entertainment nonfiction prior to *The Eternal Trust* and *Breach of Trust*, her first two novels for Five Star Publishing. Her novels have won numerous awards and the praise of critics and readers alike. *Essence of Trust* is her third novel with Five Star. Visit her Web site at www.melindaruckerhaynes.com.

Gisela Nass

The Molecules of Life

translated from the German by David Jones

World University Library

McGraw-Hill Book Company
New York Toronto

To A. Butenandt

Library of Congress Catalog Card Number: 78–77019

Phototypeset by BAS Printers Limited, Wallop, Hampshire, England
Manufactured by LIBREX, Italy

Contents

Preface

This book is intended for newcomers to the study of the molecules present in organisms. For this reason no attempt has been made to describe fully all that is known of the chemistry and functions of such molecules. Instead I have taken what I believe to be some of the most important themes in biochemistry and have illustrated them with examples. The book therefore describes the part played by molecules in the life of the organism, and chemical details are presented only where they are relevant to the subject.

Where mention is made of experiments and research workers, the reader should bear in mind that other experiments and workers who are not mentioned may have been just as important in leading to a discovery.

For stimulating and interesting discussions I should like to extend my sincere thanks to Walter Berdel, Bernt Linzen, Frederick Neidhardt, Dietrich Paul, Harro Priess, Victor Rudloff, Wilfried Seifert, Widmar Tanner and Gernot Walter.

1 Introduction

I have never had the feeling that a natural explanation devalues or takes the magic from the beauty of nature. On the contrary, the wonder of nature lies precisely here – that it never violates its own laws. The magic of diversity is not reduced one iota by our ability to conceive how it came about.

KONRAD LORENZ

No philosopher or scientist has yet succeeded in defining life comprehensively. All we can do is to list a number of features that are possessed in common by living things. Taken on their own, these features may also be found in inanimate nature, but it is their combined presence that is typical of living things.

There are three very important properties that are possessed by all living things. We shall discuss these at some length in this book, but briefly, these properties take the following form. First, organisms maintain themselves and grow, which they do by breaking down and building up substances within themselves – a process called *metabolism*. Second, organisms must propagate, that is, produce offspring of the same type. This we shall call *identical reproduction*. Third, all living things react to certain changes in their environment in such a way that they survive the change. In other words, living things can *adapt*.

The smallest unit which shows these three properties of life is the living cell. Some organisms, like bacteria, consist of one cell. More complex organisms consist of many cells, each of which shows the three properties of life mentioned above.

Metabolism, identical reproduction and adaptation are broad concepts that tell us little about the molecular processes involved. But with our present knowledge of the chemistry of life we have some idea of how the three properties operate in molecular terms. We realise that the same chemical reactions are often shared among two or three of the three properties of life. Another important point that will become clear is that the same molecular building blocks are found in very different organisms and that these building blocks react in the same ways. Where special properties are possessed by particular organisms we find that there are structures present additional to these basic building blocks.

The concept of adaptation implies the importance of the environment for the organism. The environment consists of all those factors outside the organism which can evoke a response in the organism. Indeed, certain features of the environment are essential for the maintenance and propagation of life. The environment and organism interact in the simplest forms of life – the single-celled organisms – no less than for the most complex organisms, such as man. But each organism reacts to only certain factors in the environment. Some environmental factors, such as sunlight, affect many organisms; other factors affect only certain types of organism. In the following chapters we shall try to relate the needs of a particular organism to its particular environment.

2 A few chemical concepts

It is not possible to gain even a rudimentary idea of the structure and functions of the building blocks of life without some knowledge of the fundamentals of chemistry. We shall consider only a few chemical principles here, enough to provide a frame of reference for describing the chemistry of some phenomena of life. This is necessary because the living organism is built up of the same chemical elements which we find in inanimate nature and in the universe.

It was established long ago that the smallest particles of matter are *atoms*. These were thought to be indivisible, which is what the word *atomos* means in Greek. Later it was found that these particles could be divided into an atomic nucleus and a shell of electrons, and in modern physics the latter can be still further divided and their properties investigated.

There are many different sorts of atoms which make up the chemical *elements* and today we know over a hundred different types. Perhaps more will be discovered in the future. The elements are presented in the form of a periodic table on page 221. All the elements that are important for an organism are known. The atoms of the elements can react and combine with one another to give larger units – the *molecules*. Thus molecules are built up from atoms and, in turn, some of them may react and combine with one another to form larger molecules, or *macromolecules*. Figure 2·1 depicts the build-up of such large units from smaller ones. It is important to understand that all these units – atoms, molecules and macromolecules – are present in the smallest unit of life, the cell, and participate in the vital processes of the cell, and that

2·1 Diagrammatic scheme of the build-up of molecules and macromolecules. Macromolecules actually consist of many more units than is shown here.

molecules or macromolecules possess properties which differ from those of the units from which they are built up. We shall not, however, discuss the forces of the bonds which unite the building blocks of molecules and macromolecules.

It is fundamental that the building blocks of the smallest unit of the organism, the cell, are often energy-rich compounds. Now it has been known for a few decades that all the physical and chemical processes in the universe that we can observe, including those on earth, obey three thermodynamic laws. These laws are given on page 221, and it is only the following simplified outline of the laws that really concerns us. Every energy-rich system tends to break down into a more disordered state. However, the addition of suitable energy from outside the system can hinder the disappearance of organised structures, such as cells, or can enable them to form themselves into functioning units. The tendency of individual molecules or macromolecules to decompose can be

2·2 Energy flow in the living world.

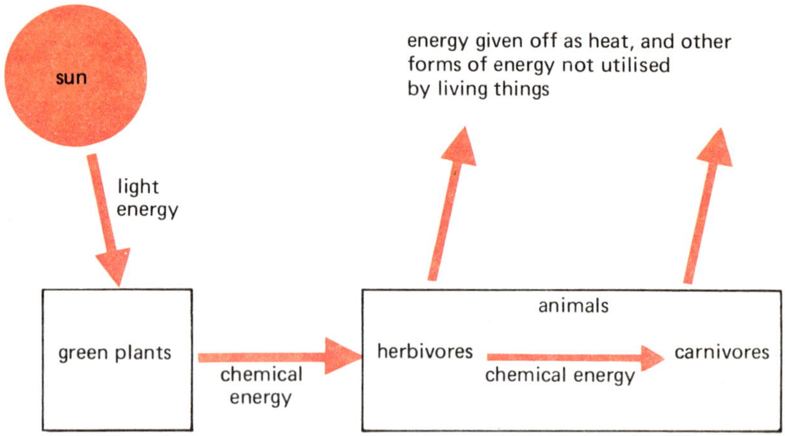

measured and is different for different molecules. It follows that the quantity of energy needed in order to maintain or build up the individual cell components differs for different components.

Figure 2·2 summarises the flow of energy through living things. Note that the energy for the maintenance of life derives ultimately from the sun. Further, the figure shows that only green plants are able to convert the radiant energy of the sun to chemical energy, which can then be used by other organisms for the build-up and maintenance of their cells. The formula of the molecule responsible for 'trapping solar energy' – chlorophyll – is given in the appendix (p.222).

Summary The smallest unit of life – the cell – is, like inanimate matter, composed of atoms which are present largely in the form of molecules or macromolecules. The properties of composite structures, such as molecules, differ from the sum of the properties of their components – the atoms. Many of the cell components are energy-rich compounds and so tend to decompose into units of lesser order and energy. The addition of suitable energy to the organism from its surroundings can prevent the disappearance of cell components and allows new structures to be built up.

3 The bacterial cell as the simplest organism

We shall now examine the structure of the simplest living creature – a unicellular organism. As may be seen from figure 3·1, some one-celled organisms are more complicated than others. The single-celled *Paramecium*, for example, has a larger number of structures than is found in a bacterial cell, such as one belonging to the *coli* group. We have to bear in mind that although single-celled creatures are the simplest forms of life, they differ in complexity among themselves. However, certain structures are common to all types of cells. We shall regard these structures, which are also present in the bacterial cell, as the minimum equipment of the single-celled organism. In this chapter, the structure and functions of these elements of the minimum organism will be explained. The *coli* cell is chosen as an example because it is one of the simplest and most thoroughly investigated of unicellular organisms.

One of the reasons for investigating *coli* bacteria as a model for the simple one-celled organism is that it is possible to culture a very large number of identical *coli* cells in the laboratory within a very short time. This means that we can study the properties of cell components, which are present only in small number in a single *coli* cell, by isolating them from a large number of identical *coli* cells and observing their properties. Also, *coli* cells do not cause disease, either in man or in most other organisms. They live in the intestine of various organisms without causing injury to the host, and occasionally they are advantageous, since they help in the degradation of residual food in the intestines. They also deposit vitamins in

3·1 The structures of bacteria and *Paramecium* visible under the light microscope at an approximately one thousand-fold magnification. *Paramecium* is a very complex unicellular organism, and contains structures which are also found in the cells of multicellular animals. These structures permit specialised functions to be carried out inside a single cell.

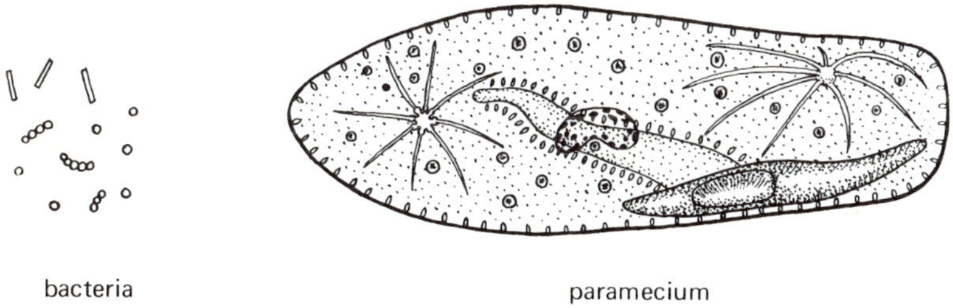

the intestines which can be absorbed and used by the host.

First we shall outline the morphological and chemical structure of the *coli* cell, of which an electron microscope picture is shown in figure 3·2. The magnification of 32,000 reveals the details of the cell. In the following description of the components of the *coli* cell it will become clear that there is no sharp dividing line between the morphology and the chemistry of the cell. Individual molecules also have a spatial structure and the shape of visible structures is conditioned by the spatial arrangement of the molecules which compose them. Our present knowledge of the constitution of cells has been attained by combining the discoveries of morphologists and biochemists who have worked in this field for many decades.

3·2 Electron micrograph of a *coli* cell. The approximately 32,000-fold magnification allows us to discern some of the macromolecular structures of the cell, such as deoxyribonucleic acid and ribosomes. The diagram identifies some of the structures visible in the micrograph.

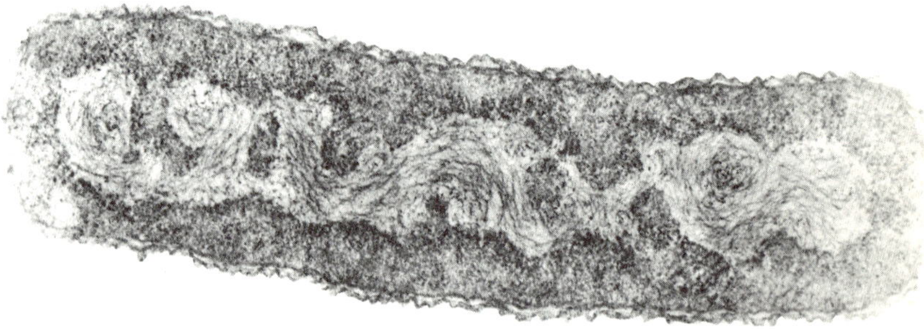

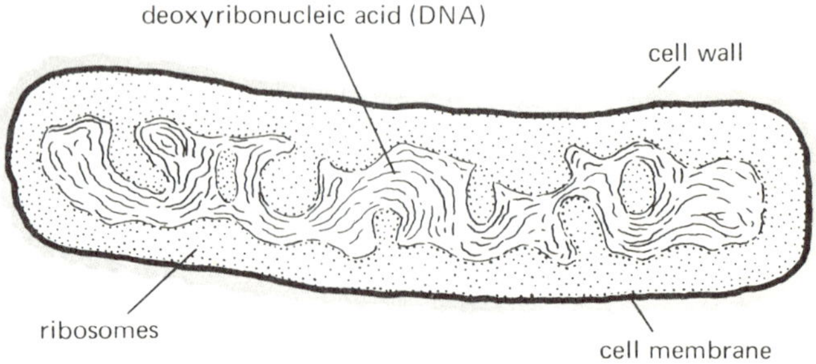

The electron miscoscope picture of the *coli* cell shows that the cell is separated from its surroundings by a cell wall and inside this, a cell membrane. Within the cell, the molecules and macromolecules are of a characteristic type and number. Not only is the type of these components the same in simple unicellular organisms but the number of each component is constant and characteristic of *coli* cells. Several of the macromolecular structures, such as ribosomes and deoxyribonucleic acids, are visible under the electron microscope. However, many of the components have no recognisable structure and form the 'liquid' parts of the cytoplasm.

An analytical chemist could describe the *coli* cell by enumerating the type and number of atoms which can be isolated from it or from its components. But the resulting table would not show the essential properties of the cell since most of the atoms of the cell are present in the form of molecules and macromolecules, and as explained in chapter 2, the properties of molecules differ from the sum of the properties of their constituent atoms. A list of the number and type of molecules and macromolecules in the *coli* cell gives much more information about its properties (table 3.1). Additional information is obtained when the composition of the cell is tabulated, not in terms of atoms and molecules, but according to its functional units, as in table 3·2. In this table, only those functional units are listed which are important for our further understanding of the chemical processes of the cell; it is not meant to be comprehensive. There are many other functional units or building blocks in the cell, for example the trace

Table 3·1 Molecules and macromolecules in a *coli* cell

(Modified from J. D. Watson in *Molecular Biology of the Gene,* W.A. Benjamin Inc., New York, 1965)

component	percentage of cell weight	approximate number per cell	number of somewhat modified forms
water	70	4×10^{10}	1
salts	1	$2{\cdot}5 \times 10^{8}$	20
carbohydrates	3	2×10^{8}	200
amino acids and their precursors	0·4	3×10^{7}	100
nucleotides and their precursors	0·4	$1{\cdot}2 \times 10^{7}$	200
fats (lipids)	2	$2{\cdot}5 \times 10^{7}$	50
other molecules (decomposition products, etc)	0·2	$1{\cdot}5 \times 10^{7}$	
proteins	15	10^{6}	2000–3000
Nucleic Acids			
deoxyribonucleic acid (DNA)	1	4	1
ribonucleic acid (RNA)	6		
ribosome-RNA		6×10^{4}	2
transfer-RNA		4×10^{5}	40
messenger-RNA		10^{3}	1000

Table 3·2 Some functional units of the *coli* cell

unit	functions	macromolecular components
cell membrane and cell wall	selective boundary between the cells and its environment	phospholipids, proteins, polysaccharides
chromosome	determines all the possible vital phenomena of the cell	deoxyribonucleic acid
ribosomes	site of protein synthesis	ribonucleic acid, proteins
messenger-RNA transfer-RNA	indispensable participants in protein synthesis	ribonucleic acid
enzymes	catalyse many chemical reactions of the cell, such as the build-up of macro-molecules and their building blocks, or the conversion of food-stuffs for gaining energy	proteins

elements iron and magnesium, and these are not listed in the table although they are essential for many important reactions. We shall occasionally have to refer to tables 3·1 and 3·2 and gradually their significance will become clearer.

Returning to the *coli* cell, the cell wall and cell membrane (figure 3·2) separate the *coli* cell from its environment, and these two layers are made up of characteristic components. Their function is to control the exchange of molecules between the cell interior and the environment. The ribosomes are

Table 3·3 Minimal environmental conditions for the growth of *coli* cells

(Modified from J. D. Watson in *Molecular Biology of the Gene,* W. A. Benjamin Inc., New York, 1965)

substance	**quantity**
ammonium chloride	1·0 g
magnesium sulphate	0·15 g
potassium dihydrogen phosphate	3·0 g
disodium hydrogen phosphate	6·0 g
glucose	40·0 g
water	1 litre

The necessary traces of certain ions such as iron are contained in water. Oxygen is obtained from the air.

visible in the interior of the cell, and play an essential part in the maintenance of the cell since they help in the synthesis of protein. One can also make out the chromosome, which determines all the possible reactions and properties of the cell.

This description of the elements of the *coli* cell that are visible with the electron microscope is incomplete, and is merely intended as an introduction to the next chapter, which gives a more detailed explanation of the interrelations of the functional units of the *coli* cell and their properties.

There is one more thing to add to what has been said about the composition of the environment of the *coli* cells. The maintenance and propagation of life is possible only in an environment which is characteristic for each organism. Just as the *coli* cell may be regarded as an example of the simplest form of life, so its essential environment is composed of relatively few factors. Table 3·3 shows the minimum environment necessary for the maintenance and propagation of *coli* cells. It consists of certain salts, oxygen, a nitrogen and a carbon source, all dissolved in water. The carbon source also supplies energy to the cell, as is described in the next chapter.

Summary The *coli* cell is an example of the simplest organism. Some of its structures are visible under the electron microscope. Other components of *coli* cells are also mentioned, and their role in the vital processes of the *coli* cell will be described in the next chapter. Other bacteria and simple one-celled organisms have structures resembling those of the *coli* cell. For these simple organisms, the same functions depend on the same chemical components and their similar spatial arrangement. It is only with the differentiated multicellular organisms that the same function can be attributed to more than one type of chemical structure.

4 Energy and the synthesis of the building blocks of macromolecules

ATP as an energy store and supplier of energy to the cell

In the second chapter we said that cells, or rather their building blocks, are energy-rich systems of high order and that they tend to break down into components of lower energy. It was also mentioned that the intake of energy from the environment can prevent this decomposition of the cells. We shall now look more closely at the form in which energy is supplied to the cell, how it is stored there, and how it is used. Once again the *coli* cell will be used as an example. Table 3·3 shows the environmental conditions which the *coli* cell exploits for its maintenance and propagation. Of the environmental factors listed, the only molecule which can supply energy to the cell is the sugar molecule, glucose, this being an energy-rich compound. In order that the energy contained in the glucose molecule may become available to the cell, the glucose must undergo a step-wise degradation. In this process, a characteristic series of energy-poorer molecules are produced from the glucose and the energy which is set free is partly captured by ADP molecules, leading to the formation of energy-rich ATP molecules. The chemical structure of ATP is given in the appendix (p. 223). If no oxygen is available in the cell, then the following reaction occurs:

$$1 \text{ glucose} + 2 \text{ phosphate} + 2 \text{ ADP} \rightarrow 2 \text{ lactic acid} + 2 \text{ ATP}$$

This reaction summarises eleven individual steps and thus neglects the real complexity of the reaction; the details of the

4·1 The build-up of more complex structures from simpler molecules in the *coli* cell. Only a few examples are given of each category.

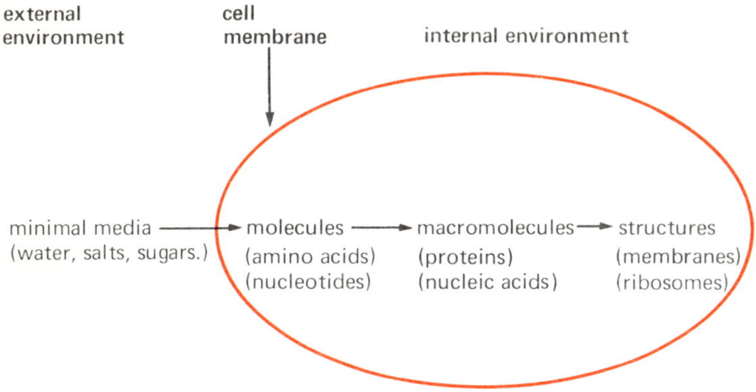

reaction are given on p. 224. It is only one example of several possible pathways occurring in various cells for obtaining energy from energy-rich compounds such as glucose and for storing energy in a form which may be used by the cell, that is, as ATP. If oxygen is available in the cell, then other routes may be adopted for the break-down of glucose and the production of ATP; the glucose may be degraded to carbon dioxide and water with the production of a maximum of thirty-eight molecules of ATP. One of these routes for the oxygen-consuming degradation of glucose is shown on p 225.

The building blocks of macromolecules

Figure 4·1 shows the hierarchy of the building blocks of the cells mentioned in chapter 2. From this diagram it may be seen that the molecules absorbed by *coli* cells from their en-

Table 4·1 Types of macromolecule present in the *coli* cell

type of building block	number of similar building blocks	macromolecule
amino acid	20	proteins
ribonucleotide	more than 4	ribonucleic acids
deoxyribonucleotide	4	deoxyribonucleic acids
simple sugars	more than 10	polysaccharides

vironment are converted into the building blocks of macromolecules. The production of the necessary molecules involves several intermediate stages.

Before passing on to one of the many possible routes of synthesis, we must first deal in more detail with the macromolecules present in the cell and their building blocks. Table 4·1 summarises the important macromolecules in the *coli* cell and their building blocks. In the main, each type of macromolecule is formed by the bonding together of identical building blocks, characteristic of the macromolecule concerned. The synthesis of macromolecules from their building blocks will be described in more detail in the next chapter. For the present, it is enough to say that there are three classes of macromolecules – the proteins, the nucleic acids and the polysaccharides. The proteins are made up of amino acids, the nucleic acids of nucleotides and the polysaccharides

of sugars. The chemical structures of the twenty building blocks of the proteins, the amino acids, and of the eight building blocks of the nucleic acids are given on pp.226–9. However, the principles involved in the composition of macromolecules may be understood without a knowledge of the chemistry of the individual building blocks. As indicated in figure 4·1, the building blocks are built up from the molecules of the environment and ATP is consumed in the process.

There is a specific route for the synthesis of each of the twenty building blocks of proteins, each proceeding via several intermediate compounds. This is equally true of the building blocks of other macromolecules. Figure 4·2 outlines the synthesis of one of the protein building blocks, histidine, and the appendix (p.231) shows its synthesis in greater detail, with the chemical formulae. The simplified scheme in figure 4·2 shows that this protein building block is synthesised in the cell via several intermediate stages and that the necessary energy is supplied by ATP.

Enzyme catalysis in reaction series

The stages in the conversion of glucose into molecules of lower energy, whereby ATP is formed from ADP, or into the formation of the building blocks of macromolecules, would be very slow if it were not for the presence of molecules which accelerate these reactions. These are the *enzymes*. They are proteins, and accelerate chemical reactions by bonding with the reaction partners, the reactants. When the reaction has

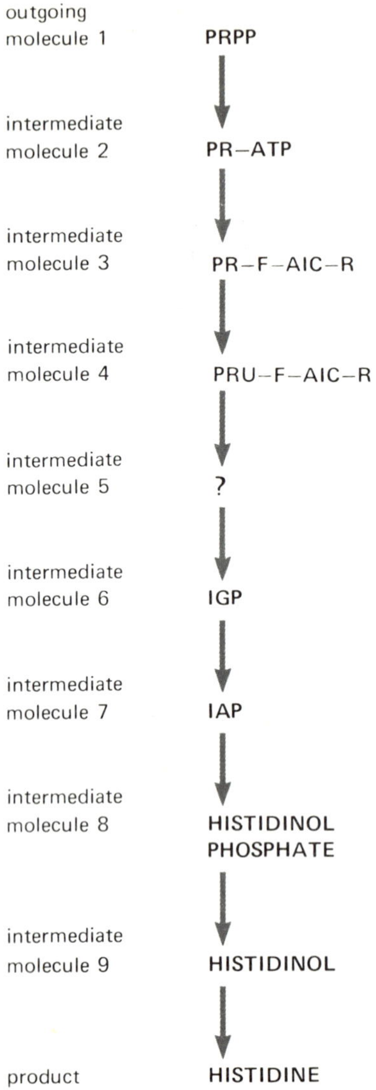

4·2 Synthesis of a protein building block, the amino acid histidine. A precursor molecule undergoes a characteristic sequence of stepwise changes. (The letters are the abbreviations of the intermediate compounds). Such a sequence could be drawn for the syntheses of other building blocks of molecules, but the number and type of intermediates would be different.

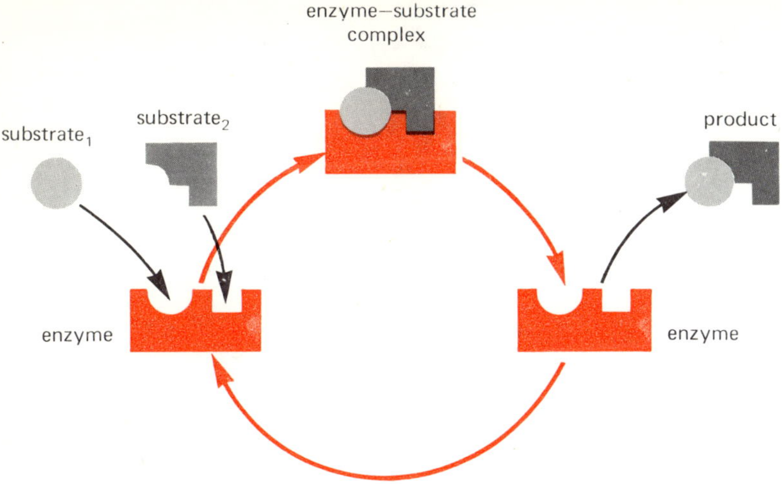

4·3 Diagrammatic illustration of how enzymes work. The reversible bonding of the substrates to their corresponding enzyme allows for a faster conversion of the substrates to the product.

taken place the products detach themselves from the enzyme. Molecules which attach themselves to enzymes and are converted are called *substrates,* the converted molecules the *products*. Following the conversion of the substrate to the corresponding products, the enzyme remains unchanged and is available for reaction with other molecules of the same type. The conversion of molecules by enzymes is shown schematically in figure 4·3.

The bonding of the reactants to the enzyme is highly specific and a different enzyme is responsible for each reaction. Thus, in a *coli* cell, there will be several hundred specific protein catalysts; their formation and structure will be described in the next chapter. From what has been said, the reactions for the synthesis of the building blocks of macromolecules shown

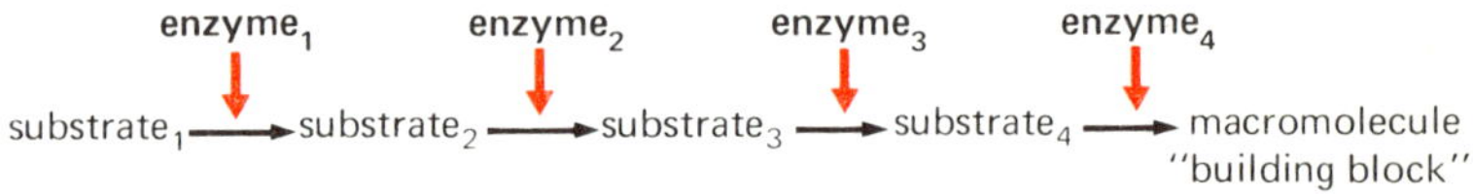

4·4 Each step in a series of reactions leading to the synthesis of a macromolecule is catalysed by a different enzyme. The product of one step becomes the substrate for the next.

in figure 4·2 are actually incomplete for they do not show the enzymes which give the reactions the velocity necessary for the maintenance of life. Figure 4·4 is a better way of representing the actual processes taking place in a chain of reactions in the cell.

The imaginative and intensive research of many scientists over the last few decades has resulted in our present knowledge of several of the chains of reactions for the build-up or degradation of cell components; we also know the relevant enzymes. In 1897 H. Buchner managed to initiate the reactions for the build-up of a cell molecule outside the cell, in a test-tube. He isolated enzymes from cells and added these to their substrates. The result was surprising in that it showed that reactions, either individually or consecutively, resulting in the

degradation of glucose or in the synthesis of building blocks of macromolecules could happen *outside* the cell.

We have seen that cells must acquire energy from the environment in order to prevent the loss of energy-rich components. ATP is the molecule which stores energy, and supplies it to the cell. This seems to be the right moment to explain what is meant by this 'loss' of molecules and structures of the cell. If we observe a resting *coli* cell over a long period of time it always presents the same picture. However, if we observed the individual molecules or structures we should find that they decay and are replaced by new molecules of the same type. This continuous build-up and degradation of molecules may be followed by supplying the cell with radioactively 'labelled' foodstuffs. To determine the life-span of components of the organism by using 'labelled' foodstuffs was the idea of G. von Hevesy. He used molecules labelled with a radioactive atom – that is, an atom which emits radiation. In this way von Hevesy followed the uptake of the labelled molecules into the cells, their incorporation into various structures and the subsequent decomposition of the structures followed by the discharge of the degradation products into the environment. The same method showed that individual cell molecules and structures survive for a time which is characteristic for each type. The fact that a cell does not appear to change over a given time is due to the equal rate of build-up and degradation of its components. In other words cells are in a state of dynamic equilibrium; they always present us with the same picture; however, the

structures and their building blocks are not the same ones but identical copies of each other.

Summary The ATP molecule is central to the storage and supply of energy in all cells. It provides energy for the build-up of molecules and macromolecules and during the process is converted into ADP and phosphate.

The building blocks of macromolecules are formed from foods via several characteristic reactions. These reactions proceed with the velocity necessary for life because they are accelerated by catalysts called enzymes. Characteristic series of reactions for the build-up or degradation of cell components operate in the cell and each step in such a chain is catalysed by a specific enzyme. These are the basic chemical requirements for *metabolism* – one of the three properties of life mentioned in the first chapter concerned with the maintenance and growth of a cell.

The fact that reactions may also be performed outside the cell, in a test tube, by addition of the substrates to the corresponding enzyme isolated from cells, shows that for metabolism it is not essential that the cell is intact.

5 The structure, function and synthesis of macromolecules

Now we must consider how the macromolecules are produced from the building blocks described in chapter 4. Table 4·1 shows that three important groups of macromolecules are present in the *coli* cell – the proteins, the nucleic acids, and the polysaccharides. Each of these macromolecules is composed of a definite number of similar units linked together in a definite order by many bonds of the same type. The function of each macromolecule is determined both by the number of its units and by the sequential order of these units. However, each type of macromolecule has a different function and they are produced in different ways inside the cell.

Deoxyribonucleic acid (DNA)

The units of DNA are four deoxyribonucleotides. As shown in figure 5·1, these units are made up from three types of molecule and the units differ only in the presence of the *bases*, symbolised by the letters A, C, T, G.

It is the DNA molecules of the cells which determine the properties of the organism. This conclusion is based on the experiments made by O. Avery, C. MacLeod and M. McCarty in 1944. They isolated DNA from bacteria which formed a smooth cell colony and added it to a culture of bacteria with a rough cell colony. The recipient bacteria took up the DNA and their cell colonies became smooth. Other macromolecules isolated from the cell, such as proteins or polysaccharides, cannot convey properties from one type of bacteria to other cells. How DNA controls the properties of the cell

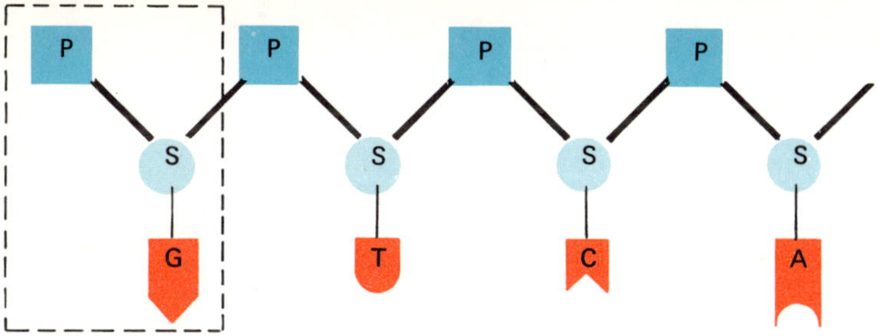

5·1 Above The composition of a DNA molecule. Four bases are linked to a backbone of alternating sugar and phosphate molecules. The box encloses a DNA building block, a nucleotide, which consists of a phosphate, a sugar and a base.

5·2 Right The structure of biologically active DNA, which is present in cells as a double-stranded helix. Because of the energy properties and the spatial characteristics of the bases in DNA, linkages are formed between each two bases of the two strands, causing the latter to assume the double helix configuration.

Far Right The replication of DNA. The two strands separate, and complementary nucleotides attach themselves to both strands by means of base pairing. Subsequent linking of these nucleotides gives rise to two new DNA double helices. The sequences of the nucleotides of the new DNA double helices are identical with those of the original helix. Each new DNA double helix consists of one DNA strand from the original double helix and one newly synthesised strand.

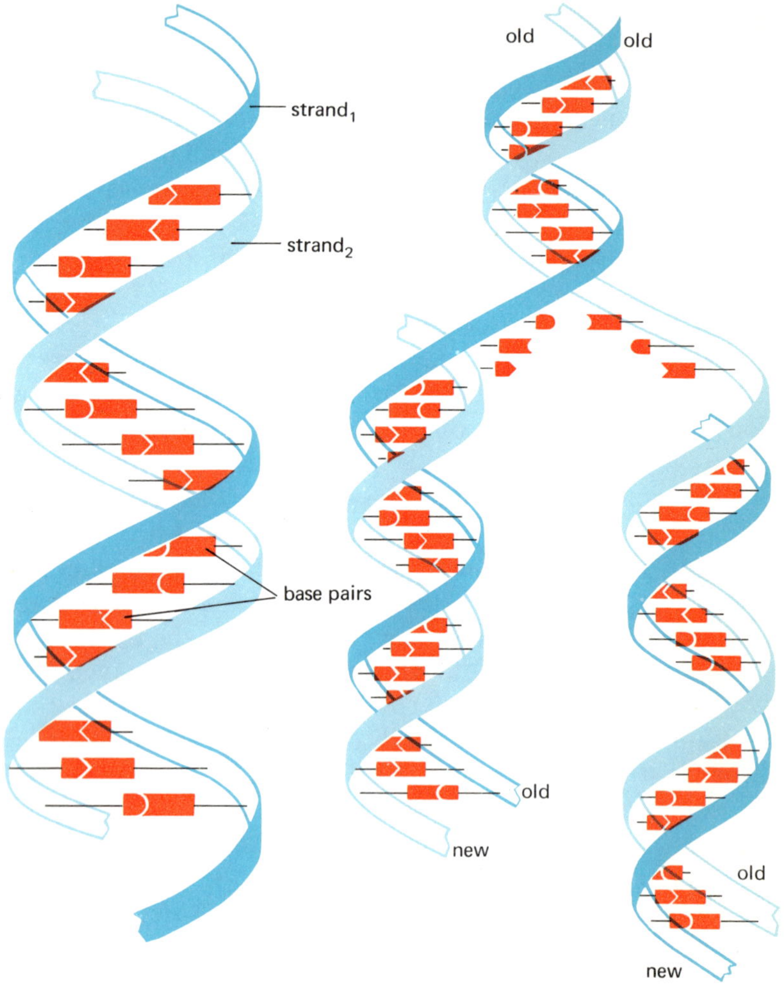
strand$_1$
strand$_2$
base pairs
old
old
old
new
old
new

will be explained in the next chapter.

Experiments by other research groups then showed that alteration or exchange of one single unit in a long DNA molecule can bring about the loss of a particular cell property. We now know that it is the sequential order of the component units in DNA that determines the properties of cells.

This conclusion prompts us to ask how new yet identical DNA molecules are formed during the reproduction of *coli* cells, since if the sequential order of the units of DNA determines the properties of the cells, then cells with the same properties must possess identical DNA molecules. In order to understand the replication of DNA we shall first take a closer look at its structure. In the cell, DNA is not present as simple threads but in the form of a helical double-strand (figure 5·2). This structure was predicted by J. Watson and F. Crick in 1953 on the basis of the chemical and physical properties of the four units of DNA, and it has since become a well-established fact. As figure 5·2 shows, the four components are always paired, so that the base A is linked to the base T and C with G. The shape of the units is such that the linkage of A with T and C with G produces a helix in which the two DNA molecules are twined around one another at a uniform distance; the backbone of the helix is made up of the sugar-phosphate part of the building units and the bases of the pairs A-T and C-G are opposite one another on the inside. This structure of the DNA molecule inside the cell means that not only does the sequential order of the units determine the properties of the cell, it means that once the order of the units

in one of the DNA strands has evolved, the order of the units in the second strand is fixed. The DNA strands are complementary to one another.

Our knowledge of this structure of DNA allows us to say a little about the processes which take place during its replication. The two complementary strands become separated and free units of DNA may now attach themselves to the corresponding units of the DNA strands and are there coupled together. When this process – separation of the complementary strands, attachment of new building units by the pairing of A with T and of C with G, and finally coupling of these units to form a new DNA strand – has taken place over the whole DNA molecule (figure 5·2), we then have two DNA double helices, each of which contains a newly synthesised strand. The experimental proof of this mode of DNA replication was obtained in 1958 by M. Meselson and F. Stahl, who followed the course of the regeneration of labelled DNA molecules. The presentation of cell replication of DNA shown in figure 5·2 does not include the other essentials for the reaction, such as energy sources and enzymes.

In 1967 A.Kornberg and his team were able to conduct the replication of DNA molecules outside the cell, in a test tube. They isolated the necessary factors from cells and then put them together. The DNA produced in the test tube was biologically active, that is, it made other cells perform certain functions according to the sequential order of its units.

Summary The DNA macromolecules of a cell are made up of four units and the sequential order of these determines the properties of the cell. DNA is present in the cell in the form of a double helix. This structure results from the tendency of the four different units to pair up opposite one another. This base-pairing also makes possible the replication of the DNA molecules, a prerequisite for the transmission of identical properties from one cell to its descendents.

The synthesis of biologically active DNA *in vitro* is further proof that individual characteristics of life such as the replication of DNA are not restricted to intact cells.

Ribonucleic acids (RNA)

In some respects the structure of ribonucleic acid resembles that of deoxyribonucleic acid. Most ribonucleic acids (RNA) contain four building blocks, and like deoxyribonucleic acid, they consist of three parts. The sugar is different from that in DNA; the phosphate part and three of the bases (A, C, G,) are identical, while the fourth base of the RNA-building blocks (U) has a somewhat different structure (see p.229) from its DNA counterpart (T). In addition, the manner of linking the building units to form macromolecular RNA corresponds with that for DNA so that we may assume that a stretched-out ribonucleic acid molecule has the structure shown in figure 5·1. None of the RNA molecules exhibit the helical double stranded structure of DNA. Ribonucleic acids in cells are classed into three groups according to their function.

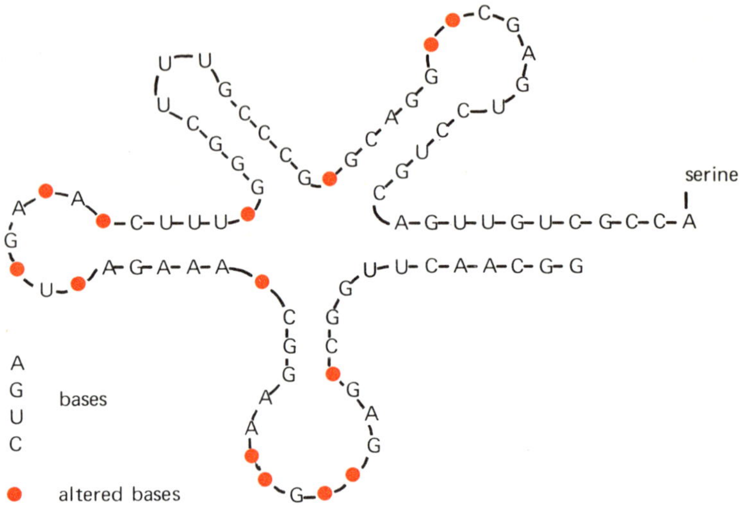

5·3 The sequence of building blocks and the folded arrangement of a serine transfer-RNA from yeast cells. The letters A,C,U and G are symbols for the bases of RNA. Note that some of the nucleotides contain other, so-called rare bases.

The structures of the soluble ribonucleic acids are the best known. In recent years R. Holley and H. Zachau and their research group have worked out the nature and sequential order of the building blocks of three of the soluble transfer-ribonucleic acids, of which more than sixty are known. Figures 5·3 shows the structure of serine transfer-RNA. As yet little is known of the sequential order of the building blocks in the other two ribonucleic acids, messenger-RNA and ribosomal-RNA. Their functions will become apparent when

we describe protein synthesis.

As will be seen from the way in which RNA molecules are formed in the cell, the sequential order of the building blocks of RNA is determined by the DNA of the cell. In many respects the synthesis of RNA resembles DNA replication; using the mechanism for base-pairing described earlier, complementary building blocks of RNA attach themselves to certain sites on the DNA and these units are then linked together with the aid of a certain enzyme which is different from that involved in the replication of DNA. How the choice of the DNA strand for making the RNA copy is made, whether the two strands have to separate in the process and how the beginning and end of the RNA copy on the long DNA molecule are determined are questions which are at present being studied in many laboratories.

Proteins

The building blocks of proteins are the amino acids and the structure of the twenty different amino acids are given in the appendix (p. 226). The properties of proteins are determined by the number and sequential order of their building blocks. The change of only one amino acid in a chain of more than a hundred can destroy or change the function of a protein.

As yet, the entire amino acid sequence is known for only a few proteins. Figure 5·4 shows the sequential order of the amino acids in the protein lysozyme, an enzyme which can be isolated in large quantities from the white of hen's eggs.

Just as with the nucleic acids, proteins in the cell do not exist as extended threads but as three dimensional spatial structures, each characteristic of a particular protein. This is shown schematically in figure 5·5. This figure also shows that several spatially arranged protein molecules can join with one another to form compound macromolecules. This behaviour is characteristic of proteins.

The amino acid sequence of the protein chains determines their spatial structure and their association to form compound macromolecules, for which process no energy need be supplied from outside the system. In the case of the enzyme lysozyme, its enzymatic property is performed by a single, folded protein chain; other enzymes function only if they are made up of a number of associated protein chains. We shall learn more about this in chapter 8. Figure 5·6 shows a model of the structure of active lysozyme. Following the development of very difficult techniques, such as X-ray structural analysis (see p. 219), it has also been possible to determine the position in the molecule to which the appropriate substrate is attached. This is indicated by the arrow in figure 5·6. Figure 5·7 shows the atomic structure of the model. These techniques have also shown that the three dimensional structure of lysozyme undergoes characteristic changes when acting as an enzyme (see also chapter 8).

If several folded protein chains associate to form a complex protein, the molecule ultimately becomes large enough to be visible at a 160,000-fold magnification using the electron microscope. Figure 5·8 shows the electron microscope picture of

1 10
lys — val — phe — gly — arg — cys — glu — leu — ala — ala — ala — met

20
ser — tyr — gly — arg — tyr — asn — asp — leu — gly — his — arg — lys

30
leu — gly — asn — try — val — cys — ala — ala — lys — phe — glu — ser

40
asp — thr — asn — arg — asn — thr — ala — gln — thr — asn — phe — asn

50 60
gly — ser — thr — asp — tyr — gly — ile — leu — gln — ile — asn — ser

70
ser — gly — pro — thr — arg — gly — asn — asp — cys — try — try — arg

80
arg — asn — leu — cys — asn — ile — pro — cys — ser — ala — leu — leu

90
lys — ala — cys — asn — val — ser — ala — thr — ile — asp — ser — ser

100
lys — ile — val — ser — asp — gly — asp — gly — met — asn — ala — try

120 110
val — asp — thr — gly — lys — cys — arg — asn — arg — try — ala — val

129
gln — ala — try — ile — arg — gly — cys — arg — leu

5·4 Left The sequential order of amino acids in a protein – the enzyme lysozyme. The twenty different amino acids are represented by the first three letters of their names. This protein consists of a characteristic sequence of 129 amino acids.

5·5 Below Diagrammatic representation of the build-up of enzymes.

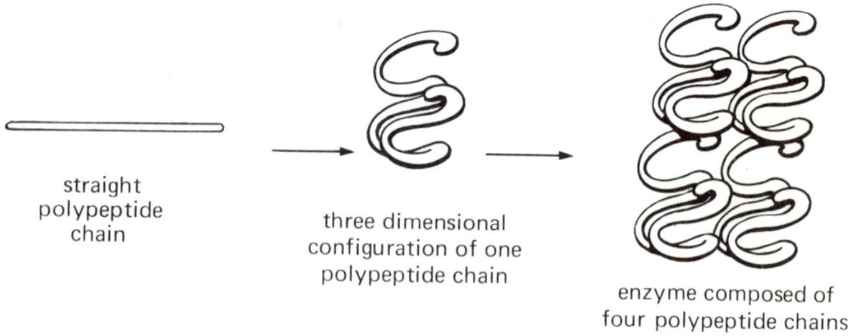

5·6 A three-dimensional model of active lysozyme to show the arrangement of the atoms. The red spheres represent oxygen atoms which participate in cleavage of the substrate.

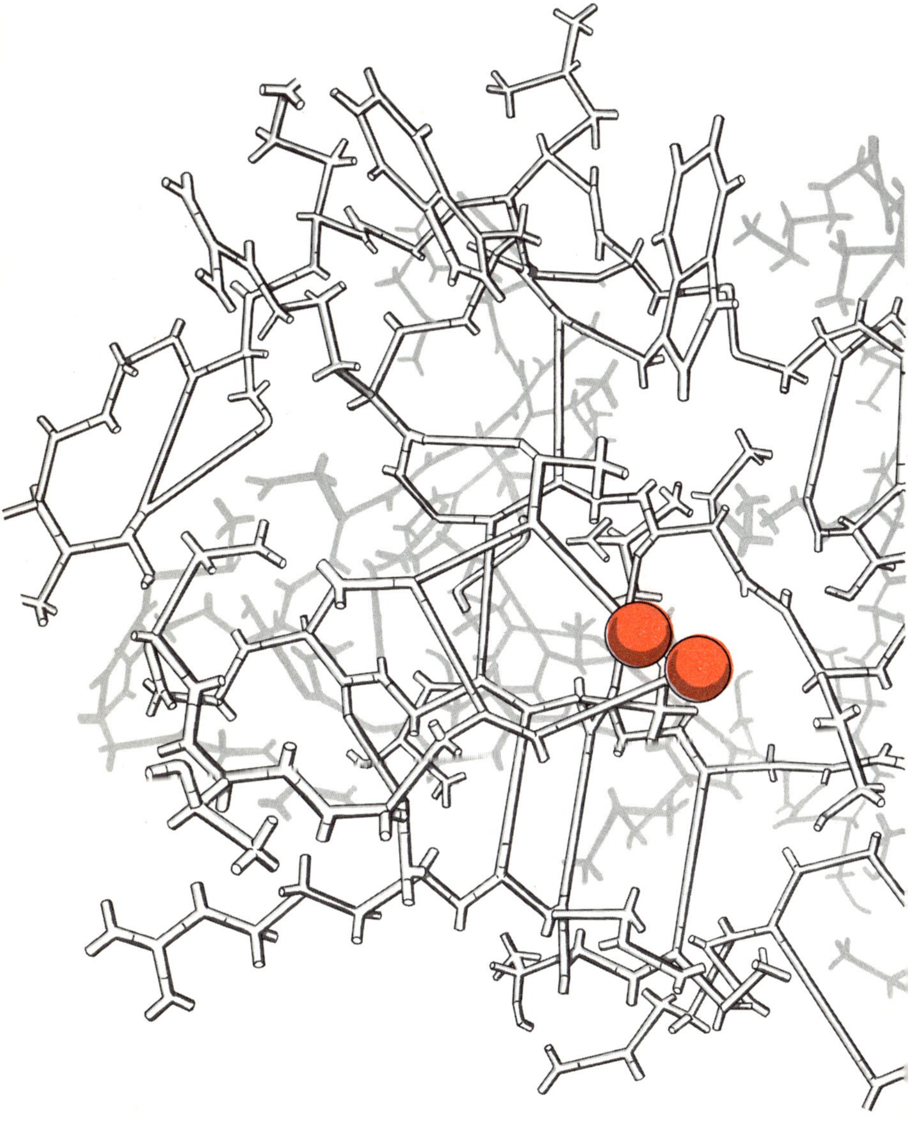

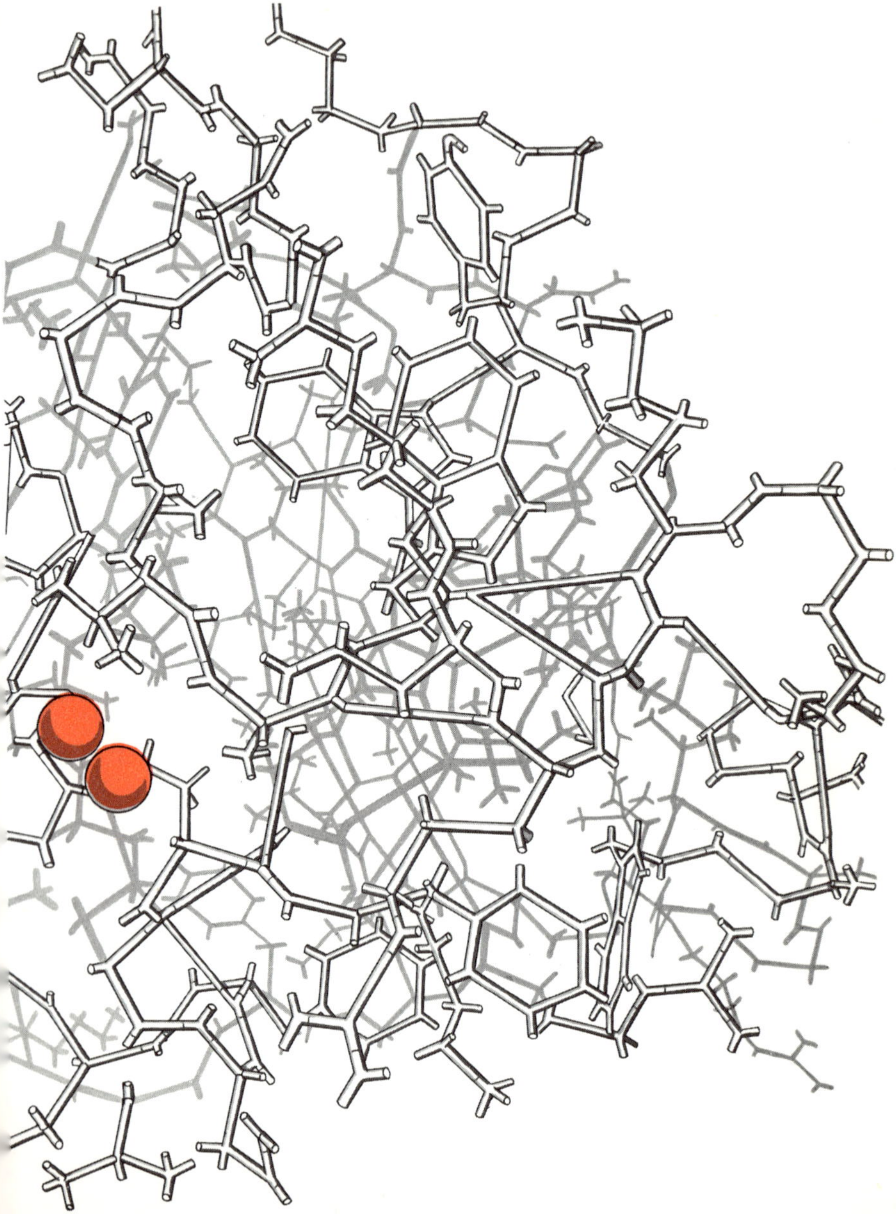

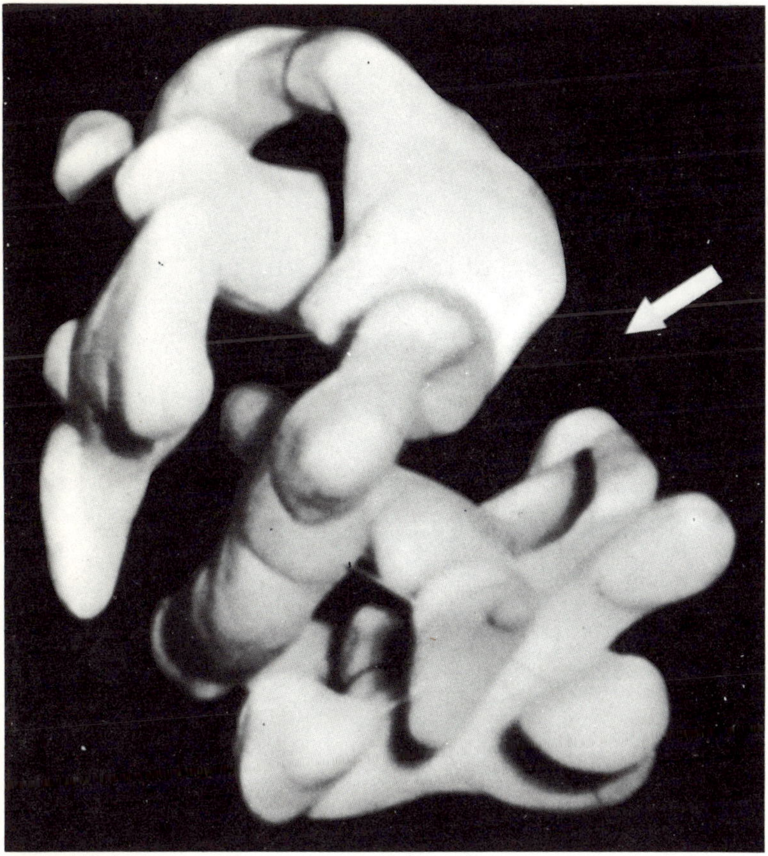

5·7 A three-dimensional model of a lysozyme molecule. The arrow indicates the site of attachment of the substrate to the enzyme during the conversion of substrate to product.

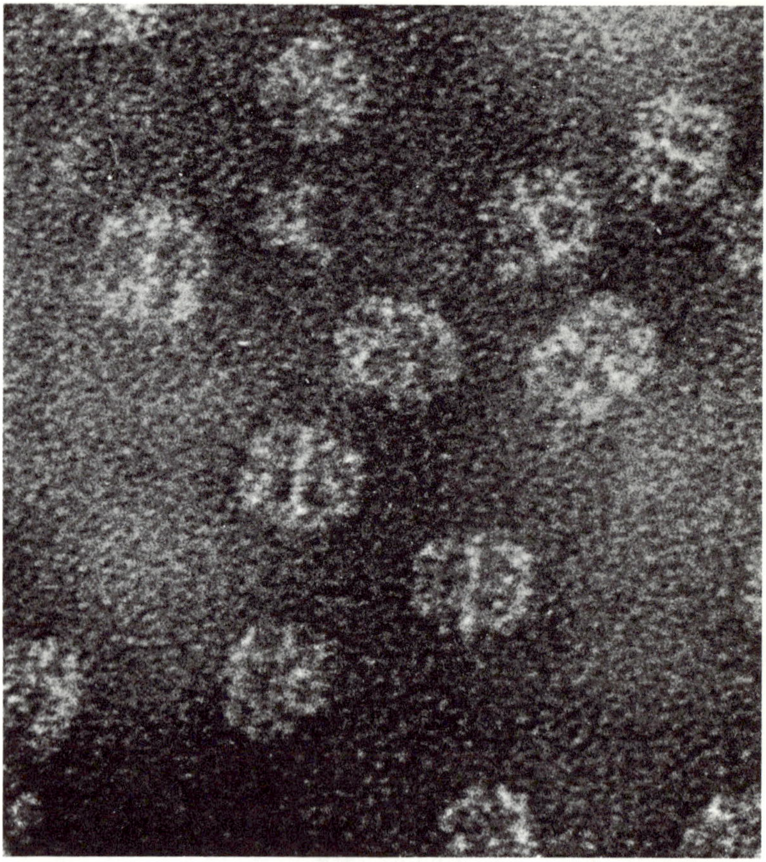

5·8 Electron micrograph of multi-enzyme fatty acid synthetase, which catalyses the synthesis of fatty acids.

5·9 Electron micrograph of ribosomes from red blood cells. Some ribosomes can be seen grouped together.

fatty-acid synthetase from *coli* cells, which catalyses the synthesis of fatty acids.

Not all proteins present in the cell are enzymes; that is, not all proteins act as catalysts for reactions which build up, rearrange, or break down building blocks. For example, several proteins are found in the cell wall and as components of the sites of protein synthesis, the ribosomes.

Before considering the steps in protein synthesis we shall look at the structure of these ribosomes. They are cell structures made up mainly of two types of macromolecule, that is, ribonucleic acid which is surrounded by a layer of protein. Figure 5·9 shows an electron microscope picture of ribosomes and indicates that ribosomes are made up of two sub-units.

Protein synthesis is the production of various proteins with a definite number of amino acids arranged in a definite sequential order. Once again it is the deoxyribonucleic acid of the cell which contains the information for the composition of proteins; the sequential order of the building blocks in DNA also determines the amino acid sequence of proteins. At first sight this appears rather a problem because a sequence of four building blocks in DNA has to determine the sequential order of twenty amino acids in proteins. It is clear that a single nucleotide cannot decide the place of an amino acid

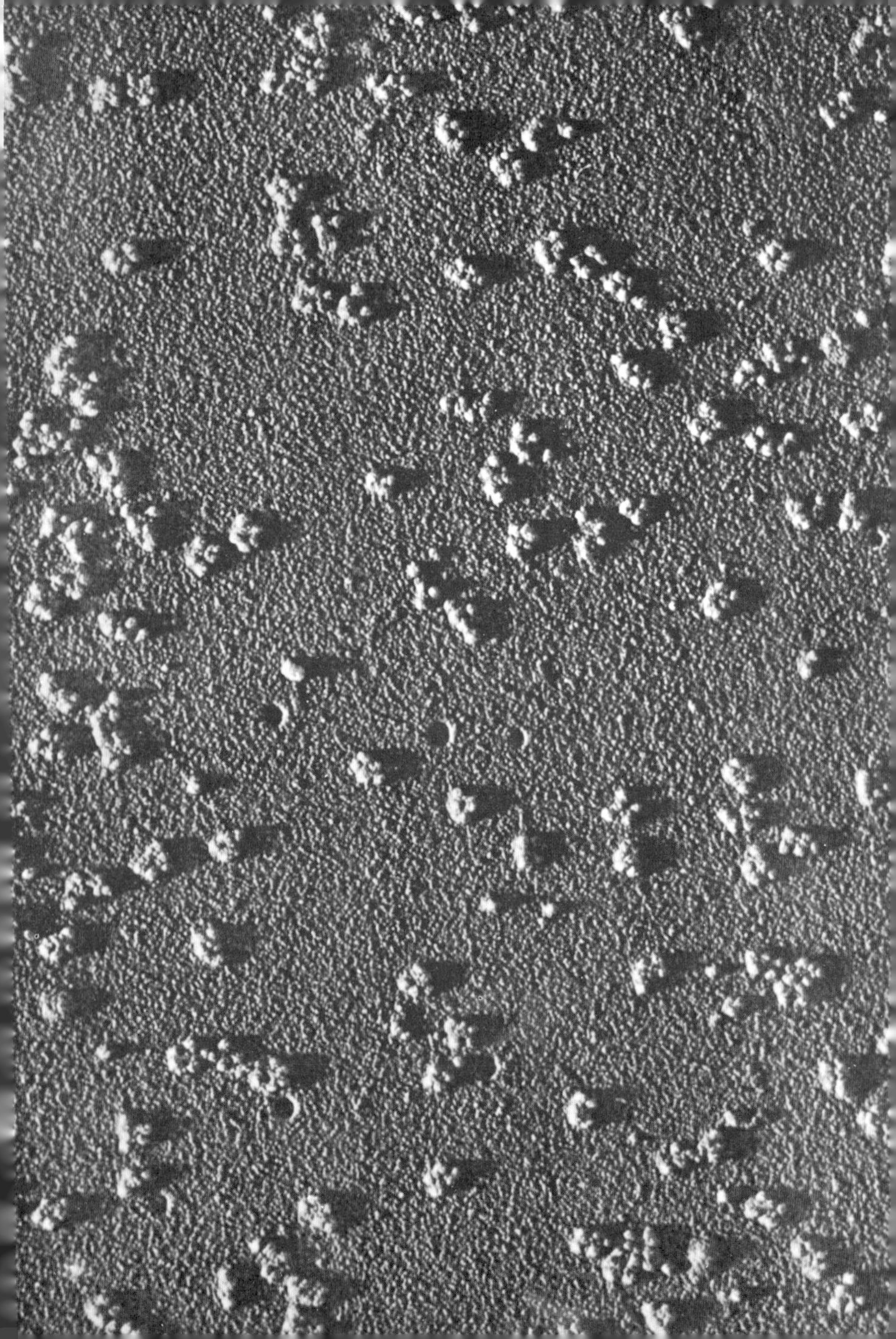

5·10 The various stages of protein synthesis.
Below Transcription : from one of the DNA strands the deoxyribonucleotide sequence containing the code for a polypeptide chain is transcribed as a complementary messenger-RNA molecule. The diagram does not show enzymes such as RNA-polymerase, nor other essential factors.
Right Translation : here the nucleotide sequence of messenger-RNA is translated into the corresponding amino acid sequence

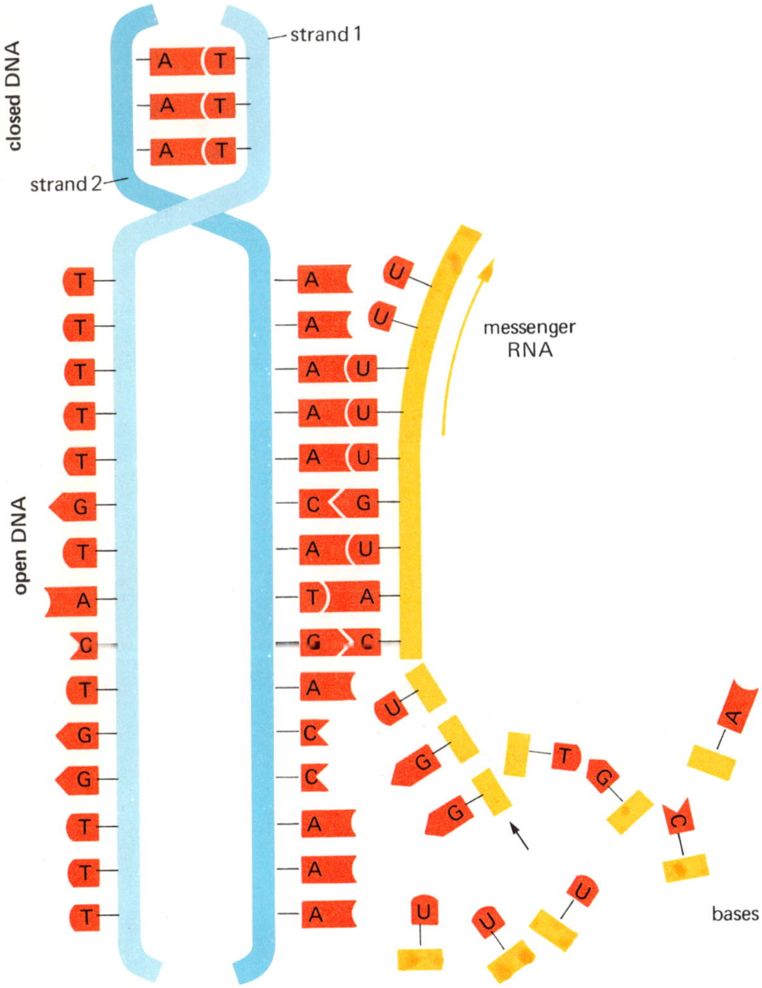

of the polypeptide chain. Messenger-RNA attaches to the ribosomes and, by means of base-pairing, transfer-RNSs carrying the appropriate amino acid bind themselves to the corresponding positions in the messenger-RNA. One by one the amino acids are added to the growing polypeptide chain and are released from their transfer-RNA. By means of the appropriate synthetase, transfer-RNA then links up with another molecule of its corresponding amino acid.

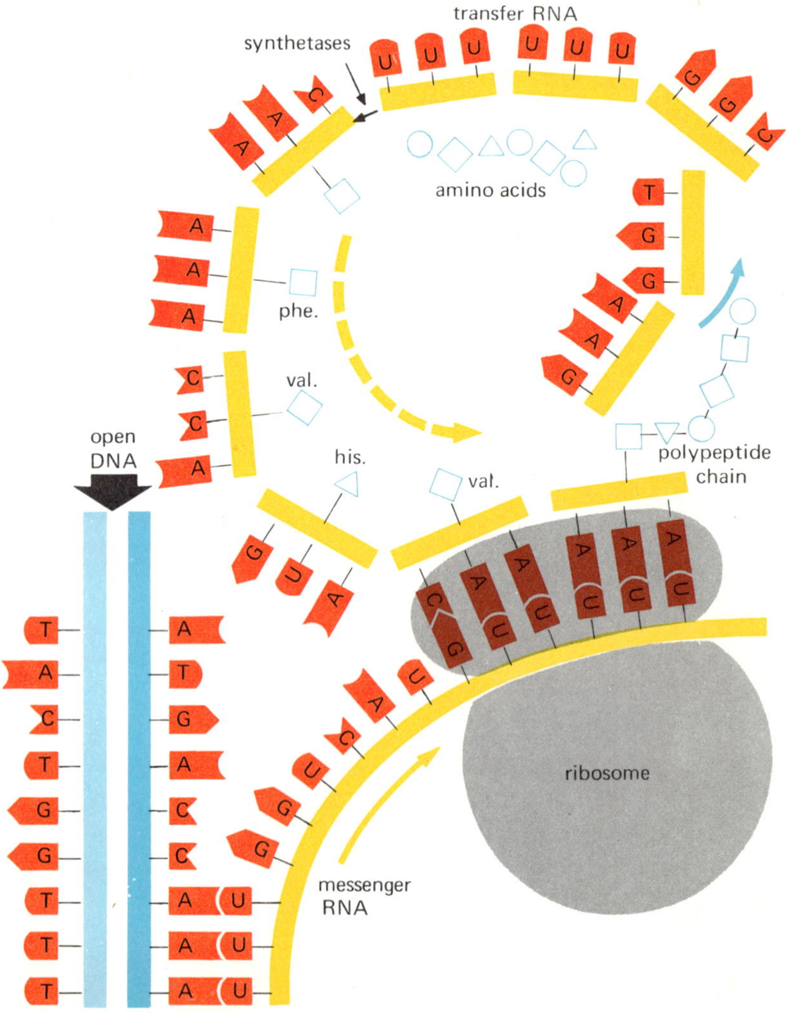

in the protein. The system also would not work if a sequence of two nucleotides determined the amino acid sequence because there are only sixteen combinations of four nucleotides taken two at a time. However, it has been shown experimentally that a sequence of three nucleotides in DNA determines the place of one amino acid in a protein. Furthermore, from thorough investigations in several laboratories, we now know which sequence of three nucleotides in DNA determines which amino acid. The allocation of the amino acids to sixty-four possible nucleotide triplet combinations of DNA is given in the appendix (p. 232). Not only is this code valid for *coli* cells but for the cells of all organisms investigated so far, including man. In other words, the code is universal. Since there are sixty-four possible trinucleotide combinations, several amino acids are coded for by more than one triplet.

The statement that the order of three nucleotides in DNA determines the position of an amino acid in a protein says nothing as to how the sequence of, for example, 180 deoxyribonucleotides in DNA becomes translated into a corresponding order of 60 amino acids in a protein.

In general, the process is as follows: messenger-RNA is sent from the DNA to the ribosomes, the site of protein synthesis. Messenger-RNA is formed in the following way: complementary ribonucleotides attach to that part of the DNA which contains the information for the amino acid sequence of the protein to be made and are there linked together with the aid of the appropriate enzyme, RNA-polymerase. The next step is that messenger-RNA attaches itself to the ribosomes (figure

5·10). This is where the translation of the nucleotide sequence to the corresponding amino acid sequence actually takes place and once again it is the association of the corresponding complementary bases that accomplishes this. The amino acids arrive at the ribosomes, attached to small nucleic acid molecules called transfer-RNA. Each amino acid is bound to one specific transfer-RNA molecule, which bears the appropriate trinucleotide sequence, so that it can attach to the corresponding position in the messenger-RNA by the mechanism of base-pairing.

We still need to know the step in protein synthesis which couples the correct amino acid to the appropriate transfer-RNA. This is accomplished with the aid of enzymes, the so-called synthetases. The specificity of these enzymes is such that they link up with a certain amino acid and with the appropriate transfer-RNA and dissociate from them after they are coupled together. Thus these enzymes play an essential part in the translation of the nucleotide sequence into the correct amino acid sequence. At least one specific synthetase is present for each amino acid. To date, neither the amino acid sequence nor the spatial structure of any of these enzymes is known.

The processes involved in protein synthesis shown in figure 5·10 do not mention such equally indispensable factors as, for example, the suppliers of energy and factors involved in binding messenger- or transfer-RNA to the ribosomes. The process of protein synthesis is not yet known in all its details. For example, which of the two strands of the DNA double helix

is read off in the formation of messenger-RNA for only one of them will give a meaningful set of instructions for the formation of a protein. Also, how is one messenger-RNA formed on a DNA strand delimited from the adjacent one?

It is to some extent possible to synthesise DNA, RNA and proteins by using molecules and structures isolated from cells. However, protein synthesis carried out *in vitro* using material isolated from cells is much slower than the process in living cells. Further research will show whether more refined knowledge of the factors involved in protein synthesis will allow the process to be carried out with isolated building blocks outside the cell with the same velocity. It might be found to be impossible in principle because the spatial orientation of the molecules and structures in the cells is all-important for these complicated processes.

Polysaccharides

The structure, function and synthesis of these macromolecules will not be given more detailed coverage in this book than is summarised in table 3·3 since a detailed knowledge of them plays no part in the themes of this book. However, this does not mean that polysaccharides are not just as necessary for the life of the cell. All we need add here is that their building blocks are attached to one another by means of specific enzymes. No complex mechanisms of synthesis are involved as in the case of nucleic acid and protein synthesis.

Summary The structure, function and synthesis of nucleic acids and proteins is described in more detail because these macromolecules participate in all the important processes of life. This will be further stressed in the next chapter. The reactions are as valid for the simplest forms of life as for complicated organisms, including man.

DNA is decisive for all properties of the organism, since the sequential order of its building blocks determines the structure and hence the function of ribonucleic acids and hence those of proteins.

The sequence of deoxyribonucleotides in DNA which determines the structure of a protein chain or RNA chain is called a *gene*. The gene concept is much older than its molecular interpretation. Since the discovery of the laws of heredity by G. Mendel in 1865 it has constantly changed and we now know what a gene is in molecular terms. A historical description of the changes in the gene concept would show that our present knowledge of the significance of DNA in living things is due to the combined efforts of many scientists working in several branches of science.

In our description of the synthesis of macromolecules it was shown that the principle of pairing of two of the four building blocks respectively of deoxy- and ribo-nucleic acids plays a decisive role. Also, the step in protein synthesis in which the amino acids are coupled to transfer-RNA requires specific enzymes showing that proteins participate in the synthesis of proteins and drawing attention to the relationships between various reactions in the cell.

6 Regulation of the synthesis of macromolecules and their precursors

In the preceding chapters we looked at the structure, function and formation of the cell macromolecules and their building blocks. In addition we mentioned that the number of components of the cell, although different for each molecule or macromolecule, is constant. The characteristic composition of the cell is valid only for a certain environment. If the environment changes, for example the culture medium of the *coli* cells, then the number and type of some of their molecules also change. In other words, the composition of cells is to some extent a response to their environment.

How does the cell regulate its composition? Put simply, the cell household shows a tendency to manage itself as economically as possible. In other words, whatever is superfluous under certain environmental conditions ought or will not be synthesised inevitably by the cell.

It is easiest to understand the regulation mechanisms in the cell by means of examples. Figure 4·2 shows the steps in the synthesis of histidine – one of the building blocks of proteins. Since we have dealt with the formation of proteins in chapter 5 we can now also include the essential steps in the synthesis of each of the enzymes involved (figure 6·1). If the protein building block, histidine, is added to the cell from outside, it passes into the cell and so the cell does not then need to synthesise more. The synthesis of histidine is retarded in two ways: first, the enzyme which catalyses the first step in the series of reactions leading to the synthesis of histidine has a structure such that its activity is inhibited if the concentration of histidine molecules in the cell exceeds a certain

6·1 Synthesis on an amino acid, such as histidine.
The deoxyribonucleotide sequences (genes) encoding the amino acid sequences of the histidine-synthetic enzymes are arranged linearly on the DNA. Enzymes 1-4 are produced according to the process of protein synthesis via messenger-RNA 1-4. These enzymes catalyse the steps in histidine synthesis, the number of steps shown having been reduced for simplicity. Histidine regulates its synthesis in two ways.

1. By inhibiting the enzyme of the first reaction.
2. By repressing the production of the enzymes which catalyse its synthesis. Both regulation mechanisms require a certain histidine concentration in the cell – symbolised by histidine 1 + n.

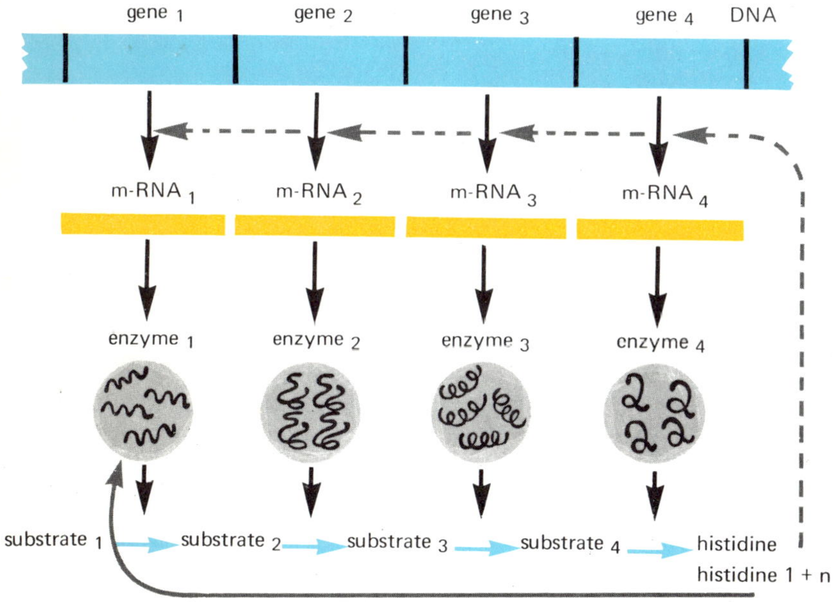

value. This inhibition of the first enzyme means that there is no substrate for the next step in the reaction so that the subsequent enzymes involved in the series of reactions have nothing to work on. This principle – the inhibition of the first enzyme in a chain of reactions by the end-product of the chain – applies to the synthesis of many building blocks of macromolecules and in metabolic energy cycles. It was first described by H. Umbarger in 1956 for the synthesis of the amino acid isoleucine.

Recently a great deal of knowledge has accumulated on the molecular processes involved in the inhibition of enzymes by substances of lower molecular weight, such as what structure the enzyme must have and how its structure is changed by the inhibitor so that its action is switched off. These are physicochemical aspects which fall outside the scope of this book, but we should mention that research has also shown that in the presence of certain molecules the activity of some enzymes is not inhibited but increased, while some only function in the presence of these activators. The molecular processes involved in the inhibition and activation of enzymes appear to be similar: the inhibiting or the activating substance binds itself to the enzyme and so changes its structure and activity. These substances are called *effectors*. It is becoming increasingly fascinating to learn how the majority of the metabolic pathways in cells are economically regulated by this mechanism of inhibition or activation of enzymes by effectors.

There is a second regulation principle by which the cell

suspends the synthesis of building blocks when these can be obtained ready-made from the environment. To continue with our example of histidine synthesis, we saw that if the histidine concentration in the cell reaches a certain value then the enzyme of the first reaction in the chain is inhibited by the histidine and so histidine synthesis stops. In this way the cell certainly conserves the energy and materials involved in histidine synthesis but the enzymes which participate in the synthesis would still be produced. The second regulating principle operates in such a way that the formation of the enzymes involved in histidine production is also repressed if the cell has more than sufficient histidine. It is not the histidine itself which represses the synthesis of these enzymes but a substance which is formed only when histidine is present. This *repression* of the formation of enzymes by the end-product of a metabolic pathway is another regulatory mechanism which is frequently used in regulating the synthesis of the building blocks of macromolecules or the reaction chains for gaining energy.

Not only is the formation of certain enzymes in the cell specifically repressed but the enzymes of other metabolic pathways are produced only if their substrate is actually present in the cell. To take another example, this time one of the routes for gaining energy. Just as glucose can be used for providing energy, so lactose, another sugar, can be put to the same use. The enzymes which break down this sugar are found only in *coli* cells if lactose is present in the culture medium and enters the *coli* cells. That is, lactose *induces* the formation of the enzymes which degrade it – once again very economical for

the cell household.

F. Jacob and J. Monod in 1961 suggested a molecular mechanism for the regulating principles of repression and induction, which is summarised in figure 6·2. Their suggestion stimulated research in many laboratories to gain a better understanding of the molecular processes involved in these processes. The repression and induction of enzyme formation in their model is supposed to take the following form: there is a specific repressor for the formation of the enzymes of a certain metabolic pathway; the synthesis of those enzymes is hindered if their repressor molecule is present. In cases where the end-product of a metabolic pathway prevents the formation of enzymes, the end-product converts a repressor precursor to the actual repressor. To go back to the example of histidine: the histidine acts upon a repressor precursor to give the repressor itself and this prevents the synthesis of the ten histidine synthetic enzymes. In the case of induction of the enzymes by the lactose substrate, the lactose inactivates the repressor for the lactose degrading enzyme. Thus the essential difference between repression and induction is that in repression the repressor molecule is made active by a lower molecular-weight molecule while in induction a corresponding lower molecular-weight molecule inactivates an active repressor.

Until recently no one knew what step in the formation of the enzymes was interfered with by the repressor. However, in the case of the induction of the lactose-degrading enzyme, it has recently been possible to isolate the repressor molecule

6·2 Regulation of enzyme formation by repression and induction. In induction, low molecular-weight substances inactivate repressor molecules formed intracellularly. For example, the sugar lactose leads to the inactivation of the repressor molecules which suppress the synthesis of the lactose-degrading enzymes; formation of lactose degrading enzymes is then unhindered.
In the case of repression, a low molecular-weight

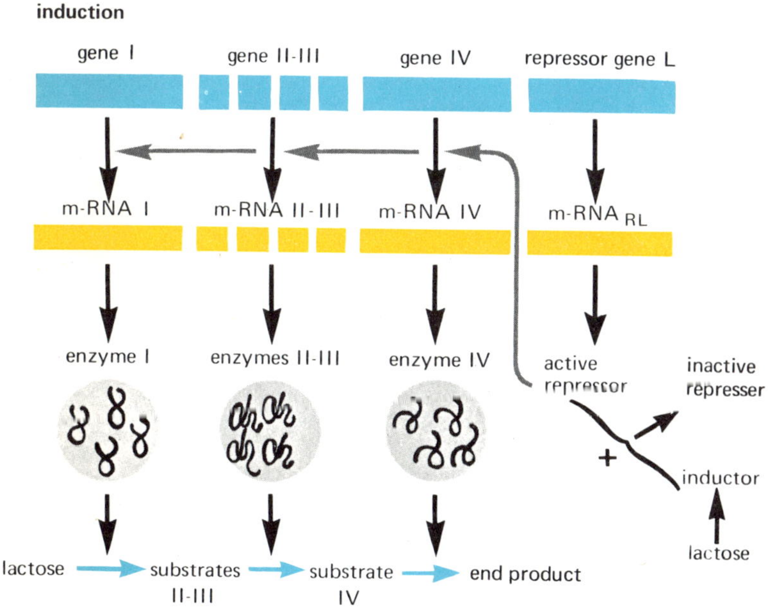

substance activates an intracellularly formed repressor precursor. For example, histidine causes the conversion of the appropriate repressor precursors to an active repressor, which prevents the production of those enzymes which catalyse histidine synthesis.

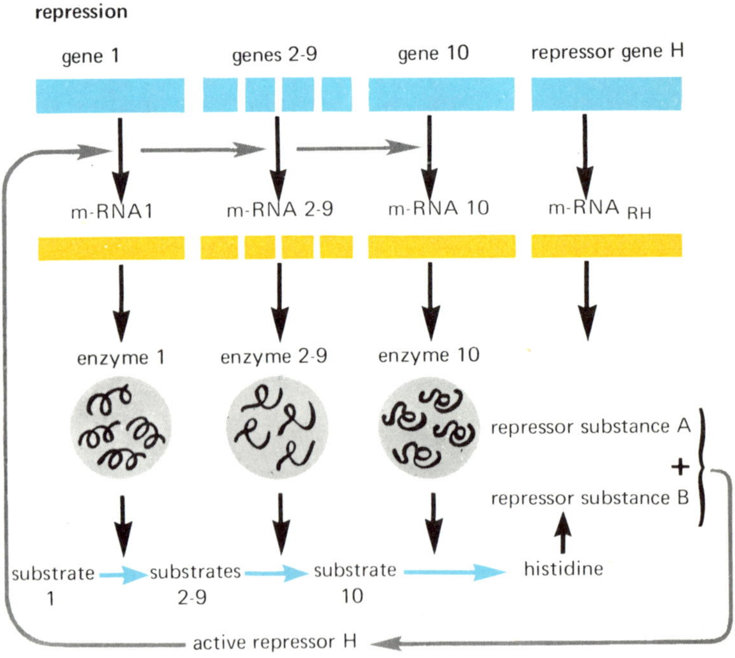

and to identify it as a protein. Furthermore, it has been observed that the repressor protein probably hinders the synthesis of the lactose-degrading enzyme by bonding with that portion of the DNA which contains the nucleotide sequence for the structure of the degrading enzymes. The structure of the repressor protein is determined by a different section of DNA (the repressor gene), as mentioned several times for other proteins. It now appears certain that the mechanism suggested by F. Jacob and J. Monod for the induction of the lactose-degrading enzyme is correct. Whether the same mechanism is true in all details for other inductions and for the repression of enzyme formation is being investigated in several laboratories.

From what has been said about the regulation of enzyme formation it could be inferred that the only enzymes that are repressed or induced are those where the end-products (in the case of repression) or the substrates (in the case of induction) can enter the cell from outside. However, the substrates of certain enzymes cannot be supplied from outside the cell since they cannot pass through the cell membrane. The synthetases may be mentioned as an example, which play a crucial role in the translation of the nucleotide sequence of DNA into the amino acid sequence of proteins (figure 5·10). The rate of formation of these enzymes is also regulated, and researchers are trying to find the repressor molecule responsible.

The formation of other macromolecules in the cell is also regulated but little is known of the molecular processes involved and so we can only make a few brief remarks about the

regulation of the syntheses of DNA and RNA. The regulation of DNA synthesis appears to be important for the rhythm of cell division, while the production of messenger-RNA is probably influenced by the regulation of enzyme formation. Since environmental conditions are known which vary the number of ribosomes, the rate of synthesis of ribosomal RNA and of their associated proteins must also be regulated. In addition, there is experimental evidence that there can be variations in the rate of formation of the third type of RNA – transfer-RNA.

Enzyme inhibition or activation by effectors can take place outside the cell. The processes of repression and induction of enzyme formation, however, have so far been possible only within the intact cell. Once again the question arises whether the spatial arrangement of the cell components is crucial for these processes.

Summary In the cell there are sensitive mechanisms which limit the synthesis of certain molecules (for example, histidine) if these reach a certain concentration in the cell, for example by intake from the environment. This reduction in the synthesis of a molecule may be achieved by inhibiting the activity of the first enzyme of a metabolic pathway, or it may occur by the formation of a repressor substance which represses the formation of all the enzymes of the pathway. The final product of the metabolic pathway, histidine, takes part in the inhibition of the enzyme and in the formation of the repressor.

In addition, there are enzymes which are formed only when

their substrate is present in the cell, for example, the lactose-degrading enzymes. The induction of enzyme formation is achieved in such a way that the substrate suspends the action of the corresponding repressor molecules.

The regulation processes described should also be regarded as the response of the organism to the composition and changes of its environment – that is, as an *adaptation*.

7 The structure and organisation of multicellular organisms

It has been mentioned that the same building blocks found in the *coli* cell are found in complex organisms, including man, where they have similar properties. The following chapters are devoted to the description of some additional structures or functions found in multicellular organisms.

It is obvious that complex organisms, such as beetles or elephants, have species-specific structures in addition to those structures found in simple organisms. Complex organisms also consist of different cells with specialised structures and functions. Cells of the same type are grouped to form tissues, which are sometimes held together by connective substances. In organs, several specialised cell types or tissues are coordinated to form a functional unit, as for example in the liver, lung or brain (figure 7·1).

Table 7·1 lists the functions and chemical composition of a few cellular structures found in complex organisms. Figure 7·2 shows an electron microscope picture of a specialised cell of man, a cartilage cell, and a diagram of the same cell.

The molecular processes of some processes of multicellular organisms are described in the following chapters, but before passing on to these we must elaborate on table 7·1 and figure 7·2 From these it may be seen that differentiated cells of multicellular organisms contain in their complex structures the known functional units of single-celled organisms. This is indicated again in figure 7·3, in which the cell nucleus is progressively broken down into smaller structural units. The nucleus contains besides other structures the chromosomes which contain the DNA; just as for single-celled organisms,

7·1 Photomicrograph of a nerve cell (central pyramid shaped cell) from the human brain (*below*) and liver cells (*right*).

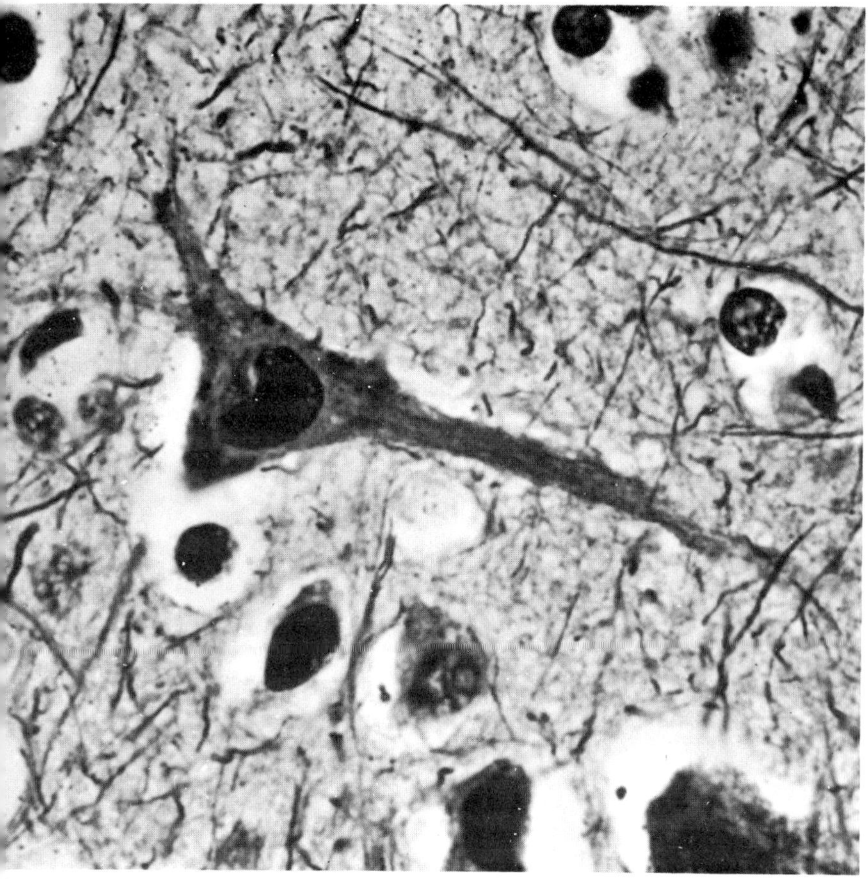

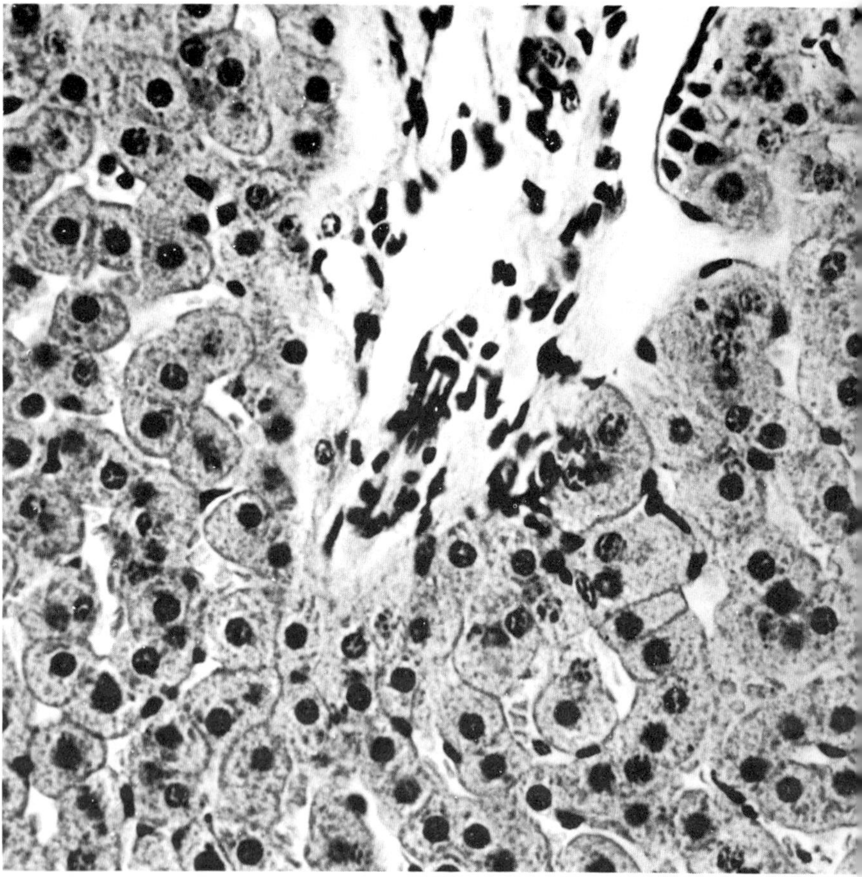

Table 7·1 Some structures in the cells of multicellular organisms

structure	function	molecular components
Cell membrane	selective boundary between environment and cell interior	proteins, lipids, polysaccharides
Cell nucleus		
Chromosomes	determine the possible properties of the cell	DNA, proteins
Nucleolus	mediator between cytoplasm and nucleus	proteins, RNA and others
Cytoplasm		
Mitochondria	the site of enzymes for obtaining energy from energy-rich molecules	proteins, lipids, DNA, RNA
Lysosomes	contain enzymes for the break-down of certain substances	proteins, lipids
Endoplasmic reticulum	the site of attachment of the ribosomes, and subdivides the cytoplasm	lipids, polysaccharides, proteins
Golgi apparatus	secretory	lipids, polysaccharides, proteins

the DNA molecules determine the properties of the cells. Their nucleotide sequences contain the information for the structure and, consequently, the function of the proteins and the nucleic acids. However, the chromosomes contain additional molecules, for example certain proteins called histones; it is assumed that these proteins influence the activity of the genes. The number of chromosomes is characteristic for each species of animal and plant; thus the nuclei of the cells of the fruit fly *Drosophila melanogaster* contain eight chromosomes, the nuclei of cells from man, forty-six. Another structure found in the cell nucleus is the nucleolus, which acts as a mediator between the cell nucleus and the cell cytoplasm and contains such structures as ribosomes and messenger-RNA.

The cells of differentiated organisms also contain mitochondria (figure 7·4), cell structures with well-developed membranes containing enzymes which take part in the metabolic energy cycles. Recent investigations have shown that the enzymes are arranged on the membranes so that their spatial location largely corresponds with the order in which they catalyse the various steps of a metabolic pathway. In view of this directional component they are called vectorial enzymes. Like the membranes of cells, the membranes of mitochondria select the molecules they take in. Also, in recent years it has been shown that DNA, ribosomes and other molecules taking part in protein synthesis are present in these organelles and their full significance is still being investigated.

Lysosomes are another type of structure bounded by a membrane and are found in the cells of higher organisms

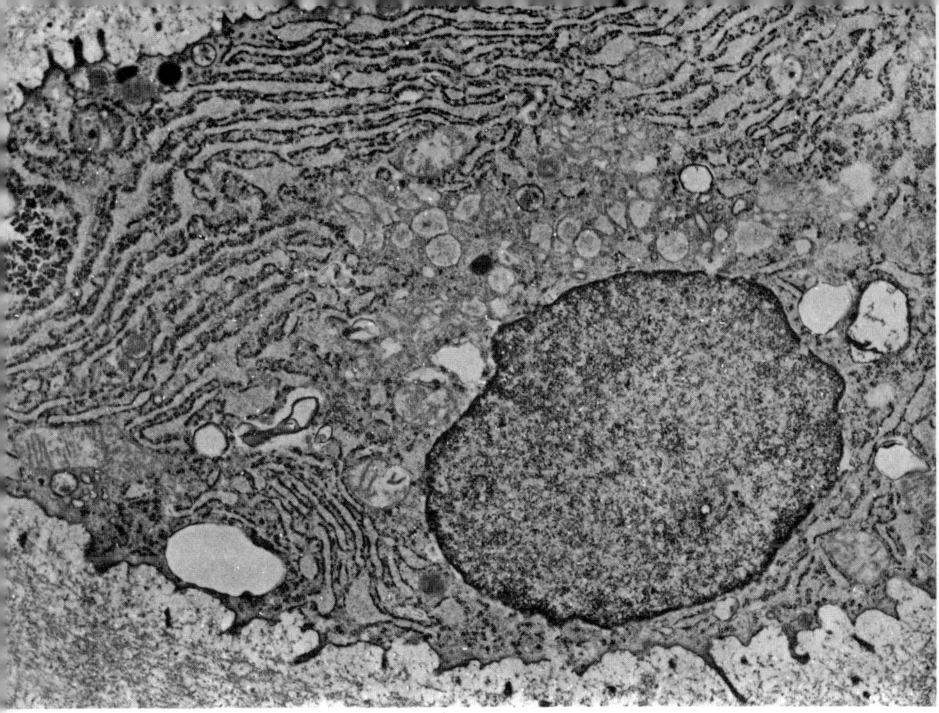

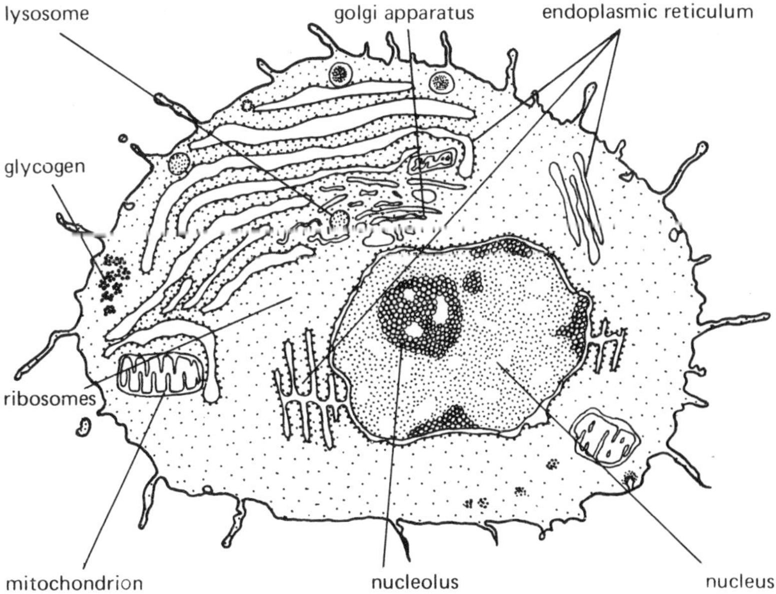
lysosome
golgi apparatus
endoplasmic reticulum
glycogen
ribosomes
mitochondrion
nucleolus
nucleus

7·2 Left Electron micrograph of a human cartilage cell (*top*) (x 16,000) and a diagram to show the main parts of the above cell (*bottom*).

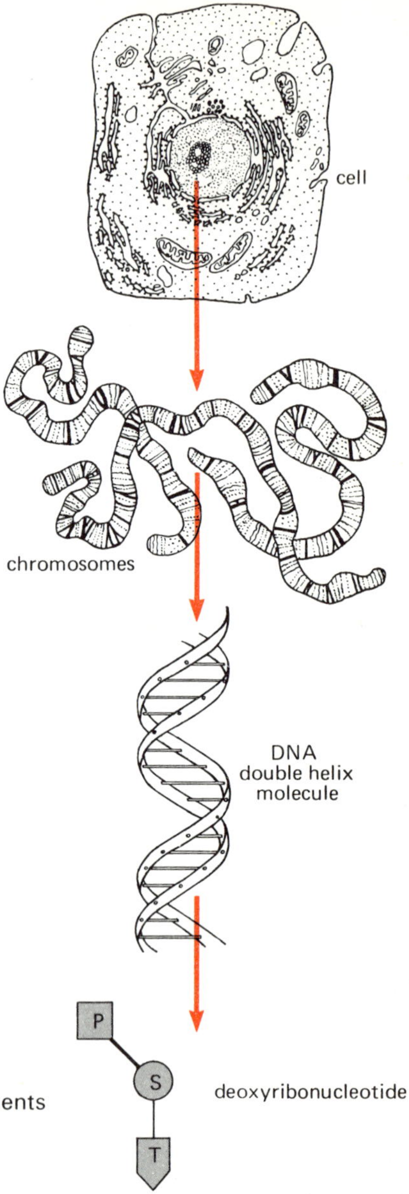

7·3 Right Successive enlargements of a part of the cell nucleus.

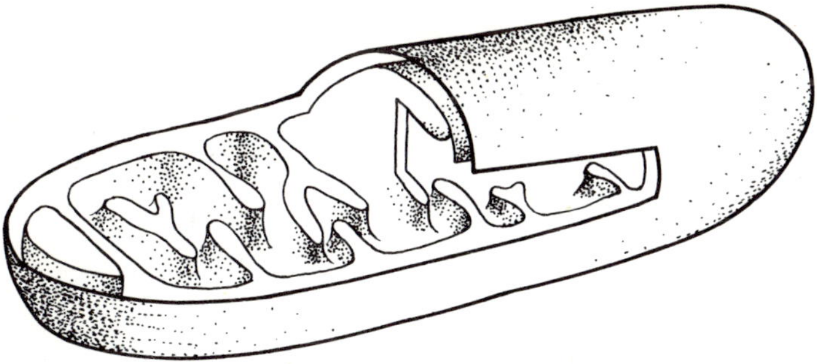

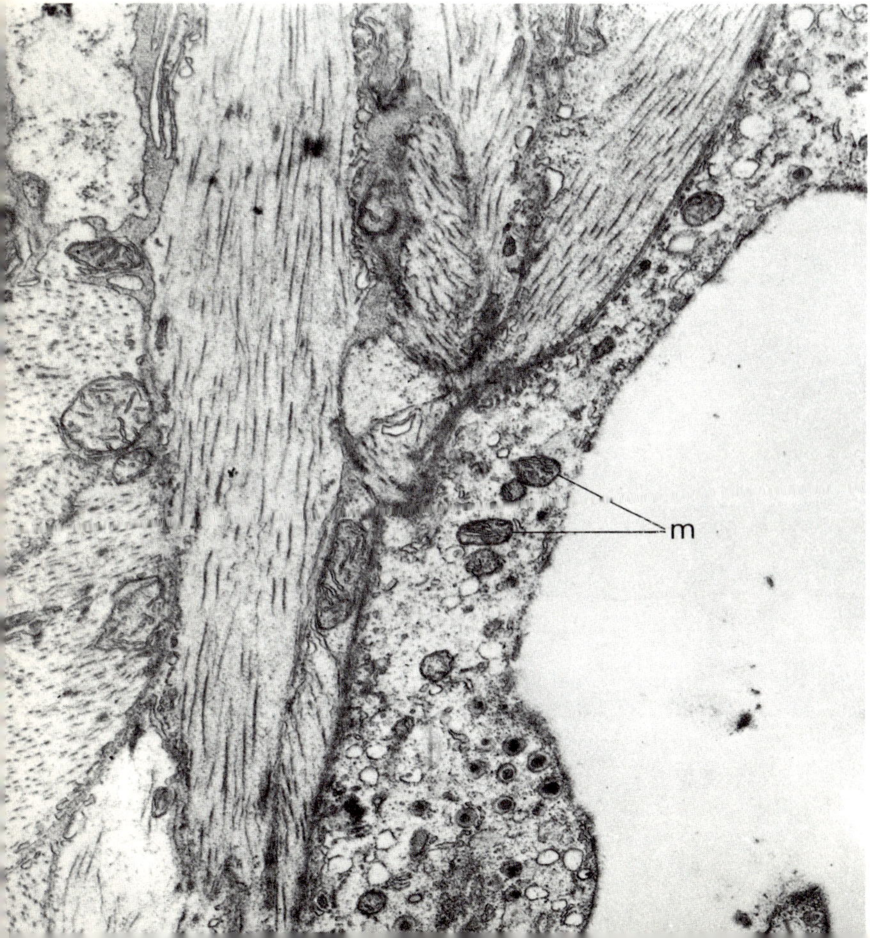
m

7·4 Left model of a mitochondrion. The enzymes which participate in the cell's energy metabolism are attached to the membranes in a definite order. Also shown is an electron micrograph of a cell containing mitochondria.

7·5 Below Electron micrograph of lysosomes. These contain enzymes which catalyse the breakdown of certain substances.

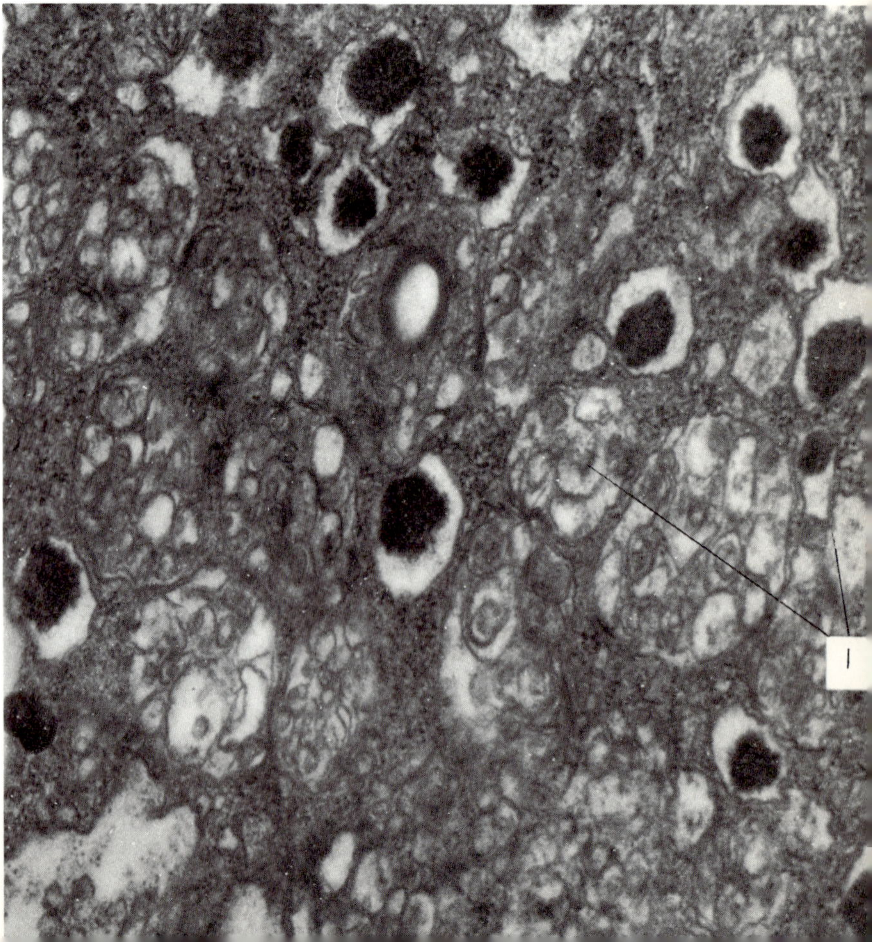

7·6 Electron micrograph of chloroplasts, which are cellular organelles of green plants. They contain the chlorophyll and other compounds necessary for synthesising glucose and other energy-rich substances, by utilizing the energy of sunlight.

(figure 7·5). They appear to contain functionally related enzymes which catalyse the degradation of macromolecules and other substances.

The electron microscope picture of the cells (figure 7·2) also shows the endoplasmic reticulum, a membraneous structure extending throughout the cytoplasm, to which the cell ribosomes are attached. The list of cell structures of multicellular organisms in table 7·1 is by no means complete; for example it does not mention the chloroplasts of plant cells, which contain the molecules necessary for photosynthesis (figure 7·6). Then, again, other cells contain the so-called basal bodies which are a part of the cilium or flagellum which are sometimes locomotory organelles.

In the following chapters the molecular basis of a few of the vital phenomena of complex organisms are described. We shall also learn that many proteins are present in these cells which are not present in *coli* cells. This is also reflected in the difference between the DNA-content of the *coli* cells and of the cells of multicellular organisms. However, the cells of complex organisms never contain all the possible cell proteins; each individual tissue has its characteristic pattern.

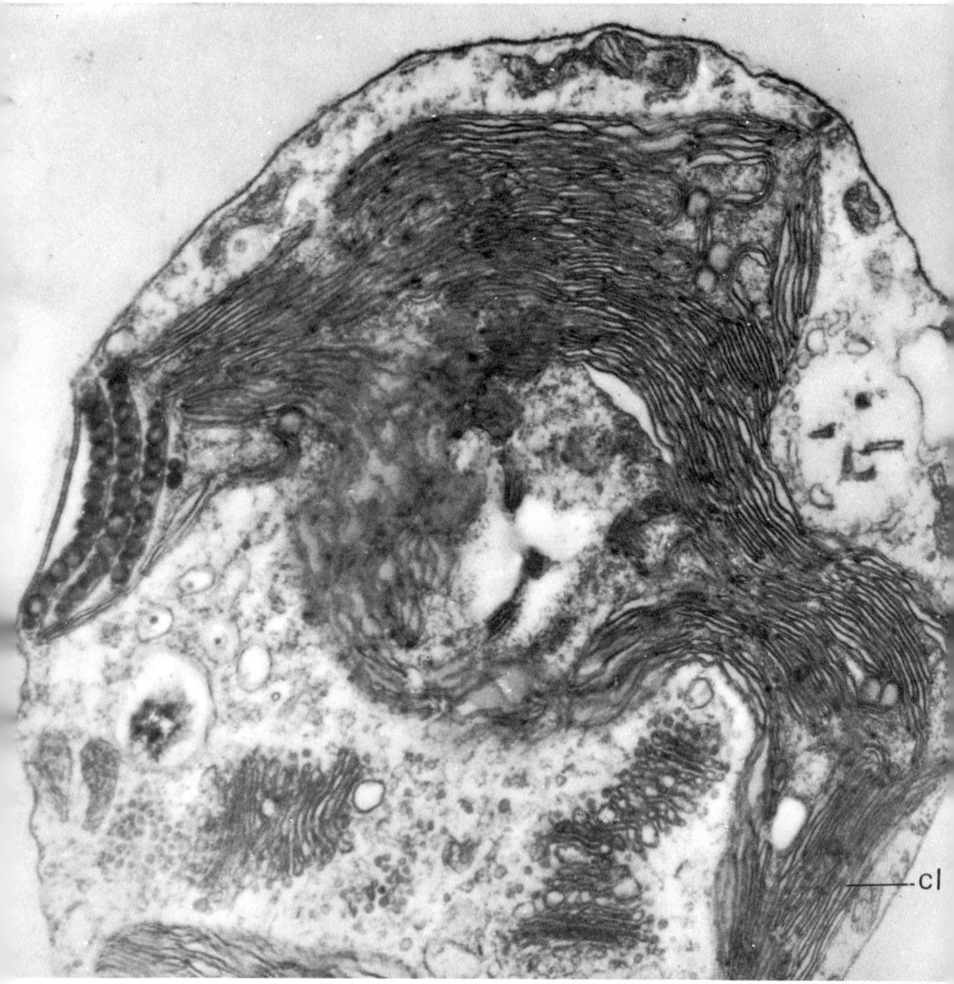
cl

Summary The cells of more complex organisms contain structures and molecules additional to those of simple unicellular organisms. Several of these new structures contain building blocks which are present in the unicellular organism in a disordered manner but which are here assembled to form new ordered structural units. For example, functionally related groups of enzymes are localised in lysosomes or in mitochondria. The additional cell structures and the specialisation of cells in more complex organisms to form organs permit other vital phenomena. A few of these will be described in the following chapters.

8 Communication routes in more complex organisms

Here we shall describe a few of the structures and molecules of multicellular organisms that not only enable life-processes, such as metabolism and adaptation, to proceed in the cell, but which also co-ordinate these processes in the entire organism.

Systems having physical connections with the entire organism

One important and specialised system which extends throughout the body in many differentiated organisms comprises the blood vessels and the blood within them. Its task is to co-ordinate the functions of the individual organs and tissues of the organism and to act as a route of communication for the transport of substances. Figure 8·1 shows the circulatory system in vertebrates. Starting from the heart, the vessels branch repeatedly until they reach the individual cells. Then they join up again and return via the heart to the lungs, and finally enter the heart again. We shall not describe the chemical composition of the blood vessels, but deal with the blood itself. This consists of specialised cells and the blood plasma. It would take too long to list all the cells of the blood, the many different molecules which make up the plasma, and to describe fully their functions and formation. The most that can be done within the scope of this book is to select a few examples.

We know from the description of *coli* cells that nutritive substances, for providing energy and for the build-up of the

8·1 Much simplified circulation of the blood of a vertebrate.

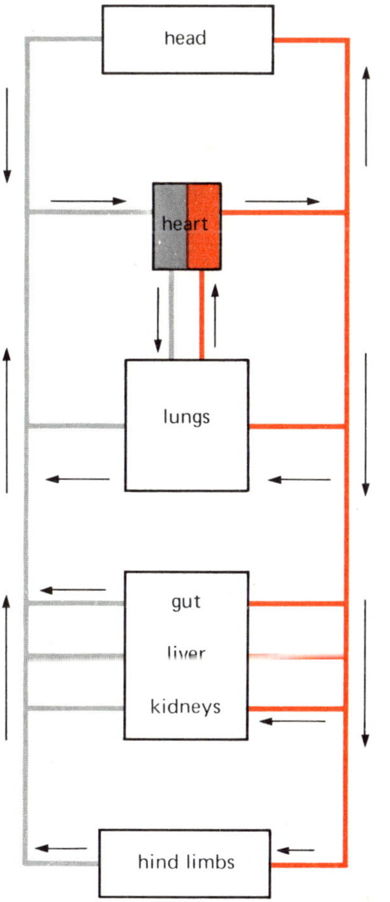

cell components, reach the cell interior by selective passage through the cell membrane and that waste products are removed in the same way. It is clear that in the case of more complex organisms nutritive substances cannot pass directly from the environment to the individual cells. Nevertheless, every cell of a multicellular organism, as in single-celled organisms, must be supplied with oxygen, energy-rich compounds and other nutritive substances. These processes are performed in multicellular organisms by means of organs, such as the stomach, intestines, lungs and kidneys, and each organ consists of specialised cells. The blood serves to transport oxygen, foodstuffs and other substances to the cells and removes yet other substances from the cells.

All the components of the blood are present at a certain concentration, which is kept constant by various complicated regulation mechanisms. Human blood contains five million red blood cells per cubic millimeter. These cells carry oxygen bonded to a protein called haemoglobin. The protein consists of two parts – a protein made up of four polypeptide chains, and a non-protein part, namely four haem groups, each of which contains an iron atom (see p. 233). It is the haem group which causes the red colour of red blood cells and therefore of the blood as a whole. The protein part of the haemoglobin of man is composed of two protein chains of one type, the so-called alpha chains, and two of another, the beta chains. These polypeptide chains are among the few for which the entire sequence of amino acids is known. The primary structure of the haemoglobin chains was elucidated simultane-

ously a few years ago by G. Braunitzer in Germany and by A. Konigsberg in the USA. The amino acid sequence of the two haemoglobin chains is given on p. 234. As already mentioned for enzymes, individual protein chains tend to associate to form complex structures; this is also the case here – the two alpha and the two beta chains form the framework of the haemoglobin molecule which encloses the four non-protein haem groups. The three-dimensional structure of the active haemoglobin molecule was first described in England by M. Perutz in 1960. As a result of this work we now have a detailed picture of the spatial structure of haemoglobin. The haemoglobin molecule is composed of two of each of the alpha and beta chains and four haem groups. We know which amino acid sequences of the haemoglobin molecule are especially important in bonding oxygen and delivering it to the tissues and what must be the state of the blood in order that the haemoglobin can carry out this function properly. In addition, the site at which oxygen is attached to the haemoglobin molecule is known. The iron atoms of the four haem groups each bind one molecule.

The structure and properties of haemoglobin illustrate two more principles, which also apply to other protein molecules. The reversible bonding of oxygen to the iron atoms in haemoglobin is made possible only by the combined action of the protein and the haem part. Isolated iron atoms or haem residues can only bind oxygen irreversibly, which would prevent its delivery to the cells; isolated protein chains cannot bind oxygen at all. This brings us to a generalisation: several pro-

teins can function only in combination with a molecule which is not a protein (for example, haem); individually neither part can perform the function. So this is another case of our often-quoted dictum: the properties of molecules are different from the sum of the properties of their components. The combination with a non-protein part also occurs in the case of many protein enzymes.

The function of haemoglobin can be described in the following, somewhat simplified, fashion: the four polypeptide chains and the haem groups are present together so as to change the nature of the bonding of the oxygen to the iron atom from an irreversible to a reversible linkage. However, this statement neglects the secondary functions of haemoglobin – it must participate in other processes of the organism and it possesses structural elements to meet these needs. The influence of the structures of the protein chains on the bonding of oxygen to haemoglobin will be treated in more detail in chapter 13, where we shall find that even the exchange of one amino acid for another in one of the polypeptide chains can lead to an astonishing loss of function and result in illness.

The studies made by M. Perutz' group on the spatial structure of haemoglobin have also shown that during the bonding of oxygen to haemoglobin the protein chains are displaced into and towards one another. This change of shape of the haemoglobin molecule following the bonding of an oxygen molecule changes its chemical properties in such a way as to favour the bonding of additional oxygen molecules. This is a further example (although in a different form) of the principle

8·2 The main stages involved in blood clotting, in which the blood clotting protein, fibrin, is formed as the final product. The last two steps are labelled with the names of the factors which are actually involved. It is characteristic of this series of reactions that the product of one reaction becomes the catalyst for the next.

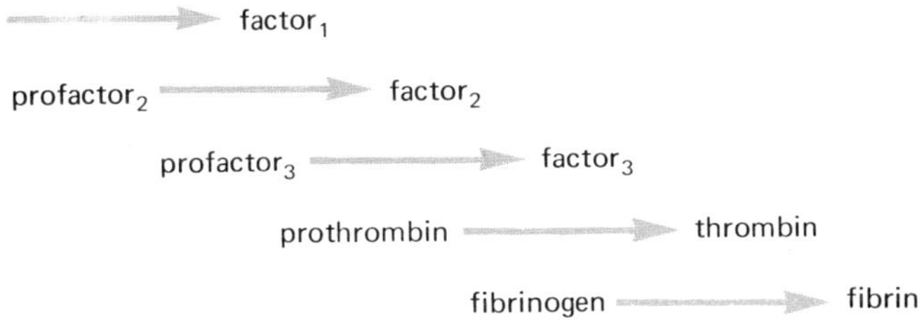

of a change of spatial structure due to the bonding of reaction partners, as described for lysozyme on p. 41.

Now that we have described the structure and function of one of the components of red blood cells we ought to mention a functional unit of the blood plasma. As we know, no sooner does blood emerge from the blood vessels than it begins to clot. The series of reactions responsible for this process is summarised in figure 8·2. In its basic features this series of events reminds one of enzyme substrate chains (for example figure 4·4), except that in blood clotting, proteins are modified and the product of one reaction becomes the catalyst for the next. After several specific modifications, the last step is the conversion of the protein fibrinogen to fibrin. In this process,

sequences of nineteen and of twenty-one amino acids are split off from fibrinogen, leaving fibrin – a protein which cements itself to form threads which close the ruptured vessel. Space does not allow us to consider the many cellular and molecular mechanisms stimulated by the formation of fibrin in order, for example, to replace the fibrin clot of a wound by vessels and skin. One of the reasons for mentioning the factors involved in blood clotting is that some of the molecules involved can be genetically altered, and as such cause certain well-known human illnesses, as will be described later in chapter 13.

A third type of molecule found in blood demonstrates a further property. Many cells need certain metals; thus iron is required by the tissues in which red blood-cells are made, while other tissues, such as the liver and certain parts of the brain, are rich in copper. These essential metals are also carried in the blood bound to specific proteins. The protein which contains bound copper is called coeruloplasmin because when isolated the pure form yields blue crystals (figure 8·3).

Fascinating as it would be to consider the structure and function of the many different components of blood – today more than a hundred different proteins of the blood plasma are known – these three examples will have to suffice.

Another cell system which embraces all parts of the body in more complex organisms is the nervous system. This also serves to co-ordinate the functions of the organism and to release characteristic reactions to certain environmental stimuli. The brain occupies the foremost place in the hierarchy

8·3 Crystals of coeruloplasmin. The blue colour of the crystals of this blood protein is due to copper.

of the nervous system. Some of the chemical processes involved in the conduction of stimuli and other functions of the nerve cells are known. However, our knowledge of the molecular basis of nervous activity is much the same as was our knowledge of genetics at the turn of the century. We are far from a molecular understanding of phenomena such as sleep, memory and passion. However, during the last few years, intensive studies using new biochemical methods suggest that in future the chemical reactions of even these phenomena will be understood.

Hormones Hormones are another group of substances in multicellular organisms which effect communication between cells. Apart from this, some are essential participants in the development of the organism and in the co-ordinated reaction of the body cells to changes in the environment. Most hormones are formed in differentiated body cells and from there pass into the blood stream which carries them to where they are needed. They may therefore be considered as components of the blood, where they are present at a definite concentration which is kept constant by sensitive regulation mechanisms.

Although hormones have several properties in common, their chemical structures may be very different from one another. Table 8·1 lists hormones found in vertebrates and gives their broad molecular structure and some of their

Table 8·1 Some hormones of vertebrates

(Modified from P. Karlson in *Kurzes Lehrbuch der Biochemie,* Thieme Verlag, Stuttgart, 1967)

chemical structure	name	place of origin	acts on
steroids	glucosteroids	adrenal cortex	sugar metabolism
	halosteroids	adrenal cortex	salt balance
	oestrogen	ovary	development of sex characteristics
	progesterone	ovary	
	testosterone	testes	
derived from amino acids	thyroxin	thyroid gland	energy metabolism, development
	adrenalin	medulla of suprarenal gland	blood pressure, sugar metabolism, intestinal activity
proteins	parathormone	parathyroid gland	calcium control
	thyrocalcitonin	thyroid gland	bone development
	insulin,	pancreas	sugar metabolism
	glucagon	pancreas	
	erythropoietin	kidneys	formation of red blood cells
	ocytocin	pituitary-occipital lobe	contraction of the womb
	vasopressin	pituitary-occipital lobe	salt and water balance
	somatotropin	pituitary-anterior lobe	growth, metabolism
	corticotropin	pituitary-anterior lobe	hormone production in adrenal cortex
	thyrotropin	pituitary-anterior lobe	function of the thyroid gland
	follicle-stimulating hormone	pituitary-anterior lobe	germ cell formation
	luteinizing hormone	pituitary-anterior lobe	production of sex hormones

functions. We shall look at a few of them a little more closely, starting with the hormone insulin. This was discovered in 1921 by the Canadians F. Banting and C. Best. Insulin is formed in certain cells of the pancreas and plays a vital role in sugar metabolism in mammals. If for any reason the production of insulin should cease, the individual develops a very serious condition called diabetes (see chapter 13).

Chemically insulin is a protein. Its structure was elucidated in 1951 by F. Sanger and his co-workers, following the development of methods which are still used today for determining the primary structure of other proteins. Insulin consists of two polypeptide chains; the amino acid sequence and the cross linkages of the two chains are given on p. 235. Because of the relatively few links of the chains, this protein was one of the first biologically active proteins to be synthesised in the laboratory using chemical methods without the aid of cell components, such as enzymes. After a great deal of experimentation, its synthesis was achieved in 1964 almost simultaneously by three different research groups. However, at present a greater yield of the active hormone is obtained in the same time by isolating insulin from the pancreas of animals, so that the insulin used medicinally is of animal origin. Although the structure of insulin and its participation in sugar metabolism is known, the precise molecular action of this hormone is still a topic of research: there is evidence that insulin aids the transport of the sugar glucose through the cell membrane. In addition, insulin appears to stimulate the synthesis of proteins in many cells, such as liver cells. It is

not yet known whether insulin directly affects the activity of certain genes.

Among the most interesting results of research in recent years is the finding that at least several hormones activate certain genes. This became especially clear from the elucidation of the structure and mode of action of an insect hormone, called ecdysone. This hormone initiates the shedding of the skins of insect larvae and pupae, that is, affects moulting during their development to the mature insect. Chemically ecdysone is a steroid and its formula is given on p. 236. The administration of ecdysone to insect larvae results in intensive RNA synthesis at certain positions on the chromosomes. This is interpreted as follows: in certain DNA regions ecdysone initiates the synthesis of the corresponding messenger-RNA, which in turn, leads to the production of the corresponding protein. The synthesis of RNA at certain positions in insect chromosomes can be observed under the microscope since several insect cells contain so-called giant chromosomes, formed by doubling of the chromosome without subsequent separation into two. Figure 8·4 shows the action of ecdysone and figure 8·5 a microscope picture of a giant chromosome from an insect cell; the positions of RNA synthesis are marked with an arrow. What is important is that following administration of ecdysone to insects, RNA synthesis is stimulated only at definite positions on the chromosomes.

Mammals also contain hormones which have a structural resemblance to the insect hormone and belong to the class of steroids. These are the sex hormones, testosterone and oestra-

8·4 When the hormone ecdysone is administered to insect pupae it initiates the shedding of the pupal skin and leads to the next stage in development – the maturė insect. Ecdysone works by activating some genes, resulting in the synthesis of certain messenger-RNA molecules.

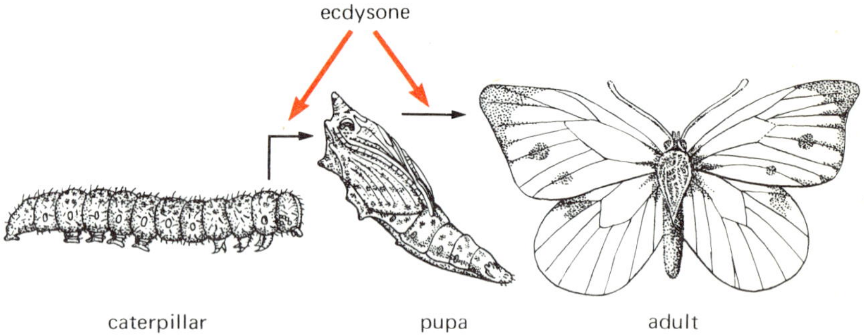

diol; their structures were elucidated by A. Butenandt in 1931. They are essential for the development of the secondary sexual characteristics. Other steriod hormones include the glucocortico-steroids, which take part in sugar metabolism, and the halosteroids, which help in the regulation of salt concentration. The mode of action of some of these hormones is apparently by either direct or indirect action upon the genes, because following their application to mammals RNA or protein synthesis is initiated in certain cells.

Table 8·1 demonstrates that substances of widely different chemical structure can act as hormones, as, for example, adrenalin, which takes part in several processes in mammals,

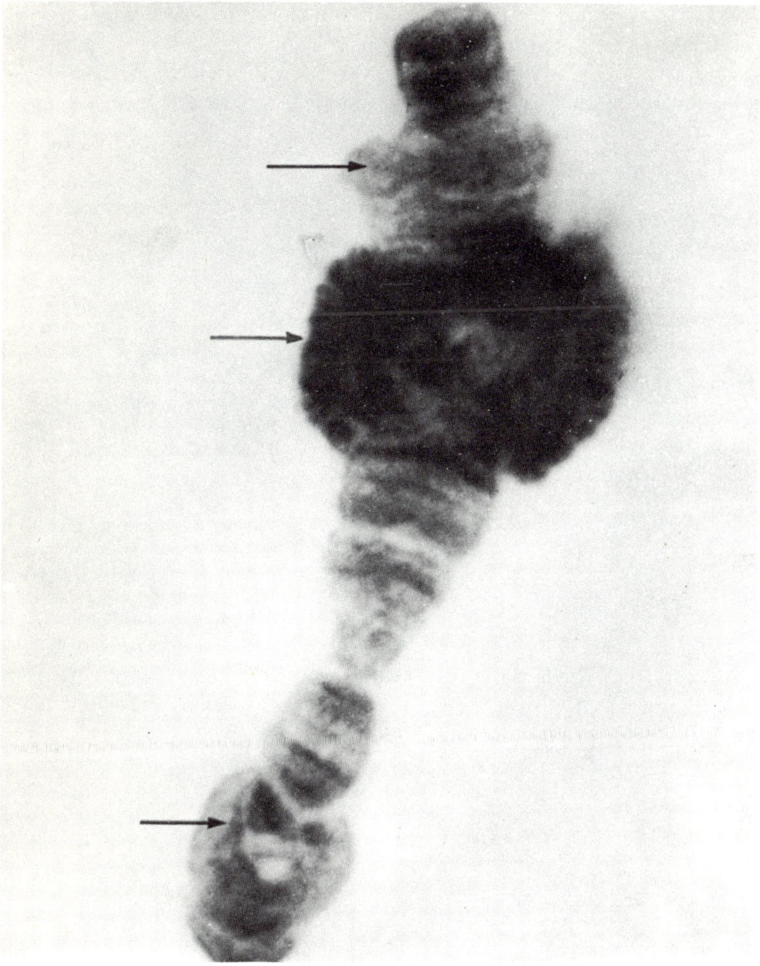

8·5 This photomicrograph of an insect chromosome shows that, following the administration of ecdysone, intensive RNA-synthesis occurs at certain places on the genetic substance (DNA). The arrows show the main regions of synthesis.

such as the regulation of blood pressure, intestinal activity and the activity of several enzymes of the metabolic energy cycles. This list of hormones shows that there are many hormones that are essential for the differentiated organism; we shall not discuss their structure and action any further here but they are critically involved in various processes in the development and maintenance of the organism. Whether such chemically different substances all operate by gene activation remains an open question, but several hormones appear to act via a direct alteration of enzyme activity.

Summary The structure and function of a few components of the blood is described in order to show some of the routes of communication of the cells of differentiated organisms. Our present knowledge of the composition and spatial structure of the oxygen-carrying molecule, haemoglobin, and of the change in its structure while it performs its function, allows us to hope that in the future other vital phenomena which appear to be especially complex will be explicable in terms of a sequence of interactions between parts of the molecule and its environment. Each component of the blood is present in constant characteristic amounts. Environmental changes are met by a change in the amount of the components: thus the

number of red blood cells increases in human beings who live for a period in regions of low oxygen concentration, such as high mountains.

Hormones are also components of the blood, and chemically belong to various classes of substance. They take part in regulating the development and maintenance of organisms. Some of them act by activating the genes of certain body cells.

9 Molecules for communication between organisms

This chapter deals with the properties of a few molecules that are formed in organisms and are then passed to the environment to be picked up by other organisms, which then show a characteristic reaction. These substances affect certain metabolic or regulatory processes in the organisms that receive them. In order to be effective, the molecules must reach their site of action at a suitable concentration. Some substances produce a reaction in every cell, for example, molecules which change the energy metabolism of the cell. Other substances block only particular reactions in certain cells in some multicellular organisms.

Drugs are compounds, partly of natural origin, partly developed by chemists, which can interfere in human metabolic or regulatory processes. Although their use and misuse is of considerable importance, we shall give little attention to this large group of compounds.

The poison most toxic to humans, that is, which is active in the lowest concentration, is a protein secreted by the bacillus *Botulinum clostridium*, the botulinus toxin. Relatively few molecules are enough to kill a man or animal, and it acts by paralysing important nerve reactions. Many of the toxins known today belong chemically to the proteins and most of the molecular processes involved in their action are still topics in research. We shall now give a more detailed description of the structure and mode of action of a few groups of molecules which effect communication between organisms.

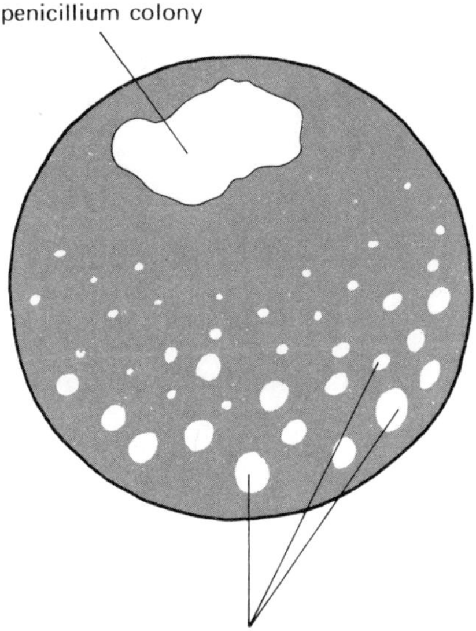

9·1 Above Secretions from the fungus *Penicillium* inhibit the growth of colonies of *Staphylococci* bacteria. This observation led Fleming to the discovery of the first antibiotic, penicillin.
9·2 Right Inhibition of protein synthesis in bacteria by antibiotics. The point at which a particular antibiotic interferes with protein synthesis is shown by red arrows. Actinomycin inhibits the synthesis of messenger-RNA; chloramphenical, the formation of the active m-RNA-ribosome complex; streptomycin, the formation of functioning ribosomes; puromycin, the further growth of the polypeptide chain; borrelidin, the bonding of the amino acid threonine to transfer-RNA.

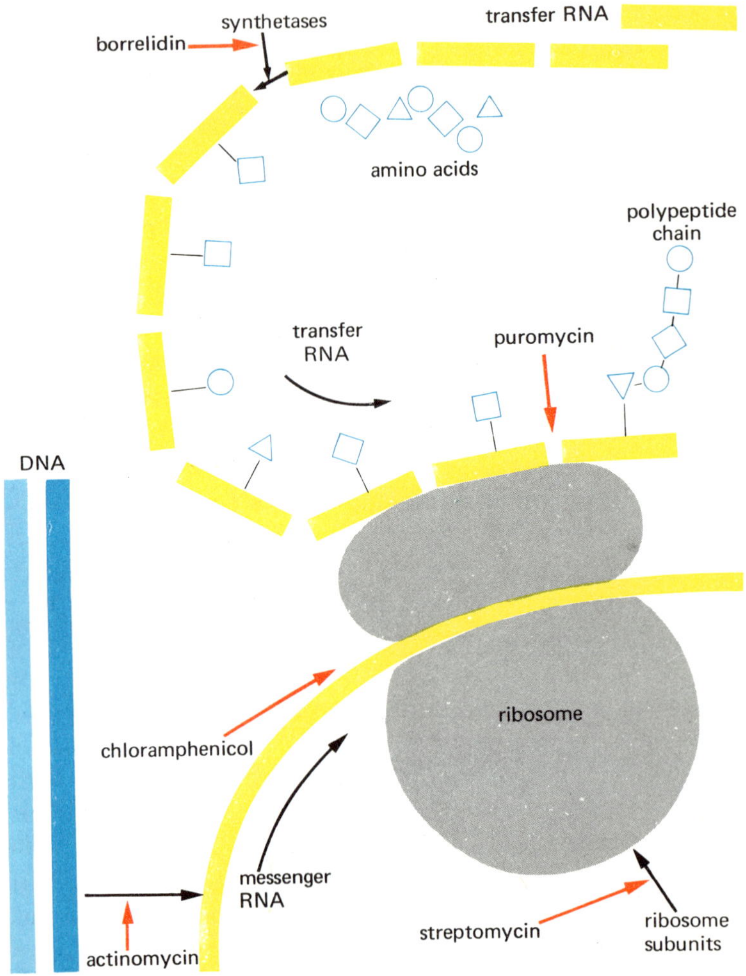
synthetases
transfer RNA
borrelidin
amino acids
polypeptide chain
transfer RNA
puromycin
DNA
ribosome
chloramphenicol
messenger RNA
streptomycin
ribosome subunits
actinomycin

Antibiotics

In 1929 the English scientist A. Fleming observed that bacteria were destroyed in the neighbourhood of the fungus *Penicillium*. Figure 9·1 shows the dissolution of bacterial colonies by a substance secreted by *Penicillium*. Following this discovery, there was a systematic search for substances having similar action from other types of fungus or bacteria. As a result, a whole series of antibiotics which inhibit the growth of bacteria are known today. Furthermore, many of the infectious diseases of mankind have lost their terror; thus, illnesses such as pneumonia and typhus that are caused by bacteria can now be effectively controlled with the aid of antibiotics.

The chemical composition and the mode of action of a few antibiotics are known in detail. As examples, the structures of two antibiotics, streptomycin and chloramphenicol, are given on p. 236. Many antibiotics inhibit the growth of bacterial cells by blocking certain steps in their protein synthesis. The simplified scheme of protein synthesis shown in figure 9·2 indicates the points of attack for a number of antibiotics.

One necessary property of antibiotics to control infectious diseases in man is that the antibiotic should block protein synthesis only in the invading bacterium and not in human cells. For the majority of antibiotics this is guaranteed by the impermeability of the cell membranes of mammalian cells to antibiotics. One complication in the treatment of infectious diseases with antibiotics is that bacteria can develop a re-

sistance towards the antibiotic so that they are no longer destroyed. In recent years a race has developed between the pharmaceutical industry discovering and synthesising new antibiotics and the acquirement of resistance by many disease-causing bacteria.

The molecular changes in the bacterial cells responsible for resistance are partially known. Will shall explain how the resistance of several strains of bacteria towards streptomycin is molecularly conditioned. Figure 9·2 shows that streptomycin inhibits protein synthesis in bacteria at the stage of ribosome formation. It changes the smaller ribosome subunit in such a way that some trinucleotides of messenger-RNA will no longer bond with the corresponding transfer-RNA. For example, the triplet for the amino acid phenylalanine binds with isoleucine transfer-RNA; this means that isoleucine takes the place of phenylalanine in the resulting protein. Since the function of a protein depends on its amino acid sequence, the necessary protein is produced in a non-functioning form, thus causing the death of the bacterial cell. This mechanism also expands our knowledge of the processes of protein synthesis. We said that the sequential order of the amino acids in proteins is determined by the sequential order of the trinucleotides in DNA. The mode of action of streptomycin now shows that the structure of ribosomes can be so changed by certain lower molecular-weight substances that the same messenger-RNA can be read in different ways, resulting in the incorporation of a 'wrong' amino acid. This indicates that the ribosomes should not only be considered as the site of the

translation of the nucleotide sequence into the amino acid sequence; their structure affects this translation. Bacteria in which protein synthesis is no longer disturbed by streptomycin possess changed ribosome proteins: the nucleotide sequence in DNA which encodes the structure of the ribosome proteins has changed, resulting in a change in certain ribosomal proteins. The changed ribosome structure prevents the streptomycin from taking effect, so that in these cells protein synthesis proceeds undisturbed even in the presence of the antibiotic, and the bacteria do not die; they have become resistant.

There are even bacteria the ribosomes of which undergo such a change that they are not only resistant to streptomycin, but their ribosomes can also carry out protein synthesis properly only in the presence of streptomycin – these are streptomycin-dependent bacteria. The build-up of resistance by bacteria is not restricted to the case of streptomycin but has been observed with all known antibiotics. Various mechanisms are responsible. Thus, resistance to penicillin is caused by an enzyme, called penicillinase, which degrades penicillin.

Vitamins

Vitamins are another group of substances which are secreted by one organism and affect another. They are not involved in the destruction of life but in its maintenance. Some organisms are able to produce them but others are not and these latter must therefore assimilate them with their food. Besides vitamins, there are other molecules which cannot be synthesised

by certain organisms, such as some of the building blocks of proteins, for example the amino acid histidine; these must be taken in daily by the rat in fairly large quantities. However, as far as vitamins are concerned, small quantities suffice. This is because their function is usually to bond, for example, to enzymes, thus enabling enzymes to function. Not all enzymes, though, need vitamins to be active.

From the definition of vitamins it may be seen that there are no vitamins *per se*, but only in relation to specific organisms. Thus, many of the substances which are vitamins for humans can be synthesised by other organisms. Man assimilates his vitamins with his food; certain vitamins may be contained in vegetables or milk, for example. From this it may be deduced that an unbalanced diet will not supply certain vitamins and will result in the corresponding deficiency symptoms. This was very much the case when the chemical nature of vitamins was unknown. Thus, one of the longest known diseases due to vitamin deficiency is scurvy, a particular affliction of sailors in the past. Vitamin C was not present in the dried food of sailors but is found, for example, in fresh vegetables and fruit. Today the structure of vitamin C is known (p. 237) and the substance may be synthesised in the laboratory. As with many other vitamins, it is important in that it takes part in catalysing several metabolic reactions. If it is lacking in the diet, deficiency symptoms occur, expressing themselves initially in changes of the skin, teeth and joints. It is a vitamin for man, apes and guinea pigs; other mammals are able to synthesise it.

Today, more than ten vitamins are known to be essential to man. As in the case of hormones, these substances are classed together not because of their chemical structure but because of their related functions. We shall now consider the structure and mode of action (p.237–8) of vitamin A. The precursors of this vitamin are synthesised in plants and assimilated by mammals from their food. The vitamin precursors are then split in the animal to give active vitamin A. As a component of visual purple in the retina it is essential to vision. Light produces a chemical rearrangement in the vitamin A molecule and this in turn results in a spatial re-organisation of the protein part of the visual purple, thus stimulating certain nerves. This is therefore a further example of a system which functions only by the co-operation of a non-protein and a protein part. Neither of these parts alone is capable of carrying out the function which they perform together – a phenomenon we noted in the case of the oxygen-carrying haemoglobin. The stages involved in the process of vision are shown on p. 238.

Pheromones

These substances are found mainly in insects. They are very interesting biologically because they enable insects to communicate with each other in certain ways. Their chemistry and action have not long been known, and there are two reasons for this. In the first place they are produced in exceedingly small quantities, which makes their isolation very

difficult, and secondly, this method of communication is rarely met with in other animal groups.

In 1959 A. Butenandt's research group worked out the chemical structure of the sexual lure of the silk-moth *(Bombyx mori)* after working for years to isolate sufficient quantities of the pure substance. It is a lipid and its formula is given on p. 239 together with the chemical formula of a very similar molecule synthesised in the laboratory. The latter differs from the natural lure only in the spatial arrangement of a few atoms in the molecule. However, this molecule is well-nigh inactive as a lure for the silk-moth. The natural lure secreted by the female silk-moth entices male silk-moths from a distance of several kilometres; it cannot be more than a few molecules that reach the receptors of the males and which send them in the direction of the female.

The non-attractive lipid, differing from the active form merely by a small difference in its spatial arrangement, brings us to a principle which needs emphasising again. The spatial arrangement of the groups in molecules is just as decisive for their biological function as is their composition. In the appendix (p. 240), this principle is illustrated with the amino acid alanine.

Pheromones are not restricted to the sexual lures of the insect world. The important issues in an insect colony, such as communication between insects on the position of profitable sources of food, dangers and recognition of the queen, are all controlled by specific substances. These pheromones are also lower molecular-weight compounds and are often deri-

9·3 Head of the male silk moth, showing the super-sensitive antennae which carry thousands of sensory cells. The latter respond specifically to lures and air movements. The stimulated sensory cells send nerve impulses to the brain, which are then translated into corresponding behaviour patterns of the animal.

vatives of fatty acids; the chemical structures of several of these pheromones have been elucidated. Several research groups are presently concerned with the analysis of the molecules in that part of the chain of reactions which bridge the gap between the arrival of the pheromone at the receptor and its translation into a complex mode of behaviour in the recipient animal, such as fleeing or searching for food (figure 9·3).

A curiosity

Here we shall give another interesting example of the molecular weapons used between different animal species. If the yellow brand-beetle, a water beetle, is approached by a predatory fish, it secretes a liquid which paralyses the fish. An analysis of this defence liquid has shown that the substance responsible is a steroid which resembles the hormones (halosteroids) which regulate the salt balance in fishes, as they do in all vertebrates. In the appendix (p. 240) the chemical structure of a hormone from vertebrates is compared with the defence substance of the beetle. The sudden and excessive quantity of this hormone absorbed from the beetle's defence liquid seriously upsets the fish's salt balance, which produces a temporary paralysis. This happens because the concentration of a hormone in an organism is as critical as its structure. The steroid has no effect on the beetle itself since, for this animal, it does not act as a hormone.

Summary Some molecules synthesised by living organisms produce a definite reaction in other organisms of the same or of a different species. Some of these substances act as defence substances, others as a means of communication.

Antibiotics inhibit the growth of bacteria by, for example, interfering with the reactions that synthesise proteins in bacteria. The investigation of the mode of action of the antibiotic streptomycin has also increased our knowledge of the function of ribosomes in protein synthesis: the structure of the ribosomal protein can change the translation of the nucleotide sequence of messenger-RNA into the correct amino acid sequence.

Vitamins are a group of lower molecular-weight substances which some organisms synthesise in their cells but others cannot. The latter must therefore assimilate these substances in their diet. Only small quantities of vitamins are necessary since these substances act mainly as catalysts in important reactions, such as in metabolism or in the process of vision.

Pheromones serve for communication between organisms of the same species. Certain environmental stimuli such as danger, the urge to find food, can cause insects to secrete pheromones which come into contact with certain receptors in other members of the species and cause the latter to adopt similar modes of behaviour, such as to flee, or to search for food.

10 Antibodies

Structure and mode of action

If foreign compounds are administered to vertebrates, then within a few days their blood is found to contain protein molecules which bind specifically with the foreign compounds which induced their formation. These proteins are called *antibodies*. Figure 10·1 shows how an injection of foreign compounds brings about the formation of antibodies. In the case illustrated, rabbits were injected with polysaccharides from the cell walls of bacteria. If blood is taken from the animals after a week and mixed with the same polysaccharide in a test tube, a precipitate is formed. This precipitate is composed of the polysaccharides and the antibodies that have been formed. The interesting feature of antibodies is their high specificity: antibodies produced by the injection of certain polysaccharides react only with these polysaccharides and not with others from the cell membranes of other bacteria. The molecular components of a macromolecule with which the antibody reacts can be analysed in more detail: in each case, the specificity of the antibody is directed towards the arrangement of a few sugar molecules in the polysaccharide. These molecular configurations of the large molecule are called antigenic determinants, and all molecules which cause the formation of antibodies are called *antigens*.

So far we have mentioned polysaccharides as antigens. However, the ability to produce antibodies in certain organisms is not restricted to polysaccharides. Other molecules, for example, proteins, or complex molecules such as lipopoly-

10·1 The formation of antibodies in rabbits. Antibodies are found in the blood plasma.

saccharides, administered to vertebrates also result in the formation of specific antibodies.

The chemical structure of antibodies has been recently intensively investigated. Figure 10·2 shows a model of an antibody molecule. It consists of four protein chains, two smaller and two larger, held together by certain linkages. Once again we meet the principle described for haemoglobin: the complete function of the antibody, that is, its bonding to the appropriate antigen, is possible only through the co-operation of the four chains. The reactive sites of the antibody molecule are indicated with an arrow and it may be seen that two identical reactive sites are present in each antibody molecule. Now we can understand the formation of a visible precipitate when the antibody reacts with the appropriate antigen molecule to form a cross-linked network, as shown in figure 10·3.

The amino acid sequences of the protein chains of antibody molecules are at present being investigated in several laboratories and those of a few smaller chains of some antibodies are

3 polysaccharide added to blood plasma

4 polysaccharide precipitated by antibody within hours

known. Their comparison shows that certain parts of their amino acid sequence in the chains is identical and it is now assumed that antibodies differ only in that part of the chain which is close to the bonding sites and that these differences are principally responsible both for the specificity of the antibody and its bonding to the antigen. It is still not clear, though, how chemically similar antibodies, such as proteins, can bind so specifically with antigens that are chemically so different, like polysaccharides or some proteins. Also, the function of a small sugar residue in the antibody is unknown.

Biological significance

The significance of antibodies for the maintenance of organisms, including man, was known long before their chemical structures. It was known that antibodies play a crucial part in the resistance to every infectious disease. For example, if the body is infected with the germs of measles, then within

10·2 Above A model of an antibody molecule which consists of two short and two long polypeptide chains. The arrows indicate the areas on the antibody molecule which are the bonding sites for the appropriate antigen. Different antibodies possess different amino acid sequences in those parts of the four polypeptide chains which are close to the antigen bonding sites. The sugar part of the antibody is not shown.

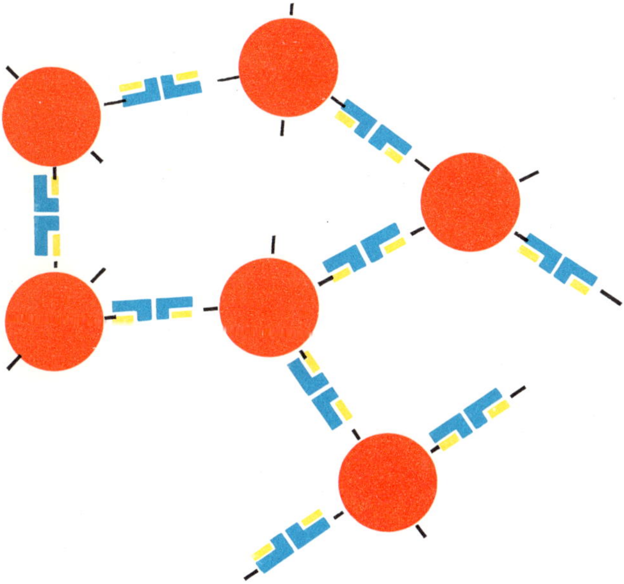

nine days this results in the production of antibodies which react specifically with the measles germs, preventing them from spreading further among the body cells and thus localising the symptoms. A person who has suffered from measles contains the antibodies for the measles germs in the blood. This explains why measles generally occurs only once in a lifetime: if there is a new infection by measles germs, they are immediately bound by the antibodies already present in the blood stream and their effect is nullified before they can give rise to the symptoms of the illness.

The knowledge that antibodies prevent infectious diseases is the basis of all modern vaccination. The practice is to inoculate with germs related to those of the illness but which are not dangerous. Since the antigenic determinants of these germs are the same as those of the disease-causing germs, the organism produces antibodies which are specific to the latter. These antibodies remain in the blood and if the individual should become infected with the germs of the actual disease, they are immediately bound by these antibodies. This principle of *active immunisation* was introduced in 1796 by E. Jenner, who

10·3 Left Antigen-antibody precipitation. Here red blood corpuscles are used as the antigen. Each of the blood corpuscles possesses several antigenic determinants on its surface. The reaction of the antibody with the antigenic determinants produces an immuno-precipitate, which consists of red blood corpuscles linked by antibodies. Thus it is a condition for the formation of a visible immuno-precipitate that there is more than one antigenic determinant per antigen.

discovered that the germs of cow-pox did not produce illness but prevented the subject from catching small-pox at a later date. The germs of cow-pox and small-pox are sufficiently similar that a person innoculated with cow-pox germs produces antibodies which react also with the germs of small-pox and therefore prevent the outbreak of the disease. The introduction of vaccination with cow-pox has meant that severe epidemics of small-pox are now unknown in Europe and the USA.

Active immunisation has also lessened the terrors of other infectious diseases, such as diphtheria or yellow fever. We no longer wait for the chance discovery of harmless germs related to those of the disease. Many laboratories specialise in isolating disease-producing germs and then modifying them to make them harmless but capable, following inoculation, of inducing antibodies which will react with harmful germs. The first successful modification of a disease-producing germ in the laboratory was achieved by M. Theiler in 1930, when he developed germs for innoculation against yellow fever.

However, it is easy to see that it would not be possible to inoculate every person in time to avoid infection with germs. At the end of the last century, E. von Behring conceived the idea of keeping a store of antibodies for certain illnesses, ready to inject into a patient at the time of the illness. This procedure supplies the body with antibodies immediately, whereas the formation of antibodies takes up to nine days following infection and is often very slight when the person is already suffering from the illness. Inoculation with pre-

pared antibodies often prevents diseases such as tetanus or diphtheria. The antibodies for injection are obtained from animals such as horses or sheep which have been infected with the germs of the disease and which contain the appropriate antibodies in their blood stream. The blood plasma of the animals may be kept for many years at minus seventy degrees centigrade. The prevention of disease by inoculation with antibodies is called *passive immunisation* – passive because the subject is supplied with prepared antibodies.

The molecular processes involved in the synthesis of antibodies are still largely unknown. Antibodies are formed in cells specialised for this purpose, which are to be found in, among other places, the lymph nodes. How antigens, such as certain sequences of sugars or amino acids, cause the formation of specific antibodies is still not clear in detail. Our knowledge of the molecular processes of antibody synthesis is in much the same state as was protein synthesis a few years ago, when the puzzle was how the sequence of nucleotides in nucleic acids was translated to a specific sequence of amino acids in proteins.

Human blood groups

In 1900 K. Landsteiner discovered that there are four main types of blood groups in man, and that the blood of any human belongs to one or other of these groups; the groups are named by the letters A, B, AB and O. The groups differ in the arrangement of certain molecules in the surface of the red blood cells.

In the appendix (p. 241) it is shown that these four blood groups are the result of a certain arrangement of various sugars in the cell wall. These arrangements of sugars are passed on from parents to offspring and are not affected by environmental factors. This is why the distribution of blood groups amongst the world's peoples is so interesting, since it gives some information on the relationships between peoples and on their migrations. Thus there is a characteristic distribution of the individual blood groups over the world; figure 10·4 shows the frequency distribution for the blood groups A and B, that is, the frequency of the occurrence of certain sugar groupings in the blood cell wall of people in different countries.

A knowledge of human blood groups is very important in medicine. People with blood group A carry no antibodies for the sugar molecules of their own red blood cells but their blood plasma does contain antibodies for those molecular arrangements which are not present. Thus a person with blood group A carries antibodies for the B sugars; these antibodies react with the red blood cells from a person with blood group B, binding the foreign cells and causing them to clump together, as shown in figure 10·3. This knowledge is used in blood transfusions: the blood donor and the receiver must both have the same blood group.

For a long time it was a puzzle how a person with blood group A could have antibodies for blood group B and vice versa. These antibodies were present even if the person had never come into contact with the cells of persons with blood

group B, and this apparently contradicted the rule that antibodies are produced only if the corresponding antigen, in this case the B-substance, has entered the organism. This apparent contradiction has now been solved: our intestinal bacteria, the *coli* cells, have cell walls which contain sugar units similar to those of the A and B blood group substances. Degradation products of the bacterial walls find their way from the intestine into the organism and these evoke the formation of specific antibodies. Since the antigenic determinants – the sugar groupings – in the cell walls of the red blood cells and the *coli* cells are the same, the antibodies resulting from the components of the *coli* cells also react with the corresponding structures of the red blood cells.

Here we have an interesting biological phenomenon: people with blood group B contain antibodies only for the A substance in their blood although the *coli* bacteria produce both A and B groupings as antigens. Thus, antibodies are normally not produced for substances which are contained in the organism's own cells or tissues; for this would be incompatible with the maintenance of the organism since it would result in a clumping and destruction of the body's own cells. The fact that organisms do not produce antibodies against their own compounds has been theoretically and experimentally investigated by M. Burnet and P. Medawar, who found that the organism recognises as its own all those substances present in the body up to about the time of birth. All substances entering the organism after this time are regarded as alien and therefore result in the formation of specific anti-

bodies. The molecular processes which prevent the formation of antibodies against the body's own substances are still the object of research.

Since, with the exception of identical twins, no two persons are exactly alike, it is understandable that the transplantation of tissues or organs from one person to another leads to the formation of antibodies in the recipient against the transplanted foreign substances; these antibodies then react with the antigens of the alien cells and destroy them. This is why the replacement of defective organs of one person by sound organs from another is seldom successful. The difficult techniques involved in the transplantation of organs from one person to another have been developed to such perfection that surgeons can now transplant organs such as the heart or the kidney. However, after about nine days, antibodies are formed in the recipient which destroy the transplanted organ. Now it is certainly possible to prevent the production of all antibodies in an organism, for example, by irradiation of the tissues which produce antibodies or by the use of certain drugs. But since antibodies are essential as a resistance against infectious diseases, the prevention of all antibody formation can lead to severe infection. Thus it is easy to see that the transplantation of organs can hope to be a permanent success only if it is possible to prevent the formation of antibodies for very specific antigens – those contained in the transplanted organ.

In human medicine cases have been known that break the rule that antibodies are not formed against the organism's

10·4 Overleaf Geographical distribution of A and B blood groups. The distribution corresponds with the blood groups of the original inhabitants of these countries, and therefore reflects the presence of certain sugar molecules in the membranes of the red blood corpuscles.

own substance. These syndromes are grouped under the name of *auto-immune* illnesses. They include, among others, several forms of rheumatism and the destruction of red blood cells. It appears that alien molecules usually combine with the native molecules and antibodies are produced against the combination, and then, ultimately these antibodies react with the native molecules as well and so lead to a destruction of certain cells of the patient.

Apart from the blood group factors described so far, there are blood groups for which antibodies are formed only after the foreign blood has entered the organism. The so-called rhesus factors are the most significant because, in some cases, they can complicate the normal course of a pregnancy, but we cannot go into this any further.

Summary Antibodies are proteins produced in vertebrate organisms in response to foreign substances entering the body. The substances which lead to the formation of antibodies are called antigens. Chemically, these substances may be very different from one another. Thus both proteins and polysaccharides stimulate the formation of antibodies if they are foreign to the organism. The antibodies bind specifically with the molecules that cause their formation. The specificity of the antibodies is always directed towards specific regions of the antigen – the antigenic determinants. The organism's own molecules do not cause antibody formation. At present, research is directed towards understanding the molecular processes involved in the recognition of molecules foreign to the

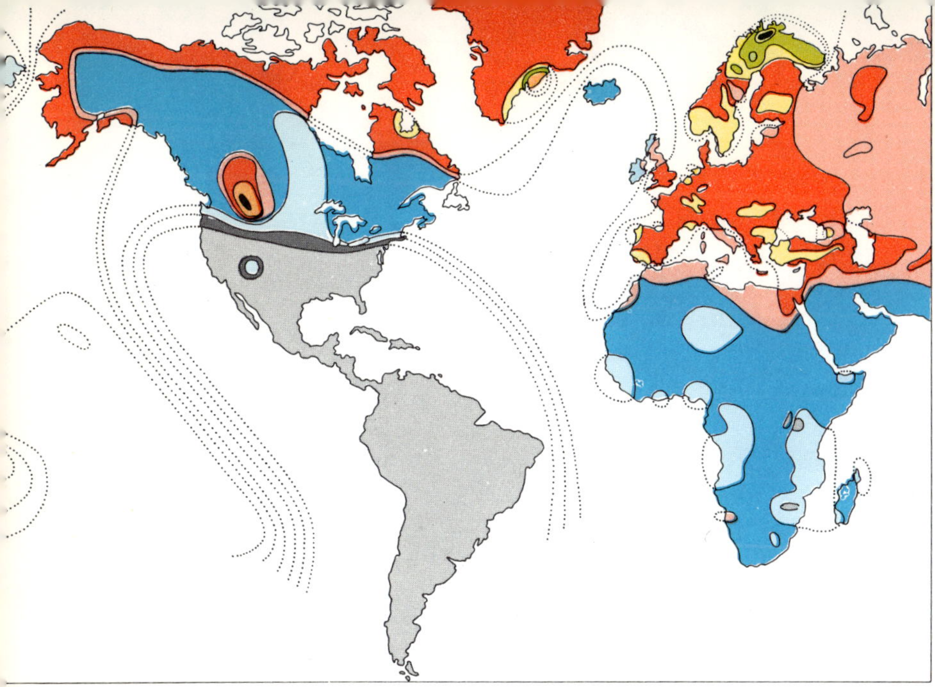

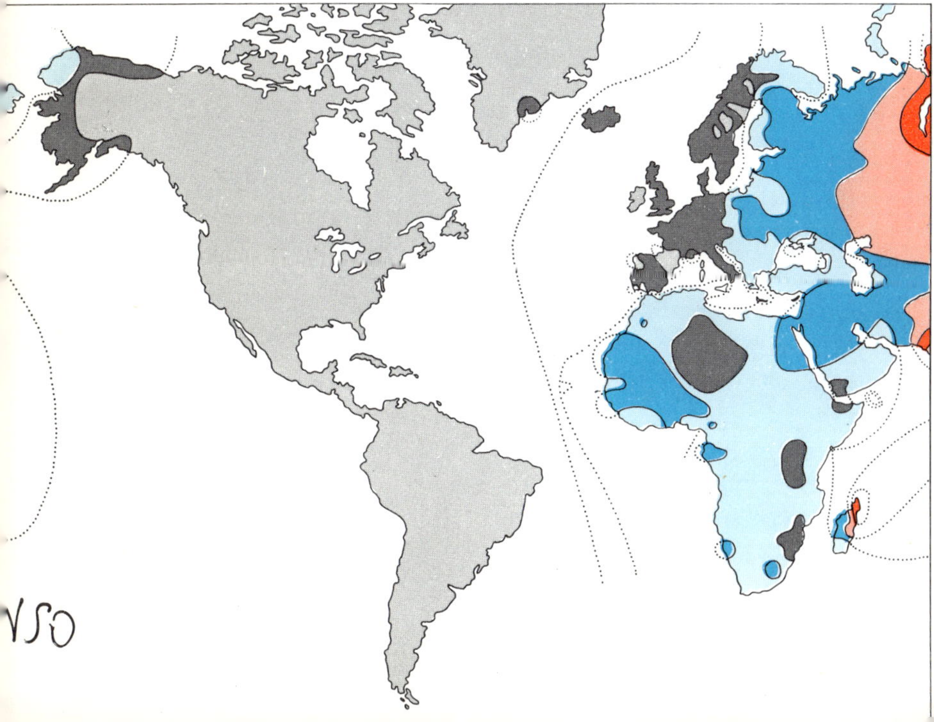

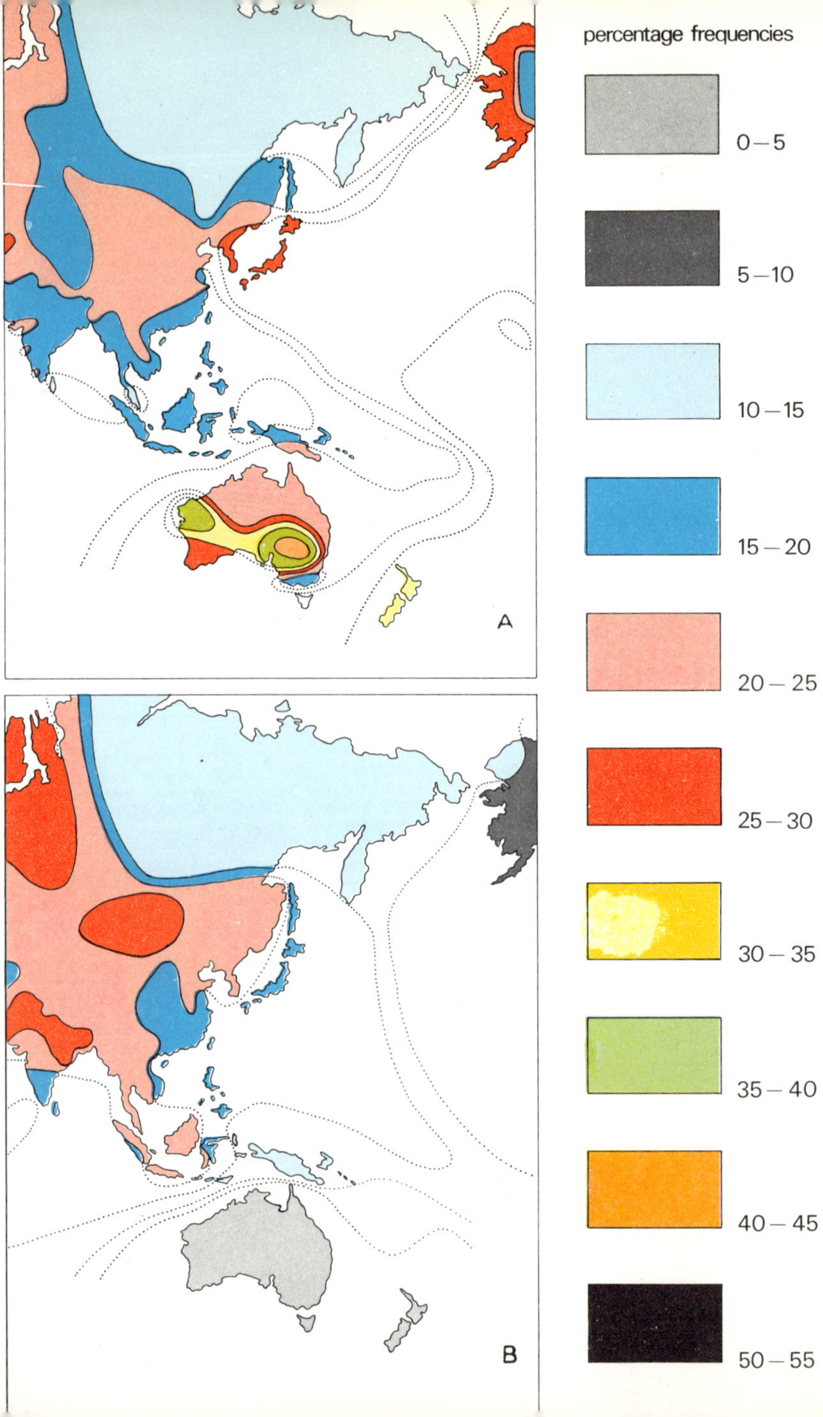
A
B
percentage frequencies
0 – 5
5 – 10
10 – 15
15 – 20
20 – 25
25 – 30
30 – 35
35 – 40
40 – 45
50 – 55

body, and of the structure and synthesis of antibodies in specialised cells.

The main significance of antibodies is their vital participation in the resistance to infectious diseases. In the last decade, active or passive immunisation, ensuring the presence of antibodies for the particular infectious diseases at the right time, have saved the lives of many persons who would otherwise have died in epidemics.

The description of the ABO-systems of human blood groups has revealed some disadvantages entailed in the formation and action of antibodies, such as the problems posed in the transplantation of organs from one person to another and the participation of antibodies in human auto-immune illnesses.

11 Phylogeny – the evolution of complex organisms from simpler ones

As described in chapter 1, the number and type of molecules in simple unicellular organisms are constant in a particular environment. Apart from this, we learned that different types of molecules in *coli* cells have different functions. All possible vital properties of the cell are determined by the macromolecule DNA. During protein synthesis, the nucleotide sequence of DNA is translated into a specific sequence of protein building blocks. Many proteins in their role as enzymes determine the course of the reactions which are involved in producing energy, and in the synthesis of cell wall structures, the building blocks of macromolecules and the macromolecules themselves. Thus the functions of the macromolecules in cells are interrelated and are controlled by DNA.

The same basic processes operate in multicellular organisms, and so there is a constant and certain uniformity in the cellular structures and reactions in more complex organisms. But the specialised cells of more complex organisms have additional structures and functions which are not present in simple one-celled organisms. The question we have to consider now is how this multiplicity of different organisms came about.

In the middle of the last century C. Darwin realised that organisms have evolved from one another. A comparison of the macroscopic structures and forms of different organisms alive today and information from fossils enables us to draw up a phylogenetic tree (figure 11·1). Many of the branches of this tree may be sub-divided and analysed further, as shown in figure 11·2 for the development of the modern horse from

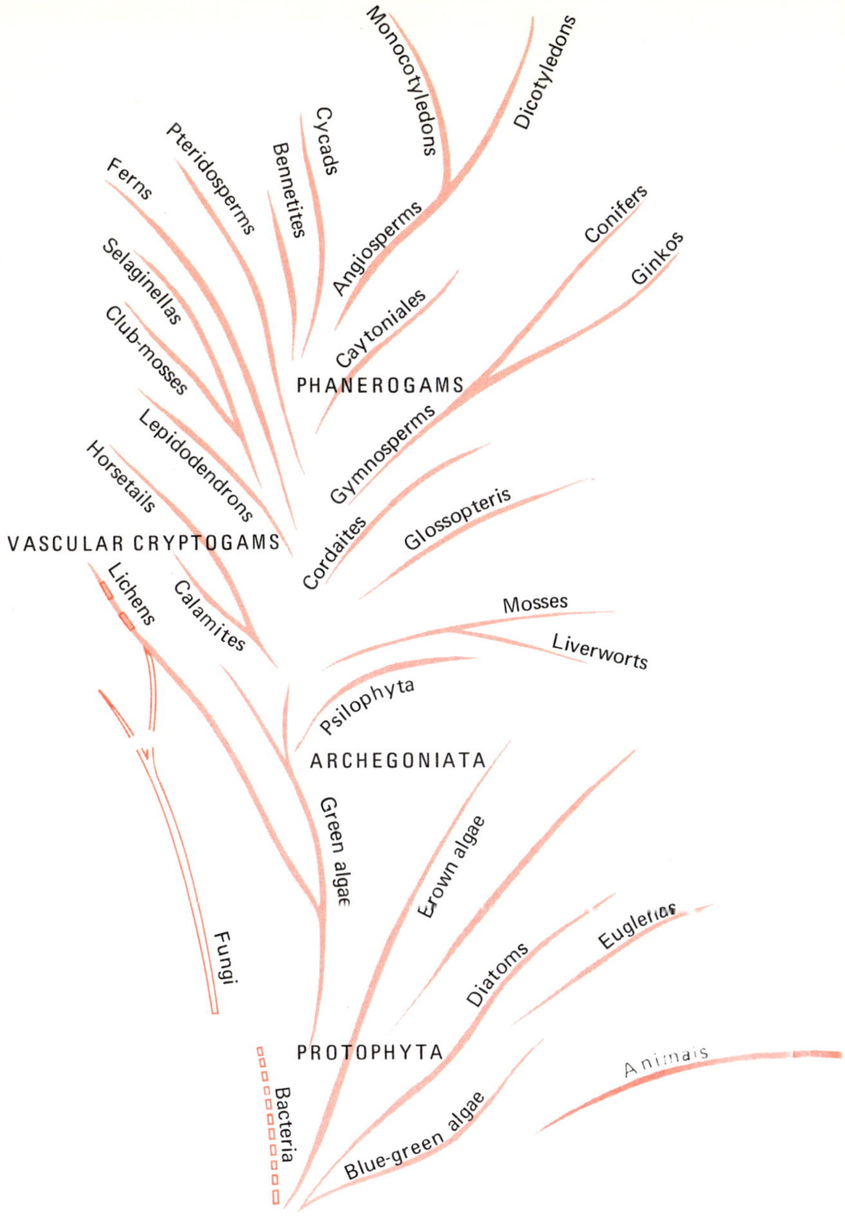

Monocotyledons
Dicotyledons
Cycads
Pteridosperms
Bennetites
Ferns
Angiosperms
Conifers
Ginkos
Selaginellas
Caytoniales
Club-mosses
PHANEROGAMS
Lepidodendrons
Gymnosperms
Horsetails
Glossopteris
Cordaites
VASCULAR CRYPTOGAMS
Lichens
Calamites
Mosses
Liverworts
Psilophyta
ARCHEGONIATA
Green algae
Brown algae
Fungi
Euglenas
Diatoms
PROTOPHYTA
Animals
Bacteria
Blue-green algae

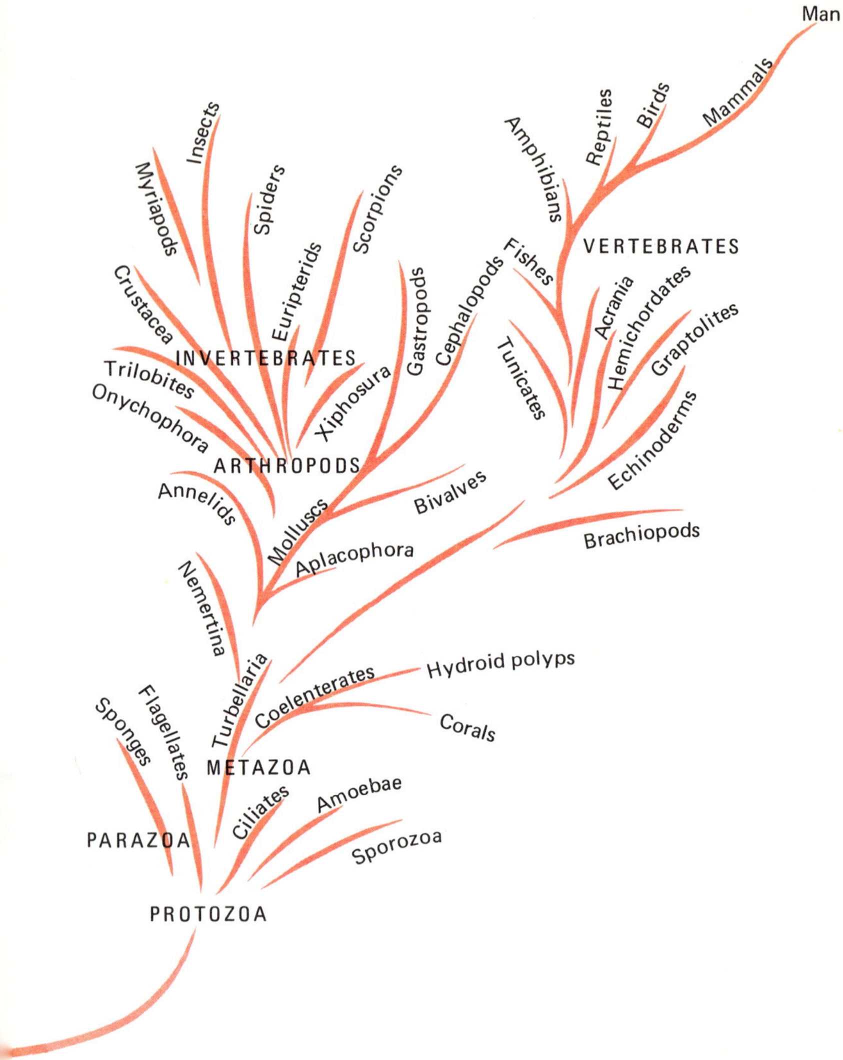

11·1 This phylogenetic tree shows the development of present-day organisms from simpler precursors.

11·2 The evolution of the horse represents one of the terminal branches of the phylogenetic tree. The other branches of the tree shown in figure **11·1** also end in similar detail.

its ancestors. The essence of Darwin's findings was not merely that organisms have evolved from other organisms; he also recognised the mechanisms which produced this evolution. In 1858 C. Darwin and A. Wallace read a joint paper to the Linnaean Society of London called *On the tendency of species to form varieties and on the perpetuation of varieties and species by natural selection*. Here they stated that variation and selection are the processes responsible for the development of more complex organisms from simpler ones. It appears to me to be one of the most inspired ideas ever conceived by man, if you consider that Darwin grasped these principles with no knowledge at all of the molecular processes responsible. Today, research on the molecules of life has resulted in our understanding variation and selection in molecular terms to a considerable extent; if this had been so in Darwin's time, his ideas would not have been doubted so often.

The production and maintenance of mutations

The prime chemical requirements for the occurrence of variations among organisms are mutations. Molecular processes are at work which change the genetic substance, the DNA, to give new or changed proteins. These proteins are often capable of changing some properties of the cell.

south america
north america
old world
recent
pleistocene
pliocene
miocene
oligocene
eocene
equus
equus
equus
hipparion
pliohippus
hypohippus
anchitherium
merychippus
mesohippus
palaeotheres
eohippus
hyracotherium

11·3 The three main types of mutation. The four different symbols represent the four building blocks (deoxyribonucleotides) of DNA. In point mutation, there is an exchange of one DNA building block for one of the other three. In deletion, there is a loss of one or a sequence of several DNA building blocks. In gene duplication, the sequence of building blocks comprising a gene is duplicated, either in part or wholly.

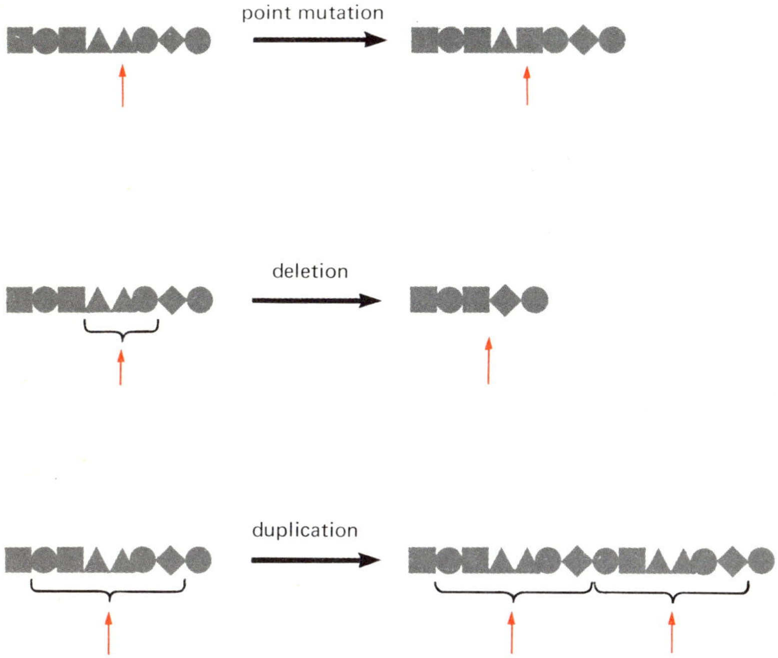

It is the sequential order of the building blocks of DNA which determines the sequential order of the amino acids, and as we have often pointed out, it is the sequence of amino acids which determines the function of the protein. Other proteins with different properties are produced because of a new or different sequence of nucleotides in DNA.

The genes of DNA may be affected by the following changes (see figure 11·3): 1. Exchange of a DNA building-block – point mutation. 2. Complete or partial disappearance of a gene, called deletion. 3. Simple or multiple duplication of a gene or part of it. All three types of mutation change the amino acid sequence of proteins and therefore their function. Molecular changes in DNA can, in fact, be corroborated by observing the correspondingly altered proteins. Before considering the modification of the amino acid sequence of a protein by mutation in detail, we must give some attention to the origin of mutations.

In 1927 A. Muller reported that X-rays increase the number of variations of each characteristic in a fly, including properties like eye-colour and ability to fly (figure 11·4). The occurrence of hitherto unknown variations was also observed. Today we know that certain short-wave radiations or certain chemicals bring about changes in DNA. The so-called spontaneous mutations, observable in a definite percentage in every population of identical individuals, are thought to be due mainly to the action of cosmic radiation, which is a normal part of our environment. Extensive investigations by several groups of workers on the detailed molecular action of muta-

genic agents, such as certain radiations or chemicals, have also shown that mutations often only achieve their final form by the co-operation of processes concerned in the replication of DNA. Duplication of a gene makes this especially clear: this could be caused by a short segment of the DNA strand being copied twice during replication.

From the nature of the molecular processes that produce mutations, and the construction of DNA from four building blocks in a characteristic order, it should be clear that the result of a mutation is not necessarily adaptive. The sequential order of the DNA building-blocks is changed; what effect this has upon the properties of cells cannot be estimated from this change. One and the same chemical change at different positions in the DNA molecule can have completely different consequences for the cell.

Theoretically, all of the possible variations of the many proteins found in cells ought to be found in nature but this is not the case; only certain variations are encountered. To understand why this should be so we must recall that Darwin stipulated that selection was essential for the formation of species. According to this principle, only a few of the variations caused by mutations persist and these are the ones which are adapted to their environment and which favour the survival of the species and its reproduction. Let us clarify this point by taking an extreme case. If a mutation so changes the DNA that an important protein suffers such a change in its amino acid sequence that it can no longer fulfill its function, then the cell dies and is excluded from reproduction. For example, an

11·4 Some wing and eye mutations in the fly *Drosophila.*

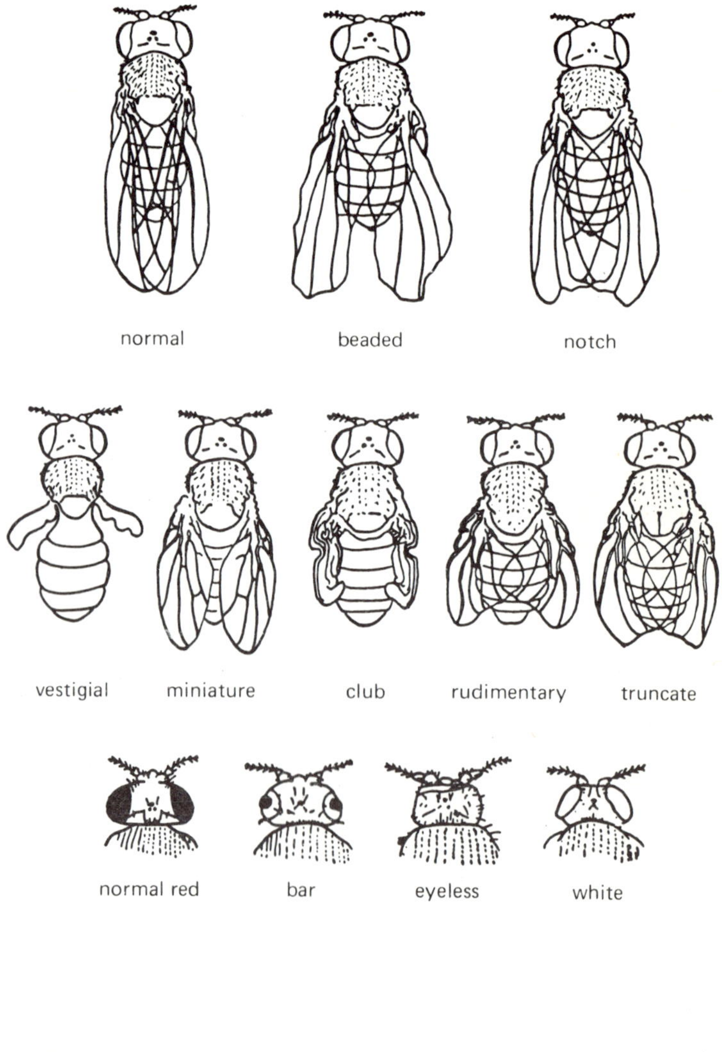

11·5 A case of industrial melanism. In areas with little air pollution the trunks of trees are covered with light-coloured lichens (*left*). On these the light-coloured form of the moth *Biston betularia* is found, and is well camouflaged against predators; the dark form of the moth, being conspicuous to predators, is very rare. The trunks of trees in polluted areas are devoid of lichens and have dark trunks (*right*). This has led to the selection of mutations which result in a darker pigmentation, so that here the darker form of the moth is better camouflaged and is therefore more numerous than the light form.

enzyme incapable of functioning and yet essential for protein synthesis leads to the complete break-down of the metabolism of the cell and to its death. A similar situation is true for more complex organisms. For example, if the oxygen-carrying molecule, haemoglobin, is so changed by a mutation that it can no longer bind oxygen, then this will also lead to an inviable organism. Actually, most of the changes in DNA caused by mutations are detrimental to the organism. This statement implies that only a limited number of mutational changes in DNA can occur, otherwise there will be a great deterioration in the properties of the individual; on the other hand they must be numerous enough to allow the further evolution of the organism. It is easy to see that this balance between a necessary and harmless rate of mutation can be sensibly disturbed if we suddenly increase the mutation rate through radioactivity or other mutagenic agents in the environment.

The principle of selection says that the only modified functions (variations) to persist over several generations are those which improve the properties of the organism, that is, improve its survival under the prevalent environmental conditions (figure 11·5). Now the environment of an organism consists not only of inanimate matter but also of other organisms. A change in the properties of one animal species can change the environment of another species sharing the same habitat to such an extent that it can no longer find sufficient food. Thus the extinction of a species is conditioned not only by its own gene mutations but by the improved survival of another

warbler finch
large tree finch
medium tree finch
small tree finch
tool-using finch
mangrove finch
large ground finch
medium gound finch
small ground finch
sharp beaked ground finch
cactus ground finch
large cactus ground finch
vegetarian tree finch

11·6 The shapes of beaks found in finches of the Galapagos Islands. The beak-shape is related to the type of food eaten by each finch, demonstrating a particular case of adaptation.

species or its intrusion into the same habitat. In other words, the species which has undergone variation is a new environmental factor both for the original form and also for the other organisms in that habitat. Thus the degree of adaptation, the selection value, is always relative to the particular environment.

From this we can understand that the existence of diverse vacant niches can lead to the evolution and maintenance of separate varieties of animal specially adapted to occupy them. A striking example of this is seen in the case of the finches of the Galapagos Islands. The original population comprised a few migrants from the mainland of South America. However, their descendants have become specialised in various ways according to the food they eat. Thus there is a great diversity of beak forms (figure 11·6), and as the birds are adapted to eat different foods, they are no longer in competition with each other. These islands represent so-called ecological niches which maintain several variations which could not have evolved in other environments. It was this observation which led Darwin to realise that variation and selection are the basis of the evolution of species.

From our understanding of the molecular processes which lead to variations, namely changes in DNA produced by short-wave radiation or certain chemicals, it is possible to conclude the protracted argument among scientists as to whether the

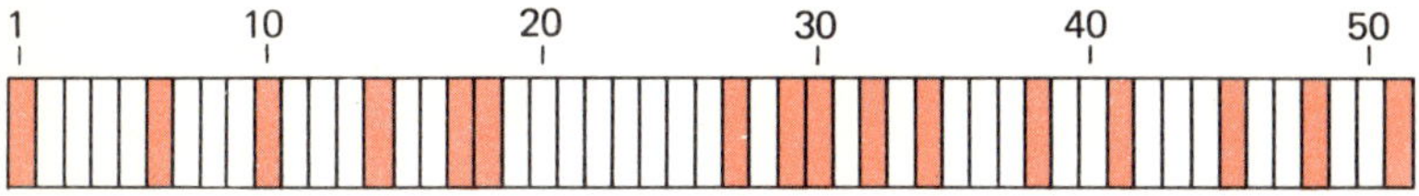

11·7 Comparison of the amino acid sequence of cytochrome C from various species. In this diagram each box represents the position of one of the 104 amino acids in the cytochrome polypeptide chain. The amino acid sequences of the cytochromes of 25 different species have now been analysed; the red boxes enclose the amino acids which are identical in the cytochromes of all 25 species.

stimulus which produces the change is identical with the factor which determines whether a given alteration is to survive. The inspired experiments of S. Luria and M. Delbrück answered this question before anything was known of the molecular relationships. Today their findings seem obvious: the stimuli resulting in mutations and the environmental factors which select the newly formed properties are fundamentally different.

The effect of mutations on the structure of proteins

We shall now compare the basic structures of a few proteins from different species and show that the formation of these proteins via the mechanisms of point mutation and, to some extent, by gene duplication is reflected in their amino acid sequences. First we shall consider a protein which is present in one-celled organisms and throughout the phylogenetic tree up to and including the mammals – cytochrome C, an enzyme

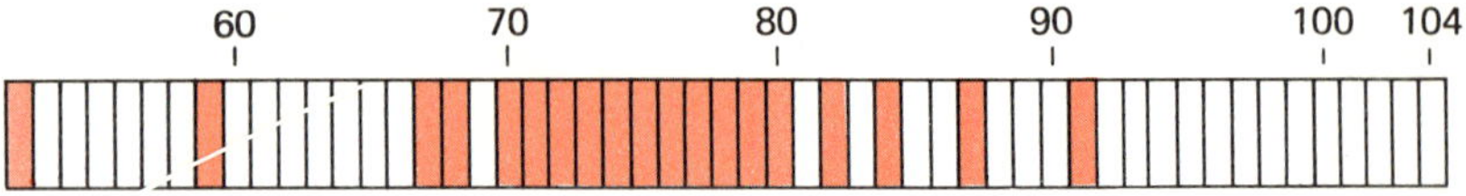

Table 11·1 Different amino acids in cytochrome of various organisms compared with those of man.

cytochrome	number of different amino acids
Chimpanzee	0
Rhesus monkey	1
Rabbit	9
Kangaroo	10
Whale	10
Cow, pig, sheep	10
Dog	11
Donkey	11
Horse	12
Hen, turkey	13
Rattlesnake	14
Tortoise	15
Tunny	21
Dogfish	23
Fly	25
Moth	31
Wheat	35
Neurospora	43
Yeast	44

11·8 Evolution of human haemoglobin chains. Duplication of an existing gene has occurred at each branch; subsequent point mutations have resulted in the haemoglobin chains found today. Thus, for example, the β-chain has developed from the precursor of the γ chain. The sequence of the forks with respect to the vertical axis indicates the relative sequence of their phylogenetic appearance.

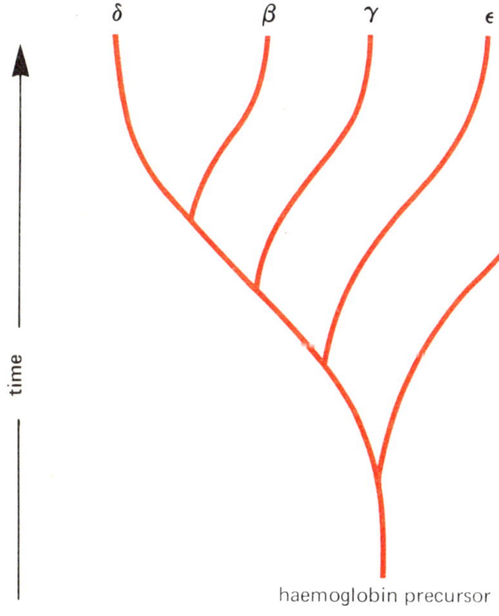

involved in obtaining energy from glucose. It consists of a characteristic sequence of 104 amino acids and figure 11·7 shows that roughly half the amino acid sequence in this enzyme from yeast cells is identical with that from human cells. Table 11·1 shows that the number of amino acids which are different, increases for organisms more widely separated on the phylogenetic tree. If point mutation is assumed to be responsible, it is possible to explain the evolution of the cytochromes from common precursors.

The production of new protein chains by the duplication of a gene already present is especially well demonstrated by the evolution of the polypeptide chains of haemoglobin. Analysis and comparison of the amino acid sequence of the haemoglobin proteins indicates that the earliest molecule resembling the haemoglobin chain was formed by repeated duplication of a short DNA segment. During the course of evolution of animal species, point mutation and deletions have produced further changes. In addition, further gene duplication took place to permit the formation of new, similar protein chains. Figure 11·8 shows the development of the protein chains of haemoglobin.

The analyses and comparison of the amino acid sequence of other proteins in different animal species has supported the general validity of the process just described: longer and new protein chains can be produced during phylogeny by the duplication of an existing gene and subsequent point mutations. Gene duplications allow new proteins to develop while preserving the original gene.

Selection and interrelated functions

The question of what is the basis of selection (that is, the maintenance and multiplications of variations) now arises. Is it the amino acid sequence of proteins, their three dimensional structure or their function in relation to the entire organism? This question has been discussed, and today we can answer it in the following way: the function of proteins is due to their characteristic spatial structure which, in turn is conditioned by their amino acid sequence. From the investigations of J. Kendrew, M. Perutz and J. Watson, we know that the replacement of some amino acids in a protein by certain other amino acids does not alter the spatial structure of the protein. For example, haemoglobin chains of different animal species have some altered amino acid sequences but the same spatial structure. On the other hand, all the possible exchanges in the amino acid sequence (preserving the same spatial structure) are not always realised in nature. As described for cytochrome C, about 50 per cent of the amino acids are in identical positions in the protein chain in various organisms. This means that the corresponding nucleotide sequences of the DNA in these particular genes have been maintained unaltered for many generations over some millions of years. In the same period of time other genes have changed greatly and new genes have evolved. This demonstrates that there must still be other factors to account for maintenance and adaptation of proteins in addition to their spatial structure and primary function. Some of the unchanging amino acid

sequences of cytochrome c are probably important for the reactions of the entire organism, such as certain regulation processes. In other words, it is the entire organism which persists and multiplies in its environment. For this reason a mutated gene can survive in the population or be selected for only if the corresponding proteins, in addition to producing an improved primary enzymatic function, are also equally or better suited to the vital functions of the entire organism. In other words, it is this effect of a mutation on the entire organism and its interaction with the environment which determines whether the mutation will persist (figure 11·9).

Many of the intermediate stages in the evolution of macroscopic structures in organisms are missing, and the same is true of the intermediate forms of proteins. This is understandable if we recall that today we encounter only the terminal forms of the branches of the phylogenetic tree; the transitional forms were at first present in small numbers and then, over a long period, involving many generations they have spread over a wide range and in doing so evolved further (figure 11·10).

At this point it ought to be mentioned that earlier evolutionary stages were necessary for the development of structures present in modern organisms, as for example, the eye or the wing of an animal. On the other hand, each single evolutionary step must have been adapted to the environment of the time in order to persist and spread. The stages of evolution which lead up to a later functional unit are not therefore directed *towards* the final result but rather *away* from the ancestors.

11·9 The wings of a bird, a bat and a reconstruction of a fossil pterodactyl. These three animals evolved structures for flight independently of each other. There is thus no evolutionary connection between the three wings.
11·10 The fossil *Archaeopteryx* (bottom right)

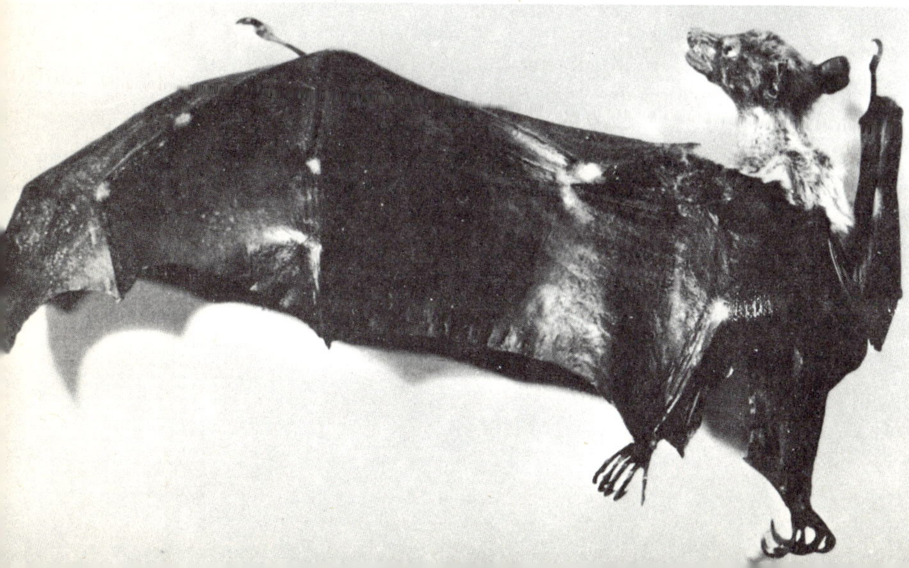

is intermediate between reptiles and birds. The tail with its 20 vertebrae reminds one of reptiles, while the arrangement of the wing feathers is the same as in birds. *Archaeopteryx* thus represents an evolutionary link between reptiles and birds.

11·11 *Proteus*, a salamander which lives in dark caves. The skin of the mature salamander contains no pigment and its eyes are so atrophied as to be blind.

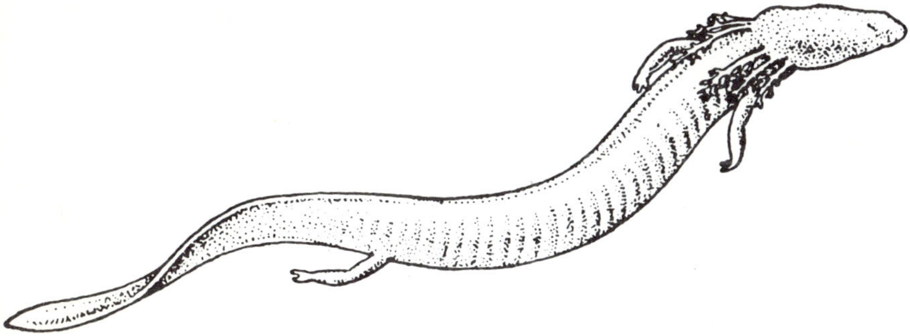

The significance of the continued presence of selection factors for the maintenance of structures or of certain molecules, even after their spread in a species over many generations, is made clearer if one compares the functional units of individuals of a species living in an environment which has changed in such a way that the functional unit has become useless. If, for example, a species has spread to live in caves, then the eyes, including the molecules involved in the process of vision, are no longer necessary (figure 11·11). Various forms of eye atrophy are encountered among individuals. This means that cessation of the selection factors can cause an atrophy of functions and structures; in this case, mutations which change the

functionless structure have no effect on the survival of the animal and result in a larger number of vestigial structures.

Summary The processes of mutation and selection control the evolution of an organism from simpler forms. In the processes of mutation, either the building blocks of existing genes change to produce proteins with different properties, or certain genes or gene sections are duplicated. These duplications may then be the site of further point mutations. These processes give rise to additional proteins with functions quite different from their precursors. Knowing the construction of DNA from four building blocks, it is understandable that one and the same chemical change (exchange of a base in various positions in the DNA) can have various biological consequences. Mutations are produced by certain types of radiation, by chemicals and by faulty reproduction of the DNA during cell division.

From the large numbers of mutations which occur, the only ones to survive and give rise to new species are those which enhance the adaptation of organisms to their particular environment. Thus, every individual of a species contains mutations, but the only mutations that are selected are those which improve the functions of the organism and these are the ones that are found in all the individuals of a species after a long period.

It is the interplay of organisms and their environment which determines which properties are propagated. Selection acts on the functions of an organism. If the same sorts of function

are conditioned by two components, as for example, eye structures in the case of insects and mammals, then in the process of selection both are treated in the same manner. If they should be useless, as in the case of cave-dwelling creatures, then they atrophy in future generations. This also shows that once a property has formed, it persists owing to the maintenance of the selection factors which allowed it to spread at an earlier date. The amino acid sequence of proteins and their spatial structure are essential for the function of proteins. However, their persistence and spread over generations is also determined by the integration of individual functions into other vital processes of the organism.

12 Ontogeny – the development of the individual

As described in chapter 11, the chemical reactions involved in the evolution of one organism from another over millions of years are largely known. We know less about the chemical processes in the development of more complex organisms from the fertilised egg to maturity. The morphological stages which must be passed through during this process were, however, extensively analysed at the beginning of this century.

Figure 12·1 shows one of the stages in the development of the human embryo. The specialised cells and structures typical of a human being develop slowly via characteristic intermediate stages from a one-celled egg. Each egg cell must therefore contain all the genes for the many different structures and molecules of the complex organism. Clearly these genes become active one after the other in a definite order. Several structures and molecules are formed in the development of the individual; others disappear at a later stage. Now what are the key substances which selectively time the functioning of the genes responsible for the occurrence of the molecules and structures? One clue to the molecular explanation of the development of the individual is the knowledge that certain hormones initiate certain stages of development.

Some stages in the development of insects are stimulated by the hormone ecdysone. Another hormone, thyroxin, is involved in the development of the tadpole to the frog. These hormones allow certain gene groups to become active. However, the presence of substances, known as *inductors*, cannot explain in molecular terms the precise sequence of stages of development from the fertilised egg to the mature organism.

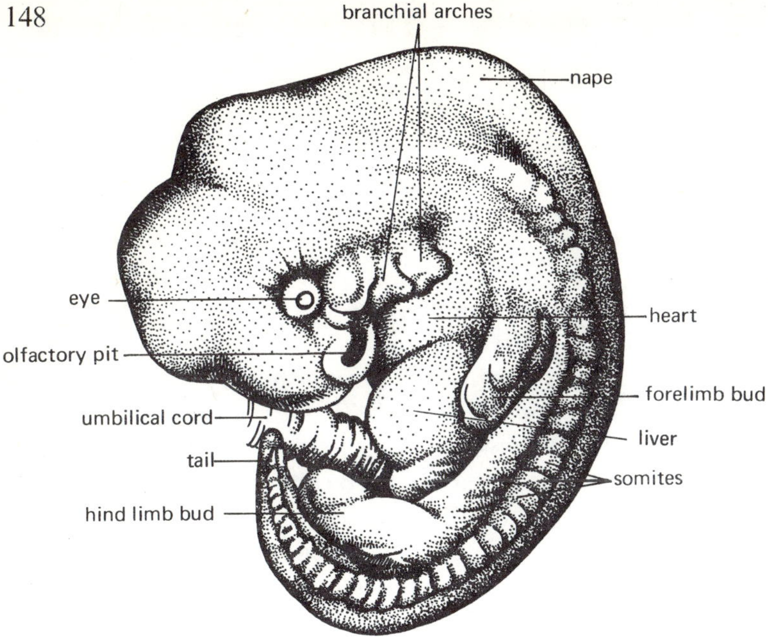

In our study of unicellular organisms we learned of a selective switching on and off of genes in the repression or induction of enzyme synthesis. Reactions towards changes in the environment comparable to these responses also occur in multicellular organisms. Some aquatic plants, for example, develop differently-shaped leaves according to the depth of water they live in. The regulation of the development of a multicellular organism differs from these regulation principles in that the external environment remains constant during certain developmental processes, and in that most developmental stages are irreversible, even if earlier environmental conditions are repeated later in the development of the organism.

In 1886 E. Haeckel proposed the rule that the individual

12·1 The diagram represents a human embryo 8 millimetres long, that is, roughly one month after fertilisation of the ovum.

development of the organism repeated in abbreviated forms the stages passed through during phylogeny. For example, the phylogenetic tree in figure 11·1 shows that fish are among the ancestors of the mammals, and we also find gills at certain embryonic stages of the mammal. The recapitulation during the development of the individual of structures from previous evolutionary stages may also be demonstrated at the molecular level. For example, during human embryonic development, oxygen-carrying haemoglobin is built up from different protein chains. During the embryonic period, these appear in an order that probably corresponds with the sequential order of their phylogenetic occurrence (figure 12·2). Also, certain metabolic processes, such as the excretion of nitrogen, are accomplished in a phylogenetically earlier form in the tadpole than in the adult frog.

An interesting question is whether, during the development of the individual, there is also a recapitulation of the protein chains of enzymes whose phylogenetic modifications can be understood as a series of point mutations, like those of cytochrome c. If this should be the case, then a doubling must also have occurred with these genes during phylogenesis in order that the older genes in the organism should have persisted. This would prove the causal significance of the recapitulation

12·2 Time-sequence of the development of human haemoglobin chains. In humans each haemoglobin molecule consists of four polypeptide chains, two α chains and two other chains. During embryonic development, the non α chains supersede one another in a characteristic order: after the ε chain the γ chain follows and at the time of birth, the γ chain is superseded by the β chain. The sequence of occurrence of the non-α chains during the development of the human corresponds with the order of their appearance in phylogeny.

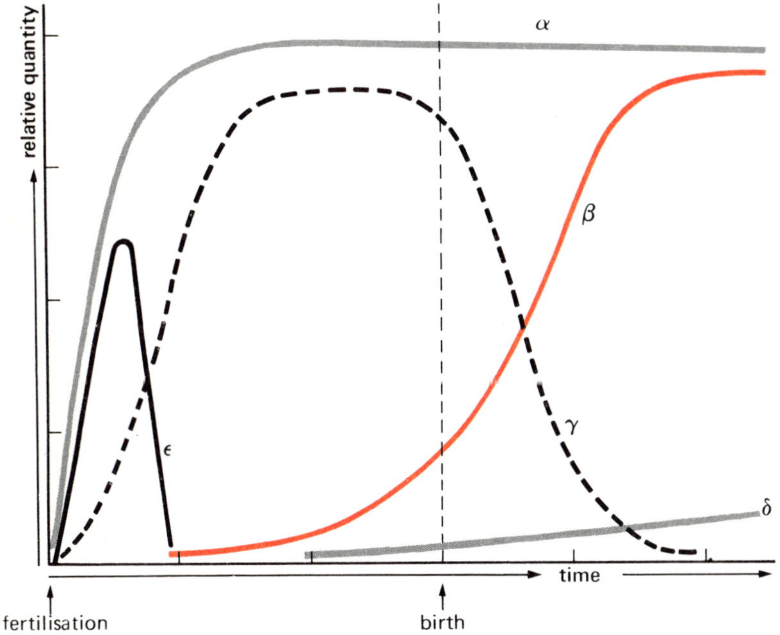

of the sequential order of phylogenetically earlier structures and molecules for the individual development of the organisms. It would also be interesting to trace the key reactions responsible for the formation of characteristic enzyme patterns of the mature organs of organisms.

The process of ageing cannot yet be described in molecular terms. It is true that we know a few of the chemical changes that occur during ageing. For example, human cells accumulate increasing quantities of a dyestuff called lipofuscin. However, changes in the individual building blocks of the organism do not provide any information on the molecular causes of ageing.

Summary One of the first steps toward understanding the molecular relationships in the development of more complex organisms from a fertilised egg is the realisation that several hormones act as inductors at various stages of development. A causal significance of the phylogenetic history for the development of individuals is demonstrated by the fact that several structures and molecules from evolutionary ancestors are transiently present during the ontogeny of the individual. The appearance in time of these characteristics in ontogeny corresponds largely with that of their occurrence in phylogeny. The molecular causes of ageing and death are still the subject of experimental and theoretical research.

13 Genetically determined molecular illnesses in man

In order to gain a better understanding of the significance of genetically determined illnesses, it is necessary to mention a few facts about how hereditary features are transmitted in complex organisms. As described in chapter 7, DNA is contained in the chromosomes, and the functional sections, the genes, are arranged linearly along these. Each species of organism contains a definite number of genes, which is why there is a constant DNA-content in cells. The genes are distributed among a number of chromosomes, characteristic for each species. It was mentioned on p. 71 that human somatic cells contain forty-six chromosomes but it is biologically more useful to give their number as twice twenty-three, that is, twice the number in the germ cells. Each individual receives a set of twenty-three chromosomes from each parent when it arises by the union of the male and female sex cells. Thus each gene is represented twice, either identical or slightly modified, in the somatic cells of a multicellular organism; the genes are referred to as homologues. Our knowledge of the distribution and significance of the genes among the twenty-three chromosomes is the result of decades of research by geneticists and cytologists. One feature of the presence of double chromosome sets in somatic cells which is especially important in our discussion of genetic illnesses is that where one of a pair of homologous genes becomes so changed by mutation that it produces a defective protein, there is normally a second homologous gene present which is able to produce the normal protein.

A large number of human illnesses have been discovered

13·1 Differential migration of haemoglobin A and haemoglobin S in an electric field. A mixture of haemoglobin A (HbA) and haemoglobin S (HbS), applied to a foil, is separated into its constituents by passing an electric current. HbS differs from HbA in that one negatively charged amino acid in HbA is replaced by a neutral amino acid in HbS. This causes HbS (red) to migrate more slowly towards the positive pole of the electric field.

that are caused by a change in the structure of an essential building block. In another group of genetically determined illnesses, it is not the chemical structure of a molecule which is changed, but its quantity. It has been said repeatedly that the building blocks of organisms are present in a characteristic number and variety of types. For example, the number of red blood cells is kept constant by sensitive regulation mechanisms. This is also true of the cellular components of individual tissues and organs.

As our first example of an illness ascribable to a molecular change, we shall describe some of the symptoms which result from a change in the amino acid sequence of the oxygen-carrying haemoglobin molecule. In 1949 L. Pauling reported that haemoglobin molecules isolated from certain humans migrated more slowly than was usual in an electric field (figure 13·1). The different migration rate in an electric field indicates a variation in the electrical charge of the molecules; the red blood cells from which the haemoglobin had been isolated appeared to be sickle-shaped instead of round under

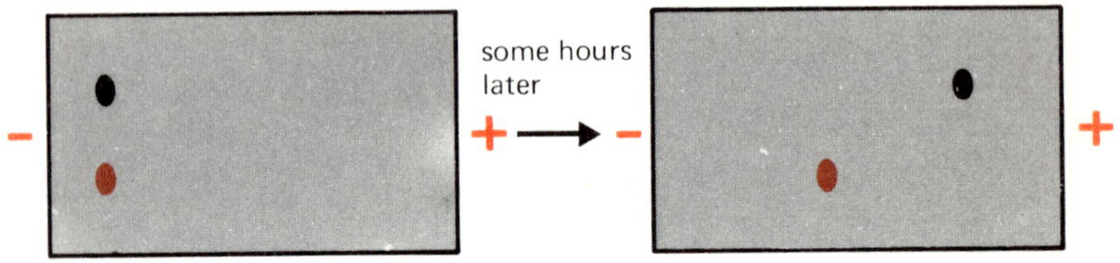

certain conditions (figure 13·2). For this reason the changed haemoglobin is called haemoglobin s. The different migration of haemoglobin s was given a molecular interpretation following its chemical analysis: V. Ingram in 1959 showed that in one of the polypeptide chains of haemoglobin s a positively charged amino acid is replaced by a neutral one. (see appendix, p. 242).

Haemoglobin s, which produces the harmful sickle-cell anaemia, is especially prevalent among native Africans. However, its presence protects them from malaria since the malarial parasite is less easily able to penetrate their red blood cells. Thus the chance of survival of persons possessing sickle cells in malaria-infested parts of Africa is actually increased compared with that of persons with normal haemoglobin. The molecular connexion between the changed haemoglobin molecule and the changed permeability of the cell membranes of the red blood cells is still largely unknown. The more frequent occurrence of the sickle-cell carriers in Africa also supports what was said in chapter 11 – that the production

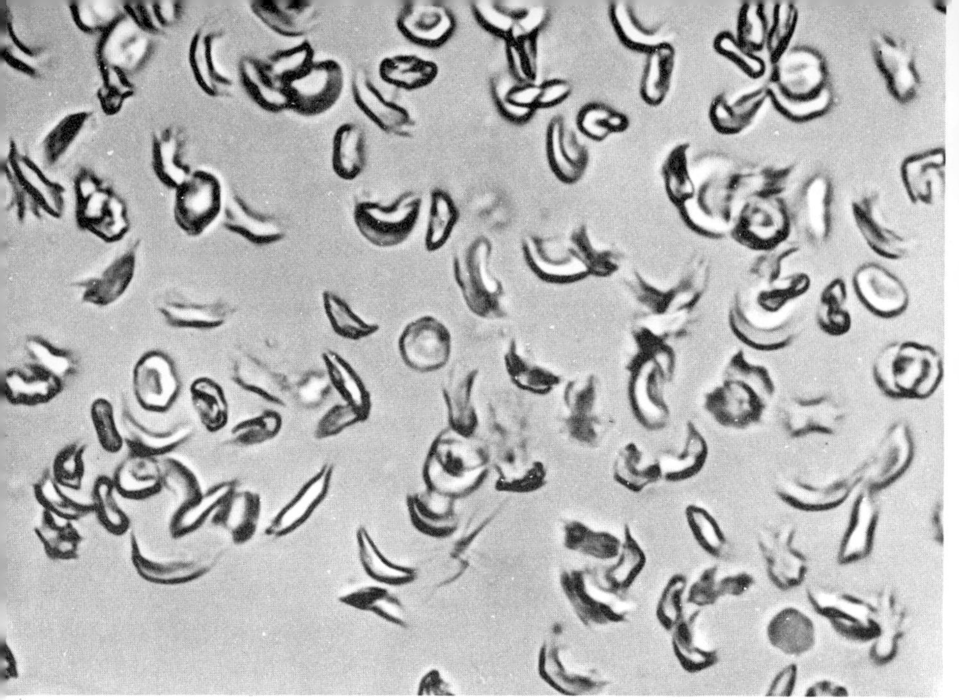

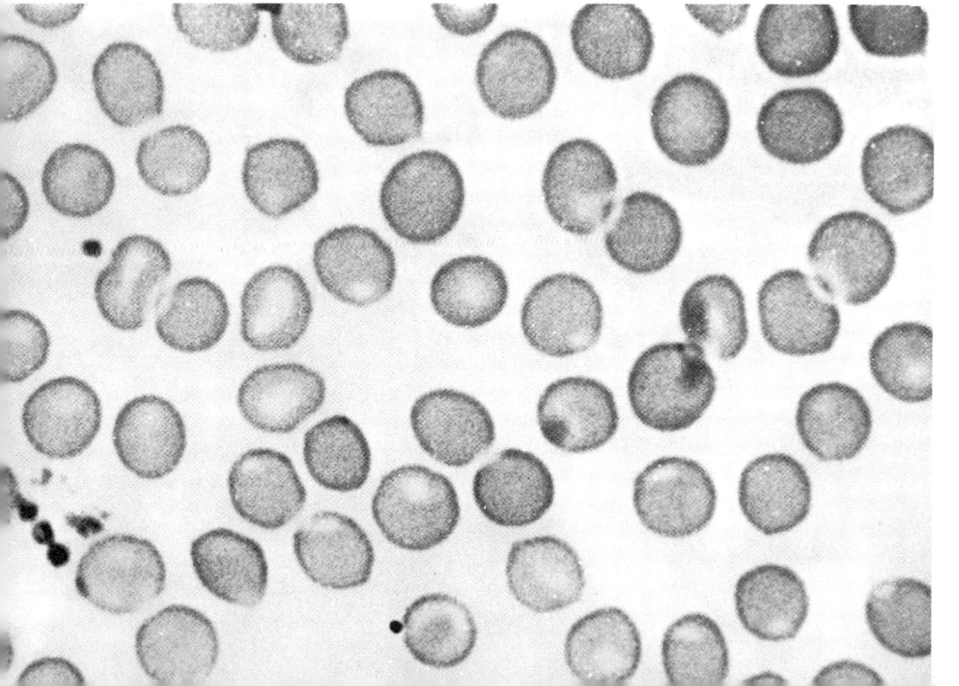

13·2 If the oxygen concentration of the environment of red blood cells containing HbS is lowered, the HbS becomes insoluble and forces them into a sickle shape (*top*). The normal round shape of blood cells is shown below.

of mutations is non-adaptive. The environment, however, acts as a selection factor and controls their spread in the population. The carriers of sickle cells in those parts of Africa most prone to malaria are better adapted to their environment than other persons. Certainly the sickle-cell mutation occurs occasionally among persons in regions not infested with malaria, such as in northern Europe, but the selection factor which encourages the spread of the mutation is lacking.

Only part of the haemoglobin is changed in sickle-cell carriers; one of the two genes responsible for haemoglobin chains is mutated so that it produces a changed protein chain. Individuals who receive a sickle-cell gene from both parents have red blood cells changed to such a degree that they usually die soon after birth.

The chemical analysis of the amino acid sequences of haemoglobin chains of many persons have shown that one amino acid in the chains is occasionally replaced by another. Once more this agrees with the presence of non-adaptive mutations and the fact that each person is a mutant, some in respect of the protein chains of the haemoglobin molecule. But only a few persons with changed amino acid sequences in haemoglobin show any symptoms of illness. Table 13·1 gives a survey of exchanges in the amino acids in haemoglo-

bin; several positions in the protein chains are excluded from amino acid exchange and these are obviously indispensible to the function of haemoglobin. Apart from this, the table teaches us something which also applies to certain observations made in chapter 11: the exchange of an amino acid reflects a change in the corresponding trinucleotide in the appropriate gene. It is understandable that several amino acid exchanges may be interpreted in terms of the alteration of only one of the building blocks in the trinucleotide, while other exchanges require several consecutive mutations. Thus, exchanges in the haemoglobin of persons alive today may be mostly interpreted in terms of the exchange of only one DNA building block (point mutation).

We shall now consider a few human diseases caused by the formation of substances in insufficient amounts. Thus, several forms of human diabetes are the result of a deficiency of the hormone insulin (p. 89) in the blood. The tendency for the illness to run in families suggests that it has a genetic origin. Other important proteins may also be present at too small a concentration, for example, fibrinogen involved in blood clotting (p. 84). In addition, other factors involved in blood clotting may also show a family deficiency. The chances of survival of such persons are determined by the extent of their tendency to bleed.

This small selection of genetically determined human molecular diseases also shows the power and impotence of medical treatment. Human diabetes caused by insulin deficiency is easily treated by injecting the patient with insulin which

Table 13·1 Amino acid substitutions in the α and β haemoglobin chains of humans due to point mutations. (Modified from H. Lehman 1967).

Name of haemoglobin	Altered chain	Position in the chain	Amino acid change	Nucleotide change
S	β	6	Glu → Val	GAG → GUG
C	β	6	Glu → Lys	GAG → AAG
D Punjab	β	121	Glu → $GluNH_2$	GAG → CAG
D ibadan	β	87	Thr → Lys	ACG → AAG
E	β	26	Glu → Lys	GAG → AAG
G Galveston	γ	6	Glu → Lys	GAG → GCG
G San José	β	7	Glu → Gly	GAG → GGG
G Chinese	α	30	Glu → $GluNH_2$	GAG → CAG
G Accra	β	79	Asp → $AspNH_2$	GAU → AAU
G Philadelphia	α	68	$AspNH_2$ → Lys	AAU → AAG
G Galveston	β	43	Glu → Ala	GAG → GCG
I	α	16	Lys → Asp	AAG → GAG
J Baltimore	β	16	Gly → Asp	GGU → GAU
J Medellin	α	22	Gly → Asp	GGU → GAU
J Oxford	α	15	Gly → Asp	GGU → GAU
M Boston	α	58	His → Tyr	CAU → UAU
M Saskatoon	β	63	His → Tyr	CAU → UAU
M Milwaukee	β	67	Val → Glu	GUG → GAG
M Iwate	α	87	His → Tyr	CAU → UAU
N Baltimore	β	95	Lys → Glu	AAG → GAG
O Indonesia	α	116	Glu → Lys	GAG → AAG
O Arab	β	121	Glu → Lys	GAG → AAG
Hikari	β	61	Lys → $AspNH_2$	AAG → AAU
Mexico	α	54	$GluNH_2$ → Glu	CAG → GAG
Norfolk	α	57	Gly → Asp	GGU → GAU
Shimonoseki	α	54	$GluNH_2$ → Arg	CAG → CGG
Sriraj	β	7	Glu → Lys	GAG → AAG
Tokuchi	β	2	His → Tyr	CAU → UAU
Zürich	β	63	His → Arg	CAU → CGU

has been isolated or produced synthetically. It has the same action as insulin produced by the patient and under normal environmental conditions it restores good health. However, complications may occur in the case of changes in the external or internal environment, such as excitement or the intake of large amounts of sugar, since the patient cannot make use of the normal regulation processes that vary the rate of formation of insulin. Thus, treatment with insulin does not cure the illness but merely supplies the deficient molecules. The same is true of the other illnesses mentioned, such as deficiency in the blood-clotting factors: here again the symptoms of the illness may be avoided by supplying the missing molecules. Apart from this, an additional complication occurs in many of these treatments: as described in chapter 10, more complex organisms react to the administration of extraneous proteins by forming antibodies which bind the alien substances and render them functionless. Since blood-clotting factors used therapeutically, such as fibrinogen, are derived from animals, it is understandable that antibodies for these alien proteins may complicate the treatment.

Even more difficult is the treatment of illnesses caused by a modified intracellular protein, for example haemoglobin. An injection of isolated haemoglobin would not be successful because this molecule cannot reach the interior of the red blood cell, where it is needed. A blood transfusion would bring only temporary relief. In spite of our understanding of the cause and action of several molecular illnesses, substitution therapy is therefore not possible.

It is easy to see the dangers involved in substitution therapy: effective treatment does not cure the actual cause – the modified gene – but keeps it in the population. There has been much discussion in recent years on how to prevent the increase of defective genes in the population while not interfering with the life of the individual. This problem grows as we learn more and more about genetically determined illnesses and their treatment.

Before finishing our discussion of genetically determined diseases, we might make a few remarks about human cancer. This disease is particularly important since it accounts for roughly twenty per cent of human deaths. Cancer is a malignant growth of certain abnormal somatic cells. The cancer cells multiply and since their increase is not co-ordinated by the regulation processes of the entire organism, they destroy the tissues around them. Intensive research on the molecular causes of cancer has shown that certain environmental factors, such as high doses of short-wave radiation or certain chemicals, may lead to this condition. However, the causative agents are so varied that they provide no clue as to what key reaction is responsible for producing uncontrolled cell growth in tumours. Like research on ageing, cancer research is still at the stage of collecting together data on the numerous molecular changes in cancer cells and as yet there is no data to link all the molecular changes into a co-ordinated and understandable sequence of events.

Summary Diabetes caused by insulin deficiency, several forms of blood-clotting disorders, and the exchange of an amino acid in a protein chain of haemoglobin are all genetically determined molecular diseases of man. If the molecule exists outside the cell, as does insulin and fibrinogen, the deficiency may be made good by replacement. Functional deficiencies of proteins inside cells, as in haemoglobin or certain enzymes, cannot be remedied by such substitution therapy.

14 Viruses as parasites of single-celled and multicellular organisms

Viruses are structures which can exist outside the cell but can reproduce only inside living cells. There are various sorts of virus, which differ from one another in their chemical composition and host-specificity. Like cells, all viruses contain nucleic acids as their genetic material, but in viruses this is usually enclosed in a protein coat. Figure 14·1 shows a model of a virus particle which uses *coli* cells as its host and forces it to produce more virus. On the outside there is a coat of protein which surrounds the genetic material, deoxyribonucleic acid. The protein fibres are important for attaching the virus particle to the cell wall and subsequently for injecting the viral nucleic acids into the interior of the *coli* cells. Figure 14·2 shows an electron microscope picture of a *coli* cell infected with viruses. Essentially it shows three virus particles: two are still filled with nucleic acid but the protein shell of the third is empty. The nucleic acid injected by other viruses is visible as dark flecks inside the cell. The nucleic acid of the virus is sufficient to force the cells to build new protein-containing virus particles.

Other types of virus appear to have a completely different structure when observed under the electron microscope. Figure 14·3 shows an electron microscope picture of the tobacco mosaic virus. In this virus the nucleic acid is also enclosed in a protein coat. It is noteworthy that the genetic material of the tobacco mosaic virus is ribonucleic acid, whereas deoxyribonucleic acid is the genetic material of the cell. This virus has been studied by several groups of workers. In 1956 A. Gierer and G. Schramm showed that nucleic acid

14·1 A model of a virus particle. The fibres attach the virus to the host bacterium wall. The genetic material, the DNA, is surrounded by a protein shell. DNA is injected into the host cell, where it initiates the formation of virus particles of the same type.

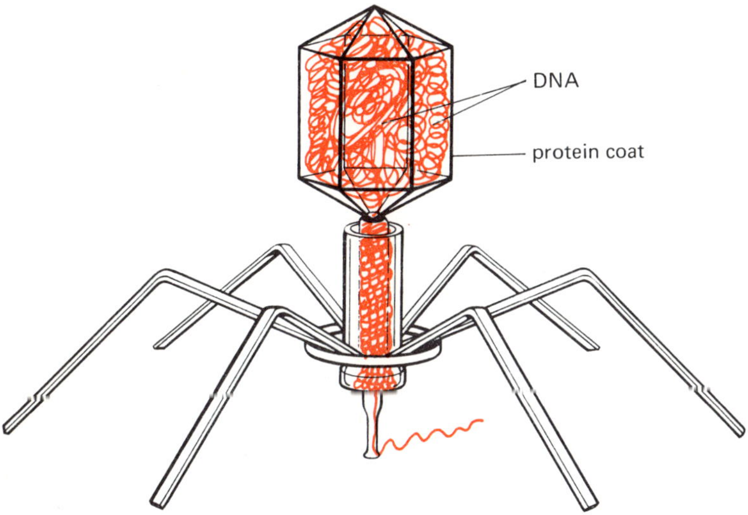

isolated from the virus particle was sufficient to cause the tobacco-plant cells to produce new tobacco mosaic virus. This was proof that the viral nucleic acid carries the genetic information for the formation of new virus particles – a finding which has since been shown to be true of other viruses, including the virus of *coli* cells (figure 14·4).

The protein part of the tobacco mosaic virus shows special features. The protein shell is built up of many identical subunits, and in fact it was one of the first protein chains to be analysed for the entire amino acid sequence. With this information it was possible to make controlled chemical changes, or mutations, in the ribonucleic acid, and to compare the amino acid sequence of the changed protein shell with the original. These investigations made a decisive contribution to understanding the genetic code, that is, to the allocation of the trinucleotide sequences of nucleic acids to certain amino acid sequences in the protein chain.

Viruses may be classed into three groups according to the type of host. Some viruses multiply only in certain bacteria, others only in the cells of plants and a third group only in the cells of animals or human beings. The viruses of the latter group are important because many of them cause diseases, including measles, poliomyelitis, small pox, mumps and yellow fever, to mention but a few.

From what has been said about the structure of viruses, it follows that antibiotics can have no effect on them. As described in chapter 9, most antibiotics block a specific reaction in the metabolism of bacteria. Viruses, on the other hand, use

14·2 Electron micrograph of a *coli* cell infected with a virus. Several virus particles have already injected their genetic material (dark spots inside the cell) into the bacterium. The empty protein shells of some particles can be seen outside the cell. Other virus particles attached to the cell wall or in the vicinity of the *coli* cell are as yet unchanged.

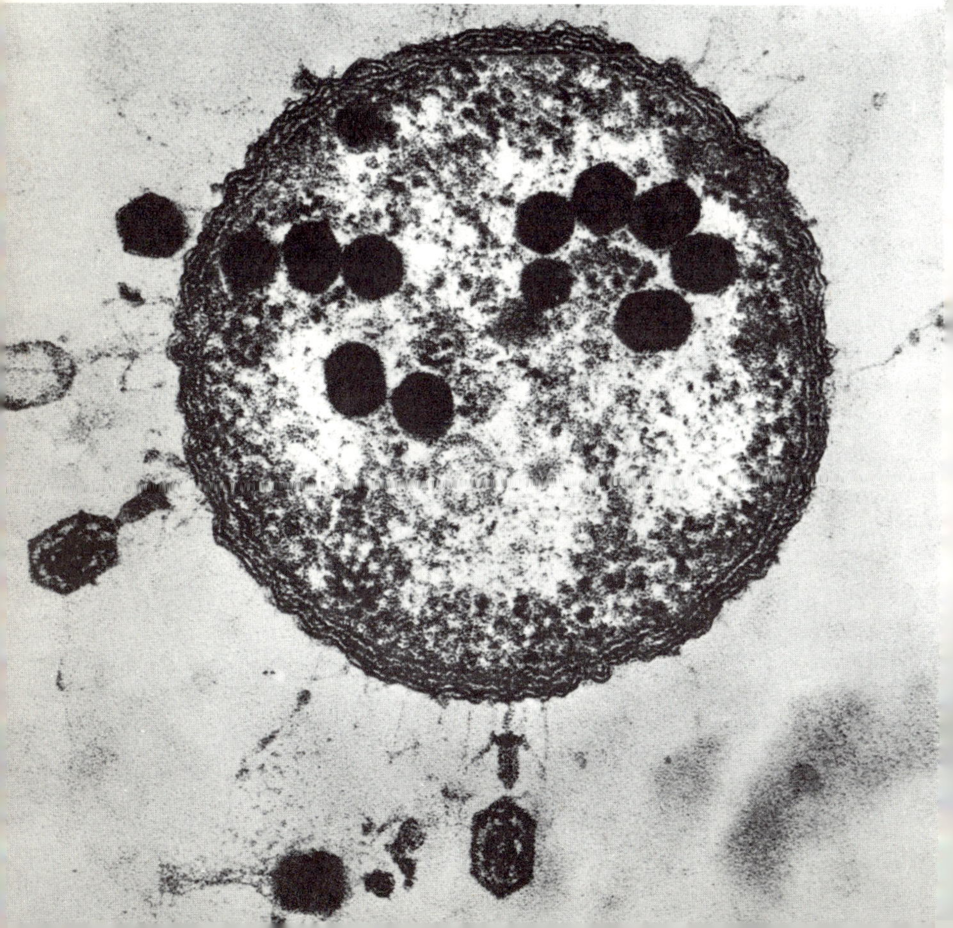

14·3 Electron micrograph of the tobacco mosaic virus (x 150,000). Some of the protein chains have been removed from the virus particle to expose the nucleic acid thread inside.

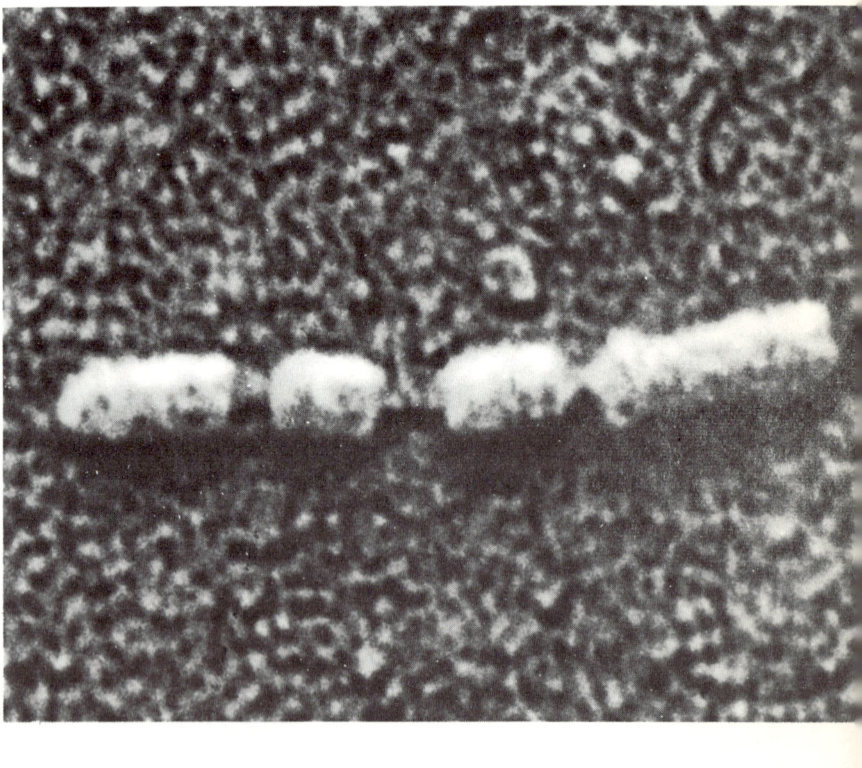

the metabolism of the host cell for their reproduction, and so antibiotics cannot affect them. This is why it is so important to culture strains of virus which do not produce illness, but which lead to the formation of protective antibodies. The production of such forms is therefore concerned with the isolation of mutants of the inimical virus with nucleic acids which are so changed that although the antigenic properties of the shell proteins remain they do not damage the host cell.

Viruses are very specific for their host cells. Thus they require for their reproduction not only certain organisms but definite cells within those organisms. The germs of poliomyelitis attack mainly certain nerve cells and produce paralysis; the mumps virus invades mainly the cells of the parotid gland. The cell-specificity of the viruses is due to two things: the virus requires suitable receptors at the surface of the host cell to allow the injection of the viral nucleic acid, and the host cell must be able to change over its metabolism for virus production.

One of the most important topics of research at the moment is the processes involved in the production of new virus particles in host cells. Among other reasons such research should give additional information on some regulation mechanisms in cells. The nucleic acids of viruses, as said before, force the host cell to adapt its metabolism to the production for the virus of building blocks, mostly viral protein, and nucleic acids. The nucleic acid of the virus contains the information for the amino acid sequence of its shell protein as well as for all the other proteins and components needed to produce new

14·4 Electron micrograph of DNA drawn out of two virus particles. The two ends of one of the DNA molecules is visible, indicating that the genetic material of the virus consists of DNA thread. The two empty protein shells of the virus can be seen at top and bottom of the photograph.

virus particles. Thus the equipment for protein synthesis of the host cell is used to produce new virus particles, which destroys the normal functioning of the cell so that the cell finally dies. We are just beginning to understand the details of the molecular steps caused by the invasion of a virus that force a cell to malfunction and lose its own identity.

Summary Viruses are particles which must invade intact cells for their propagation, but unlike isolated cell structures, they can exist outside the cells. The reproduction of the virus can occur only in certain specific cells. Many infectious diseases of man are due to the destruction of body cells during the reproduction of a virus strain. The genetic material of the virus, the nucleic acid, contains the information which forces the host cell to produce new virus particles of the same type, to the exclusion of its own metabolic reactions.

Viruses are not capable *per se* of performing the basic functions of life, such as metabolism or reproduction. They require intact host cells for this purpose, so viruses can neither be regarded as the simplest organisms nor as their ancestors.

15 The origin of cells

The last chapters have outlined the chemical basis of a few vital phenomena, using as our starting point the smallest unit of life, the cell. We also tried to understand how more complex organisms evolved from simpler ones. But how did the first cells originate? The answer to this question will probably never be more than hypothetical because the environmental conditions prevailing on earth at the time when the first building blocks of cells formed must have been quite different from those today. Nevertheless, the suggestions as to the nature of the conditions prevailing on the earth several thousand million years ago, when the first organisms evolved, have been made. A description of the elegant methods for calculating the age of our planet and dating the appearance of the first organisms would be out of place here, but we may mention that radioactivity methods are mainly used for this purpose, just as they are used for determining the life-span of cell components. Table 15·1 shows a time-table of cosmic and biological evolution. The earth was formed roughly five thousand million years ago; the first organisms emerged about three thousand million years ago, and anthropomorphic beings very roughly one million years ago. This table is expressed pictorially in figure 15·1.

In the last few decades, investigations in many laboratories have tried to simulate the environmental conditions prevalent at the time of the production of the first organisms, in an attempt to observe the formation of some cell component or cell organisation from simple molecules by supplying suitable energy. Thus attempts are being made to produce the building

15·1 Time-table of the earth's history. Each storey of the building represents a period of 100 million years. Using this as a time scale for evolution, we can see at what a late stage organisms have developed on our planet. A thick book lying on top of the building would represent the era of mankind.

Table 15·1 Some data on cosmic, biological and human evolution

(Modified from T. Dobzhansky in *Evolution, Genetics and Man*, John Wiley and Sons, New York, 1963)

approximate age in years	event
100	publication of Darwin's *Origin of Species*
100–200	industrial revolution
300–400	Galileo and the development of modern science
2000	birth of Christ
3000	beginning of the Greek civilisation
3500	beginning of the Chinese civilisation
5400	beginning of civilization in Mesopotamia
5400	first dynasty in Egypt
6200	introduction of the calendar in Egypt
15–25 thousand	man in America
20–50 thousand	Cro-Magnon man in Europe
20–75 thousand	stone age in Europe
500–800 thousand	first man-made tools
75 million	beginning of the age of mammals
125 million	appearance of the first mammal
500 million	first fossil evidence
2·5 thousand million	appearance of life on earth
5 thousand million	appearance of atoms of the chemical elements and subsequent formation of the stars and planets

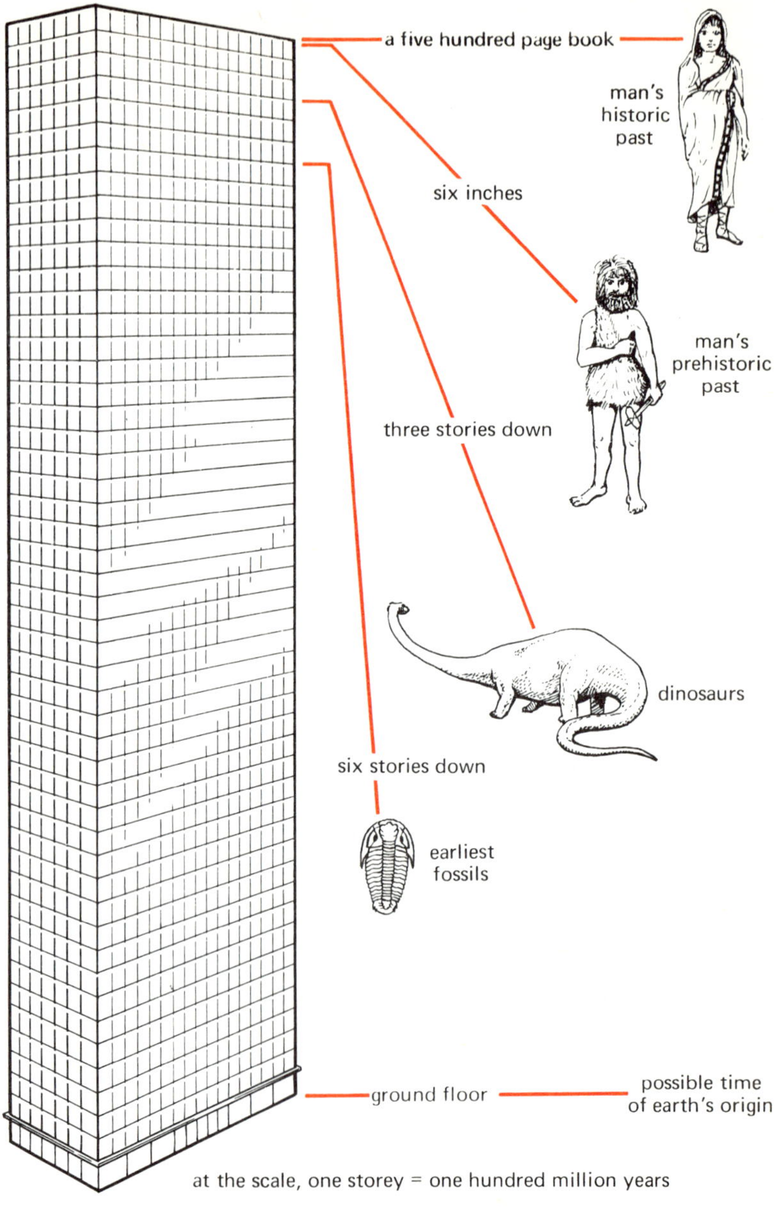

at the scale, one storey = one hundred million years

15·2 Electron micrograph of 'artificial cells', or microspheres. Under appropriate environmental conditions, certain elements combine to form amino acids and these in turn produce protein-like macromolecules. Under different environmental conditions these macromolecules adopt the configuration of cells, as shown here. A similar process is assumed to have taken place in prehistoric times. Several of these microspheres possess a double membrane; the morphological similarity with bacteria is striking but the chemical composition of the cell wall is much more complex.

blocks of macromolecules, macromolecules themselves, and energy-rich compounds *without* the participation of biological catalysts such as enzymes. In 1953 H. Urey and S. Miller obtained a good yield of amino acids under conditions which are thought to have prevailed at the time of the beginning of life. Since then, the building blocks of other macromolecules, such as nucleotides, sugars and fatty acids, have been produced under similar conditions in the laboratory (p. 242).

The next step is to combine these building blocks into larger molecules in the laboratory, so imitating what must have happened in prehistoric conditions. Thus proteins are formed from amino acids, and nucleic acids from nucleotides. Similarly, energy-rich compounds similar to ATP, or the components of chlorophyll, and the haem group of haemoglobin, have been synthesised under similar conditions in the laboratory.

The greatest problem in understanding the origin of cells centres around the occurrence of the first cell-like bodies. Many years ago, A. Oparin suggested that for the further evolution of the precursors of cells, there must have been some

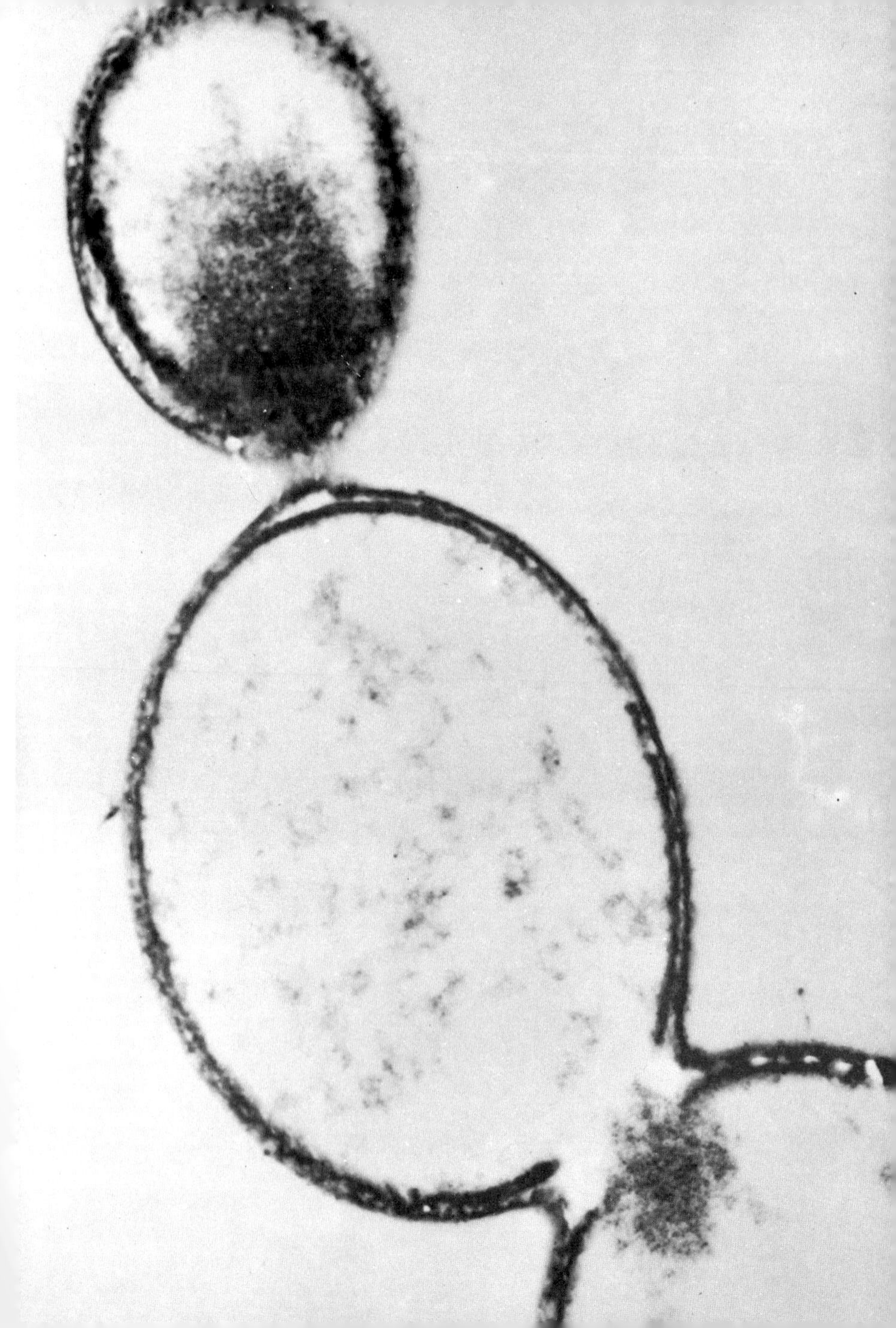

interaction between these and the environment. His suggestions have stimulated research which has shown that under suitable conditions, bodies bounded by double walls can be formed from proteins (figure 15·2). This result may be the first step towards understanding the formation of the spatial organisation found in cells today. Selection processes must have played a part in the evolution of cells from simpler precursors, just as they did in the formation of more complex organisms. In order that the first cell-like entities might be progressively modified they must also have acquired the ability to undergo almost identical reproduction. As the earth's atmosphere changed in such a way that it was no longer possible for new cell components or cell structures to be created, the cell precursors must have achieved a degree of independence which allowed their reproduction and further evolution by interaction with the environment of that time.

The fact that some building blocks, such as those of DNA, occur in all existing organisms, and that ATP is the universal source of energy, suggests that organisms evolved from a 'primaeval cell'. On the other hand, it is known, especially through the investigations carried out by M. Eigen's research group using new methods, that of the many possible building blocks of the nucleic acids, the four used in DNA are especially suited to the processes of replication and mutation, which are necessary for the development and evolution of organisms. The base-pairing is unstable to an extent that the two processes can occur sufficiently often, on the one hand to maintain life (replication) and on the other hand to allow for

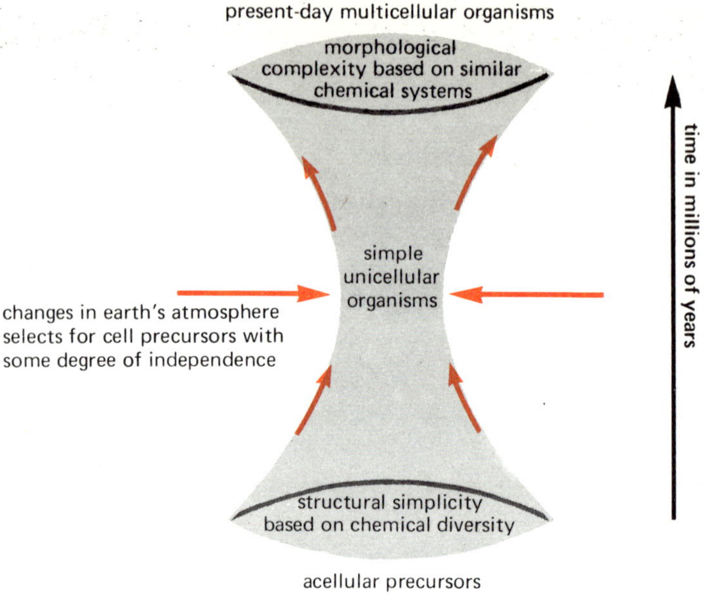

15·3 Under suitable environmental conditions, simple one-celled organisms are produced from acellular precursors and in the course of many millions of years, complex organisms have evolved from these simpler ones. The degree of 'narrowing' in this diagram would be different according to how many acellular precursors actually evolved into the first unicellular organisms.

evolution (mutation). Thus it is possible that the same sort of cell precursors were repeatedly formed roughly three thousand million years ago. Figure 15·3 symbolises these ideas on the origin of life; the intersection for the formation of the first cells would be thicker or thinner according to the number of similar precursors.

Summary The laboratory simulation of conditions prevailing on earth at the time when the first cells arose, roughly three thousand million years ago, produces the following biological molecules: building blocks of macromolecules, macromolecules themselves and certain compounds which supply energy. Also, the occurrence of cell-like bodies can be observed under suitable conditions in the laboratory. Thus the formation of the first cells would appear to have been possible in the earth's atmosphere at that time. As the conditions on earth changed, cell-like entities must have achieved an organisation which allowed them to continue to evolve more independently. The interaction between organism and environment may also be deduced from the present composition of the earth's atmosphere: the oxygen in the air derives almost entirely from chemical reactions in plants. The oxygen is consumed by other organisms and is replaced by plants.

16 Conclusion

In the introduction we avoided giving a comprehensive definition of life, and just listed three properties that, present together, make life possible. These properties are identical reproduction, metabolism and adaptation. The molecualar reactions which participate in these processes guarantee the maintenance, propagation and evolution of organisms, and we find them both in the simplest forms of life, the single-celled bacteria, and in more complex organisms, including man.

We have also seen that similar types of basic molecules and structures are found in all organisms. The same genetic material, deoxyribonucleic acid, is responsible for the formation of all the molecules and structures, and thus brings about all the properties of the organism. The sequence of nucleotides in DNA determines the number and types of the possible ribonucleic acids and proteins. In turn, the proteins catalyse the synthesis and degradation of other parts of the cell. Certain proteins, such as the RNA-polymerases, synthetases and ribosomes must be available for the translation of the nucleotide sequence of DNA to the amino acid sequence of proteins. This means that the functional interconnextion of the cell components is essential for life. Of all the cell molecules and structures it is predominantly the nucleic acids and proteins which enable the organism to maintain itself, reproduce and evolve, and all these processes are controlled by DNA. Also, we have shown that a suitable environment is essential for these processes to occur.

Thus the three minimal characteristics of the living organism, identical reproduction, metabolism and adaptation, rely

16·1 Top The energy cycle in cells. Cells take in energy-rich substances from the environment in the form of food. Metabolism of these compounds produces ATP in the cells – a substance which stores energy for use in building macromolecules–during which it decomposes into ADP and P. The organism excretes the waste products of these energy-gaining processes into the environment. Over a period of time the energy cycle presents the same picture. The participating molecules are identical copies of each other. In green plant cells it is the radiant energy of the sun which maintains the cycle of metabolic reactions.

16·2 Bottom The water cycle in inanimate nature. As shown for the energy-flow in cells, the water-flow presents over a period of time the same picture ; here too the participating molecules are identical copies of each other and the driving force for the water cycle is the radiant energy of the sun.

on the interrelations of certain combinations of molecules and structures in the organism. In more complex organisms the molecular processes involved in these three properties are correspondingly more complex.

We have not so far inquired as to whether any of the three characteristics of life are found in inanimate nature. Certainly this is so for reproduction. For example, the appearance of the first crystal in a saturated salt solution initiates the formation of further crystals. Processes related to metabolism may also be demonstrated in inanimate nature. In chapters 1 to 4 it was mentioned that the continual build-up and degradation of energy-rich molecules and structures of the

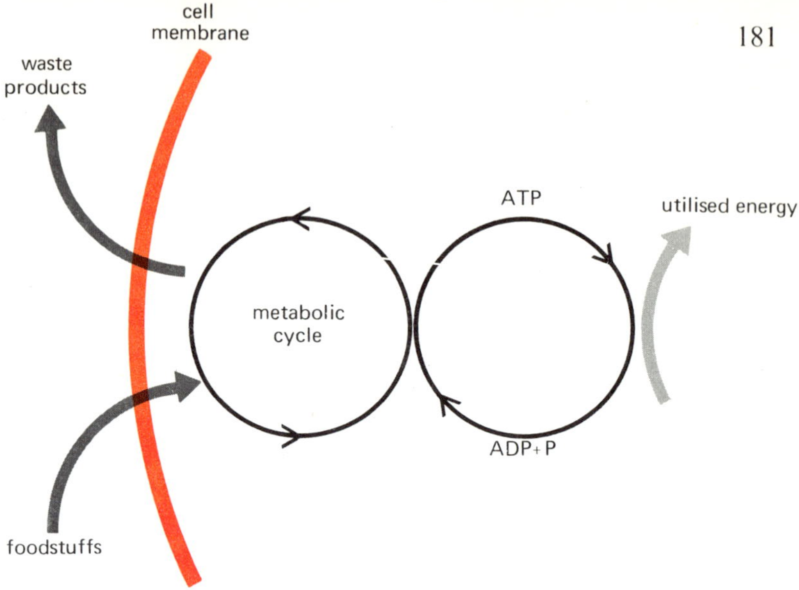
cell
membrane
waste
products
ATP
utilised energy
metabolic
cycle
ADP+P
foodstuffs

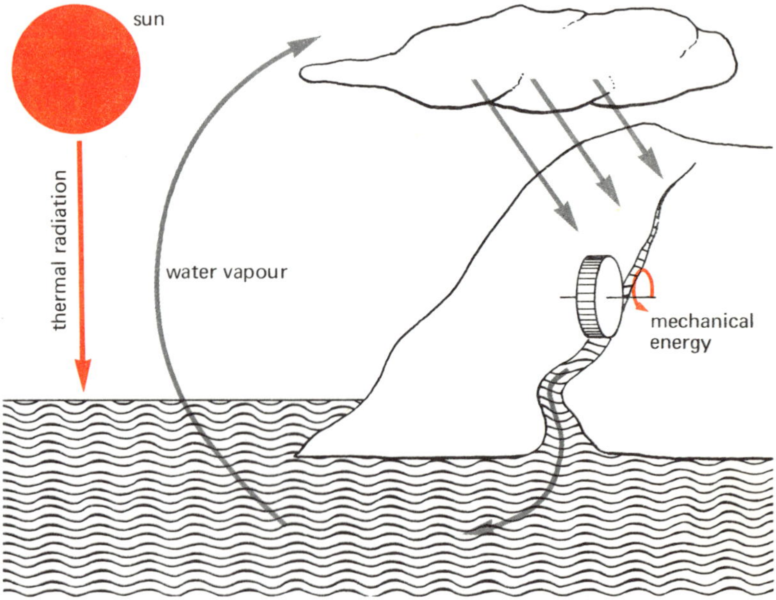
sun
thermal radiation
water vapour
mechanical
energy

cells were metabolic reactions. Observed over a long period of time, cells present us with the same picture but the molecules and structures are identical copies of each other.

The energy cycle is shown again in figure 16·1: cell metabolism is maintained by the addition of energy from the environment. Plants make use of the radiant energy of the sun for this purpose while other organisms take in energy in the form of the energy-rich molecules of food. Figure 16·2 shows the energy cycle for water in inanimate nature. Although the appearance of a river may be the same over a given period of time, the water molecules are always different. In this case the energy cycle relies on thermal radiation from the sun. These two pictures were conceived by F. Lipmann in order to demonstrate that a cycle for the conversion of energy could exist in inanimate as well as in animate nature. The ATP molecule formed in the cell may be used for the build-up of energy-rich molecules; the fall of water making the river flow can be used for operating a power station.

It is also possible to find an equivalent for adaptation in inanimate nature. In the introduction, this characteristic was described as the ability of an organism to react to changes in its environment, so that new environmental conditions should not reduce its viability. At the same time, our definition shows the wide scope of its interpretation. We shall now mention a few adaptation processes again since they relate to a common principle, the regulation cycle with negative feedback.

Regulation mechanisms for maintaining a constant concentration of cell molecules were encountered in the des-

cription of the reactions in *coli* cells, the main example used being the regulation of the concentration of histidine. Later we learned that, in more complex organisms, components of the blood, such as red blood cells and hormones, were each adjusted and maintained at a characteristic concentration according to environmental conditions. These adaptation processes for maintaining the constancy of the internal environment of the cell or organism are dependent upon the common principle of a control system with *negative feedback*, a principle well known in engineering. The principle is used, for example, in devices for maintaining a constant room temperature or a constant water level in a tank. Figure 16·3 shows that the water level in a tank may be kept constant by means of a float which actuates an electrical contact; when the water level reaches a given value the pump is switched off. If the water level falls, this contact is broken and the pump switches on again. This is one of the simplest examples of a control system involving negative feedback. Figure 16·4 shows a general plan of this type of regulation. Its most important characteristic is that the effects relayed by the controller result in the opposite action: too much water in the tank causes the water supply to be turned off. In the simplest devices using negative feedback, the measuring equipment directly influences the controlled variable; thus, in several thermostats it is the thermometer which switches off the heating current. However in most cases there are intermediate stages so that the controlled variable is indirectly influenced by the measuring device.

16·3 Top Regulating the water level in a tank by means of negative feedback. When the water level falls, a float on the surface makes an electrical contact, causing the water pump to be turned on. When the water level rises, the upper electric contact is broken. Further upward movement of the float results in contact being made with the lower electric point, which causes the water pump to be switched off. These operations repeat themselves in a time sequence.

16·4 Bottom Circuit diagram of a biological control system. Changes in a factor to be kept constant are registered by a measuring device (receptor) and passed on to a regulating centre (controller) where this information is translated into an opposing reaction (negative feedback). This reverses the change in magnitude.

Repression – the regulation process for maintaining a constant concentration of, for example, histidine in *coli* cells – may also be regarded as a control system with negative feedback: too much histidine inside the cells results in a cessation of histidine production. There are also examples of this sort of adaptation in the case of more complex organisms (figure 16·5): the concentration of the hormone cortisone is kept constant by means of the hormone ACTH which stimulates the formation of cortisone in the suprarenal cortex. If the concentration of cortisone in the blood exceeds a certain value, this stops further production of ACTH in the pituitary so that there is no more ACTH to stimulate cortisone production in the suprarenal cortex. If the cortisone level in the blood falls, then formation of ACTH in the pituitary starts

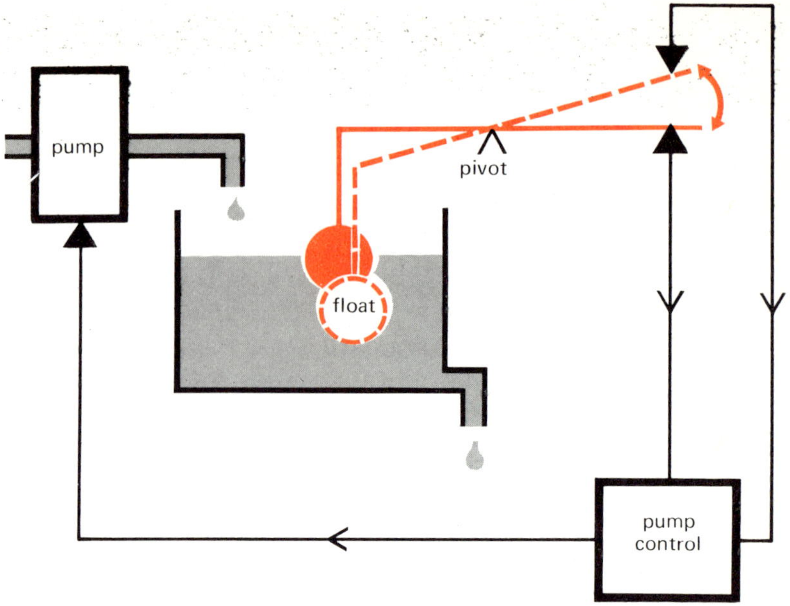
pump
pivot
float
pump control

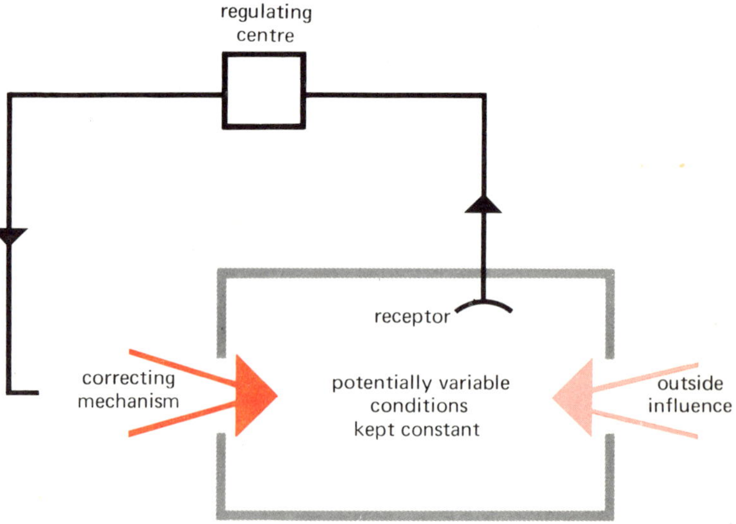
regulating centre
receptor
correcting mechanism
potentially variable conditions kept constant
outside influence

16·5 Regulation of the formation of the hormone cortisone by negative feedback. The hormone ACTH, produced in the pituitary gland, activates the formation of cortisone from its precursors in the suprarenal cortex. When the concentration of cortisone in the blood exceeds a certain value, this inhibits the production of further ACTH. Too low a drop in cortisone level in the blood ends the inhibition of ACTH production, so that more cortisone is produced.

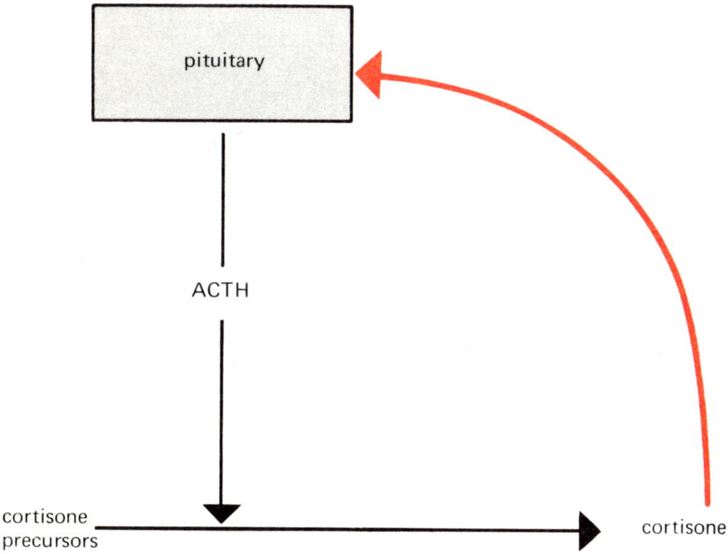

again. Once again the principle of negative feedback is obvious here: too much cortisone in the blood ultimately leads to a cessation of cortisone production.

Every engineer knows many devices which use complicated variations of this principle. For example, several control systems of this sort may be linked so that each activates the other or operates in contrary directions. The consideration of biological adaptation processes from the standpoint of control systems with negative feedback was introduced independently by the physiologist R. Wagner and the mathematician N. Wiener a few decades ago. Since then, similar work by other researchers has led to an understanding of many biological phenomena; for example, the co-ordinated reactions of insects which orientate them in space, or the way in which the semi-circular canals of the ear work.

Thus we have seen that the three characteristics of life – reproduction, metabolism and adaptation – may be found individually, in some form at least, in inanimate nature. But it is their combined presence that is characteristic of living organisms. But the possibility of interpreting the concepts of reproduction, metabolism and adaptation in different ways obscures the significance of some biological phenomena. For this reason we shall return to a concept which is vital to the existence of many organisms living together, especially to man. This vital process is evolution, once again a concept open to wide interpretation. In chapter 11 it was stated that mutation and selection are responsible for the evolution of organisms from simple forms to the many complex organisms living

today, and that mutations are alterations of the genetic substance of organisms, the DNA. As a result, one or more properties of the bearer of the mutation may change, resulting either in the same adaptability to the environment as before, a reduced viability, or, in rare cases, improved viability. It is the latter result which by selection has produced the present variety of organisms.

The genetic basis of those characteristics peculiar to man, which we call his spiritual and cultural abilities, has also evolved over thousands of years by mutation and selection. T. Dobzhansky, in particular, has pointed out that during the evolution of man, gene combinations have evolved which have made our cultural development possible, namely the ability to master and have a feeling for the thoughts or inventions of other persons and to act on them in various original ways. Cultural knowledge or ways of life once acquired are passed on to subsequent generations and other peoples through the media of speech and writing. These human capacities enable the cultural abilities of one person to be passed on to a larger number of people than to his direct descendants. Thus cultural evolution may be more effective in a given time than biological evolution based solely on transmitting genes. It is just this combination of biological and cultural evolution which is unique to the evolution of human beings and explains his dominant position in the biological world. Of course, some animals show some learning ability and the capacity for invention in communication between each other, as in the learning of a specific bird song from other members of the

species. However, in man the ability to learn and to think has reached a peak of development which distinguishes him from other organisms and allows him, to a very large extent, to control the rest of nature. It was mentioned in chapter 12, that, in general, organisms recapitulate their phylogenetic history during their ontogenic development. Certain parallels are also observable in the spiritual and cultural development of individuals: we need to learn some stages of the evolution of our present culture if we wish to participate in it and to develop it further. Each of the earlier stages of cultural evolution was essential for the formation of our present-day culture, but only a few of these will be recapitulated.

These considerations lead us to a fact that we have already mentioned several times: our individual biological and cultural development requires an adequate environment and this environment includes other human beings. It is our environment which realises our physical and psychical potential. Experiments in which men remained voluntarily in a room protected from any environmental stimulus showed that they reacted with psychological and physical disorders which compelled them to terminate the isolation. In this context it is interesting that it is a common feature of all organisms not only to react to some changes in their environment by means of adaptation processes, but to use various environmental factors as stimuli for provoking certain modes of reaction in their development, even in an environment which remains constant. This also occurs with man and is in part an unconscious process. It makes it all the more important that those persons who have a

critical influence on our lives because of their position in society should be aware of the environmental effects of their behaviour and sayings; the same words or acts may produce different effects on persons of different biological or cultural stages of development. I would like to conclude these reflections with a quotation from T. Dobzhansky:

> I am an optimist because I know that mankind, the living world, and the whole universe have evolved and are evolving. Look into yourself and look at the world around you. Everywhere there is a tremendous amount of ugliness as well as of beauty, much that is good and admirable and a lot that is evil and horrible. My point is that the knowledge that we are evolving bestows hope. Whether one feels that beauty and good or that ugliness and evil predominate in the world, one knows that this world was not created all at once, fixed and unchangeable forever. Creation is not an event, but a process, not complete but continuing. Progress and betterment are by no means guaranteed or vouchsafed in evolution. However, man may strive to bring them about, and this striving is what gives meaning and dignity to human life, individually and collectively. So, let me repeat, evolution bestows hope.

Glossary 1: Some scientific terms

Adaptation — adjustment to changes in the environment. Adaptation enables the organism to cope with environmental changes in a way that is advantageous to its existence. Some examples of adaptation are: the repression or induction of enzyme formation, the maintenance of the concentration of components of blood at a value characteristic for the particular environment. Apart from this, adaptation permits animals and humans to live in different environments. The degree of adaptation differs for different species, and is one of the minimal properties of life.

Adenosine triphosphate (ATP) — is formed in cells during the break-down of energy-rich compounds, such as glucose, and is called on when energy is required for the formation of macromolecules or other energy-rich components of the cell. ATP plays the vital role of energy storage and is the energy supplier in various chemical reactions in the cell.

Amino acids — the building blocks of proteins. Proteins are made up of twenty different amino acids. The basic structure of all amino acids is similar and they are linked together by the same sort of chemical linkage to form polypeptide chains and proteins.

Amino-acid sequence — sequence of amino acids in polypeptide chains or in proteins; the amino acid sequence determines the spatial structure and the properties of the proteins.

Antibiotics — lower molecular-weight substances from various species of fungus or bacteria, or molecules

synthesised in the laboratory. By blocking vital processes such as protein synthesis or cell-wall synthesis they hinder the growth of several bacteria. Penicillin and streptomycin are antibiotics, and these and many others are used medicinally to combat infectious diseases.

Antibodies	proteins formed in more complex organisms, including man, in response to the intrusion of antigens, substances alien to the body. Each antibody binds itself specifically to the appropriate antigenic determinant. Antibodies are involved principally in resisting infection.
Antigens	substances foreign to the body which lead (in more complex organisms, including man) to the formation of specific antibodies. Most antigens contain several antigenic determinants. Chemically antigens may belong to the proteins, the polysaccharides or to other classes of substance.
Antigenic determinants	chemical groupings in antigens which stimulate the formation of a specific antibody. Each antigen may possess several antigenic determinants and may therefore be responsible for the formation of various antibodies. In the reaction of the antibody with its corresponding antigen, the antibody bonds to the antigenic determinant.
Atoms	there are more than 100 different atoms, and they are listed in the periodic system of the elements on p. 221. Atoms, whether different or alike,. may bond with one another to form molecules.

ATP — *see* adenosine triphosphate

Bases (of nucleic acids) — one of the three building blocks of nucleotides. The bases determine the specificity of the nucleotides. Five different bases predominate in the nucleotides of organisms: adenine, guanine, thymine, cytosine and uracil. They are represented by the letters A, G, T, C and U. The first four are present in deoxyribonucleotides; A, U, C and G in ribonucleotides.

Base pairing — the specific linking of two nucleotides. Nucleotides containing base A link with those containing either the base T in DNA or U in RNA and a nucleotide containing C links with a G nucleotide. This rule of base pairing is fundamental: it conditions the intracellular double-stranded structure of DNA, the replication of DNA and the translation of the nucleotide sequence of DNA or of messenger-RNA into the amino acid sequence of proteins.

Blood — consists of the blood plasma, containing over a hundred different proteins and other substances, and blood cells. It carries vital substances, formed in specialised cells of organisms or absorbed from the environment, to wherever they are required in the organism.

Blood groups — molecular arrangements in the walls of red blood cells. In man, four main groups are recognised, referred to as A, B, AB and O. The blood plasma of humans contains antibodies which bind with all blood groups other than that of the particular individual (apart from blood group O). Thus a person with blood

	group A possesses antibodies which react with red blood cells of a donor with blood group B. Blood groups are important in human blood transfusions.
Botulinus toxin	a protein from the bacillus *Botulinum clostridium*. Relatively few molecules of this toxin are sufficient to paralyse the nerves in human beings with fatal results.
Cell	the smallest unit of life. The cells of all organisms possess a similar basic molecular equipment to carry out the minimal properties of life – identical reproduction, metabolism and adaptation. Additional molecules and structures are characteristic of particular species of organism. The type and number of the cell components is constant over a given period of time and characterises the various organisms.
Chlorophyll	a molecule contained in green plant cells. It is involved in photosynthesis, in particular, in the conversion of solar energy into chemical energy.
Chloroplasts	chlorophyll containing cell structures in plant cells. Among other processes, the chemical reactions of photosynthesis take place in these organelles.
Chromosomes	structures of the cell nucleus. Besides other types of molecule, they contain DNA, that is, the genetic material of the cell. The chromosome number is constant and characteristic for each species of organism.
Coeruloplasmin	a protein of the blood plasma; it binds copper

and takes it to wherever it is needed in the organism.

Coli cell — a species of bacterium. The *coli* cells are among the simplest of single-celled organisms. Their chemical composition and reactions are known in great detail from the research of many scientists.

Cytochrome C — an enzyme involved in metabolic energy-cycles which consume oxygen. It is present in simple unicellular organisms and in more complex ones, including man. The amino acid sequence of cytochrome C isolated from various species is known.

Cytoplasm — the part of the cell interior other than the cell nucleus. The cytoplasm consists of ribosomes and other cell structures, and many cellular molecules and macromolecules.

Deletion — one of the possible types of mutation; the loss of a certain nucleotide sequence of DNA. According to the length of the piece lost, the cell will lack a whole or a part of a polypeptide chain. The effect of the deletion on the viability of the individual depends on the part played by the changed protein in the life of the organism.

Deoxyribonucleic acid (DNA) — the genetic material of cells. DNA determines all the possible properties of the organism. It is made up of four deoxyribonucleotides and their sequential order determines the sequential order of the amino acids in proteins. The position of a particular amino acid in the polypep-

	tide chain is given in each case by the sequence of three nucleotides (a triplet). The sequence of deoxyribonucleotides in DNA also fixes the sequence of ribonucleotides in RNA.
Deoxyribo-nucleotides	building blocks of deoxyribonucleic acids; each consists of a sugar (deoxyribose), a phosphate group and a base. There are four different deoxyribonucleotides, all containing deoxyribose and phosphate and differing in the bases A, T, C and G.
DNA	*see* deoxyribonucleic acid
Ecdysone	an insect hormone involved in the shedding of the skins of pupae and larvae. It acts by activating certain of the insect's genes. Chemically it belongs to the steroids.
Effectors	lower molecular-weight substances which promote (activators) or inhibit (inhibitors) the activity of enzymes.
Environment	the entire surroundings of an individual, provoking certain vital responses at some stage in its development. Both animate and inanimate objects are environmental factors.
Enzymes	catalysts of biochemical reactions commonly involved in the build-up or degradation of biological molecules. Enzymes are proteins but occasionally the presence of a molecule which is not a protein may be necessary in order that the enzyme can function. Molecules whose reactions are catalysed by enzymes are called substrates.
Fibrin	a protein which is produced from fibrinogen

during blood clotting.

Fibrinogen — a component of the blood plasma. During the clotting of the blood a few amino acids are enzymatically split off from the fibrinogen to leave fibrin.

Gene — the nucleotide sequence of cellular DNA which determines the amino acid sequence of a polypeptide chain or the ribonucleotide sequence of a RNA molecule. In certain viruses, RNA is present as the genetic substance.

Genome — the sum of all the various genes present in an organism.

Glucose — a sugar molecule. In plants it is produced, among others, from precursors of lower energy by the absorption of the radiant energy of the sun. In many organisms glucose is degraded by reactions of the metabolic energy cycles for the production of ATP.

Haem — the non-protein part of the oxygen-carrying molecule haemoglobin. Structures related to haem are found in several enzymes concerned in metabolic energy cycles and in chlorophyll.

Haemoglobin — molecule occurring in red blood cells which transports oxygen. It consists of four haem groups, and two unlike pairs of polypeptide chains. The amino acid sequences of the four polypeptide chains and the spatial structure of human haemoglobin have been thoroughly analysed.

Haemoglobin S — abnormal haemoglobin differing from the normal human type by the substitution of a single

amino acid resulting from a point mutation. Under low oxygen tension red blood cells containing haemoglobins assume a sickle shape.

Histidine — one of the twenty amino acids which are the building blocks of proteins.

Hormones — a group of molecules produced in specialised cells and transported to other places where they are needed, classed according to their modes of formation and functioning. Their primary action may result, for example, in the activation of certain genes or in a change in the activity of several enzymes. Some hormones, for example thyroxin, are involved in the induction of certain stages in the development of the organism. There is considerable variation of chemical structure among the hormones.

Induction — 1. stimulation of enzyme formation by certain lower-molecular weight substances (inductors). 2. the actuation of new stages of development during the evolution of the individual (ontogeny) of more complex organisms is also known as induction. Substances which effect this type of induction include several hormones.

Infectious diseases — diseases of man or animals, caused, for example, by bacteria or viruses. To overcome such a disease, the presence of antibodies is essential; the antibodies bond with components of the germ.

Insulin — a hormone present in complex organisms. It is involved in sugar metabolism and is formed in the pancreas whence it is conveyed by the blood to wherever it is needed. It is a protein and its

amino acid sequence is known.

Lactose — a sugar composed of two sugar molecules. In *coli* cells it induces the formation of enzymes which catalyse its degradation.

Lipids — molecules composed, amongst other substances, of fatty acids.

Lysosomes — cell structures found in more complex organisms. They are collections of enzymes which catalyse the degradation of certain structures or molecules.

Lysozyme — an enzyme isolated from the white of hen's eggs. It was one of the first proteins whose amino acid sequence and spatial structure were solved.

Macromolecules — giant molecules built up from many smaller molecules either of the same or of different types. Proteins, nucleic acids and polysaccharides are macromolecules. Their spatial structure and function is determined by the number and the sequence of the molecules of which they are made.

Messenger-RNA (m-RNA) — the ribonucleotide copy of a piece of DNA. m-RNA is involved in protein synthesis – it encodes the amino acid sequence of one or more polypeptide chains. Base-pairing and the catalysing action of RNA-polymerase are two essentials for its formation.

Metabolism — one of the essential characteristics of all organisms. Includes chemical reactions for the maintenance and propagation of the body. Some reactions are synthetic, such as the build-

	up of proteins and macromolecules. Others are break-down reactions, such as when glucose is broken down to liberate energy.
Mitochondria	organelles found in more complex organisms. They are the site of the respiratory enzymes that catalyse most of the reactions of the metabolic energy cycle.
Molecular diseases (genetically determined)	illnesses produced by the mutation of at least one gene. As a result of the mutation, some molecule is produced in a different form causing direct or indirect interference with some vital process.
m-RNA	*see* messenger-RNA.
Mutagens	agents inducing mutation, for example, short-wave radiation and certain chemicals.
Mutation	a change in the genetic material, the DNA, of an organism, which involves changes in the sequence (change of type or number) of the DNA building blocks, the deoxyribonucleotides. This may result in proteins or ribonucleic acids with altered structure and function. Together with selection, mutation is the basis for the evolution (phylogeny) of organisms.
Mutation rate	the number of mutations produced in a given time.
Nucleotides	building blocks of the nucleic acids. A distinction is made between ribonucleotides, the building blocks of ribonucleic acids, and deoxyribonucleotides, the building blocks of deoxyribonucleic acids.
Ontogeny	the development of more complex organisms

from the fertilised egg to the mature individual.

Organs — functional units in multicellular organisms; they are assemblages of various specialised cells.

Penicillin — the first antibiotic to be discovered. It inhibits the propagation of certain types of bacteria.

Pheromones — low molecular-weight substances used for communication between individuals of the same species. For example, the substances responsible for sexual attraction in beetles and for communication between bees are pheromones.

Photosynthesis — a process in green plants resulting in the formation of energy-rich compounds (such as glucose) from carbon dioxide and water, utilising the radiant energy of the sun. The oxygen liberated in the process is released by plants and is taken up by other organisms.

Phylogenetic tree — a schematic representation of the relationships between different organisms; it also shows the course of the evolution of the organism.

Phylogeny — the evolution of organisms from simpler forms over a period of several million years. Modern knowledge on the evolution of organisms and the relationships between them may be depicted as a phylogenetic tree. Phylogeny is caused by mutation and selection.

Point mutation — one of the possible types of mutation. One nucleotide of DNA is replaced by another; in the cells, this may result in a changed RNA or in a changed protein, possibly with different properties.

Polypeptide chains	macromolecules consisting of a characteristic number and sequence of amino acids. The term polypeptide is often used in the same sense as the term protein but the concept of protein includes additional characteristics.
Polysaccharides	macromolecules built up from sugar molecules. They form part of cell membranes.
Primary structure	the sequential order of the building blocks in macromolecules without taking their spatial structure into consideration; for example, the sequence of nucleotides in nucleic acids or the sequential order of the amino acids in proteins.
Proteins	macromolecules consisting of one or more polypeptide chains. Each polypeptide chain is built up of a characteristic number of amino acids in a characteristic sequence. This sequence determines the spatial structure and function of the proteins. Many proteins act as enzymes.
Protein synthesis	all the processes involved in the production of proteins from their building blocks, the amino acids, in cells. This entails the translation of the nucleotide sequences of DNA, the genes, into the amino acid sequences of polypeptide chains. Among others, messenger-RNA, synthetases, transfer-RNA are all involved in protein synthesis.
Radioactive radiation	particulate decomposition products or short-wave electromagnetic radiation of radioactive atoms or molecules; they may have a mutagenic action. Radioactive molecules are used to trace the path of these molecules within the

	organism by measuring the radiation produced by their decay.
Replication	production of an identical or near identical DNA strand from a pre-existing strand.
Repression	the inhibition by repressor substances of the formation of enzymes in cells.
Repressor	a substance which prevents the formation of one or more enzymes in cells.
Reproduction	producing similar offspring – one of the essential properties of life.
Ribonucleic acids (RNA)	macromolecules composed mainly of four blocks, the ribonucleotides. There are three groups of nucleic acids which have different functions: messenger-RNA, transfer-RNA and ribosomal RNA. All three types of ribonucleic acid are involved in protein synthesis.
Ribonucleotides	building blocks of the ribonucleic acids; each consists of the sugar, ribose, a phosphate group and a base. Four different ribonucleotides predominate, all of which contain ribose and phosphate; they are distinguished by their different bases, A, U, G and C.
Ribosomes	cell particles composed of ribosomal RNA and various proteins. During protein synthesis, messenger-RNA is bound to the ribosomes and this is where the translation of the nucleotide sequence of m-RNA to the amino acid sequence of the proteins takes place.
RNA	*see* Ribonucleic acid.
RNA-polymerase	an enzyme which catalyses the formation of RNA. Under the influence of RNA-polymerase,

the ribonucleotides attached to the DNA by base-pairing are linked together to form messenger-RNA, ribosomal or transfer-RNA.

Selection — together with mutation, the crucial mechanism for the evolution of organisms from simpler forms. Organisms which, by mutation, have acquired properties giving them an improved chance of survival and propagation in a certain environment, persist and multiply, often at the cost of the viability of their earlier forms. They are better adapted to environmental conditions. Selection processes embrace all stages of adaptation of organisms to their environment, from non-viability due to the loss of a vital building-block or due to sudden changes in the environment, to considerably improved viability and propagation because of a mutation or new environmental factors.

Shell protein — the protein coat of viruses which surrounds the virus genetic material, the nucleic acid.

Sickle cells — sickle-shaped red blood corpuscles. They may be present in people whose red blood cells contain haemoglobin S instead of the normal haemoglobin. Haemoglobin S results from a point mutation in the gene for one of the polypeptide chains of the haemoglobin molecule.

Steroids — chemical compounds, all derivatives of the sterane skeleton. Some hormones are steroids, such as ecdysone in insects and sex hormones in vertebrates.

Streptomycin — an antibiotic much used medically to combat germs.

Substitution therapy treatment of an illness by administering the missing or modified substance to the sick individual. This treatment may not be applied in the case of molecular diseases caused by the misfunction of an intracellular macromolecule, since the molecules administered cannot pass through the cell membrane.

Synthetases abbreviation for aminoacyl-t-RNA-synthetases. Each of these enzymes catalyses the bonding of one amino acid to the appropriate transfer-RNA molecules. They are involved in the translation of the nucleotide sequence of m-RNA to the corresponding amino acid sequence of the proteins.

Tissues associations of cells of the same type.

Transfer-RNA one of the three types of ribonucleic acid playing an essential part in protein synthesis. The amino acids are bonded to transfer-RNA molecules and, by means of base-pairing, arrive at the position of the messenger-RNA which indicates their place in the protein molecule. There are at least sixty-four different transfer-RNA molecules, corresponding to the number of possible triplets.

Triplet a trinucleotide. A sequence of three nucleotides in DNA or m-RNA encodes an amino acid in the corresponding protein. Since there are four different nucleotides in DNA and in m-RNA, there are sixty-four different triplets. This means that several of the twenty amino acids are coded for by more than one triplet.

Vaccination (inoculation)	(a) Active: the administration of harmless or relatively harmless germs to produce specific antibodies in the organism. The antibodies nullify the injurious effects of a later infection by similar germs which cause illness. (b) Passive: an individual suffering from an infectious disease is given the corresponding antibody which has been produced in another organism.
Viruses	non-cellular structures which are able to survive outside cells for long periods. However, they require intact cells to reproduce, which often destroys the host cell. Many germs of infectious diseases are viruses. Their genetic material may be DNA or RNA and this is surrounded by shell protein.
Vitamins	substances which many organisms cannot synthesise and which are essential to life. These are mostly involved as catalysts of important reactions, such as the metabolic energy-cycle and the process of vision, and so only small quantities are necessary. They must be ingested with the food. The absence of a vitamin in the diet can lead to characteristic deficiency illnesses.

Glossary 2: Some methods used in molecular biology

We shall now outline some of the methods which are frequently used in research into the chemistry of life. We cannot describe the wide range of theoretical and experimental ideas used in various scientific disciplines which have resulted in the standard methods used today. Often, a question is solved only after the development of a suitable method which may result from the combined contributions of several scientists.

We may distinguish four main approaches to research into the chemistry of life, although in practice these categories are partly combined in the work of a scientist. Research may be either theoretical or experimental, and both types may be classified further according to whether the approach is more analytical or more synthetic.

To the synthetic approach belong, for example, experiments to determine how certain cell components function, such as attempts to synthesise proteins in a test tube using isolated molecules, or the variation of the environment of organisms in order to discover the key substances for the development of the fertilised egg to the mature complex organism.

However, the synthetic approach often requires the presence of isolated cell components. For this reason we shall include a description of some analytic methods which are used mainly for the isolation of components of organisms and for establishing their purity. The substances must be pure before they may be identified and analysed by determining their molecular weight or atomic composition. The composition of the *coli* cell tabulated in table 3·1, for example, is the outcome of many ideas and experiments, including the development of special methods, which has kept several research groups busy for many years. Often, it is the idea or the quest which allows the scientist to forget the monotonous routine of some series of experiments.

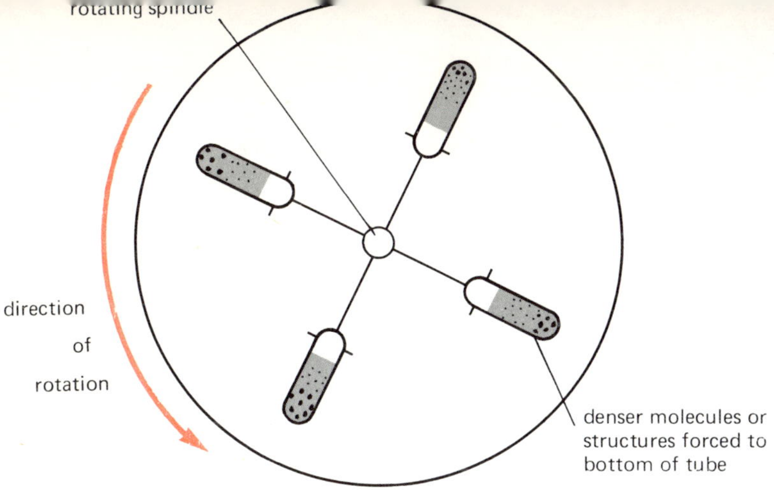

Centrifugation Here molecules and structures are separated according to their differences in weight. The mixture of molecules to be separated is rotated in a specially designed container, a rotor; this is motor-driven and may be rotated at a definite velocity. The gravitational pull on the molecules increases with the number of rotations per minute; sedimentation to the bottom of the vessel, away from the axis of the centrifuge, takes place at different rates. The sedimentation rate of molecules or structures is also affected by the density of the solvent.

The successful use of the ultracentrifuge for determining molecular weights is based upon a difficult mathematical and physical theory which cannot be mentioned here. Rotor speeds of more than 40,000 revolutions per minute indicate the great technical demands made on the ultracentrifuge.

Low-speed centrifuges (3,000 revolutions per minute) are used, for example, to separate the red corpuscles from the blood plasma or bacterial suspensions from their culture medium. High speed centrifuges are used to separate cell components and, for example, to isolate ribosomes or in the determination of molecular weights. The centrifugation of molecules through salt density-gradients considerably improves their separation.

Chromatography This method is used to separate molecules of different substances present together in a solution. The solution is applied to an insoluble medium which has a different affinity for the individual molecules of the solution so that the molecules migrate through the medium at different rates.

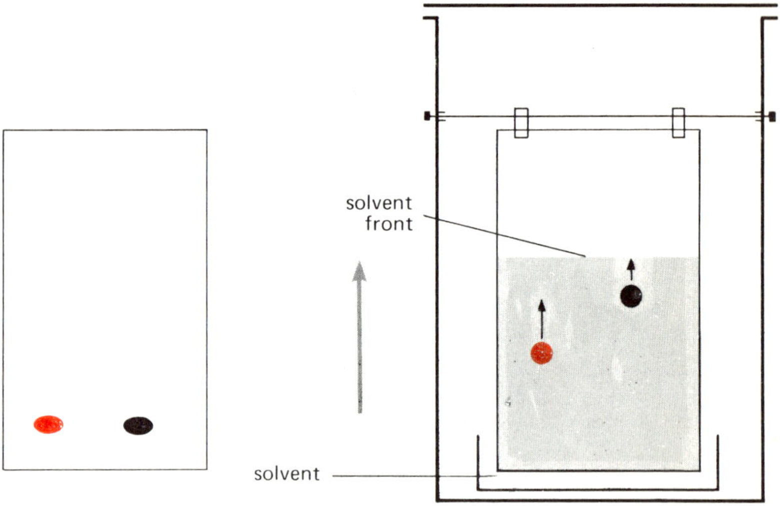

1 *Paper chromatography:* a simple method for the separation of smaller molecules from one another. The molecules to be separated are applied to sheets of suitable paper, which are subsequently placed in a vessel which contains a suitable solvent. A distinction is made between ascending and descending paper chromatography according to whether the solvent migrates on the paper from below or above. Highly soluble components of the sample mixture will migrate at the solvent front; other substances move more slowly according to their solubility. From this it follows that the choice of solvent determines the speed of migration of the individual molecules and is crucial for a successful separation.

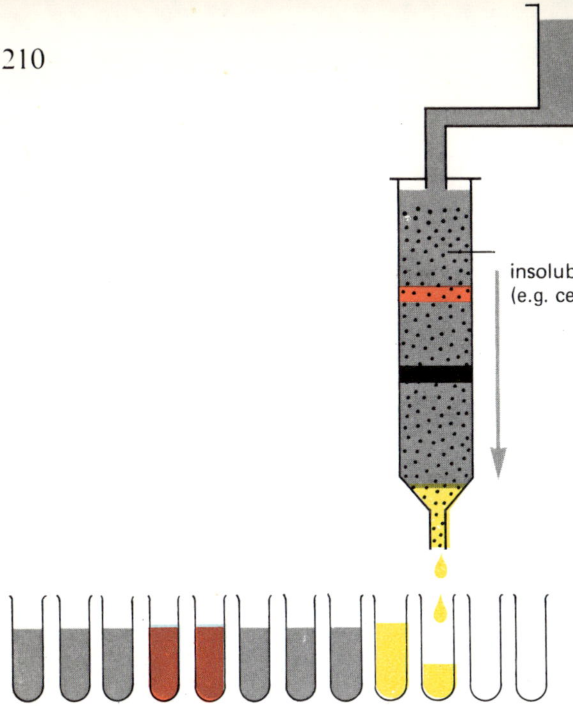

2 *Column chromatography:* an insoluble medium is packed into a glass tube; the length and width of this tube influence the separation of the molecules. The molecules to be separated are applied to the top of the column and their migration is started by adding a solvent. The characteristic separation which results depends on the choice of solvent and carrier material. A positively charged carrier binds negatively charged molecules; other carriers contain pores which are penetrated by the smaller molecules, which are therefore slowed down. The solution which flows from the column is collected in small fractions, which contain the separated classes of molecules.

Paper chromatography may be used for the separation of amino acids, nucleotides and other lower molecular-weight metabolic products. Column chromatography is, for example, important for the separation of mixtures of proteins, that is, for the isolation of enzymes such as cytochrome C or RNA-polymerase.

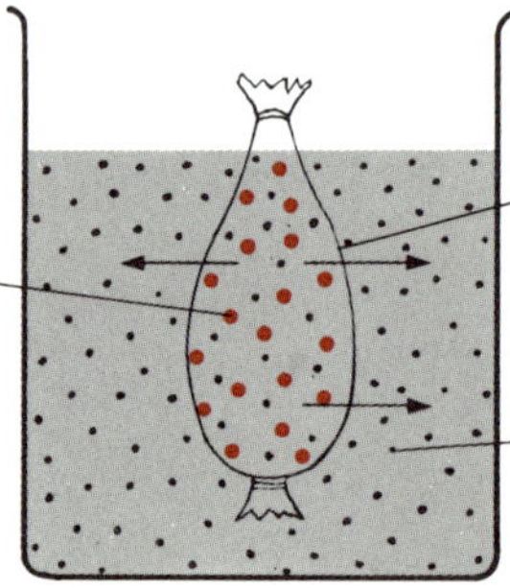

Dialysis A sensitive method for separating lower molecular-weight components from macromolecules. A thin membrane in the form of a tube is filled with the solution containing the molecules to be separated. The pore size of the membrane allows the diffusion of small molecules such as salts or amino acids; larger molecules such as proteins or nucleic acids cannot pass through the pores and so remain inside the dialysis tube.

Dialysis is a convenient method of exchanging solvents in the isolation of enzymes or other macromolecules.

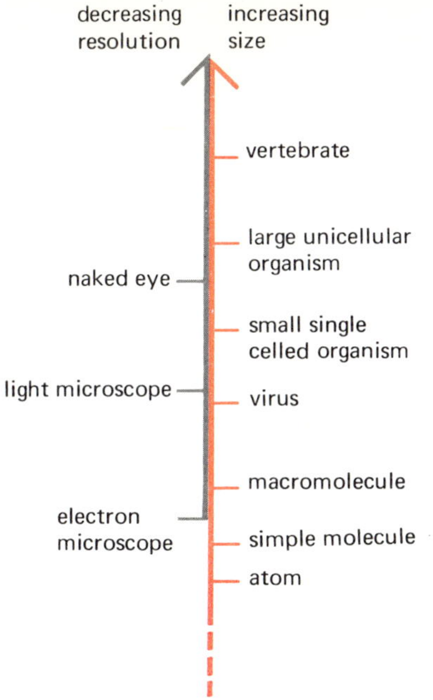

Electron microscopy This provides pictures of structures which cannot be resolved by the eye or the optical microscope. The figure shows a few components of the universe arranged according to their size. It also shows the range of sizes which can be resolved with the eye and the optical and electron microscopes.

The principle of the electron microscope is similar to that of the optical microscope. In the former, an electron beam replaces the beam of visible light in the optical microscope and instead of a system of lenses there is a suitable arrangement of magnetic fields. However, the preparation of the sample is often accompanied by great technical difficulties.

With the electron microscope, cellular structures or molecules may be enlarged more than two hundred thousand times (figure 5·9 or 7·2).

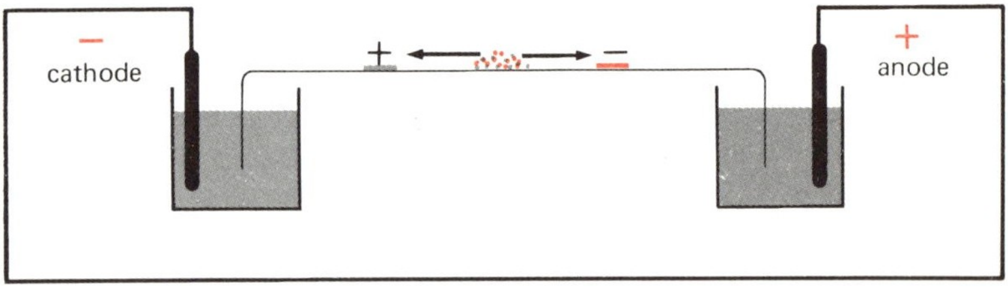

Electrophoresis Molecules or macromolecules may be separated in an electric field if they are charged to different extents. The mixture of compounds is applied to supporting films which dip into two containers filled with a salt solution. One of the containers holds a cathode, the other an anode. On passing an electric current, the negatively charged molecules migrate to the anode and the positively charged molecules to the cathode. Paper, agar and starch are examples of substances which may be used as supporting films.

The rate of migration of a molecule in an electric field is determined by its size and the number of charged groups per molecule.

This method is used in the separation of proteins, nucleic acids and their building blocks. The method is especially well suited to testing the purity of an isolated molecule.

Immunological methods The specific reactivity of antibodies allows them to be used for the detection or the isolation of molecules or structures.

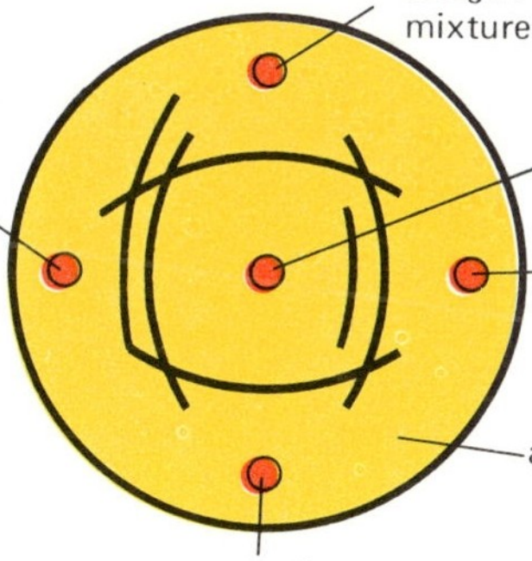

1 *Immunoprecipitation:* if to a mixture of molecules, antibodies are added which react with one type of molecule, then a specific precipitate is formed, consisting of the antibody and the corresponding antigen molecule. The pure antigen is obtained by isolating the immunoprecipitate and splitting it into antigen and antibody.

If immunoprecipitation is carried out in agar, it is possible to make an analysis of the number or type of the different antigens present in a solution. A small dish is covered with agar and the antiserum is added to a central hole in the agar; the antigen mixture to be analysed is applied to surrounding holes. Antigens and antibodies diffuse into the agar and wherever an antibody comes into contact with the corresponding antigen a specific precipitate forms; this shows up as a line of turbidity in the agar. The form and number of the lines gives information on the number and structural relationships of molecules in the various samples.

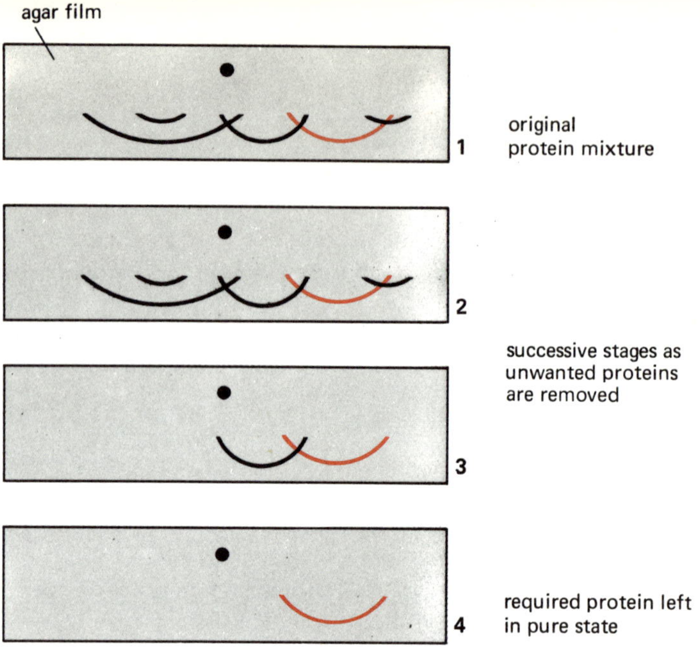

2 *Immuno-electrophoresis:* here immunodiffusion in agar is combined with electrophoresis. First of all the mixture of molecules to be identified is subjected to electrophoresis using agar as a supporting film. Then a groove is made in the agar and this is filled with the antiserum. As the antiserum diffuses through the agar it encounters the molecules separated by electrophoresis; wherever the antibody comes into contact with its corresponding antigen, an immunoprecipitate forms as a characteristic line.

Particularly when combined with characteristic colour reactions, this technique permits the analysis and comparison of components of mixtures of molecules. Also, it allows one to follow the purification of a specific protein of, say, the blood plasma, by monitoring the disappearance of other proteins after each stage of purification.

Isotopic labelling This can be used to follow the routes and conversions of molecules in organisms. Many atoms are obtainable in slightly changed forms known as radioactive isotopes. They are stable only for a definite period and decompose to give other atoms or fragments of atoms. During their decomposition, many atoms emit radioactive radiations which may be quantitatively and qualitatively measured by special devices. Different radioactive atoms have different but constant rates of decay.

The path of molecules within the organism can be followed especially well with molecules containing radioactive atoms with a low rate of decay; radioactive carbon, C^{14}, is one such atom. For example, if C^{14}-labelled glucose is fed to *coli* cells, it is possible to deduce which metabolic products are formed from glucose by observing the radioactivity appearing in other molecules; the results are improved by analysing the conversion products at given time intervals.

This technique can be used to determine the type and sequence of metabolic reactions. It has been used, for example, for analysing the conversion products of enzymatic reactions, either in the organism or in a test tube. Several radioactive radiations blacken photographic plates, and so this method can be used to locate radioactive molecules within the organism.

Precipitation The different solubility of molecules in various salt solutions, or in organic solvents such as alcohol or acetone, permits a fractional separation of a mixture of molecules in solution. If the salt concentration of a solution is gradually increased, then at each stage, certain types of molecule become insoluble and sink to the bottom of the vessel as a precipitate. The insoluble molecules are separated from the remaining solution by centrifugation before each increase in salt concentration.

The method is used in the fractionation of protein solutions, for example the blood plasma, or in separating different types of molecule, such as proteins and nucleic acids by means of organic solvents.

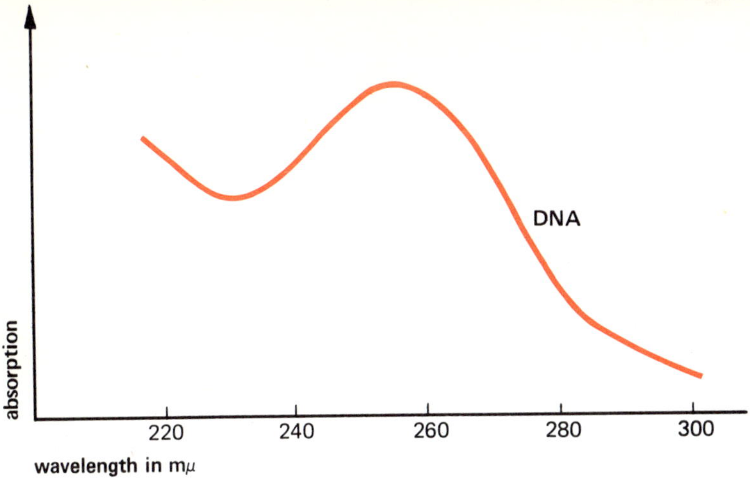

Spectrophotometry This may be used for the qualitative and quantitative analysis of mixtures of molecules in solution.

In ultraviolet spectrophotometry, dissolved molecules are irradiated with light of a definite wavelength. According to the type of molecule, there will be maximum absorption at a characteristic wavelength. The figure shows the absorption spectrum of nucleic acids; the absorption maximum lies at a wavelength of 253mμ. The absorption spectra of the substances to be analysed may be compared with the spectra of known molecules and in this way a qualitative analysis of a mixture of substances can be carried out. The concentration of the absorbing substance can be calculated from the quantity of light absorbed.

We shall not mention the physical theory behind this method or the apparatus involved. The same goes for other spectrophotometric methods, such as infrared spectroscopy or nuclear-magnetic-resonance spectroscopy. By means of chemical relaxation spectrometry it is possible to follow the time-course, the kinetics, of chemical reactions to within fractions of thousandths of a second.

These methods may be used in the qualitative and quantitative analysis of molecules in a solution; for example, the reaction products in enzymatic reactions.

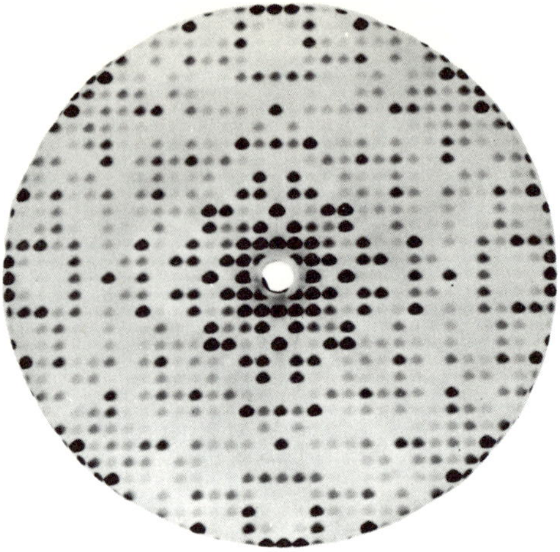

X-ray structural analysis The main application of this method is in the analysis of the three-dimensional structure of molecules and macromolecules. The molecule to be investigated must be present in crystalline form. In the crystal, identical molecules are packed together in a regular pattern. The wavelength of X-rays is sufficiently short for the rays to be diffracted in a characteristic manner according to the arrangement of the atoms in the molecules of the crystal. Thus for each type of molecule X-rays produce a characteristic diffraction pattern. We cannot here go into the extensive apparatus and mathematical requirements necessary for carrying out this method or for translating the diffraction pattern into an actual spatial model of the molecule (figure 5·6).

X-ray diffraction has been used for the structural analysis of macromolecules such as lysozyme or haemoglobin. Treatment of the enzyme with substrates or inhibitors before X-ray structural analysis shows the influence of these substances on the spatial structure of the enzyme and thus clarifies the molecular changes within a macromolecule during its reactions.

Appendix

A2·1 The periodic table of elements.

	0	**I**																	**II**	
1	0 Nn	1 H																	2 He	**1**
	Oa	**Ia**	**IIa**	**IIIa**	**IVa**	**Va**	**VIa**	**VIIa**	**VIIIa bzw. Ob**			**Ib**	**IIb**	**IIIb**	**IVb**	**Vb**	**VIb**	**VIIb**	**VIIIb**	
2	2 He	3 Li	4 Be											5 B	6 C	7 N	8 O	9 F	10 Ne	**2**
3	10 Ne	11 Na	12 Mg											13 Al	14 SI	15 P	16 S	17 Cl	18 Ar	**3**
4	18 Ar	19 K	20 Ca	21 Sc	22 Ti	23 V	24 Cr	25 Mn	26 Fe	27 Co	28 Ni	29 Cu	30 Zn	31 Ga	32 Ge	33 As	34 Se	35 Br	36 Kr	**4**
5	36 Kr	37 Rb	38 Sr	39 Y	40 Zr	41 Nb	42 Mo	43 Tc	44 Ru	45 Rh	46 Pd	47 Ag	48 Cd	49 In	50 Sn	51 Sb	52 Te	53 J	54 Xe	**5**
6	54 Xe	55 Cs	56 Ba	57 La	72 Hf	73 Ta	74 W	75 Re	76 Os	77 Ir	78 Pt	79 Au	80 Hg	81 Tl	82 Pb	83 Bi	84 Po	85 At	86 Rn	**6**
7	86 Rn	87 Fr	88 Ra	89 Ac	104 —	(105) —	(106) —	(107) —	(108) —	(109) —	(110) —	(111) —	(112) —	(113) —	(114) —	(115) —	(116) —	(117) —	(118) —	**7**
	Oa	**Ia**	**IIa**	**IIIa**	**IVa**	**Va**	**VIa**	**VIIa**	**VIIIa bzw. Ob**			**Ib**	**IIb**	**IIIb**	**IVb**	**Vb**	**VIb**	**VIIb**	**VIIIb**	

A2·2 The three laws of thermodynamics:

1 The total energy of a closed system remains constant.

2 In a closed system, all processes proceed in such a way that the entropy increases (entropy is a measure of disorder).

3 At the absolute zero of temperature, the entropy of a pure, solid substance tends to zero.

A2·3 Formula of chlorophyll *a*. In chlorophyll *b* the formyl group replaces the methyl group. The chlorophyll molecule enables green plant cells to convert the radiant energy of the sun into chemical energy.

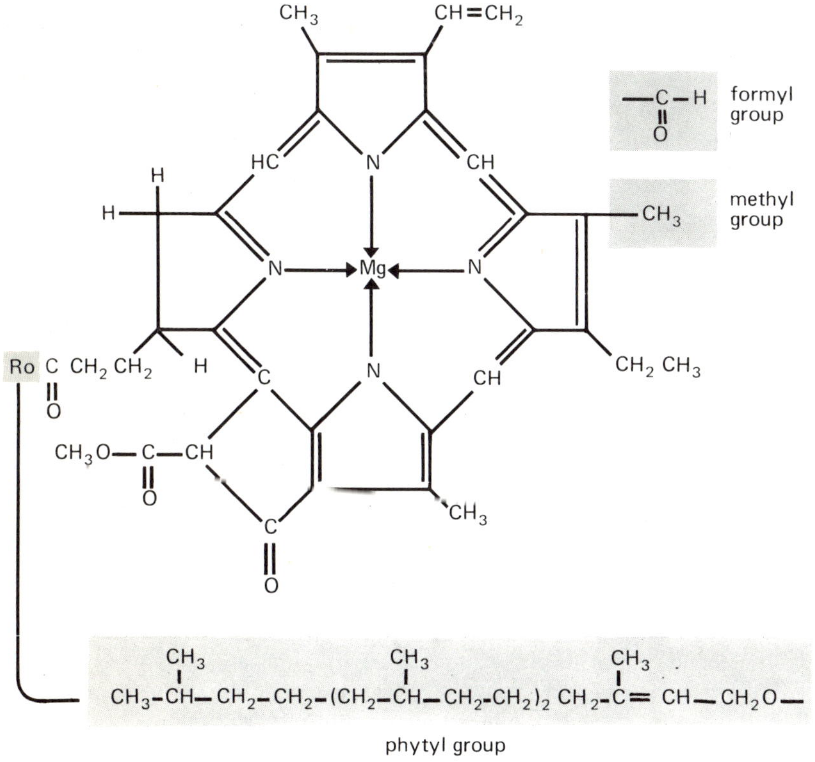

A4·1 Formula of the ATP molecule. ATP acts as the store and supplier of energy in both unicellular organisms and in the cells of more complex organisms, including man.

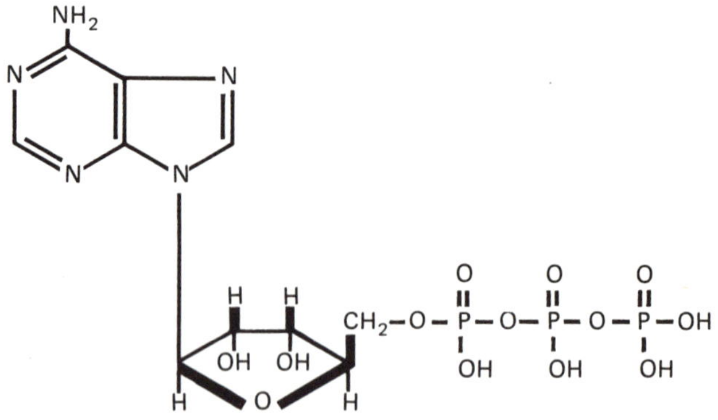

A4·2 Reaction chain for the degradation of glucose for the formation of ATP. The degradation of glucose proceeds via several intermediate stages, with the liberation of four molecules of ATP. Two of these ATP molecules are consumed in the degradation of a further molecule of glucose, so that the degradation of one glucose molecule liberates two ATP molecules for use in other cell reactions which consume energy. The whole process is called anaerobic glycolysis.

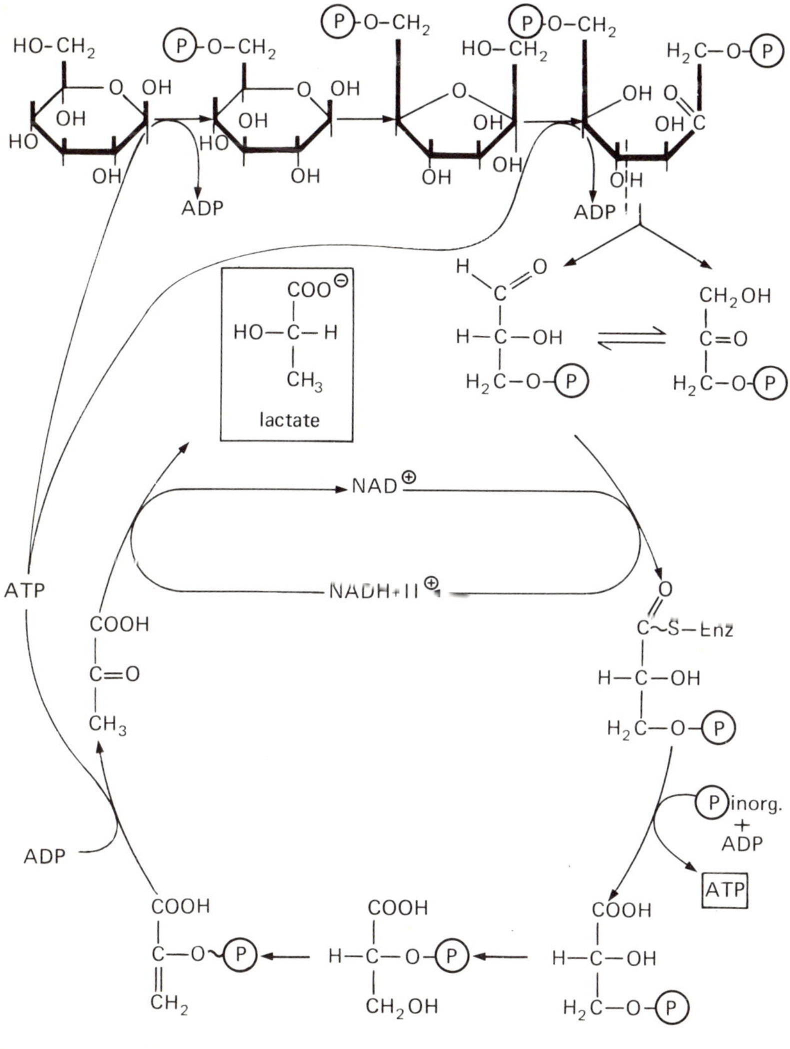

A4·3 The citric acid cycle; the individual reaction steps are not explained. A C_2-fragment (acetyl-CoA) condenses with C_4-fragment (oxalacetate) to form citric acid. After nine stages the C_2-fragment is degraded, and during these stages energy is gained. The citric acid cycle takes place only in connection with the reactions of the respiratory sequence.

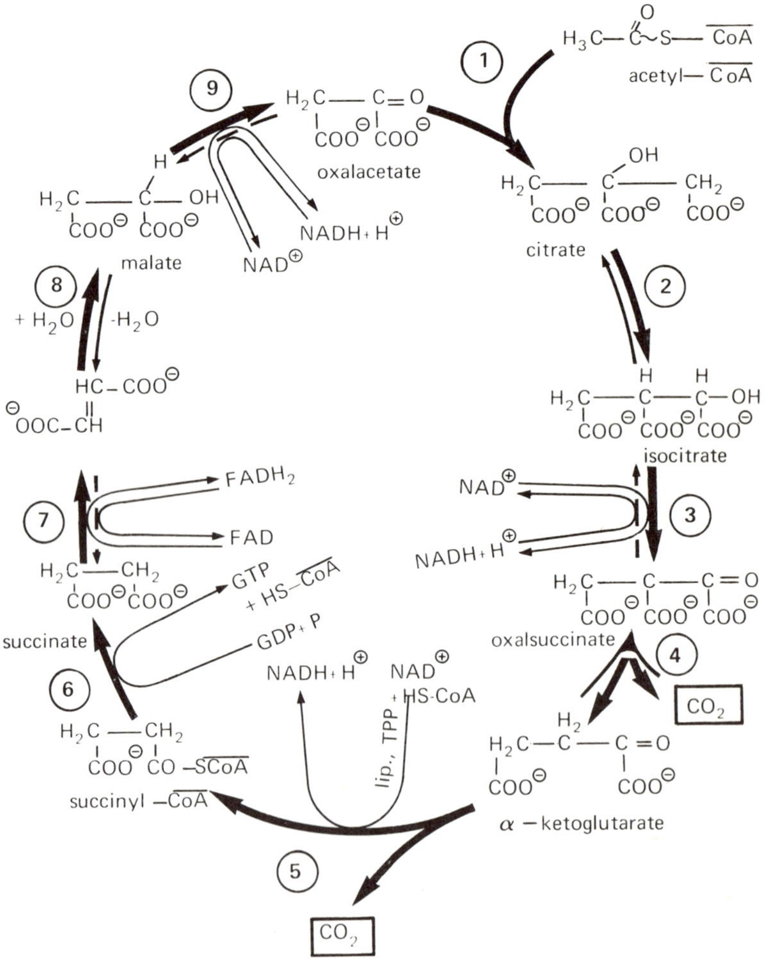

A4·4 The structural formulae of the twenty amino acids.

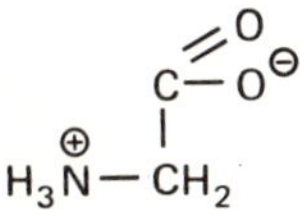

glycine
(gly)

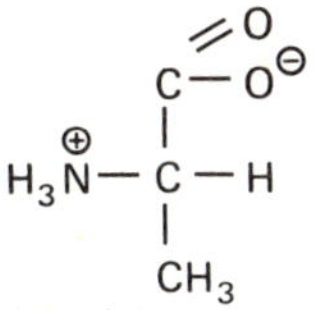

L-alanine
(ala)

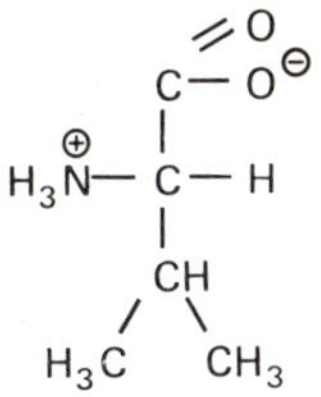

L-valine
(val)

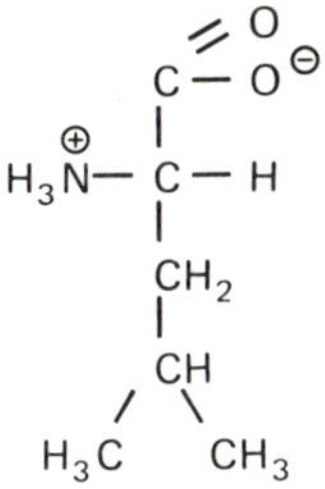

L-leucine
(leu)

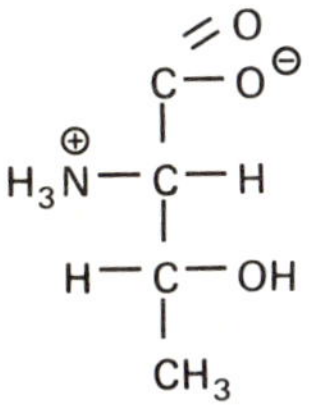

L-threonine
(thre)

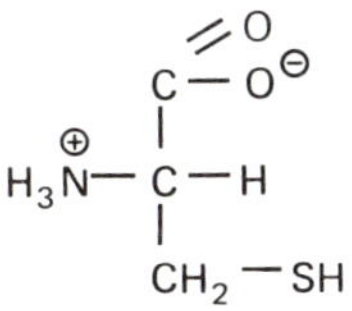

L-cysteine
(cys)

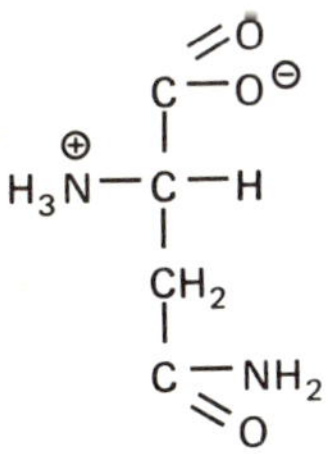

L-asparagine
(asn)

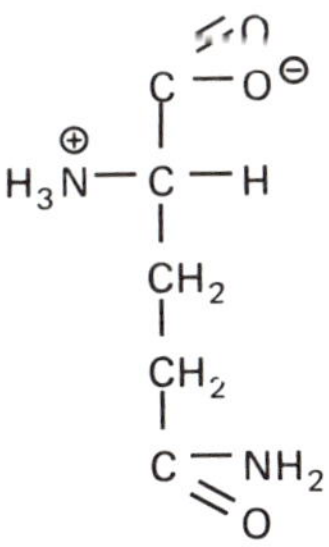

L-glutamine
(glu N)

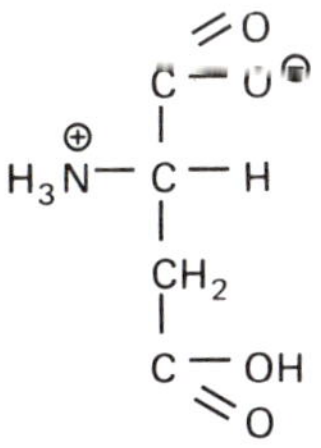

L-aspartic acid
(asp)

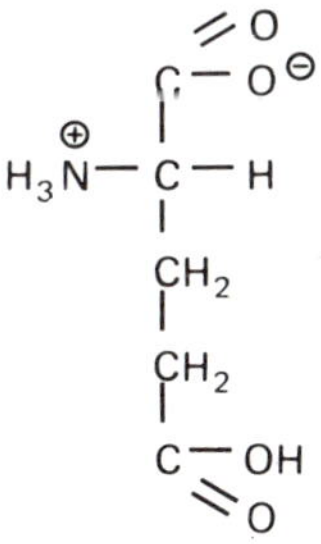

L-glutamic acid
(glu)

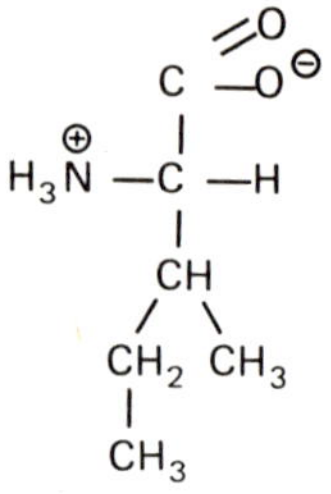

L-isoleucine
(ile)

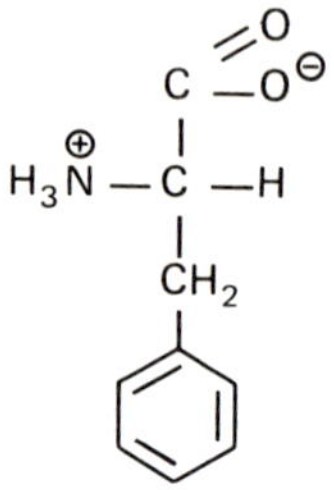

L-phenylalanine
(phe)

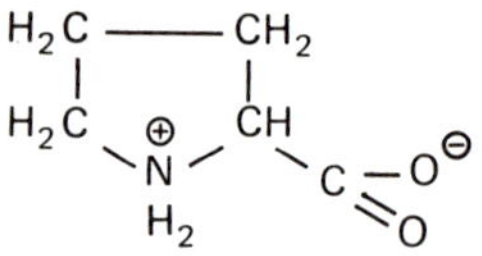

L-proline
(pro)

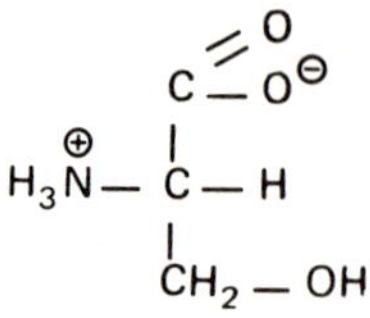

L-serine
(ser)

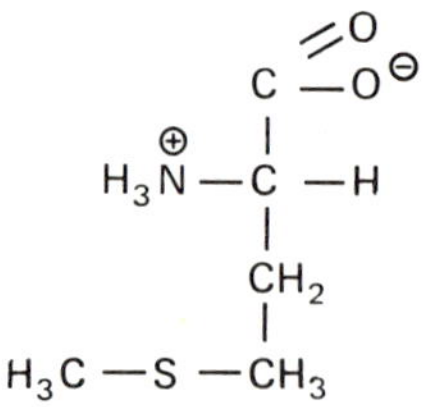

L-methionine
(met)

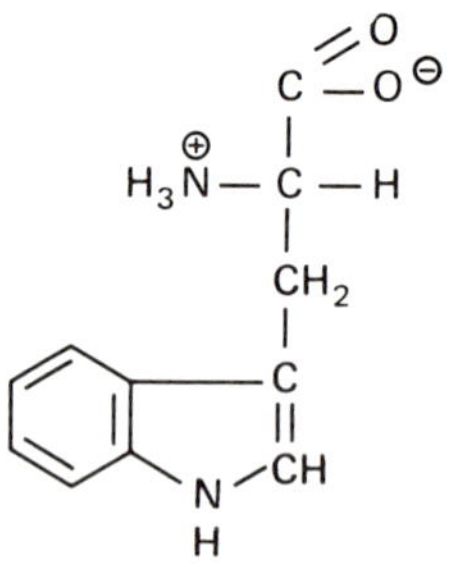

L-tryptophan
(try)

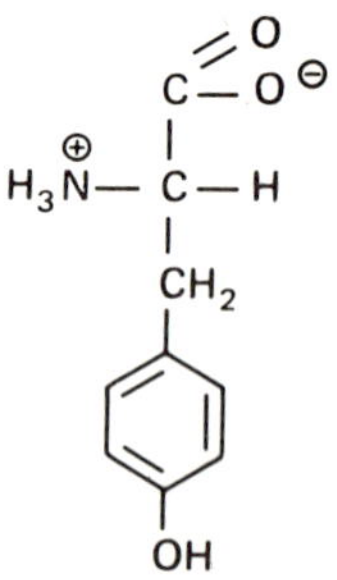

L-tyrosine
(tyr)

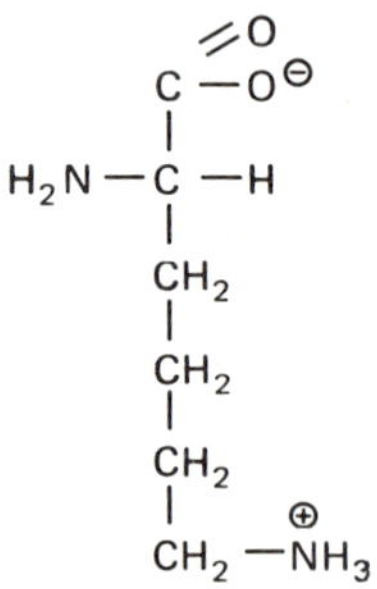

L-lysine
(lys)

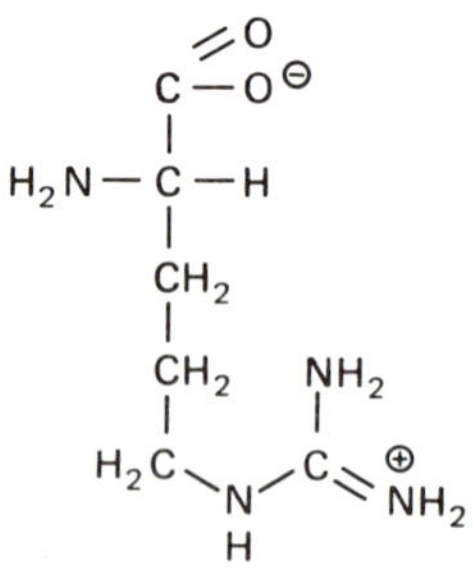

L-arginine
(arg)

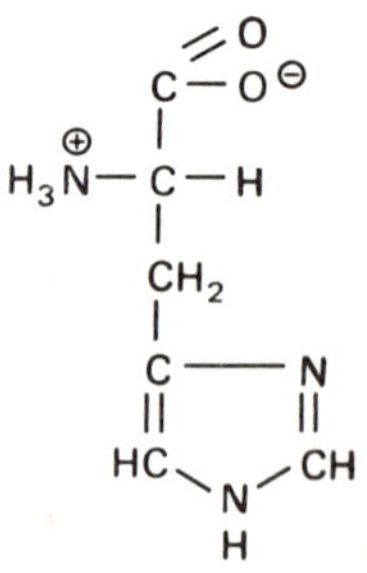

L-histidine
(his)

A4·5 The building blocks of deoxy-and ribo-nucleic acids. The building blocks of deoxyribonucleic acid are the deoxyribonucleotides, which are built up from three types of molecules : a phosphate group, a sugar residue (deoxyribose) and a base. The four different deoxyribonucleotides are distinguished by their bases, which may be adenine, thymine, guanine or cytosine. Ribonucleotides are the building blocks of ribonucleic acids, and are made up from a phosphate group, a sugar residue (ribose) and a base. There are four ribonucleotides, the bases of which differ : adenine, uracil, guanine and cytosine. Occasionally, other bases are found in ribonucleotides, particularly in those groups which compose the transfer ribonucleic acids.

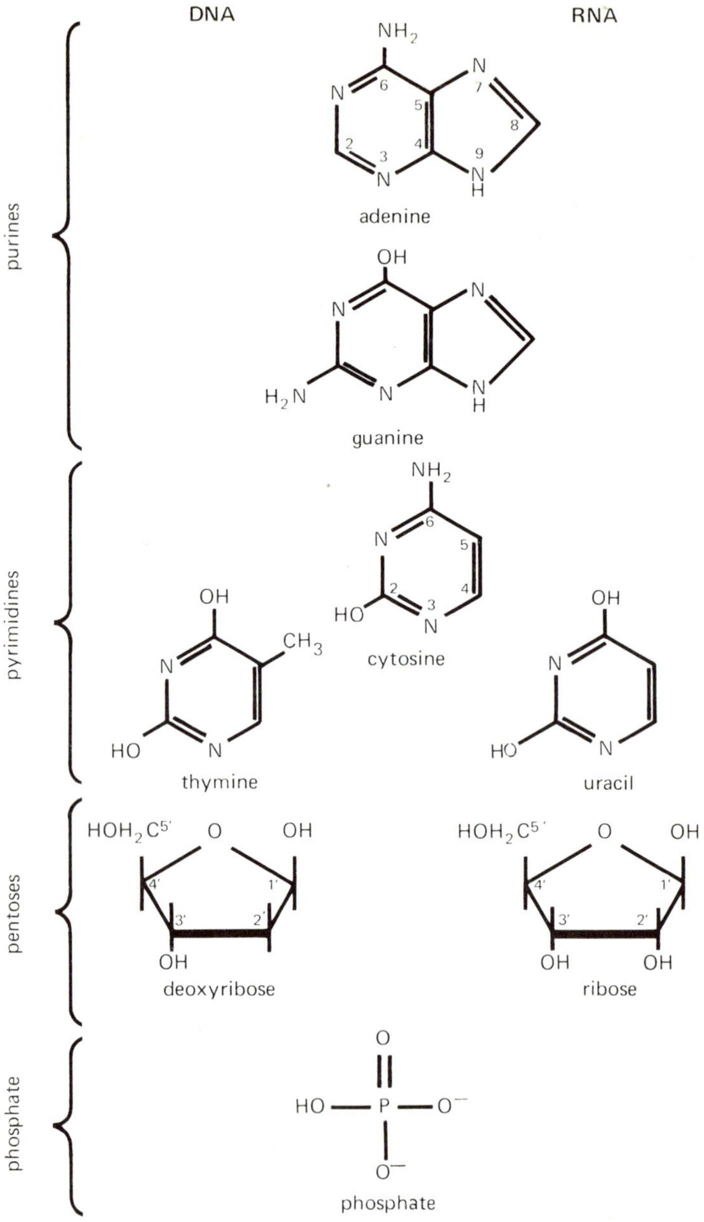
DNA
RNA
purines
adenine
guanine
pyrimidines
cytosine
thymine
uracil
pentoses
deoxyribose
ribose
phosphate
phosphate

A4·6 The synthesis of histidine in bacteria. There are ten intermediate stages, starting from two molecules present in the cells. Each step is catalysed by a specific enzyme and the product of one reaction acts as the substrate for the next. Other amino acids and the building blocks of other macromolecules are synthesised in cells by similar types of reaction series. The stages also require specific enzymes and are formed from precursors via several stages with the consumption of ATP.

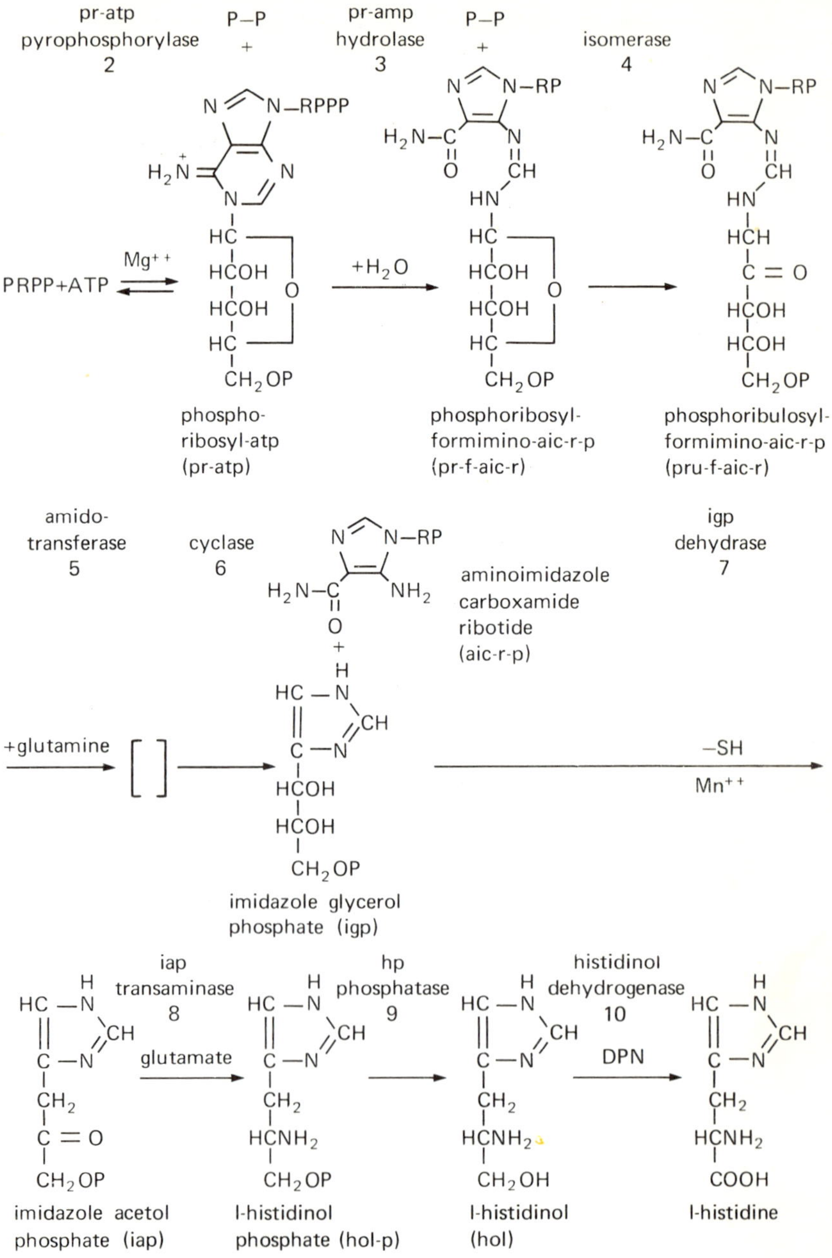
pr-atp
pyrophosphorylase
2
P—P
+
pr-amp
hydrolase
3
P—P
+
isomerase
4
PRPP+ATP
Mg++
+H2O
phospho-
ribosyl-atp
(pr-atp)
phosphoribosyl-
formimino-aic-r-p
(pr-f-aic-r)
phosphoribulosyl-
formimino-aic-r-p
(pru-f-aic-r)
amido-
transferase
5
cyclase
6
aminoimidazole
carboxamide
ribotide
(aic-r-p)
igp
dehydrase
7
+glutamine
–SH
Mn++
imidazole glycerol
phosphate (igp)
iap
transaminase
8
glutamate
hp
phosphatase
9
histidinol
dehydrogenase
10
DPN
imidazole acetol
phosphate (iap)
l-histidinol
phosphate (hol-p)
l-histidinol
(hol)
l-histidine

A5·1 The table shows which triplet of nucleotides in messenger RNA is responsible for the incorporation of which amino acid in a protein. The individual steps in the translation of this trinucleotide code to the amino acid sequence in a protein are described in more detail in chapter 5. Most of the amino acids are coded for by more than one trinucleotide of messenger RNA. The codons UAA, UGA and UAG, though not listed, are of special interest because they function as terminator codons in the m-RNA, at least in bacterial cells; no corresponding amino acids are known. The codons AUG and GUG are involved in the initiation of the synthesis of the polypeptide chain.

Amino acid	**Trinucleotide**					
Alanine	GCC	GCU	GCA	GCG		
Arginine	CGC	AGA	CGU	CGA	CGG	AGG
Aspartic acid	GAU	GAC				
Asparagine	AAU	AAC				
Cysteine	UGU	UGC				
Glutamic acid	GAA	GAG				
Glutamine	CAA	CAG				
Glycine	GGU	GGC	GGA	GGG		
Histidine	CAU	CAC				
Isoleucine	AUU	AUC	AUA			
Leucine	CUU	CUC	CUA	CUG	UUA	UUG
Lysine	AAA	AAG				
Methionine	AUG					
Phenylalanine	UUU	UUC				
Proline	CCU	CCC	CCA	CCG		
Serine	AGU	AGC	UCU	UCC	UCA	UCG
Threonine	ACU	ACC	ACA	ACG		
Tryptophan	UGG					
Tyrosine	UAU	UAC				
Valine	GUU	GUC	GUA	GUG		

A8·1 The chemical structure of haem – the non-protein part of the oxygen-carrying molecule, haemoglobin. The protein part of haemoglobin, globin, bonds to the iron atom of haem by means of the amino acid histidine. During the transport of oxygen, the oxygen molecule is reversibly bonded to the iron atom. The haem group, or molecules related to it, is also found in other composite molecules of cells, for example, in some enzymes involved in energy metabolism and in the chlorophyll of plant cells.

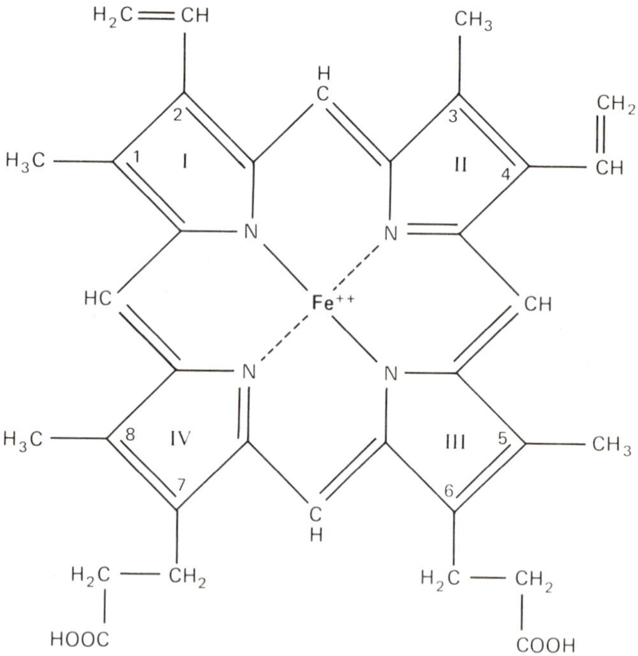

α	Val		Leu	Ser	Pro	Ala	Asp	Lys	Thr	Asn	Val	Lys	Ala	Ala	Try
β	Val	His	Leu	Thr	Pro	Glu	Glu	Lys	Ser	Ala	Val	Thr	Ala	Leu	Try
										10					

α	Gly	Lys	Val	Gly	Ala	His	Ala	Gly	Glu	Tyr	Gly	Ala	Glu	Ala	Leu
β	Gly	Lys	Val	Asn			Val	Asp	Glu	Val	Gly	Gly	Glu	Ala	Leu
					20										30

α	Glu	Arg	Met	Phe	Leu	Ser	Phe	Pro	Thr	Thr	Lys	Thr	Tyr	Phe	Pro
β	Glu	Arg	Leu	Leu	Val	Val	Tyr	Pro	Try	Thr	Gln	Arg	Phe	Phe	Glu
								40							

α	His	Phe		Asp	Leu	Ser	His						Gly	Ser	Ala
β	Ser	Phe	Gly	Asp	Leu	Ser	Thr	Pro	Asp	Ala	Val	Met	Gly	Asn	Pro
					50										60

α	Gln	Val	Lys	Gly	His	Gly	Lys	Lys	Val	Ala	Asp	Ala	Leu	Thr	Asn
β	Lys	Val	Lys	Ala	His	Gly	Lys	Lys	Val	Leu	Gly	Ala	Phe	Ser	Asp
								70							

α	Ala	Val	Ala	His	Val	Asp	Asp	Met	Pro	Asn	Ala	Leu	Ser	Ala	Leu
β	Gly	Leu	Ala	His	Leu	Asp	Asn	Leu	Lys	Gly	Thr	Phe	Ala	Thr	Leu
					80										90

α	Ser	Asp	Leu	His	Ala	His	Lys	Leu	Arg	Val	Asp	Pro	Val	Asn	Phe
β	Ser	Glu	Leu	His	Cys	Asp	Lys	Leu	His	Val	Asp	Pro	Glu	Asn	Phe
								100							

α	Lys	Leu	Leu	Ser	His	Cys	Leu	Leu	Val	Thr	Leu	Ala	Ala	His	Leu
β	Arg	Leu	Leu	Gly	Asn	Val	Leu	Val	Cys	Val	Leu	Ala	His	His	Phe
					110										120

α	Pro	Ala	Glu	Phe	Thr	Pro	Ala	Val	His	Ala	Ser	Leu	Asp	Lys	Phe
β	Gly	Lys	Glu	Phe	Thr	Pro	Pro	Val	Gln	Ala	Ala	Tyr	Gln	Lys	Val
										130					

α	Leu	Ala	Ser	Val	Ser	Thr	Val	Leu	Thr	Ser	Lys	Tyr	Arg
β	Val	Ala	Gly	Val	Ala	Asn	Ala	Leu	Ala	His	Lys	Tyr	His
					140								

A8·2 Left The amino acid sequences of the two protein chains of human haemoglobin. Globin consists of two identical pairs of protein chains, each pair consisting of an alpha and beta chain. In the alpha and beta chains from other species some of the amino acids are replaced by others.

A8·3 Below The amino acid sequence of insulin from bullocks elucidated by Sanger in 1956. Since then the amino acid sequences of insulin from other animal species and from humans has also been analysed. They differ only slightly from the protein chains given here. In the active hormone, the two protein chains are linked by disulphide bridges. Recently an inactive form of insulin has been discovered, in which the two polypeptide chains are linked to one chain by a sequence of 33 amino acids; during the change from the inactive to the active hormone, these amino acids are thought to be split off, leaving behind the A and B polypeptide chain linked by disulphide bridges.

A Chain

				NH_2						
H.Gly	Ileu	Val	Glu	Glu	Cys	Cys	Ala	Ser	Val	Cys
1	2	3	4	5	6	7	8	9	10	11

			NH_2			NH_2			NH_2
Ser	Leu	Tyr	Glu	Leu	Glu	Asp	Tyr	Cys	Asp.OH
12	13	14	15	16	17	18	19	20	21

B Chain

		NH_2	NH_2						
H.Phe	Val	Asp	Glu	His	Leu	Cys	Gly	Ser	His
1	2	3	4	5	6	7	8	9	10
Leu	Val	Glu	Ala	Leu	Tyr	Leu	Val	Cys	Gly
11	12	13	14	15	16	17	18	19	20
Glu	Arg	Gly	Phe	Phe	Tyr	Thr	Pro	Lys	Ala.OH
21	22	23	24	25	26	27	28	29	30

A8·4 Structural formula of ecdysone, showing it to be a steroid. It is an insect hormone involved in the metamorphosis of insect larvae and pupae.

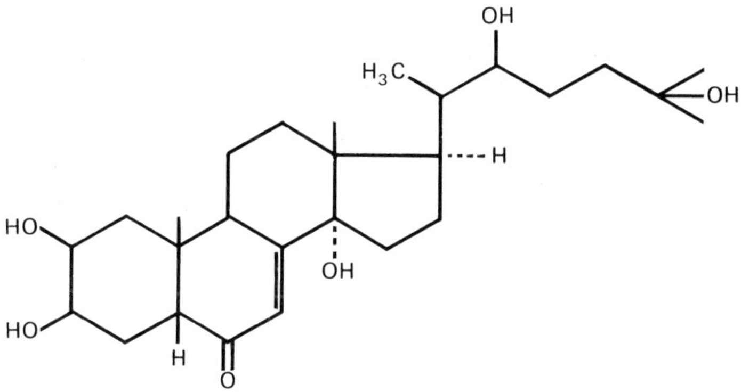

A9·1 The structural formulae of streptomycin and chloramphenicol show that substances with very different chemical structures may act as antibiotics.

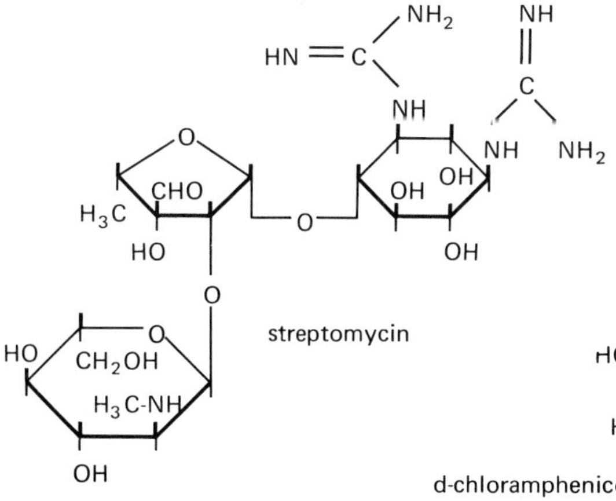

streptomycin

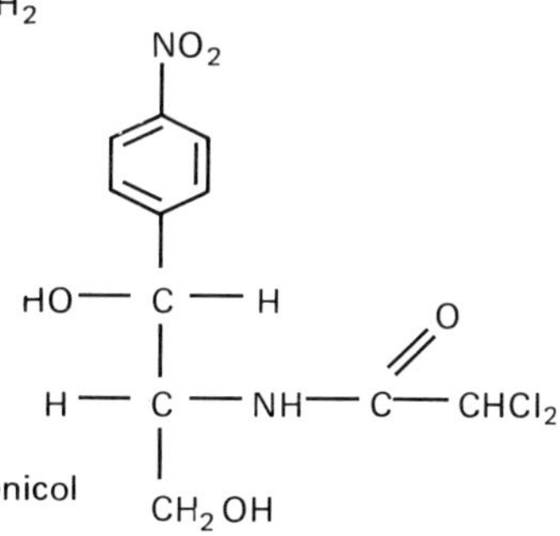

d-chloramphenicol

A9·2 The structural formula of vitamin C. Vitamin C, or L-ascorbic acid, may easily be dehydrogenated to give L-dehydroascorbic acid. It is assumed that this reversible reaction is also important in the participation of vitamin C in metabolic processes in the cells.

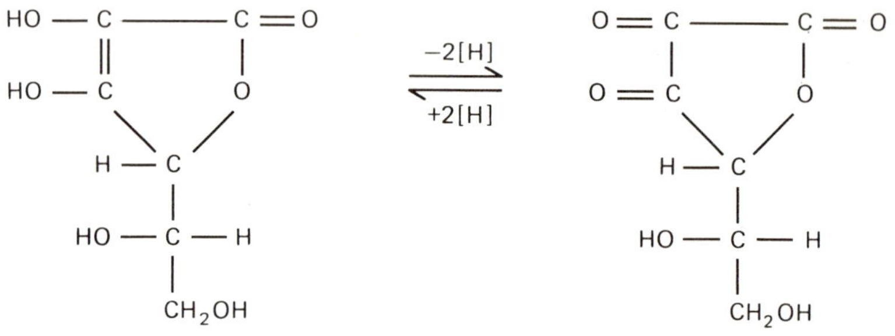

L – ascorbic acid

L – dehydro-ascorbic acid

A9·3 The structural formula of vitamin A, and its formation from the vitamin precursor. The latter is taken in with vegetable foods and the conversion to biologically active vitamin A takes place in the cells of mammals.

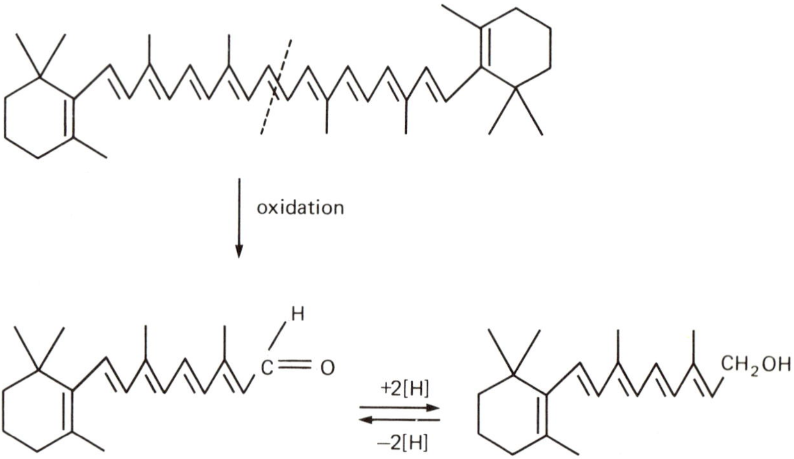

vitamin A_1-aldehyde
(all trans-retinin)

vitamin A_1

A9·4 The reaction steps involved in the process of vision, during which vitamin A undergoes several conversions.

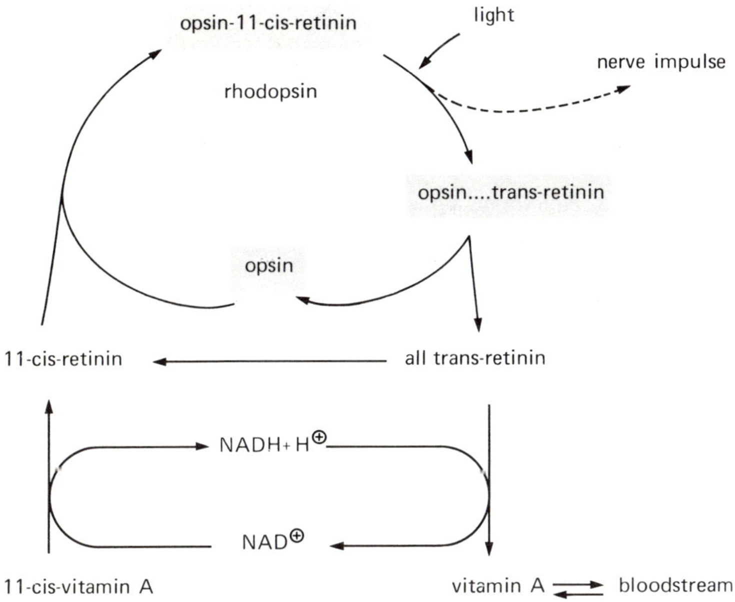

A9·5 Structural formula of the sexual lure of the silk moth *Bombyx mori*. A few molecules of bombykol reaching the receptors of the male silk moth is enough to set them flying in the direction of the female which has secreted the attractant. The isomer of bombykol is effective only if used at one million times the concentration.

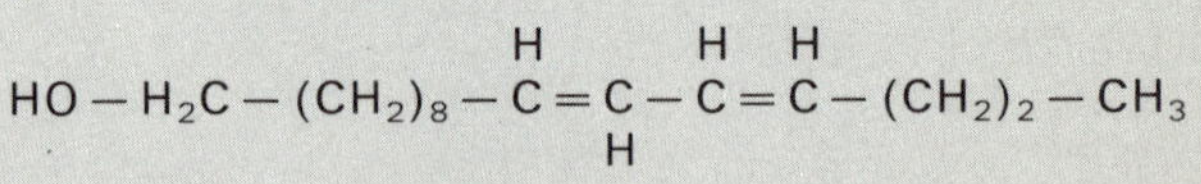

10-trans, 12-cis
Bombykol
(highly active lure)

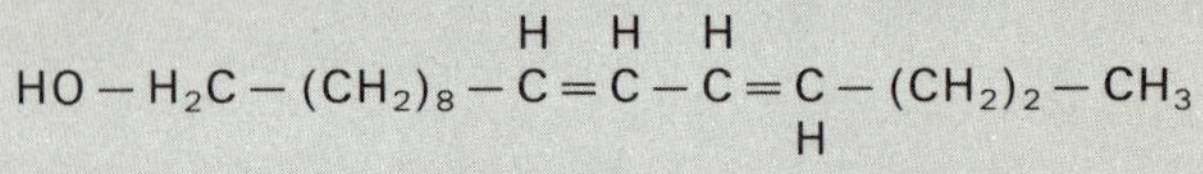

10-cis, 12-trans
Bombykol isomer
(scarcely active lure)

A9·6 Structural formulae of L- and D-alanine. All the building blocks of proteins are L-amino acids. D-alanine cannot be incorporated into protein chains in protein biosynthesis.

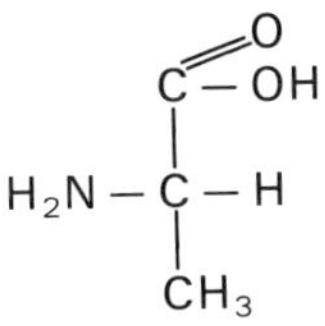

L-Alanine

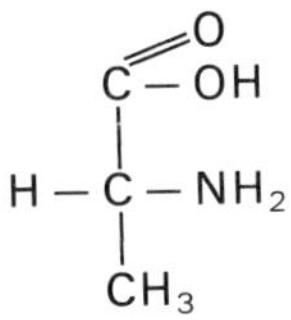

D-Alanine

A9·7 The structural formula of the defence secretion of the yellow brand beetle shows it to be steroid. The same chemical compound is known as cortexone, a substance which helps to regulate the salt-balance system of vertebrates. This explains the paralysing action of the beetle's defence secretion on fishes.

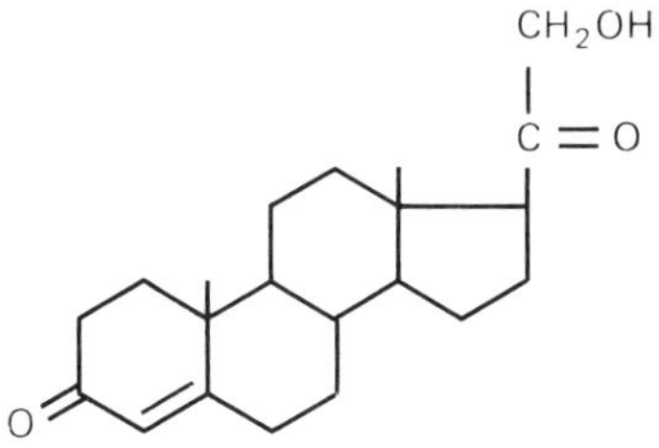

defence substance cortexone

A10·1 Blood-group active sugar molecules in the cell membrane of human red blood cells. The surfaces of the red blood cells of persons of blood group A contain sugar molecules designated in the figure as A. Blood group B is conditioned by the arrangement of sugars of substance B, while persons of blood group AB contain both A and B substances in the surfaces of their red blood cells. If, instead of the A or B substance, the sugar arrangement of substance H is present, then the blood group is O. If, for example, the red blood cells containing substance B are clumped by the action of the anti-B antibodies, the latter combine with the sugars of the B substance and so lead to the linkage and destruction of the red corpuscles.

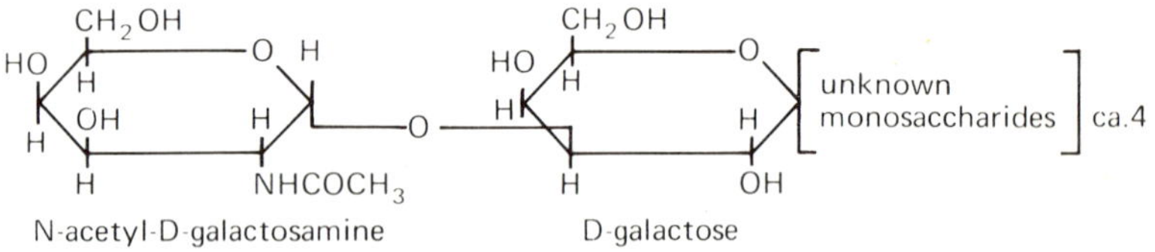

A substance

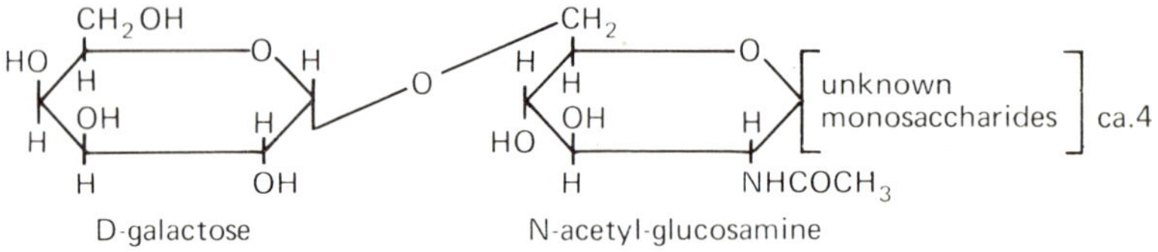

B substance

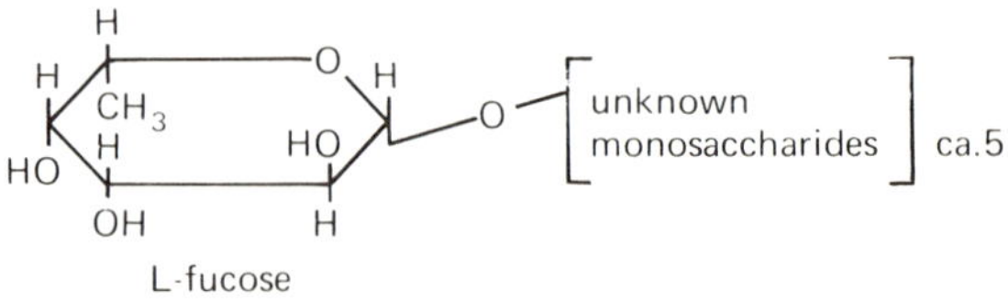

H substance

A13·1 The Difference in the amino acid sequence of the beta chain of haemoglobin A and S in man.

Beta chain of haemoglobin A :	–Thr–	Pro–	Glu–	Glu–	Lys–	Ser–
	4	5	6	7	8	9
Beta chain of haemoglobin S :	–Thr–	Pro–	Val–	Glu–	Lys–	Ser–

The exchange of only one amino acid in position 6 of the beta chain of haemoglobin converts haemoglobin A to haemoglobin S. The numerals show the position of the amino acids in the beta chain. All the other amino acid sequences in the globin (A 8.2) are identical for both haemoglobin A and haemoglobin S. A glance at A 5.2 shows that this amino acid exchange may be interpreted by a single point mutation in the relevant gene: the trinucleotide GAA for glutaminic acid is replaced by GUA for valine in the messenger RNA for the beta chain.

A15·1 Formation of organic molecules under conditions prevalent on earth about five thousand million years age. Amino acids and other substances are formed if electrical energy is supplied to a mixture of methane, ammonia, water and hydrogen in an oxygen-free atmosphere :

glycine
glycolic acid
sarcosine
aspartic acid
aminodiacetic acid
glutamic acid
aminoacetic-propionic acid

alanine
lactic acid
N–methylalanine

α–amino-n-butyric acid
α–aminoisobutyric acid
α–hydroxybutyric acid
β–alanine

succinic acid
formic acid
acetic acid
propionic acid

urea
N–methyl urea

Bibliography

2 A few chemical concepts

Lehninger, A. 1965. *Bioenergetics*, W. A. Benjamin Inc., New York.

Speakman, J. C. 1966. *Molecules*, McGraw-Hill, New York.

3 The bacterial cell as the simplest organism

Hokin, L. E. and Hokin, M. R. 1965. The Chemistry of Cell Membranes, *Scient. Am.*, **213**, No. 4.

Luria, S. E. 1960. Bacterial Protoplasma: Composition and Organization in: *The Bacteria*, Eds. P. I. Gunsalus, R. Y. Stanier, Vol. I, Academic Press, New York.

4 Energy and the synthesis of the building blocks of macromolecules

Lehninger, A. 1965. *Bioenergetics*, W. A. Benjamin Inc., New York.

Meister, A. 1965. *Biochemistry of the Amino Acids*, Academic Press, London, New York.

5 The structure, function and synthesis of macromolecules

Green, D. E. and Goldberger, R. F. 1967. *Molecular Insights into the Living Process*, Academic Press, London, New York.

Ingram, V. M. 1966. *The Biosynthesis of Macromolecules*, W. A. Benjamin Inc., New York.

Phillips, D. C. 1966. The Three-dimensional Structure of an Enzyme Molecule, *Scient. Am.*, **215**, No. 5.

Watson, J. D. 1965. *Molecular Biology of the Gene*, W. A. Benjamin Inc., New York.

6 Regulation of the synthesis of macromolecules and their precursors

Cellular Regulatory Mechanisms. 1961. *Cold Spring Harb. Quant. Biol.*, **26**.

Maaløe, O. and Kjeldgaard, N.O. 1966. *Control of Macromolecular Synthesis*, W.A. Benjamin Inc., New York.

Watson, J.D. 1965. *Molecular Biology of the Gene*, W. A. Benjamin Inc., New York.

7 The structure and organisation of multicellular organisms

Brachet, J. and Mirsky, A.E. 1959. (Eds.). *The Cell*, Academic Press, London/New York.

De Reuck, A.V.S. and Cameron, M.P. 1963. (Eds.). *Lysosomes*, Ciba Foundation, J.A. Churchill Ltd., London.

Lehninger, A.L. 1964. *The Mitochondrion*, W.A. Benjamin Inc., New York.

8 Communication routes in more complex organisms

Davidson, E.H. 1965. Hormones and Genes, *Scient. Am.*, **212**, No. 6.

Davie, E.W. and Ratnoff, O.D. 1965. Proteins of Blood Coagulation, in: *The Proteins*, vol. III, Ed. Neurath, Academic Press, London.

Gray, C.H. and Bacharach, A.L. 1967. *Hormones in Blood*, Academic Press, New York.

MacFarlane, R.G. and Robb-Smith, A.H.T. 1961. (Eds.). *Functions of the Blood*, Academic Press, London.

Perutz, M. 1966. Der molekulare Mechanismus der Atmung, *Umschau*, **66**, 597.

Zahn, H. 1967. Chemische Synthese von Proteinen, *Naturwiss.* **54**, 396.

9 Molecules for communication between organisms

Burger, A. 1960. *Medicinal Chemistry*, Interscience, London.

Gorini, L. 1966. Antibiotics and the Genetic Code. *Scient. Am.*, **214**, no. 4.

Karlson, P. 1964. Hormones in Invertebrates in: M. Florkin and H. S. Mason, *Comparative Biochemistry*, Vol. VI, Academic Press, London.

Karlson, P. 1966. Ecdyson, Häutungshormon der Insekten, *Naturwiss.* **53**, 445.

Schildknecht, H., Siewerdt, R. and Maschwitz, U. 1966. Ein Wirbeltierhormon als Wehrstoff des Gelbbrandkäfers, *Angew. Chemie*, **78**, 392.

Zähner, H. 1965. *Biologie der Antibiotika*, Springer-Verlag, Heidelberg, New York.

Zillig, W. 1966. Die Wirkung von Antibioticis auf Komponenten und Teilreaktionen des Proteinbiosynthese-Apparates, *Arch. Exp. Pharmak.* **253**, 131.

10 Antibodies

Killander, J. 1968. (Ed.). *Gamma Globulins: Structure and Control of Biosynthesis*, Interscience, London.

Landsteiner, K. 1962. *The Specificity of Serological Reactions*, Dover Publications Inc., New York, Constable, London.

Mourant, A. E. 1954. *Distribution of the Human Blood Group* Blackwell, Oxford.

Porter, R.R. 1967. The Structure of Antibodies, *Scient. Am.*, **217**, No. 4.

Springer, G.F. 1967. The Relation of Microbes of Blood-group active Substances in: *Cross-reacting Antigens and Neoantigens*, Williams and Wilkins Company, Baltimore.

11 Phylogeny – the evolution of complex organisms from simpler ones

Braunitzer, G. 1967. Primärstruktur de Eiweissstoffe, *Naturwiss.* **54**, 407.

Bryson, V. and Vogel, H.J. 1965. (Ed.). *Evolving Genes and Proteins*, Academic Press, London/New York.

Darwin, C. and Wallace, A.R. 1958. *Evolution by Natural Selection*, University Press, Cambridge.

Dobzhansky, T. 1963. *Evolution, Genetics and Man*, John Wiley and Sons Inc., London/New York.

Jukes, T.H. 1966. *Molecules and Evolution*, Columbia University Press, London/New York.

Kosswig, C. and Peters, N. 1967. Die Evolution der Höhlentiere, *Bild der Wissenschaft*, **4**, 828.

Lorenz, K. 1965. *Darwin hat recht gesehen*, Günther Neske Verlag, Pfullingen.

Mayr, E. 1964. From molecules to organic diversity, *Fed. Proc.*, **23**, 1231.

Simpson, G.G. 1964. Organisms and Molecules in Evolution, *Science*, **146**, 1535.

12 Ontogeny – the development of the individual

Spemann, H. 1936. *Experimentelle Beiträge zu einer Theorie der*

Entwicklung, Springer-Verlag, Berlin.

Strehler, B.L. 1963. *Time, Cells and Ageing*, Academic Press, New York.

Wald, G. 1963. Phylogeny and Ontogeny at the Molecular Level in: *Evolutionary Biochemistry*, Vol. III, 12.

13 Genetically determined molecular illnesses in man

Dobzhansky, T. 1965. *Dynamik der menschlichen Evolution, Gene und Umwelt*, S. Fischer Verlag.

Stanbury, J.B., Wyngaarden, J.B. and Frederickson, D.S. 1966. *The Metabolic Basis of Inherited Disease*, McGraw-Hill, London/New York.

Wolstenholme, G. 1967. (Ed.). *Man and his Future*, Ciba Foundation, J.A. Churchill Ltd., London.

14 Viruses as parasites of single-celled and multicellular organisms

Colter, J.S. and Paranchych, W. 1967. (Ed.). *The Molecular Biology of Viruses*, Academic Press, London/New York.

Luria, S.E. and Darnell, J.E. Jr. 1967. *General Virology*, Second Edition, John Wiley & Sons Inc., London/New York.

Stent, G.S. 1963. *Molecular Biology of Bacterial Viruses*, W.H. Freeman & Co., London/San Francisco.

Weidel, S. 1964. *Virus und Molekularbiologie*, Springer-Verlag, Heidelberg.

15 The origin of cells

Fox. S.W. 1965. (Ed.). *The Origins of Prebiological Systems and*

their Molecular Matrices, Academic Press, London.
Haber, H. 1967. *Unser blauer Planet*, Rowohlt-Verlag.
Oparin, A.I. 1965. The origin of Life and the origin of Enzymes, *Advances in Enzymology*, **27**, 347.

16 Conclusion

Cooper, R. 1968. The Psychology of Boredom, *Science Journal*, **4**, 38.
Dobzhansky, T. 1963. *Evolution, Genetics and Man*, John Wiley & Sons Inc., London/New York.
Dobzhansky, T. 1964. *Heredity and the Nature of Man*, Harcourt, Brace & World Inc., New York, and Allen and Unwin, London.
Frank, H. 1964. (Ed.). *Kybernetik, Brücke zwischen den Wissenschaften*, Umschau Verlag, Frankfurt.
Wagner, R. 1961. Rückkopplung und Regelung, ein Urprinzip des Lebenden, *Naturwiss*, **48**, 235.
Wiener, N. 1958. *Mensch und Menschmaschine*, Ullstein Verlag, Frankfurt.
Wiener, N. 1965. *Cybernetics*, Book Centre, London.

Acknowledgments

Acknowledgment is due to the following for the illustrations (the numbers refer to the page on which the illustration appears).

13 after A. L. Lehninger in *Bioenergetics*, W. A. Benjamin Inc., New York; 17 (top) courtesy P.H. Hofschneider; 46, 219 courtesy D.C. Phillips; 47 courtesy F. Lynen and P.H. Hofschneider; 49 courtesy A. Rich; 62–3 based on F. Jacob and J. Monod; 68 photo Ken Moreman; 69, 156 (bottom) courtesy D. Morrison; 72 (top) courtesy W.T. Becker; 74 (bottom), 75 courtesy K.M. Lyons; 77 courtesy M.J. Hobbs; 86 courtesy A.G. Morell, I. Sternlieb and M.M. Kunt,; 92 courtesy W. Beermann; 104–5 Natural History Photographic Agency, photo Stephen Dalton; 120–1 courtesy A.E. Mourant; 124–5 from *Atlas of Evolution* by Sir Gavin de Beer, Thomas Nelson, London; 127 based on A.S. Romer in *Procession of Life*, Weidenfeld & Nicolson; 131 after Morgan *et al.*; 132 copyright British Museum of Natural History; 134 after K. Lorenz in *Darwin hat recht gesehen*, Verlag Günter Neske, Pfullingen; 137–7 after E.L. Smith; 142–3 copyright British Museum of Natural History; 156 (top) courtesy H. Lehmann; 166 courtesy L.D. Simon; 167 courtesy G. Schramm; 169 courtesy R.W. Horne; 173 based on H. Haber; 175 courtesy S.W. Fox; 177 based on G.H. Dixon; 181 (top) based on F. Lippmann; 185 (bottom) based on B. Hassenstein; 224, 225, 226–7, 233, 237 (A9.2 and A9.3), 238 after P. Karlson, *Kurzes der Biochemie*, Thieme Verlag, Stuttgart; 229 after V.M. Ingram in *The Biosynthesis of Macromolecules*, W.A. Benjamin Inc., New York; 231 after J. Loper, *Brookhaven Symp. Biol.*, 17, 1964; 241 after P.L. Carpenter in *Immunology and Serology*, W.B. Saunders & Co., Philadelphia; 242 (15.1) after S.L. Miller and H.C. Urey in Organic Compound Synthesis on the Primitive Earth, *Science*, 130, 1959.
The diagrams were drawn by Design Practitioners Limited.

Index

Numerals in **bold** refer to the illustrations

02